PERKAR'S
JOURNEY

SU DP

THE
RIVER

BROTHER HORSE'S
ISLAND

DEH SHE

WESTERN
MANG

WUN

SOUTHERN
MANG

NYEL

NHOL

KINGDOMS

SWAMP
DANGUN

LHE

GULF
of
SHE CHUH

THE WATERBORN

By J. Gregory Keyes
Published by Ballantine Books

CHILDREN OF THE CHANGELING
The Waterborn
The Blackgod*
*Forthcoming

THE WATERBORN

J. Gregory Keyes

A DEL REY® BOOK
Ballantine Books • New York

A Del Rey® Book
Published by Ballantine Books

Library of Congress Cataloging-in-Publication Data
Keyes, J. Gregory.
The waterborn / by J. Gregory Keyes. — 1st ed.
p.   cm.
ISBN 0-345-40393-2
I. Title.
PS3561.E79W38   1996
813'.54—dc20   95-44073
                                                    CIP

Manufactured in the United States of America
First Edition: August 1996
10 9 8 7 6 5 4 3 2 1

For Nell

© Cherry '96

CONTENTS

PART THREE: CHANGELING

ACKNOWLEDGMENTS

Ken Carleton, Veronica Chapman, Tom Deitz,
Pat Duffy, Nell Keyes, Charles Hudson,
and Nancy Ridout-Landrum

PROLOGUE

Out of a Deep and Ancient Place

THE mountain split open with the clap of a thousand thunders, and through the rupture a cyclone of living steam screamed skyward. Blazing, many-colored lightnings rode with the wind and water, the groping fingers of an angry god.

Another god, cloaked in the flesh of an argent bird winging frantically away, was snapped like a twig by the first shock, his wings broken, the flesh seared and then stripped from bones that themselves were blown apart. The pain was awful, the fiercest agony that the god had ever known, and in eternity he had felt much pain.

Knitting a new body of air and black smoke, he redoubled his efforts to outpace the main storm, the unthinkable reservoir of power he had loosed. He rode with the blooming edge of the tempest, disintegrated and recomposed a hundred times in the wind's teeth. Jagged wounds of mountains, the pooled, dried

1

blood of plateaus hurled beneath him with hideous speed, as incomprehensible and lethal as the gaze of a basilisk.

The god felt real fear for the first time in his existence. Who
could have known his Brother held such power, such *anger*? Behind him he could see the air chewing itself to pieces, flashes like
lightning but brighter by far than the sun.

Pretty, he thought. *But it will be my death if he catches me, a
real, endless death. Perhaps—just perhaps—I have made a mistake.*

He tightened the thick strands of his heart and flew, faster than
anything save the wind had ever flown, until, like a steed run to
death, his might was gone and he fell.

The storm swept by above him, smote a mountaintop, and
shattered it.

The god struck the earth and lay there as above him the sky
became soot, the sun dimming to a pale ocher eye and then gone
altogether.

Now he finds me and I die, the god thought. *I may not be as
clever as I thought.*

But then the earth swallowed him, folded him up beneath, hid
him, kept him safe. Above, in time, the steam calmed into rain
and soaked the bone-dry hills and desiccated plains for some
score or so years.

Much more time passed, and he awoke. His flesh had grown
back. He flexed his wings, felt the warmth of golden blood in his
veins, pulled himself from his protective womb.

The world had changed, he saw. Thick boles of trees towered
about him, a thousand living mortal things, just as he had seen
in his vision, so long ago. Unleashing the Brother, he had unleashed life as well as death. He took to the air and flew above
it all, until the new world was a carpet of green below, the
blasted mountains now healed by time. In the midst of it, the
Brother was still there, but he lay quietly now, no longer angry.
He wound across the land, a serpent shimmering blue beneath
the sky. A River. He was, the bird thought, quite pretty.

But I am no longer pretty, he thought, for he had changed, as well. He was black, every feather, his beautiful argent plumage replaced by charcoal.

But he forgot that soon enough. The world was new and strange, and surely in such a place there was much mischief to be about.

And in a wink or two of his yellow eye, five more millennia passed.

PART ONE

≈≈≈≈≈≈≈≈≈≈≈≈≈≈≈≈≈≈≈≈≈≈≈≈≈≈≈≈

ROYAL BLOOD

© Cherry '96

I

The Princess
and Perfect Darkness

Hezhi confronted the black depth, felt a wind blow up from it and envelop her like the breath of a vast beast. She was seized by a sudden sensation of falling, though she could still sense the wet clay beneath her feet, slick as the back of the salamander in her mother's garden pool. Hezhi trembled; she had never been troubled by such darkness before. In the three years since she discovered the tight, narrow tunnels of the old palace, she had never ventured beyond the upper stories, the places where the ceiling was a lacework of crumbled stone, recently added sewer grills, the dense and spreading roots of O'ay trees. A ceiling that therefore let at least scraps of light drop through to guide her wanderings. Her room in the palace was likewise never dark, but always illuminated, if only by the tiny lamps of the stars peering down through the open roof of the adjacent courtyard.

But what she faced now was *chwengyu*, the perfect darkness

that she had only read about, darker than her own coal-black hair. Behind her, a faint gray light lapped at her heels, trying to call her back, like a loyal dog, knowing its mistress was heading into danger, straining at the end of its leash to reach her.

Hands against the damp, perspiring wall, Hezhi shuffled forward, her tiny bare feet squishing in the wet layer of clay. Her shoes—beautiful felted shoes—lay discarded two turnings back, where the broken stairway vanished beneath this layer of mud. How long had the lower palace been buried? She remembered the tales of the flood, but none of them really said when it had occurred. During the rule of Q'anata, she seemed to remember. One day she would find out just when that was. *Q'anata.*

She gasped as her feet slipped, and the darkness, again like a great maw, grinned to take her in. Hezhi recovered her balance, shaking. She could turn back now, as she always did. She should: Her fear was a cricket, chirping frantically beneath her breastbone. But this time she had gone farther than ever before. *This* time she had more than curiosity, she had a reason to push deeper into these tunnels. *D'en.* He was down here somewhere. The priests had taken him off, just like that. Hekes, D'en's little servant-girl, had told Hezhi as much. When the priests snatched one of the royal family, everyone knew where they took them. They took them *down*, down the staircase behind the throne room, down into the old palace, and even deeper, to where the River himself filled the hidden foundations of the city. After that, those taken were never seen again, and they were never spoken of, save with *–nata* added to their names, the suffix that denoted someone as a ghost.

D'enata, Hezhi thought, felt herself near tears. Ten years old, she had met her mother a dozen times, her father perhaps twice that. They were polite to her, but more distant than gods. D'en was three years older than she, her cousin, a kind, gentle boy. Her best friend, besides the servants who raised her. Her *only* friend in the royal family. D'en and she had spent every idle hour together, scampering about the vast empty areas of the palace, eluding their bodyguards and servants, spying on the adults. Now he was gone, taken from her.

I'll find you, she promised. She could not descend the Darkness Stair, where they had taken D'en, but she knew other routes into the underneath. There must be a way to reach her cousin, to see him again, to rescue him from whatever fate the priests had taken him off to.

Thirteen more steps she counted; the slope steepened and then leveled off flat. Her poor toes kicked against a few pieces of brick, cracked and tumbled down from above. Hezhi hugged the wall at her left, for support, for solidity. The darkness seemed infinite, though she knew the passage she was in was only an armspan across. She reached over with her right hand to confirm that.

She couldn't feel the other wall; the passage had evidently widened. Hezhi stepped over a few more feet, puzzled.

Her legs zipped out from under her as if she had been pushed. She fell roughly to the damp floor, flailing ineffectually with her arm. A shriek turned into painfully exhaled air as the wind was slapped out of her, and before she could even comprehend *that* and the agony that accompanied it, she was sliding.

Then falling. She fell for what seemed a very long time before the rush of air was replaced by a stinging explosion that seemed to burn half of her body, to push the little ghost in her up into the high air, to leave her leaden corpse as food for whatever lived in such deep, underground pools. And she *was* in a pool. The water was as warm as bathwater, and it stank of rot. Her three layers of skirt held air and kept her buoyed up for a moment— long enough for her struggling lungs to steal new breath from the fetid atmosphere. She had not yet recovered her senses, however, when the hated garments began to fill with water, to drag her down. It would have been terrifying, the speed with which her own clothes became a powerful hand, tugging her beneath the water, were she not already shocked beyond such simple terror.

She was not so shocked or stupid that she did not kick the

skirts off. Her slim, hipless, ten-year-old body shimmied easily out of them, though they grasped once more at her ankles as they sank into the deeps.

Hezhi could not really swim, but she could tread water. She was thankful that she wasn't wearing the heavy brocaded vest— that was back with her shoes. Her linen shirt did not add much to her weight.

Of course, even that weight would soon be more than enough. Hezhi was tired and numb already.

That was when she realized, for the first time, that death was not an option she would willingly take. It would have been simple, easy. The water, despite its stink, was really not unpleasant. It almost seemed to enfold her like comforting arms, like a blanket. In fact, she realized, this water must be the River, the life giver, the ancestor of the royal line. Her *own* ancestor. Didn't the River have her best interests at heart, know well her deep misery, her lonely days? So easy to go down into his belly, return to his seed. Then maybe she would be with D'en again.

But no, she wanted to live, even if she hated her life. It was a curious thing, a revelation. Even standing on the red-shingled roof of the Great Hall, staring down longingly at the neatly paved courtyard had never brought such a flash of insight. When she was on the brink of taking her *own* life, she always pulled back. She dared the roof only because she needed to know that there was at least one important choice she could make for herself. It was *control* she wanted, not death. Threatened with a death beyond her own hands, that distinction was more than plain, even to a ten-year-old.

I want to live, she thought, *but I shall not.*

That was when Tsem called for her. Tsem, her bodyguard, whom she had tricked, whom she believed too stupid to follow her.

"Tsem!" she shrieked, with what air she could bring into her voice. "I've fallen! I'm drowning."

A faint yellow glow appeared, high above her. The glow brightened along a sharp black line, like the sun rising in the east.

The line, she realized, was the edge of whatever precipice she had fallen from.

The glow suddenly had a center, the bright, glaring light of a lamp. Behind it, faintly, she could make out Tsem's rough features.

"Mistress?" he barked, his voice thick with concern. "I see you, Mistress. Come to the wall: Cling there while I come down for you."

In the faint light, she could see what wall Tsem meant. She had fallen over the edge of what must be the stairwell she had been descending. The pool drowning her was a half-submerged hall; the stairs surely continued down to its floor, which must be another ten feet or so below her. How stupid she had been! If she could only get to the wall, she could make her way to where the stair entered the water and scramble back up on it.

Except that she was *so* tired. And what was Tsem doing? The light remained where it was.

Hezhi managed to get to the wall. It was slick, very slick, and she could find little purchase on it. Kicking for all that she was worth, she tried to use her hands to push herself along it, vowing that *someone* would teach her to swim, if she survived this.

At nearly the end of her strength, Hezhi heard a thunderous splash, and the surface of the water broke into a billion shards of pale lamplight. Before she could even gasp, arms like the stone columns that held up the Great Hall wrapped around her, tilting her back so that her face was well out of the water. Beneath her, she could feel powerful muscles churning, pushing them along. It was like being borne on a cyclone or a waterspout, like being the mistress of a storm.

By the time they reached the edge of the stair, Tsem was shuddering with effort. His breath came in great, labored gasps as he threw her up onto the mud and then flopped out onto the slope himself. Hezhi listened to him wheeze like an old dog, felt the burning in her own lungs.

"Am I so heavy, Tsem?" she asked, concerned for her loyal guard.

"No, Mistress," he replied, his voice coming between gulps at first, but then waxing stronger. "No, indeed, you weigh nothing. It is Tsem who is heavy. My kind were not meant to swim, I think."

"You *have* no kind, Tsem," Hezhi said, not realizing until several years later what a hurtful thing that was to speak.

Tsem was silent for a moment, then he laughed, a single harsh grunt. "True enough, Mistress. My mother, though—*she* was not designed to swim. Giants stay far and away from the water. And my father was Human, like you, little one—and probably no better at swimming than you are." He paused and then added, "He had a lot more sense, though."

With that he scooped her up, and Hezhi found herself lifted onto Tsem's massive shoulders. He crawled up the slope on all fours, until they reached the place where the lantern still burned patiently; Hezhi could now see that it rested on a landing, five paces of level stone just where the stairs entered at the top of the room. What ancient prince had built it thus, so that he could preen and pose at the top before descending to greet his guests?

Tsem set Hezhi down by the light and began to inspect her for wounds, his thick fingers very gentle.

He was a big man, though in age no more than seventeen years. He stood a head and a half taller than any other man she knew, and his shoulders were so broad she could scarce touch both with arms spread wide. Thick boned, he was, with muscles braided like ropes and cables beneath his pale skin. His legs were short, in proportion to his body, his arms long. His jaw was both massive and receding, and when he smiled his teeth were enormous ivory cubes, like the bone dice some of the soldiers gambled with. He had been trained since birth to be what he was, a guard for the royal line. His mother, now -*nata*, had been one of her father's elite, a full-blooded Giant and terrible to see in her armor. Tsem was less large—much more manlike than the full-blooded Giants—but he was much smarter. Her father had predicted this when he ordered the mating.

The two of them made an odd pair, the half Giant and the

child. Hezhi had limbs like willow switches, her little brown face delicate, nearly heart-shaped, an elegant setting for the black opals of her eyes. Tsem could lift her with one fist if he wanted to. Instead, he prodded her long bones gently.

"You don't seem badly hurt," he said at last. "We should have Qey have a look at you, however. She knows much more of this than I."

"No, Tsem, I'm fine."

"Besides being insane, you mean."

"You should know better than to talk to me like that. I am your mistress, remember?"

"Yes, little one." Tsem sighed. "But your father is a higher master. He would be most upset with me should harm befall you. Anyway"—Tsem shrugged—"I can't help it if I say the wrong thing now and then. Tsem not too bright, you know."

Hezhi laughed scornfully. "Yes, I've seen you do *that* trick before my father and his court. 'Tsem want to help.' 'Tsem not understand such things, Master.' But *I* know better, Tsem. And you *know* I know better."

"You know too much for someone so young," Tsem said softly.

"It must be the Royal Blood working in me," Hezhi replied, through a contrived smile.

Tsem's face clouded, his thick eyebrows coming together like twin thunderstorms. But beneath the clouds, his eyes were gentle, sad. He grasped her arm. "Don't even *say* that, Princess," he whispered.

Hezhi frowned. "I don't understand. I am my father's daughter. I carry the Royal Blood—from my mother's line, too. I will be like them, powerful. One day."

"One day," Tsem said, shaking his head as if to clear it. "But now let's get you back aboveground, to a proper bath and fresh clothes."

"*No,*" Hezhi replied. She pressed herself away from the half Giant. "No. I'm going on."

"Oh? So you can keep falling into pools?"

"I should have brought a lantern, that's all. Now I have one. Say . . ." Hezhi frowned. "I thought I lost you, like always. How did you find me?"

Tsem grinned a little, showing his enormous teeth. "You not lose Tsem, little Mistress. Tsem always stay far back, always out of sight."

Hezhi reddened. "You're using your dumb voice. Because I thought you were dumb, too. But I guess I was the one who . . ." She broke off again, this time to stifle a sudden giggle.

"What?" Tsem demanded.

"I was just picturing someone *your* size sneaking around after me and D'en."

Tsem touched her lightly on the shoulder. "I'm sorry about D'enata."

"His name," Hezhi snapped, all sudden humor vanished, "is *D'en. Nn!* And I'm going to find him!"

"I knew that was what you were about!" Tsem exclaimed. "Princess, it is hopeless. Give up this notion. Try to forget your friend. It is all that you can do."

"I will not."

"Where will you go from here? Even with a lantern? Your trail ends there, in the water." He gestured at the submerged lower stair.

That silenced her. Tsem was right. Or was he? In her excitement, in arguing with Tsem, Hezhi had not looked around properly, now that she was able. But Tsem was indeed right. She could just barely see the arch of one door, there beyond the stair. If she could reach that, she might duck under it and find another room. Or she might not.

"I'll go back," she said, "but only so far as another turning. There are many ways down into this darkness. One must lead to D'en."

Tsem wagged a finger. "I will carry you out, Princess. Your father will thank me."

"And I will come back, Tsem. Again and again, until I either find him or fall too far for even *you* to save me. If you always follow me, you know what I think of doing, at times. And now that I know how smart you are, I think I may get away from you. I was never as clever as I *could* be, Tsem, since I didn't realize I had to be."

Tsem knitted his brows back together. "What do you *want* of me, Mistress? My task is to keep you safe. I can't let you run around down here. There are *things* down here."

"There are *things* up there, too."

"I don't mean ghosts, little Princess. *Those* are mostly harmless, and the priests keep the bad ones swept out. Down here there are *real* things. And the priests don't come down here to sweep."

Hezhi sighed. "My mind is made up. You can either go with me—where *I* want to go—or you can leave me alone. Which will it be? Protect me, or let me roam?"

"My head," Tsem growled, "is as likely to leave my shoulders either way."

"I wouldn't let them do that, Tsem."

"You have no control over such things, Princess."

For a moment, Hezhi nearly relented. Tsem was so good, so loyal. Almost as much a friend as D'en had been. But Tsem and all of the other servants kept a certain distance from her—even Qey, the woman who had nursed her, been all but completely her mother. Even Qey had been withdrawing from Hezhi these last few years. D'en had been unreserved with his affection.

"Tsem," Hezhi said evenly, "I *will* find D'en. With or without you."

Tsem nodded sadly, not in her direction, but out over the sunken hall. "Very well." He sighed. "With me, then. But not *now*, Mistress. Not today. Tomorrow, when you've rested, when we get you some proper clothes."

"You'll come with me?"

"Yes, though it won't do any good," Tsem said sadly.

"We will find him," Hezhi insisted.

"Maybe that will not be a good thing," Tsem gently replied.

"Do you think he is dead?"

Tsem regarded her for a long moment, then scooped her up in his great arms. "You'll catch a fever like this, Princess." He bent and took the lantern in one massive hand and carefully started up the mud-covered stair.

"Why do they take them off, Tsem?"

It seemed that Tsem considered that question for perhaps too long a time before answering. "I don't know, Princess."

"*I* think you do," Hezhi told him petulantly. "Do they take servants off, too?"

"No. Not like that. When a servant is punished, it is done publicly, with much fanfare. So the rest of us will know."

Tsem was past the slickest mud now, and gray light was beginning to filter in from farther up the tunnel, where it turned right.

"Do you *really* not know why they take them off, Tsem?"

"I really don't. Not for sure."

"Do you think that they will take *me* off?"

"No," Tsem answered, his voice curiously flat and clipped.

"If they could take off D'en, why not me?"

Tsem shrugged his massive shoulders. "You think too much, Princess. Because they won't, that's all."

Tsem could be a wall in more ways than one. Hezhi knew when he would say no more.

THE hot bathwater felt good. The angry gaze of Qey did not. Her middle-aged face was as round and tight as a fist; her hazel eyes sparkled dangerously in the lamplight as she leaned over to scrub just a *bit* too hard at the mud crusted on Hezhi's feet.

"Where is your dress?" Qey whispered after a time. Her soft voice was not conspiratorial, not pitched to trade secrets. It was reined in low only so that it would not be a shout. Hezhi winced as the less-than-kind attentions of the scrub rag moved up to her face and neck. She did not answer.

"Your dress! Do you know? Your parents will think I sold it. I may be beaten. Or Tsem! If you won't think of me, think of him. Surely someone saw him carrying you, all but naked. They might castrate Tsem!"

Hezhi wasn't sure what castration was, but she knew it couldn't be good, not if Tsem was threatened with it.

"Nobody saw us," Hezhi shot back. Soap was smarting her eyes, and more tears swam about there, as well, despite all that she had shed since the disappearance of D'en. Her eyes seemed like the River, limitlessly full.

"You can't be sure of that. You're just a child!" But her voice had begun to soften, her frantic scrubbing becoming more gentle. When Hezhi's tears finally burst forth, Qey took her in her arms, soaking the front of her simple dress with soap and bathwater.

"Child, child," Qey whispered. "What are we to do with you?"

Later, in the kitchen, Qey did not bring up the matter at all. Bright sunlight flooded the courtyard outside, washed the inner kitchen walls with cheerful color. Strings of garlic and shallots dazzled white and purple above the table as Qey kneaded huzh, the thick black bread that Hezhi loved, especially with pomegranate syrup and cream. The warm pungence of the yeast mingled with the scent of coffee warming on the indoor skillet-stove and juniper smoke wafting in from the courtyard, where the bread oven was slowly heating up. Tsem was dozing in the sunlight, a happy smile on his broad face.

"When can I learn to cook?" she asked Qey. The woman did not look up, but continued to work her callused palms against the resilient mass of dough.

"You helped me already," Qey said. "Just the other day you beat some eggs for me."

"I mean *really* cook," Hezhi said, careful not to sound cross. There had been too much trouble today already.

"No need for that, little one," Qey replied. "There will always be people like me to cook for you."

"Suppose I *want* to cook," Hezhi countered.

"And suppose I *don't*?" Qey retorted. "Neither of us chooses what we do, Hezhi. It's all decided, and you'd best get used to it."

"Who decides?"

"Everybody," Qey replied. "The River."

And that was that. If the River said, it was.

"Did the River decide about D'en?"

Qey paused. She hesitated a moment, then brushed her palms on her apron. She knelt near Hezhi and took her hands.

"Hezhi, dear," she said, "I'm sorry about him. He was a good boy; I liked him."

She took a deep breath; to Hezhi it seemed that she was trying to somehow steady herself by filling up with air.

"Hezhi," the woman continued, "what you must understand is that Tsem and I . . . we are not like you. We cannot speak and do whatever we please. There are people who watch us, all of us, and even when they *aren't* watching, the River is. So Tsem and I cannot discuss everything you want to discuss. Do you understand that?"

Hezhi looked at Qey, trying to see what was different. Because the woman who had raised her *was* different somehow. Smaller? Different.

D'en was of the Blood Royal. If something could happen to him, how much easier would it be for something to happen to Qey or Tsem? Hezhi did not want that.

"I understand, *Nama*," she answered. Qey gripped her hands, then went back to her bread. She seemed happier. Hezhi turned her gaze back out to Tsem.

I shouldn't force him, either, she considered, remembering their earlier conversation. But she *had* to. Besides, who or what could possibly take away Tsem?

II

~~~~~~

A Gift of Steel and Rose Petals

PERKAR held his new sword up toward the sun, delighting in the liquid flow of light upon its polished surface, in the deadly heft of it in his hands. He crowed aloud, a great raven war whoop, and the curious cows in the pasture around Perkar turned briefly to accuse him with their mild cow-eyes of disturbing their deep meditations. Perkar disregarded them. He had a *sword.*

He cut the air with it, once, twice, thrice, and then returned it reluctantly to the embroidered scabbard that hung on his back. Yet there, too, it pleased him, for he could feel the new weight, the mark of his manhood. A man at fifteen! Or man enough to receive a sword, anyway. He reached once more joyfully for the hilt of his sword, delight sparkling in his gray eyes.

No, his own hidden voice told him. *You were given the sword because you have shown yourself to be trustworthy. Tend to your father's cows!*

Even reminding himself of his mundane duties made Perkar feel good today. After all, that was what an adult—man or woman—did. They looked after their obligations. Dutifully Perkar crossed the low ridge in the pasture. The sun was half-way from noon to sundown, scattering gold upon the otherwise verdant landscape. Forest bunched thickly at the borders of the Cattle-Field, wild and dense as the forest at the start of the world. The pasture itself rolled on east, dotted here and there with the rust-red cattle his father preferred. Between two hills, a thin line of willow marked a stream leisurely crossing the pasture.

Perkar stopped first at the shrine on the brow of the high ridge. It was a modest affair; an altar of stone that came up to his waist, a small roof of cedar and cane sheltering it. On the altar rested a bowl of plain design. He took a cowhide bag from his waist and withdrew an incense brick, and with tinder and his bow-drill ignited it. The faint scent of cedar wafted up, and he sprinkled tallow onto the hot ember, smiling as the fat sputtered and flared. Clearing his throat, he sang, clearly and distinctly:

> Once I was a glade
> A part of the ancient forest
> When Human Beings came
> With their fourfold axes
> With their tenfold desires
> I kept to myself
> Ignored their requests
> Turned them away with
> hard thorns . . .

Perkar sang on, the short version of a long story. It was the story of how his father's grandfather had convinced the god of the forest to let him cut trees for pasture. Because he was humble and established this shrine, the spirit had eventually relented. Perkar's family had maintained good relations with the Lord of the Pasture, and with the spirits of the surrounding land.

Leaving the brick smoldering, he moved on to a second shrine just inside the edge of the woods. This invocation was a bit shorter; they owed less to the Untamed Forest, and even let deer and other creatures graze at the edge of their pasture to mollify him.

The sun was well toward the horizon when he reached the stream.

The stream had cut deep banks, etched into the pasture; the cattle had likewise worn deep trails down to it. Perkar loved this part of the land the best; when the sun was bright and straight overhead, he often came here, to cool himself in the water, to chase crawfish, to throw crickets on the surface of the water and watch the fish snatch at them from below. Humming, enjoying the feel of the sword flapping against his back, Perkar moved upstream, away from the cow-roiled waters, to where the creek flowed clear and cool from the forest. He paused there, savoring the transition from the smells of grass and cow to that of dark, leaf-strewn soil. He reached down and cupped a handful of water to sprinkle on himself. Then he took out the sacrifice he had for the water: rose petals from his mother's garden. He started the song:

> Stream Goddess am I
> Long hair curling down from the hills
> Long arms reaching down the valley . . .

Perkar finished the chant and smiled, sat down on the bank, combed fingers through short, chestnut hair. He removed his soft calfskin boots and dangled his bare feet in the water. Up the pasture Kapaka, the old red bull, bellowed, triggering a musical exchange of lowing across the hills.

Now, at last, Perkar took his sword back out. He laid it across his knees and marveled at it.

The blade was slim, double-edged, about as long as his arm. The hilt was made large enough for both hands, wrapped in cowhide, a round, polished steel pommel its only decoration.

"*I* know who made that," a girl's voice said.

Perkar nearly dropped the sword, he was so startled. Instead, he stared, gape-mouthed, at the person who had spoken to him.

She stood waist-deep in the creek, wearing no more than her dark, wet hair. Her face was pale, the color of ivory, her large almond eyes golden as the sunset. She looked to be a year or so older than he, no more.

Perkar was not fooled.

"Goddess!" he whispered.

She smiled, twirled around in the water so that her hair fanned out across it. He could not see where the silken strands ended and the stream itself began.

"I liked the rose petals," she told him.

"It's been a long time since I saw you," Perkar breathed. "Many years."

"Has it been so long? You have grown a bit larger. And you have a sword."

"I do," Perkar answered stupidly.

"Let me see it."

Perkar obediently held the sword up where she could see it. The Stream Goddess approached, revealing more of herself with each step. She looked very Human indeed, and Perkar tried his best to avert his eyes.

"You may look at me," she told him. She scrunched her eyes, concentrating on the weapon. "Yes. This was forged by the little steel god, Ko. He cooled it in me, farther upstream."

"That's right!" Perkar agreed enthusiastically. "Ko is said to be related to my family. He is said to have fathered my grandsire's sire."

"So he did, in a manner of speaking," the goddess replied. "Your family is old hereabouts, as Human Beings go. Your roots with us on the land are deep."

"I love you," Perkar breathed.

"Of course you do, silly thing," she said, smiling.

"Since I first saw you, when I was only five. You haven't changed at all."

"Oh, I have," she corrected him. "A little here, a little there. Wider in some places, more narrow in others. My hair, up in the mountains, changes most. Each storm alters it, alters the tiny rivulets that feed into me."

"I meant . . ."

"I know what you meant. My Human form will always look like this, little Perkar."

"Because . . ."

"Because someone with this shape was sacrificed to me long ago. I forget her name, though I remember a little of what she remembers . . ."

"She was lovely," Perkar said, feeling a bit bolder. When he said things like that to the girls at the gatherings, they blushed and hid their faces. The Stream Goddess merely returned him a frank stare.

"You court me, little Perkar? I am older by far than your entire lineage."

He said nothing to that.

"It is so silly," the goddess went on. "This thing about swords and men. I made my agreement with your family only because it amused me."

"Agreement?"

"There is more to receiving your sword than I suspect you know. A silly, symbolic thing, but as I said, amusing." And she reached out her long, slim arm. He took it, and felt that her flesh was indeed warm, like a Human Being's. She stepped up out of the water, glistening, her long, graceful legs nearly touching him. She smelled like—he didn't know. Rose petals?

He was certainly frightened. He had gone off, recently, with Hame, a girl his own age and Human. What they did—touching each other, exploring—had frightened him enough. The feelings it aroused had been so *hungry*. He could not see how such feelings could be sated, though he had come near to understanding once when he was alone.

But this woman drawing him down to her flesh was not Human. She was Anishu, a spirit, a goddess. Perkar was trembling as she gently tugged at the belt of his pants.

"Shhh," the Stream told him. "Don't worry."

PERKAR and the goddess lay beneath a sky gone slate gray, and the shutters of the brightest stars were opening as night threw wide her windows. Huna, the Pale Queen, was brightening but already halfway across the sky, a thick crescent. Though the night breeze should have been cool, Perkar's bare skin prickled with unnatural warmth. The Stream Goddess was tracing the lean contours of his face with her index finger. She giggled at the downy promise of beard, then cupped his cheek when he flushed in embarrassment.

"You people age so quickly," she told him. "Don't hurry it more than necessary."

Perkar nodded without understanding. His life was too full just now. He felt as if all that he had ever seen and known was about to boil up out of him, become something he had never anticipated. He was having trouble thinking. And he was in love.

"That first time, when I was so young," he asked her. "Why did you appear to me then?"

"I need no excuse to appear," she said lightly.

"You came this time to honor a bargain."

"True enough. I came last time because you were laughing, and I thought it beautiful. I wanted to hear you with Human ears."

"The stream cannot hear?"

"Oh, it can. I can hear everything, the entire length and breadth of me, from the mountains until . . ." Her lovely face clouded. "I can hear it all. But it isn't like *this*. Being tied up in one place, being just a point, a quickly moving speck—it has a different sort of appeal."

"Is that what we are to you? Specks?"

She frowned, turned over on her side, so that the curve of her hip gleamed, impossibly beautiful to Perkar. "Before, my memories are different. I remember being born, I think, long and long ago. I remember when I came through this place in the old dry bed, over there." She gestured behind them. "Mostly, though, it was all the same: swelling with the rains, greeting my little ones and taking them in. The little thoughts of all the things that live within me. The Old People—you call them the Alwat—they came and touched me now and then, but I hardly noticed them— though other spirits told me much about them. Then your people came. They annoyed me at first; they angered me. I tried to ignore them. That was when they cut this girl and put her in the water. Her blood mixed up with mine, I felt her brief little life swimming away in me. Not like a fish at all. I was very sad, sad that Human Beings thought I craved such things. That is not my nature."

"Some spirits crave death, my father says."

"The land spirits *need* it, though they care little for sacrifice. Without death, forests have nothing to eat. But I . . ."

"Streams do not crave death?"

Perkar did not understand at first. The idea of a goddess weeping was beyond his young imagination. And yet she was.

"Why are you crying?"

"My song. Do you remember the last part of my song?"

Of course, Perkar thought. *How could I ever forget your song?* He cleared his throat.

> Swollen,
> I flow across short grass
> Where the wild horses drink from
> me
> There I end, I flow on
> But I am not the same
> Not the young woman
> I am the Old Man there
> The Old Man
> And everyone fears me.

Perkar finished the stanza, gazing with wonder into her tear-streaked eyes.

"What?"

"The Old Man," she said at last, "is a terrible god. He eats me up. *He eats me up!*" She shuddered, her breath hissing.

"He swallows me each day. In time he will swallow this seed you have just put in me. He eats everything."

She rose up, a night goddess now. Huna touched her with silver.

"Stay away from *him*, Perkar," she said.

"Stop. I love you." He had begun to weep, too.

"I'm always here." She sighed, but now he heard the pain in that. As if she had also said, "and he *always* devours me." He could picture how, each moment of each day, she fell down the hills into *him*. Whoever *he* was.

She stepped onto the water, smiled at him. Then she was a sheet of silver water, collapsing. She was a ripple. She was the stream.

Perkar watched her flow, long into the night.

"I love you," he said again, before he left. He took up the sword that had been made by the god Ko, but it no longer seemed a delightful burden. It seemed heavy, somehow. Yet it was not a melancholy heaviness, not a grief. He felt strong, happy. But *sober*. Determined.

I will find out who this River is that eats her, he promised. *That is the first thing I shall discover.*

IT was morning before Perkar returned home. The rising sun banished the melancholy from his soul, lightened his step as it lightened the sturdy cedar walls of his father's damakuta. He stopped at a little shrine at the base of the hill the fort stood upon, offered a bit of wine to the little god that slept there in the stone. A rooster crowed from somewhere up beyond the wall.

The damakuta had always seemed unimaginably huge to him, but as he glanced back up the hill at it, he knew that it had become smaller. He was a man now, in every way that mattered, the first of his father's sons to come of age. Soon he would seek Piraku, a thing that had many faces: destiny, wealth, cattle, prestige—and, of course, a home. Still, he reflected, when he *did* build his own house, there could be no better model than his father's. The sturdy walls had protected his family and cattle from more than one attack by jealous chieftains and once, even, the fierce horsemen of the eastern plains. The longhouse within the walls was tightly built, warm in the harshest winter, airy and cool when the windows were unsealed in the summertime.

Perkar came lightly back to his feet and fairly bounced up the hill. The outer gate was open, of course, and Apiru, one of his father's bondsmen, waved down at him from the watchtower.

"Morning, Perkar," he shouted, a little too loudly. A little too—was that a smirk on Apiru's face?

"Morning," Perkar returned. Did Apiru *know*? Did *everyone* know? By the forest gods, did his *mother* know?

Some of the bounce was gone from Perkar's step by the time he saw his father, sitting on a stool in the courtyard. The yard was large and bare, picked clean of vegetation by the gold-and-red chickens that roamed upon it. It was large enough to hold the most valuable of their cattle, when raiders came. Still, at the moment it seemed a little cluttered. There were more people than there should be, this time of morning. Besides his father, a number of his father's bondsmen and their families stood about, apparently doing nothing. Two of his younger brothers, his sister, and *her* husband were clustered together in the doorway of the longhouse. His father's two younger brothers, *their* wives—and grandfather! He must have come over from his own fort—nearly a day's travel—last night. What was going on?

"Good morning, Perkar," his father remarked. The older man's seamed, sun-browned, angular features and hawklike nose were a worn, presently unreadable version of Perkar's own. It always made Perkar nervous when he couldn't tell what his father was thinking.

"Morning, Father. Piraku beneath you and about you." That

was the formal greeting, and Perkar guessed this to be a formal occasion, though no one seemed dressed for it. His father, in fact, was taking *off* his shirt, revealing the hard muscles and tight white scars Perkar had always so envied.

"Did your night go well, son? Do you feel more of a man?"

Perkar felt his cheeks flame with embarrassment. Father *did* know. He recalled the goddess' reference to some sort of arrangement between her and the family.

"Ah . . ." was all he could manage. A ripple of laughter fluttered around the yard. Kume, his father's oldest dog, lifted his head and yawned as if he, too, had a comment on the matter.

"One more thing, then, Perkar, and you will be a man," his father said, his eyes daunting, an ambiguous smile now ghosting on his lips.

"But I thought . . ." Perkar stopped in midutterance. When one did not *know*, it was best to keep silent. He wished desperately that he weren't the oldest son, that he had observed someone else coming into manhood. "What part is that, Father?"

"The part where I beat you senseless," the older man replied, gesturing with his hand. Padat, Perkar's cousin, came out from the doorway then, trying to keep a smile from splitting the round face all but concealed by his bushy, flaxen beard. He was carrying two heavy wooden practice swords. Perkar felt his bowels clutch. *Oh, no. Not in front of everyone.*

The swords were handed out, first to Perkar's father, then to Perkar. Perkar reluctantly moved out to face the older man.

"I, Sherye, patriarch of the clan Barku, challenge this whelp to combat. Do all of you hear this?"

There was a general chorus of assent. Sherye smiled at his son.

Perkar cleared his throat. "Ah . . . I, Perkar son of Sherye, son of the patriarch of clan Barku, take that challenge in my mouth, chew it like cud, spit it back."

"So be it," Perkar's grandfather growled from his stool.

That was that. Sherye stood immobile, waiting for Perkar to make the first move. He *always* did that, waited like a lion or a snake, and when Perkar attacked . . .

But Perkar had not even lifted his sword to fighting position, and suddenly his father was *there*, the oaken blade cutting at his shoulder, fast and hard. Perkar yanked his own sword up more by instinct than by design; his footing was all wrong, and though he caught the attack, he stumbled back beneath the sheer force of it. He let his father think he had stumbled more badly than he had: Perkar went back on one knee and then cut out at his father's extended leg. Sherye, of course, was no longer there: He was leaping in the air, the sword a brown blur. It thudded into the meat of Perkar's shoulder. The pain was immediate and paralyzing; Perkar nearly dropped his weapon. Instead he backed wildly away, amid the hoots and jeers of his family.

Sherye came on, and the expression on his face was anything but fatherly. Again the punishing blade swept down, and again Perkar's only consolation was that the weapon was wood and not sharp, god-forged steel. The blow scraped down his hasty guard, and *flick*, it whacked against his thigh. It could easily have been his hip, crippling even with a wooden weapon.

Twice struck was enough for Perkar. He was going to get hurt in this match—he might as well resign himself to it. Avoiding his father's attacks was an impossibility. The next time the blade darted at him, he ignored it, instead stepping into the blow, aiming his own attack at Sherye's exposed ribs. His father's sword caught him on his uninjured shoulder. His own weapon cut empty air.

Perkar bit his lip on a shriek. Sherye did not press his advantage, but instead stepped back and regarded his eldest son.

People were laughing at him again. Perkar set his stance and charged. The two men met and exchanged a flurry of blows; miraculously, none landed on Perkar, though he barely deflected one aimed straight at his head. Even more miraculously, one of his own strokes grazed his father's arm. Bolder, Perkar howled and leapt, committing himself to an attack that left him defenseless.

His father's blow landed first, a bruising slap against Perkar's ribs, but an instant later he felt the shock of wood meeting flesh from a more favorable perspective as his own weapon thwacked his father's upper arm. Perkar's war cry turned into a jubilant shout, but that was cut quite short as Sherye spun and laid a stinging blow across his shoulder blades. Perkar lost track, then, of how many times he was hit. In the end he thought it a miracle that nothing in his body was shattered, that the only blood was from the lip he himself had bitten.

THE heat in the sauna was delicious—it almost made Perkar glad he was hurt. Sore muscles and bruises acquired a better flavor when marinated in deep heat.

The woti didn't hurt, either. It went down his throat like a warm coal and settled warmly in his stomach a moment before venturing on out into his veins.

"You never forget your first taste of woti," his father was saying. "You never forget when you become a man."

"Likely not, after that beating," Perkar complained—but lightly, so his father would know there was no real resentment.

"You took it well. You made me proud."

Perkar bowed his head, afraid to show the fierce grin of pleasure at his father's approval. Sherye laid his palm on Perkar's back.

"Piraku," he said. "You will find Piraku, just as I did, as my father did."

Perkar nodded; he could not speak. The two of them sat in silence, let the heat work further into their bones. Sherye threw a handful of water and spruce needles onto the rocks, and fragrant steam hissed up around them.

"She's beautiful, isn't she?" his father said after a time.

"Yes," Perkar answered. "Beautiful. Father . . ."

"Hm?" The older man's eyes were closed.

"I love her, Father."

Sherye snorted. "Of course you do. We all did . . . do, though the way we love her changes. That's why our grandfathers made that pact with her, son. It's *good* to love the things in the land."

"No. No, not like that," Perkar went on. "I love her like . . ."

"Like the first woman you've ever made love to. I know. But she's *Anishu*, son. You'll see that soon enough."

"It's happened before! That song, the 'Song of Moriru,' where . . ."

"I know the song, son. But the man died, and Moriru lived on and on, always sad. That's the way it would be." He smiled and reached over to tousle Perkar's chestnut hair. "You'll find a Human girl soon enough. Don't worry about *that*."

"She's already sad," Perkar whispered, unwilling to pass over the subject so lightly. "She says . . ."

"Son." Sherye's voice was solemn, sober. "Son, let it go. There is nothing you can do for her. Let it go."

Perkar opened his mouth to speak again, but his father half-cocked one eyebrow, his signal that the matter would be pursued no further. Perkar turned his gaze down into the empty woti cup.

But he did not let it go. He could not.

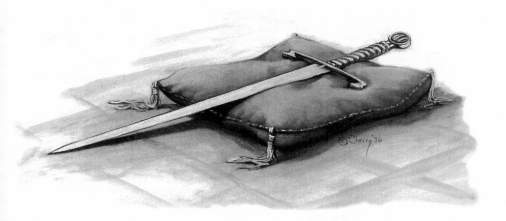

III

The Labyrinth

THE ghost hesitated at the edge of the hall, unwilling actually to venture into the light streaming down through the open roof of the small courtyard. Very little direct illumination reached the flagstones; the palace was three stories high here and the yard only ten paces across. Still, the white stucco shimmered with reflected sunlight. Ghosts did not particularly care for light.

Hezhi watched it back into the hall, hesitate near a stairwell, perhaps deciding where to go next. Qey had told her that ghosts often did not know what they were about—often forgot even that they were dead. Where and when did this one think it was? She studied it, hoping for clues, but this ghost provided few. It was less a form or even a shadow than a distortion in the air, like something seen through a glass of water—or like glass itself, for that matter. Sometimes you could see more—features, even. When Hezhi was six, she had awakened to confront the pale, nervous face of a young man. When she shrieked, he vanished quite quickly. She had never seen so clear an image since then.

Qey left little offerings for a few of the ghosts—especially Luhnnata, the one who inhabited her kitchen. Hezhi had come to be familiar with the young man who haunted her own room, though she never again saw his face.

She shrugged. This wing of the palace was strange to her, one with ghosts she had never seen. Certainly it would not be a dangerous one, not here, so close to the heart of things, where the *Sha'ghun* priests swept nearly every week.

"Let's go, Tsem," she commanded, stepping out into the light of the courtyard. The air was fragrant with sage and oregano growing from various stoneware boxes. A pigeon quickened its waddle to avoid their passage. Hezhi and Tsem brushed on past the ghost, which seemed to hug close to the wall when they came near.

"I can't believe I didn't think of this earlier," Hezhi muttered as they turned from the narrow passage onto a larger thoroughfare. Though it was a covered hallway, light streamed in from the courtyards on either side; the basic architecture of the palace made it impossible to go far from one of the alleged hundred and eighty-seven courts.

Tsem shrugged, not otherwise answering.

"You *did* think of it, didn't you?"

"Not exactly," the half Giant said reluctantly.

"Some help you are."

"Princess. Remember that you bullied me into helping you with this little enterprise. My agreement was only to go along with you into the lower cities to protect you. I never said I would do any more than that."

"You said you would help me find D'en."

"I never said that, Princess."

Hezhi thought about it. He hadn't. Still, she was in no mood to be generous. "Two years we've been running into solid walls—literally. If I'd thought to go through the library two years ago, we would have found him by now."

"Shhh, Princess. I think this is the place. You don't want anyone to hear your crazy talk."

The open doorway to their right did indeed seem to lead into the archives hall. At least, the legend on the frame said as much.

Inside, an old man sat on one of the fashionably low stools common throughout the palace. A writing board lay across his lap. On the board was a sheet of paper to which he was vigorously applying a brush and ink. Hezhi found herself instantly fascinated by the speed with which the characters flowed from his brush tip, the grace with which they lay on the paper afterward.

It took him a moment to look up.

"Yes?"

Hezhi nodded to Tsem, who bowed for her, then announced her. "Princess Hezhi Yehd Cha'dune, ninth daughter of the Chakunge—Lord of Nhol. She is here for instruction."

The old man blinked. Hezhi could see that the scarf wrapped around his head hid a nearly bald pate; his thin face crinkled naturally into a scowl as he carefully placed his brush upon the ink-mixing stone.

"Child, what do you want of me?"

Tsem started to speak, but Hezhi waved him back with what she hoped was a suitably imperious gesture. "My father wished that I should learn more of writing, of science, and of . . . architecture. You are to instruct me in these things."

The old man narrowed his eyes, as if fascinated by some strange insect he had just discovered on his morning meal.

"I've had no notice to that effect," he said at last.

"No matter," Hezhi snapped impatiently. "I'm here."

"So you are. But I am busy." He took the brush back up and began writing again.

"Who are you?" Hezhi demanded, in as imperious a tone as she could muster.

The old man sighed, paused in midstroke. He finished the character and laid the brush back down. "You may call me Ghan."

"That's not a name. That's the old word for 'teacher.' "

Ghan set the writing board aside. "At least you know that much. What else do you know, little Princess?" She did not miss the thick sarcasm in the scribe's voice.

"I can read, if that's what you mean."

"You can read the syllabary, I'm sure. Every child can read that. But can you read the old characters?"

"Some of them."

"And who, pray tell, taught you that?"

There was something accusing in the man's voice, something that made Hezhi feel suddenly insecure, cautious.

"All Royal Children are taught that," she muttered.

"Oh, no, Princess. You will not lie to me. That is the first and only thing I will teach you. With a willow rod, if necessary."

Tsem growled. "You will *not*," he said.

"Hold your tongue, servant. You have introduced your mistress. I will not hear from you again unless I ask you a question. Indeed, you will wait outside."

"He will *not*," Hezhi insisted, taking a step nearer her guardian. "Tsem stays with me, always."

"Not in here, he doesn't. Not unless he can read, that is." Ghan looked up speculatively at the huge man.

Tsem *could* read, but Hezhi knew better than to admit *that*. Servants who could read were considered dangerous and were usually punished.

"Of course he can't read," Hezhi said, hearing her own voice falter. Her manufactured confidence was rapidly failing her in the face of this terrible old man.

"Then he can wait outside."

"No."

"Princess," Ghan said testily, "he can wait outside, or I can send a message to the court, requesting to see your petition to study here. That is what I should do in any case."

Hezhi hesitated a long moment before relenting.

"Wait outside, Tsem," she said at last. Tsem said nothing, but his expression showed that he did not approve of her decision. He padded silently to the door and took up a place just beyond it, so that he could still see in.

Ghan watched him go, betraying no satisfaction at having his order obeyed. He then rose and moved to the nearest section of shelves. After a moment's study, he selected a single volume, took it down, and brought it over to Hezhi.

"Open this to the first page and read me what you see there," he demanded.

Hezhi took the book gingerly. It looked quite old, bound with copper rivets green with age. The cover was of some animal skin, which marked it as being at least a century old. The cotton paper was still white, however, if very soft from age and use. Hezhi opened the book, gazed down at the faded black characters for several long moments.

"It's something about the Swamp Kingdoms," she said at last. "This part is talking about the annual flooding of the delta."

"Read it out loud."

Hezhi brushed her hair out of her face. She glanced toward Tsem, hoping for a little courage.

"Ah, let's see. 'Herein begins our—something—we undertake to—ah—something—the many divisions of the delta lands—ah—inundated—the many dams and levees—"

"Stop." Ghan reached over and took the book from her hands, gently closed it.

"I'm sorry," Hezhi whispered. "I just didn't know all of those characters."

Ghan sat back down on his stool. "I want to know how you know *any* of them."

"I have a few books."

"*Do* you? In the old script?"

"I have a copy of the *Hymn to Bitter Lands.*"

"Who taught you to read it?"

"I also have a book *about* the old script."

Ghan crooked his mouth to one side. "You mean you taught yourself?"

"Yes."

"That would explain your awful pronunciation, wouldn't it?"

Hezhi felt herself near tears. "I didn't know my pronunciation was bad."

Ghan shrugged almost imperceptibly. "Why do you want to study here, Princess?"

"What else is there for me to do?"

"Go to parties. Court young men. You must nearly be a woman now."

"I don't like parties," she replied.

Ghan nodded. "Princess, let me tell you the truth. I'm a little impressed that you taught yourself this much of the ancient script. It shows that you have sense somewhere in that little head. It's not too rare for you royal brats to come in here and waste my time, to try to learn *just* enough to make sparkling conversation and impress the court. What is rare is a young woman who already knows how to read. If you were a man, Princess, I would not turn you away. I might teach you something. But you are not a man. In a year or two, you will be a woman, and you will marry some fair-faced fool, and he will not want you to be smarter than he is. Teaching you would be a waste of my time, and I have little enough time to waste."

Anger was lurking behind Hezhi's fear and intimidation, hidden like a cat. Now it sprang like a cat, suddenly and without warning. "I would not want to waste your time!" she snapped. "I don't care if you teach me *anything*. Just sit here with your *stupid* pen and your *stupid* ink, and I'll find whatever I need. I'll teach myself, like I always have. Just leave me alone and stay out of my way!"

Ghan shook his head. "One must be *taught* how to use a library, whether one can read or not. You want to know about architecture. Do you think the books that treat that subject are somehow going to leap out at you? You think we keep them all together?"

"I don't care! I'll find what I want!"

Ghan stared at her, and beneath his skeptical gaze, Hezhi felt her anger begin to retreat once more. Without its heat, it was difficult to withstand Ghan's scrutiny, but she forced herself to, even when her anger was stone cold and she became frightened at her own outburst. She wondered if she should add a "please?" to her last statement, but now her jaw seemed frozen in place.

Ghan nodded suddenly. "Very well. You will be very quiet. You will never speak to me. You will be *very* careful with my books, and the first time you tear *one* sheet of paper, I will send notice to your father and have you barred from this place. Do you understand these conditions, Princess?"

Hezhi nodded dumbly, at last letting her gaze stray to the richly embroidered carpet beneath her feet. "Yes, Ghan."

"Good." Ghan took his writing board back up into his lap, retrieved his parchment, brush, and ink. He did not look back up at her.

Her knees shaking a bit, Hezhi turned to confront the hundreds upon hundreds of shelves that seemed to lead back into infinite depths.

Like the darkness, she thought to herself. *Two years ago, I stepped into real darkness for the first time, searching for D'en. Into the unknown.*

Here I go again.

"Confusing," Hezhi told Tsem, as the wind fluttered the cottonwood leaves above their heads. "You could know exactly what you want and never find it. But I made progress, I think."

"What *are* you trying to find?" Tsem muttered, scratching at an ant bite on his hairy lower leg. Nearby, water gurgled in an alabaster fountain beneath a sky of lapis lazuli and gold. The roof garden of her mother's apartments was one of Hezhi's favorite places.

Hezhi snorted. "You know. Maps. *Old* maps, drawn before this city was built upon the flooded one. Maps I can use to figure out how to get to D'en other than by the Darkness Stair."

"If D'en is even . . ." Tsem cut that off; how many times in the past two years had they had this argument? The given was that Hezhi would assume D'en was alive until she had evidence that he was not.

But this time Hezhi's face clouded, not with anger, but with sorrow. "I . . . Tsem, I'm not sure I remember what he looked like any more. He had black hair like mine, and a little round face . . . Sometimes I wonder if it's even *him* I'm trying to find, now. But I loved him *so* much, Tsem. It seems like a long time ago, when I was very young . . ."

"You are *still* young, Princess," Tsem reminded her. "Master Ghan is right. You have other things you could be doing."

"Oh, yes," Hezhi responded sarcastically. "*Important* things. Like going to parties. Like meeting men."

"Qey thinks . . ."

"I know what Qey thinks, and so what? Anyway, I'm not old enough for men yet. I haven't started my bleeding."

Tsem suddenly grew a shade darker and turned his attention intently upon the fountain. Realizing she had embarrassed him, Hezhi stood and walked to the waist-high wall that encircled the rooftop garden. The city of Nhol stretched out before and around her, a bone metropolis shimmering in the westering light. Her mother's garden occupied the southern wing of the palace, and though the towers and ziggurats of the central halls soared high above her to the north, nothing obstructed her view to the west, south, or east; this rooftop was the highest on the wing.

Now Hezhi gazed off east. Behind the palace, gardens and vineyards rolled out green for a thousand paces before they were bounded by the wall. Beyond that, vast fields of millet and wheat checkered the floodplain in black fallow and viridian cultivation. Not far beyond *them*, Hezhi knew, the desert began, the vast waste her people called Hweghe, "The Killer."

Tracing her finger along the stuccoed wall, Hezhi walked south, gazed out at where the walls of the palace faded seamlessly into the city, a jumbled, chaotic tangle of streets, shops, and dwellings. Near the palace, these were of comfortable size, but they seemed to diminish with distance. Though Hezhi had never been into the city, it seemed difficult to believe that her eyes told the truth about the most distant—and most *numerous*—

houses visible to her. It seemed that they were no larger than Qey's kitchen—perhaps smaller.

East and south lay the River. Before him loomed the Great Water Temple, a seven-tiered ziggurat that blazed white, gold, and bronze, from whose sides four streams of water constantly cascaded, drawn up from the River by his own will. The two waterfalls Hezhi could see glistened like silver and diamonds. The River himself, beyond, was nearly too wide to see across. He lay heavy and cobalt, massive, unmerciful, unstoppable. A thousand colored toys bobbed upon his back: her father's great trading barges, fishing boats, houseboats, the tiny craft that could hold only one or two people. Foreign ships, beautifully clean and graceful of line, swept along beneath billowing sails, coming and going from the Swamp Kingdoms and the seacoast beyond like so many swans. All on the River, trusting—no, *praying*—that he would not capriciously choose to swallow them. People loved the River, worshipped the River, but they did not really *trust* him. The River had taken people in from the Killer, saved them, made them his own. The people of Nhol had no other god but the River—and his manifestations, the nobility. Like her father, who was part god.

Like herself. Like D'en, wherever he was.

An amazingly loud belch erupted suddenly behind her, and Hezhi smiled. Tsem was no god. He was mortal, pure-bred, despite his parents' different races. Mortal and happy to be so.

"Pardon me," Tsem said sheepishly.

Hezhi bit back a rude retort, but she did move upwind.

"It's not just the flood that buried the lower city, you know."

"No?" Tsem asked.

"I always imagined, *la*, and the flood covering the city, and then the Third Dynasty building this one upon that. But really, most of the lower city was filled in on purpose. To raise *up* the new one."

"So the next flood wouldn't be as bad."

"Right. The River isn't supposed to flood us, his children,

but . . ." Hezhi shifted uncomfortably. "I've heard the River sleeps a lot. That sometimes we just have to fend for ourselves."

"Why not wake him up?" Tsem asked.

"I think that might be worse," Hezhi replied. But she made a mental note to look for books on *that*, too. Priests wrote most books, so there should be more than a few about the River. In fact, that might be another angle to consider. The new palace had aqueducts and canals crisscrossing it, so that the sacred water would always surround them, enclose its children. The old city must have had such ducts, too.

"There must have been at least a few pipes," Hezhi mused to herself.

"You've changed the subject, haven't you?" Tsem said, his brow wrinkled.

"Hmm? Oh, yes. The one useful book I found was on the reconstruction. There were no maps, and that was a disappointment. But it talked about what they did. They filled in the courtyards with sand and rubble. Houses back then were *mostly* courtyard, and the walls were even thicker than the ones in the palace are now, so with the courtyards filled in, they could build on top of the old buildings, even if the rooms were still empty. That's why the floor cracks in the old sections, sometimes, and there are spaces underneath. That's why we haven't gotten anywhere; even when we find a suite of rooms that aren't full of sand or water, we eventually hit one of those filled-in courtyards. But you remember that one pipe? The one we found about a year ago?"

Tsem grunted. "The one I couldn't fit into?"

"Yes. I bet that was one of the sacred water tubes, built to carry water to the interior canals and fountains."

"And? It was blocked off, too."

"It had *collapsed*. Recently, I bet. If we could just find those . . . If I knew where the old temple sanctuaries were . . ."

"Princess!" Tsem's eyes were wide. "Temples? We can't go into temples!"

"Why not? After all, one day there will probably be a temple dedicated to me, like there is one for my father."

"But not to *Tsem*, Princess. Tsem is *not* safe from sacrilege, and he guesses that you aren't, either, whatever you may think."

"Hmmf. Well, I'll find that out, as well."

"Princess, you spent all day in there and found only one book."

"You have to admit, it's better than bumping around in the dark the way we have been. In one day, I understand more about the problem than I did this whole past two years."

"Well, I'm all in favor of keeping you from bumping around in the dark."

"And yourself," Hezhi added.

"That, too," Tsem admitted.

IV

A Drink with the King

Perkar's palms stung with the shock of his blow; the axe twisted off the grain of the wood and whistled down, out of his control. Angata swore and danced aside, the heavy blade barely missing his calf.

"Pay attention to what you're doing, you fool," Angata snapped, glaring at Perkar from his new vantage two strides away.

"Sorry," Perkar grunted, barely meaning it.

"Sorry wouldn't help if you'd gashed my leg down to bone," Perkar's cousin retorted. He shook back his brown hair, his green-eyed gaze still hard.

Perkar shrugged. "Sorry is the best I can do."

"It's not helping us get the fence built, either," Angata complained, waving his hand vaguely at the split-rail snake winding back into the woods, then at the half league of pasture that remained to be crossed.

"I know," Perkar sullenly acknowledged. His gaze followed the line of Angata's finger off into the woods.

Angata stared at him a moment and then shrugged. He sank down to the soft, new grass of the pasture, folding his legs up beneath him. "I say we rest, then." He sighed. "You've been like this all morning, and I have no desire to hop back to your father's damakuta on one leg."

"Father wanted this fence done by the new moon."

"He didn't say *which* new moon, did he?"

Perkar shook his head ruefully and flashed his cousin a brief smile. "You've got me there. Maybe I *should* sit down for a bit."

"Yes. Until you can get your mind back on building your fence."

"My *father's* fence," Perkar corrected him, his voice a bit sharp.

"Oh. *Oh.* So *that's* it, eh?"

Perkar chewed his lower lip a moment before reluctantly replying. "I was seventeen yesterday, Angata. *Seventeen.* And I'm still working on my father's holding."

"Your father is a great man."

"Yes, yes. My *father* is a great man. Rich in Piraku. Yet what do *I* have?"

"His good looks." Angata grinned.

Perkar glared at him. "I should know better than to talk about this." He turned his face back toward the forest. An awkward silence grew up between them. Perkar, brows knotted, clenched around his frustration; Angata's broad flat face was set in an exasperated scowl.

"You know the answer," Angata muttered, breaking the silence first. "Get yourself a woman. A woman with a good dowry, a father-in-law with a lot of land."

"Why don't you just say 'marry Bakume's daughter'?" Perkar snapped.

"All right, you stupid fool. *Marry* Bakume's daughter. The Agasapanyi Valley has some of the best pasture in the world.

Bakume offered you *two* pastures, twenty cows, and a good bull to go along with her. Not that anyone would *need* all of that to marry Kehuse. You'll find no lovelier bride."

"I don't like her."

"Perkar, I heard your father say *he* would offer you ten cows into the bargain himself, if you would marry her."

"Oh, he did? So now *I* have a dowry?"

Angata reached for him, but Perkar pulled away. "You should forget her, Perkar," he hissed, and Perkar knew they were no longer speaking of Bakume's daughter.

"Easy for you to say. You've never known her."

"No," Angata said, a little heat of his own rising into his tongue. "No, I've never lain with a goddess. But I've lain with women enough, and they're all pretty much the same, Perkar. I can't imagine that even a goddess would be *that* different."

Perkar's lips flattened into a line, and his voice quavered a bit when he whispered, "I . . . I wouldn't know."

Angata had a retort ready, but it dropped from his open mouth as he gaped at Perkar instead. "Never? Never? Wait, what about last haygathering? Kenu's girl."

"I couldn't. I just . . . I couldn't, Angata. I *tried*."

Angata touched his brow and muttered a little blessing. His intense eyes had lost their purpose, and they wandered now, embarrassed instead of certain.

"It must be some kind of witching," he said at last, almost apologetically. "There must be some way . . ."

"It isn't a witching," Perkar said. "*She* says the same things you say. Find a Human woman. Have children. Raise cattle. Be a man. But I *can't*, Angata. I don't know that I will ever be able to."

Angata shrugged again. The certainty was returning to the ridges of his brow; furrowed, they worked the problem around. Angata loved riddles, Perkar remembered. *"Sex is only the tenth part of marriage,"* Angata quoted, from somewhere. "You can learn, Perkar, over time. Learn to love a Human woman."

Perkar shook his head sharply, a dismissal. Angata nodded his own head in reply, a confirmation, a sign to move on to other ideas.

"Fine," Angata said. "A steer can be rendered by more than one tool." Then he flinched apologetically at his ill-chosen aphorism. "I mean, *many are the roads to Piraku.*"

"Better," Perkar acknowledged.

"I know more than one lad our age without a holding, or with one too small for his liking . . ."

"Like *yourself*," Perkar interjected.

"Yes. Reed Valley is nice enough, but I've not enough cattle to fill it. My point is, there are things to be done about it, things such as they sing about in epics."

"You mean we should put together a war party and go *take* someplace."

"Yes. The landless could split up the territory, the cowless could take some of the cows."

"That would have to be a *big* holding to make it worthwhile," Perkar observed. "Though, of course, some of us would probably die."

"Maybe. Though I've heard of conquest where no lives were lost."

Perkar turned to his cousin seriously. "Who, Angata? Who would you raid? Lokuhuna, whose son we hunted with as children, and who would stand with his father as we cut them down? Teruwana, whose daughter you have tumbled more than once, who gave my father a prize bull as a friendship gift? Konu of the high pastures, whose wife brings the boar to every High Gathering, whose son-in-law Hutuhan plays the harp so sweetly the children cluster about his feet rather than dash around the banquet hall, upsetting dishes and servants? Or perhaps we should take the Kapaka's own lands, the holdings of the High Chief?"

"No, no," Angata said, pushing away Perkar's objections with the flat palms of his hands. "You mention all of those close to us, near to our hearts. But there are those, far on the borders of the forest country, near the great seas of grass, with whom we hold little kinship. They spurn invitations to the High Gathering, to haygathering, to all of the festivals. We owe them nothing."

Perkar snorted. "They spurn our invitations because they dare not leave their damakutat unguarded for even a moment. They have the Mang at their backs, cousin. My father fought against the Mang once, and we nearly lost everything. And that was to a poorly organized war party. Those who live on the edges are more hardened to war than we here. They would cut us down like wheat. And if they did *not*, if we somehow triumphed, *we* would be the ones with our backs to the Mang. *You* wouldn't, I suppose, because you would be safe with your new cattle back in Reed Valley. But I have no desire to live near the plains."

"You have no desire for Piraku, then." Angata sneered. "For if you do not marry and do not conquer, you will never have any."

Perkar pursed his lips. "My grandfather married the daughter of a landless man, and he fought no one, and yet he brought enough land for a thousand cattle under pasture."

"Your grandfather struck a deal with the forest god to take land from the trees. Such a thing happens only once in ten lifetimes."

"So it does," Perkar said carefully. "Let's get back to work. I promise not to sever any of your limbs."

"Good."

"But your head may be another matter, if you don't keep quiet about what I told you."

Sunlight was deepening to gold when Perkar heard hooves beating up behind him. He gripped his axe a little more tightly; all of his talk with Angata about war made him nervous. Ironically, Angata had only just walked off across the hills toward his own holding, reckoning that his debt to Sherye was more or less paid. If the approaching horse bore some crazed Mang tribesman, Angata would miss all of the excitement.

The horse turned out to be the red and black stallion that belonged to his brother, Henyi, who rode saddleless astride him.

"Elder Brother!" Henyi shouted, his voice filled with the same excitement that flushed his face.

"You should use a saddle, Henyi. It hurts the horse to ride it bareback."

Henyi frowned in annoyance, but he did not take up his brother's complaint. Instead, he continued on with his own news.

"The Kapaka is here. Father wants you to come greet him!"

Perkar was readying a sarcastic reply when he realized his brother was not talking about Kapaka the head bull, but Kapaka, the High Chief of the nine valleys. Kapaka, the king.

"Oh," he said, to himself more than to his brother. He looked helplessly back toward the damakuta, two pastures and a forest away.

"Hop on up," Henyi said, smiling. "But don't complain about the lack of a saddle."

Perkar nodded and climbed up behind the boy. Ten years old, he had his mother's auburn hair and the same eagle nose that Perkar had gotten from Sherye, though Henyi's was still snubbed short by youth.

The powerful muscles beneath Perkar bunched and played, and then they were running, the pasture rolling beneath them.

The Kapaka. What might *he* want? Perkar's stomach felt tight.

"YOU'VE grown, Perkar," the old man acknowledged after the formal greetings were over. He accepted the first cup of woti and saluted them with it before raising it to his own lips. The Kapaka was perhaps sixty years old, perhaps a little more. His face was seamed and brown, rough with time and beard stubble. Even seated he was clearly a head shorter than Father, which made him half a head shorter than Perkar, who sat on the floor; one should be facing up when addressing a chief.

"Yes, I remember a stripling, covered in mud. But I suppose those days are past. You've become a man now."

Perkar's father clapped Perkar on the shoulder. "That he has.

One of the best sword arms I've seen, and he can work all day without letup."

"Good, good. It's good to see a boy grow up straight." The Kapaka took another sip of his woti, carefully inhaling the warm vapors as he did so. "Now," he said as he set the cup back down. "Sherye, let me ask about your cattle . . ."

Perkar found his attention wandering. His father and the Kapaka would compare their Piraku, neither boasting but each careful to list all of his assets. It was a game men played but one that—of *course*—Perkar had no part in. Rather than listening to the exchange, he instead let his gaze wander curiously over to the handful of men who had accompanied the chief from his home at Morawta.

Like the king, they seemed ordinary enough—in dress, anyway. The four of them sat together at the far end of the hall, their greetings exchanged. They were conversing in low whispers. One was about Perkar's height, heavier, with tangled black hair and a fierce smile; his hands gestured expansively. Next to him in the circle was a fellow that Perkar had met before, if only briefly: Eruka something or other, a member of the rather small Kushuta clan. He was almost skeletally lean, hollow-cheeked, with hair the color of dried hay. Perkar seemed to remember he was a singer, of sorts. The third man was older than the other two, who were not much older than Perkar. His seamed face and gray-shot red hair suggested someone about the age of Perkar's father, perhaps thirty-five or forty. He wore his hair oddly; rather than cropped at the ears, he let it grow long and braided—like a woman. Other than that, however, he did not resemble a woman in the least.

The fourth person in the company was truly eye-catching. He seemed to be speaking the least, holding a bit aloof from the others, watching their conversation with large, black eyes. His hair was white, white as a cloud, shoulder length and tied back in a tail. This had the unfortunate effect of emphasizing his forehead—what there was of it. His head sloped back sharply from rather thick brows, beneath which his eyes crouched watchful in deep sockets. His mouth was wide, expressive. If he grinned his head would probably split into two pieces. To Perkar this did not seem a real danger: This man looked as if he never smiled. If man he was. In fact, he more resembled—

Suddenly those black eyes were focused on *him*, twin tunnels empty of any clear emotion. In an instant Perkar felt himself discovered, dissected. This man was *used* to being stared at and at returning better than he got. Perkar tried to hold that gaze for a moment, but it was too cold, too unearthly. Embarrassed and with the beginnings of anger, he twitched his eyes away, turning his attention—or at least his regard—back to the Kapaka and his father.

Perkar missed the shift in conversation, but when he realized what the Kapaka was talking about, his attention became absolute.

". . . That's why I think we need some new territory. Did you know that Anawal's son over there put together a raid against my brother? Of course they didn't accomplish much, but someone could have been killed. Too many sons, Sherye, too little land. Soon they'll be going down to join the Mang out on the plains."

Perkar's father nodded. "Maybe. But it's been a long time since land was added to the Domain."

"I know. I was thinking about an expedition, Sherye."

"Against the Mang?"

"Oh, no. We tried that a few years ago, remember? How many good men did we lose?"

"I suppose it cut down on the number of landless men, though," Perkar interjected, hoping to be clever.

"Yes, well, one of those men it cut down on was my son," the Kapaka returned. His tone was light, an old grief admirably well hidden.

"I . . . I apologize, Kapaka. I spoke rudely and without thought."

The old man shrugged. "What else should the young do? No,

it's all right, friend. But I don't foresee going to war against the Mang again anytime soon. Too many fathers lost sons at the battle of Ngatakuta, and my powers of persuasion are limited." He smiled. "The best chief is the one who never tells his people to do anything they do not already *want* to do."

Perkar nodded. His mind was racing ahead, though, to the obvious conclusion. It was as if his frustration, his conversation with Angata earlier that day were both just two of a set of ripples, moving outward from where a stone had plunged into deep water. Now the ripples had come to the edge of the pool and were beginning to come together, bunch up, as if discussing the stone that made them, or perhaps the hand that threw it.

Could she have some part in this? he wondered. But it seemed unlikely. Since his manhood she had only twice come from the water to love him, and she always turned the conversation away from important matters.

"The thing is this, Perkar—this is why I had your father send for you. These men over here are going with me up into the mountains, into Balat, the old forest. I want to bargain with the Forest Lord for a few more parcels of land."

"The Forest Lord? Balati? Why not just bargain with the local spirits, the ones who live right there?"

The Kapaka raised his hands. "We've tried that, but like us, the gods in the land obey their High Chief. He has commanded his people not to give out more territory without his leave. There is also a further complication: Between our own lands and Balat there is a buffer zone of some few leagues; after that are the vast, vast countries of the Alwat. We must bargain to take land away from *them*, you see."

"Why should that be so difficult?" Perkar asked, a bit of scorn in his voice. "The Alwat are naked creatures, without Piraku. Why should they have the land over us?" Perkar had heard young men say this before—he assumed it was a general sentiment. But the Kapaka frowned at this and Sherye looked a little embarrassed.

"Because their claim is a thousand, thousand times as old as your people's," a quiet, almost whispery voice said from next to Perkar's ear. He jumped: How could anyone move so silently?

It was the strange man, the white-hair.

The Kapaka cleared his throat. "Perkar, this is Ngangata, from the west country. Probably the most valuable member of our expedition."

"You're an—" Perkar blurted, then stopped himself.

"My father was Alwa," Ngangata confirmed. "I have no clan."

Perkar nodded, wondering what that could mean, having no clan. Surely it made a man mean, hateful. To be feared.

Perkar would rather confront fear than back away from it. His eyes narrowed as he considered some insult he might give, to get it over with, to unsheath swords, if that was what it would come to. In his own home, this creature had made him to seem foolish.

"Perkar."

It was his father. It was his father, reminding him that this clanless halfling had the king's regard. It was his father reminding him that sometimes one did not *seem* foolish but instead *was* foolish.

"I'm sorry," Perkar said, perhaps without enough conviction, but an apology nonetheless. The white-haired man nodded acceptance. Perkar thought perhaps he should seem a little more grateful.

"I know very little about the Alwat," Perkar continued, more to explain his behavior to the Kapaka than to this strange person. "Perhaps you could teach me a bit, if we are to go to see them. May I call you by your name?"

"You may call me Ngangata, as the king does. It is *not* my name."

Perkar tried to ignore the slight. "You may call me Perkar," he replied softly, "and that *is* my name." *And it may be that you and I come to blows one day, no name, no clan,* Perkar felt but did not say.

V

A Forbidding and
a Compulsion

HEZHI closed her tired eyes for a moment, watched the weird play of lights beneath her eyelids. The shapes that flitted there were familiar enough—the curves and angles of faded glyphs, some known to her, better than half as mysterious as the wind from the sea. How many days now had she been staring at them, scratching at their meanings as at an itch and with as little positive effect? She simply didn't *know* enough. Ghan was right.

And yet what she *did* understand of what she read would not let her stop. Her revelations were few and hard won, but they were sweet, sweeter than anything she had known in her life thus far.

Qey was worried about her, she knew. Dragging out of bed at first light, returning when the stars came out, fingering scraps of folded paper in her pocket. With a piece of charcoal, she copied glyphs she didn't understand, and at night, in her bed, by the flicker of an oil lamp, she puzzled at their meanings. The ghost in her room took notice; he came close, as if watching her, once ruffled his invisible finger across the paper. Perhaps he had been a scribe, in life, some learned man who loved writing as much as she.

I must open my eyes, she thought. I was just beginning to understand what this page was saying. But her eyes did not open, and in a moment sleep stole up on her.

She awoke falling, hurtling down into the black depths, but it was only a sleep terror, the kind caused by small imps that lived in one's head—or so Qey said. Hezhi put one small hand to her breast, to still the beating there. In her sleep-muddled state, she feared that Ghan might hear her heart. She feared as well that Ghan might have seen her sleeping; more than once she had seen him coldly expel those who did so, even those with the royal writ of permission to be in the library. A writ that she did not have. But no, if he had seen her sleeping, she would have awakened not to falling, but to the sage's sharp tongue.

Relieved, if still a bit disoriented, Hezhi turned her attention back to the book. Horrified, she saw that it lay sprawled, splay-paged upon the floor, and bit back a little cry. Had she *dropped* it? It seemed to her that she had laid it carefully down, handled it like the precious thing that it was. But there it was, facedown, like a dead bird with wings crookedly folded. Hezhi actually shook a bit when she reached for it. When she gently turned it over, her worry became panic, for there, just near the binding, the yellowed paper had torn. It seemed a long, obvious tear to Hezhi, as wide as the River.

If you tear just one page, Ghan had told her. Just one.

Hezhi wiped at her eye when she realized a few tears had squeezed out, and she shut them tightly, willing the salty water to stay beneath her skin. If Ghan saw her cry, he would know. He might learn anyway, but he would *not* learn from her. She remained there, thinking, composing herself, for some moments more. When she felt her face settle out of distress and into what she thought was a more normal mask of indifference, Hezhi carefully closed the book. *There,* one could not tell one torn page when the book was closed. Had Ghan even seen her take this particular volume? She was deep in what she called the *tangle,* a confusing maze of shelves and tables in the back corners of the library. Ghan had not seen her asleep, and he had not seen her take down this book. Satisfied with her reasoning, feeling a little better, Hezhi replaced the volume with its dark wine binding, nestled it among its brethren. She looked about once more, saw no one through the cracks and gaps between the books and shelves.

She took down another book, one that promised to tell her of the proper consecration of First-Dynasty fanes. She reasoned that since consecration involved painting the symbol names of the River upon supporting and necessary structures of the buildings, there might be some good description of the way that such buildings were planned and constructed. After an hour of half comprehension, Hezhi saw the mistake in this; the fanes of her father's dynasty were indeed painted, but in the First Dynasty, they were merely filled with particular and complex combinations of incense. There seemed little promise of architectural description in that. Her eyelids were beginning to droop once more and, rather than risk tearing another book, she replaced the useless volume and rose. She was proud of herself when she went past Ghan, neither hurrying nor dragging, in every way her normal self. As usual, he spared her not the tiniest glance.

Once outside, she scurried to where Tsem sat, back propped against the wall. He was talking to a young man in the dress of the court, some minor nobility. When the young man saw her, he raised his brows a bit, bade a quick farewell to Tsem, and started off down the corridor, plainly having business elsewhere. Hezhi paid little mind. She rushed up to Tsem, plucking at the titan's sleeve.

"Let's go, Tsem. Now."

Tsem nodded, frowning, and climbed laboriously to his feet.

"This was a short day for you," he remarked as they crossed the increasingly busy hall. Afternoon absolutions would be offered soon, and everyone was moving toward the open fountains. Hezhi, of course, would attend no such public ceremony, and though Tsem technically *should*, she made no sign that he might be released to go and do so.

"Yes, a short day. I thought I might help Qey in the kitchen."

Tsem snorted. "There is no need to lie to *me*, Princess. Tsem is your servant."

Hezhi frowned, a bit angry that Tsem should know her so well. They crossed the White Yarrow Courtyard and then entered the royal wing, where they met fewer people going to pray.

"Did the Salamander cause you pain, Mistress?" Salamander was Tsem's name for Ghan and his smooth pate.

"No, Tsem." Hezhi was startled to feel her tears threaten to begin again. Hadn't she put them away? She was *fine*.

"Huh." The Giant grunted. They walked along a bit in silence.

"Mistress," Tsem began, then paused a moment before going on. "You know Wezh Yehd Nu?"

"What? Tsem, what are you talking about?"

"I just wondered if you knew him."

"Should I?"

"His family is wealthy and powerful."

"And unscrupulous. A century ago they acquired their land by fraud and deceit. There was a murder or two involved, as well, I think."

"*I* have never heard this," Tsem growled.

"No one talks about it. After all, *now* they have Royal Blood. It was in one of the old records—a priest wrote it, bemoaning the thinning of the River's blood with that of thieves and cutthroats."

"Ah. But this was long ago, yes?"

"Yes, long ago."

"There is a young man of the family, one Wezh . . ."

"Was that who you were talking to in the hall?"

Tsem stopped, leaned against the bright turquoise painted wall of the Wind People Hall they were just entering. "You know," he said, "that *just* may have been him."

"Now, *you* don't lie to *me*, Tsem. He scurried off like a house lizard when the cat comes around. What did this 'Wezh' want of you? I warn you, if you think I will release you, even for a day, to bodyguard some fool while he goes off to get drunk in the city . . ." Hezhi had refused such requests before.

"Ah . . . no, Princess. That is not what he wanted."

"Well?"

"He asked me to talk to *you*."

"About?" Hezhi was impatient with this conversation. What was Tsem going *on* about?

"He would like for you to . . . meet him. In the Onyx Court-yard, perhaps, or wherever you choose."

"Meet him for what . . . oh. *Oh.*"

"He asked me to tell you something else," Tsem murmured, almost inaudibly. His face was flushed dark, as dark as the time Hezhi had discovered him and the water maid who came around now and then to clean the cistern, poking and prodding one another in an old storage room.

"Something else?"

Tsem cleared his throat, his eyebrows drooping mournfully in embarrassment.

"Ah," he said. "Whither goes her brilliant beauty/My tongue cannot hold her name/More elusive than . . ."

"No! Stop *right* there," Hezhi hissed.

"I'm not very good at reciting . . ."

"It matters *not*. I don't want to hear that. This boy is *courting* me?"

"He would like to."

"No! I won't have that. No."

Tsem tightened his jaw, but then his coarse face softened. "Princess, what could it hurt?"

"I have no time for it," Hezhi answered. *Nor will I prove Ghan right about me,* she added silently.

"What shall I tell him, then?" Tsem sighed.

"Tell him whatever you like. This is no concern of mine, Tsem."

"As you say, Princess."

"Exactly so," Hezhi shot back. She strode off quickly, more than ready to be in her bed, alone, forgetting as much of the day as possible.

THE rest did Hezhi good; she slept more than in any two recent nights. But as refreshed as she felt, she also had the nagging sensation of being *behind*, of having lost time. She ate a hurried breakfast of red rice and sausage, and with barely a word to Qey, she darted off toward the library. She did not stop to get Tsem, but he followed her anyway, catching up to her before she departed the royal wing. He reached her, in fact, near the foot of the Hall of Moments, a marbled corridor scintillating in the shifting colors that glowed through its stained-glass skylights. Hezhi paused there, both to allow the Giant to join her, and also to peer down the beautiful hall. Down there were her father and mother, aunts and uncles, older siblings.

"Beautiful, isn't it, Tsem?"

"It's very nice, Princess," he answered.

"When do you think I will move down that hall, live with Father and Mother?"

"When the time comes, Princess."

"Yes, when the time comes. My sister Lanah moved down there last fall. She was thirteen, just about my age."

"Perhaps soon, then, Princess."

"Tsem, you *know*, don't you? Why we all live out here, in the royal *wing*, but not with the family. Why we move in there sometime after our tenth years. And if not that, get taken away into the dark, below the city?"

Tsem didn't answer. Instead, he seemed to be concentrating on the colors in the hall.

"It used to be that I wanted to find D'en. I still want that,

Tsem, but I wonder about myself now. Will I go down the corridor to live with Father and Mother, or will I go below the city, to wherever they took D'en? If you love me, Tsem, you should tell me."

Tsem nodded. "We have had this conversation, Princess, and I cannot answer you. I would if I could. I *do* love you."

Hezhi turned toward him, startled. His face was folded in pain, his eyes glittering like something glass and jagged.

"You *can't* tell me?" Hezhi asked. Tsem nodded. He opened his mouth to speak, but his lips worked soundlessly. He shuddered, and his eyes trembled up beneath his thick lids. He began to shake.

"No! Tsem!" Hezhi ran to him and threw her arms about his waist. She could not reach all the way around. His huge body was convulsing, shaking. As she held him, though, the shuddering quieted and finally subsided. She hugged him tighter, until two platter-sized hands reached down and gently disengaged her.

"I didn't *know*, Tsem. I'm sorry."

"It is something they do to us, when we are very young," Tsem said. His voice sounded tired, strained. "The priests—when we are chosen to work and live in the royal rooms. Me, Qey, everyone. So we can't talk about it. Do you understand?"

"I understand. I know what a Forbidding is."

Tsem acknowledged that. "I would talk to you if I could, Princess."

"I know. Come on, let us go to the library."

Her concern for Tsem ebbed as they strode on; not because she did not care for the half Giant, but because her anger began to wax. What was being hidden from her, from her siblings, her cousins? She knew no more than D'en had, and D'en was gone.

Light burst upon them again as they crossed the Ibex Courtyard, and with the real illumination came a sudden, hidden one. Hezhi grinned fiercely, her anger fitted neatly into place with purpose.

"It isn't architecture I should be studying," she whispered, not to Tsem but to herself. "It's *us*. The Blood Royal. This has to do with us." So simple, so obvious. Find the missing royalty, find D'en. Find herself. "That's what I should be studying," she whispered.

But how? She had no idea where to begin. In her meandering so far, she had encountered nothing like what she sought. Ghan was right, absolutely right. One could wander in the library for a generation and not know what one searched for; not with *her* limited skills and knowledge.

She was still sorting through that when she reached the library. As always, Tsem made his way to the hallway left of the door and sat down to wait for her. Hezhi entered, uncertain where to begin, but eager enough.

She entered and knew something was wrong. Ghan glanced up immediately from his work, met her gaze with his for the first time since that day she had entered the library. He frowned slightly and stood, holding a book with a burgundy binding. Her heart stood cold in her chest as the old man beckoned her over to him.

She went, her face burning fiercely.

"You remember what I said?" Ghan said, his voice a faint sound, a dry page turning.

"It was already torn," Hezhi said, hoping to sound confident and failing utterly.

"I told you also I would teach you not to lie," Ghan said, mildly. "How did you know what I would accuse you of?"

How had Ghan even known she had *that* book? It was impossible. Impossible, unless . . . It seemed to Hezhi that there was some way it was possible, but she was too frightened to think, and Ghan was still standing there, demanding something.

"Well?" he asked.

"I . . . I fell asleep. It tore then."

Ghan nodded. "I warned you."

"Please . . ." she began, not knowing exactly how to plead with him, what she could offer. The expression on Ghan's face stopped her, however.

"There is no bargaining with me, Princess. I am the master in this room, subject only to the word of your father. And your father will *not* speak for you."

"I may come here no longer?" *I will not cry,* Hezhi thought, and suddenly felt confident that she would not, not until later.

"Oh, no, Princess. You *will* come here. You will come here every day, and you will do as I say." He handed her a piece of rolled paper. Ch'ange paper, the kind royal business was transacted on.

"Your father was kind enough to sign this, Princess."

"What is it?" Her head was swimming, her knees seemed wobbly, unsound, and she feared she would collapse.

"It is a contract. You are indebted to the Royal Library. During the daylight hours, you will be as my servant, doing what chores I see fit. You may not complain, and you must comply or be bound by your hair to the shaming post in the Grand Courtyard. Do you understand this?"

"Servant?" Hezhi blurted. "I *cannot* be a servant. I am a princess!"

"Which means nothing to me. Not with this paper in my hands. Even the emperor, your father, serves the River, and you serve *him,* as does all of the royal family. And *he* has commanded that *you* serve me." He proffered Hezhi the document.

She took it with trembling fingers, but she could not read it. She could not concentrate. But there was her father's signature, his seal. It was real.

"I . . ." she began.

"The first thing I tell you is to be silent. You speak only when I request it."

"Yes, Ghan," she acknowledged, lowering her eyes by way of answer.

"Now. Today I will show you how to mend books. I have many for you to mend. After that, I believe . . ." He shot his gaze about the room almost hungrily. "Have you improved your command of the old script? You may speak."

"I have tried . . ." She trailed off. She could not possibly read the old script as well as Ghan would want her to.

Ghan glared. "There is much indexing to be done. Do you know what indexing is?"

"No, Ghan."

"So *ignorant.*" He sighed. "But it cannot be helped, I suppose."

"If I . . ."

"I didn't ask you to speak!" Ghan hissed, his face contorted.

"Your pardon, I—"

"Silence!"

But I am a princess, Hezhi thought, but succeeded in not retorting.

"Follow me. Do *not* stop to tear any books."

Ghan took her to a small table. There were sheets of white paper, a bowl of paste, heavy boards for pressing.

"Tears are simple," Ghan began. "Even the simple can fix them. I will show you that first, then the binding."

Hezhi nodded. Dully, she watched his smooth brown fingers deftly work with the paper.

"Use just enough glue. Just enough, and no more."

A sudden suspicion filled Hezhi. An image, even, of her sleeping, of Ghan standing over her, of him reaching down, tearing the book himself, then quietly leaving her there, still asleep. So that he could do *this,* humiliate her, punish her for invading his precious library.

Ghan's finger was a handspan from her nose, wagging angrily.

"You aren't paying attention," he accused. He looked angry.

Yes, I am, Hezhi thought. *I certainly am.*

VI

A Gift of Blood

"Please." Perkar groaned. "I'm leaving. Please, Goddess, give me your blessing."

The stream flowed on, caressing only his ankles, and them only indifferently, with no more feeling than it would a stick or a rock.

"Please," he repeated. As the sun moved on and on across the sky.

At last, near sundown, the water swirled. She was there, watching him.

"I am not for you, Perkar," she told him.

"It matters not," he answered. Her beauty would kill him, he thought. It was so terrible, so wonderful. Even in his dreams it could not be idealized, could not become greater; even in dreams it only faded.

She shook leaves from her hair. A wet, ebony tendril of it strayed down over her right eye.

"You have no right," she said. "You have no right to add to my sorrow. You are a beast like all other beasts."

63

"Yet you love me."

Her face twisted into a little smile, evil at the edges. "You don't know what I feel, Perkar. I am not a beast—or I am many. When I think of myself this way—in this form, in the form of this poor little creature whose blood was loosed in me—when I think of myself this way, I have some love for you. But it is *my* kind of love, nothing you would recognize." She shook her head, her most Human expression. "Go away, live and die, forget me."

"I *am* going away," Perkar said.

"Good. Stay away."

"Only when I *do* die."

Her face softened, and she walked over, stroked his face. But when her fingers touched him, she drew back again.

"There is talk among the spirits," she whispered. "You are going to speak to the Forest Lord."

"I am."

"You will be very near *him*, Perkar. The devourer."

"Not so," Perkar mumbled, reaching to touch her. "We go north and west. You—the great River is in the east. That is where you . . . he . . ."

"Where he takes me in. Where he kills me and chews me up. But that is down along his body. His head is farther up, up in the mountains. You will be near him, and you must be careful. He will smell me upon you, taste me. And he knows you, too, my sweet, for through me he has swallowed your seed. Promise me that you will not approach him."

"I promise you that I will find a way to kill him."

The goddess darted her hand out: It leapt quickly as a fish and slapped him hard across the face.

"You are a boy," she hissed. "You have the thoughts of a boy. Be a man and live with what *may* be, what is possible, and not what you childishly wish."

Perkar was too stunned to speak. He was still without his voice when she faded back into the water.

*　　*　　*

"I STILL say you should take old Yellow Mane," Henyi muttered.

Perkar smiled thinly at his little brother. "I don't think Yellow Mane would last very long in Balat—or any wild forest. I think Yellow Mane is fine just where she is. Happy, too."

"But I don't see why you have to take Kutasapal."

"Because Father gave him to me. What are you complaining about? You already have a fine stallion."

"So do you."

"For a journey like this, one needs *many* horses," Perkar said.

"So *you* say."

"Watch when the others arrive with the king," Perkar told him, tousling the younger boy's hair. "They will have more than one horse."

"Of course they will. There will be more than one of *them*. The king, that strange-looking man . . ."

"They will *each* have more than one horse, I mean." Perkar kicked at one of the red chickens pecking near his boots, where a few grains had dropped from the handful he had just given his horse. "I'm taking Kutasapal, here, and Mang, of course." Mang was Perkar's favorite steed. Years before, when the fierce Mang raiders had come up the valley, many had died and their kin never recovered their mounts. The beasts were hard to train—or so Perkar's father said—but one of the stallions got a mare with colt. Mang was second in that line, a proud fine horse, dun with fierce red stripes the color of dried blood on his neck.

"Henyi, give your brother a rest. He needs the finest of our horses."

Both brothers turned at the new voice.

"Hello, Mother," they said, nearly in unison.

"Henyi, the chickens need feed. See to it, please."

Perkar lowered his head, ostensibly to tighten the packs on the mare. In fact, he was avoiding his mother's troubled gaze.

"There is no need to do this, Masati," she said.

Perkar grimaced, worked harder at the packs. "It is bad luck to call a man his childhood name when he seeks Piraku."

She snorted, and Perkar looked at her for the first time. Her auburn hair was bound in three tight braids, and she wore her tall felt hat, the one that signified her marriage to Sherye. A hawk feather fluttered from the top tassel. She was dressed to send her son off to war.

"You seek Piraku too far away, son. It can be found much closer to home."

"*I* can't find it here."

"Because you are foolish; for no other reason."

"Father said . . ." Perkar began, but she cut him short with a humorless little laugh.

"Oh, I heard the two of you last night, heads full of woti and silliness. Talking about grand adventures and sword fights. But tonight, Perkar, your father will come to me. He will come to me, and he will not weep, but he will lay his head against my breast. He will not sleep."

Perkar heaved a deep sigh. "I cannot live with him forever. He knows that."

"The Kapaka is a reckless man, and he chooses reckless companions. Your father knows that, too."

Perkar answered that with a shrug only. His mother watched him tighten the already tight packs.

"They will be here soon, Mother. It will be unseemly if you are standing close enough to nurse me. They will think me less a man than they already do."

"The tower man will announce their coming. Plenty of time for me to move up onto the porch."

He nodded reluctantly. He was beginning to feel silly checking the packs. He drew his sword out, wiped it with a cleaning rag. The morning sun glinted from it.

"Four generations, but *my* son is the one to be ruined by her," his mother muttered.

"I don't want to talk about this," Perkar said, and his tone was stringent enough that she actually winced.

"Well. Well," she said.

He put the sword away, looked up to the tower man. He was gazing impassively off toward the road.

"Listen, Perkar. You men run about seeking Piraku, finding it, stealing it. Killing each other for it. My only Piraku is *you*, you and your brother. Do you understand that? If both of you die before me, I will have nothing. Do you see? So you must take care of yourself." Her voice trembled a bit; Perkar had never seen her cry—or even come this close.

"Here," she said. She was offering him something; a little wooden charm. "This is from the oak tree you were named for," she confided. "Right near where I buried your caul. Tuck it away somewhere, where the other men won't see it."

"Mother . . ."

"*Son.* Each of them will have something like this. They will just hide it, as you will. No man leaves without something from his mother."

"I have much more than this from you," he said softly.

"I'm glad you believe so," she answered.

"*Kapakapane,*" the tower man shouted. The king is coming.

"Hurry, Mother."

She turned and walked quickly up to the big porch. She was very small, his mother, as fine as a little bird. Now *he* had to fight back tears.

Be a man, he thought to himself. But everyone seemed to think being a man meant something different. Women, for instance, seemed to have *very* confused ideas about it.

Out at the gate, there was a clatter of hooves, growing louder.

THE Kapaka wasted no time setting off. The men praised each others' horses; Perkar grinned from ear to ear when the Kapaka spoke of Mang. Mang, at least, was his. During all of this Ngangata—the halfling—was silent. He sat impassively astride a coal-black mare, an ugly creature, thick of leg. Perkar suspected that the horse, like Ngangata himself, was half wild. Still, he was too excited to think much on the half Alwa and his rudeness. The morning fairly gleamed, honey light dribbled over a fresh green landscape, birds sang. The cattle watched them impassively as they made their way out across the pastures, following the road off and away from his father's holdings. His one moment of sadness, early on that ride, was the glimpse of the tree line that hid the Stream, the goddess that he loved. They did not cross her, however, but passed on west. They did stop at the pasture shrine and offer tallow to the old forest spirit; Perkar was pleased at the precise and fine manner in which the Kapaka made his offering. That even such an important man as he took the time to honor the ties forged by his ancestors.

His companions were the same five who had come to the damakuta before. Apad—the dark-haired man his own age—seemed the most talkative of the lot. He rode a double arm's length from him.

"We shall have fine lands like these, my friend," he told Perkar.

"Our grandchildren, perhaps," Perkar answered. "My father says that it takes many years and much hard work to create such beautiful pastures. In my grandfather's day, they say, this was mostly burned stumps and weeds."

"Just so," Apad gave back cheerfully. "This land is like a worn shoe; there is nothing better to wear. But we shall make our *own* shoes." Perkar was wondering if Apad were joking about his name, which meant simply "shoe," but decided not to ask. People were often sensitive about their names.

"How I shall work!" Apad went on. "I will bet all of you now—bet you a fine steer—that I will clear more of my land in my lifetime than any of you!"

Eruka tossed back his straw-blond hair and glanced back over his shoulder at them. "Apad bets you a steer he doesn't even own."

"*Yet,*" Apad said, waggling a finger at his friend.

"Hmm," Eruka replied.

"Eruka fears to take me up on the bet," Apad confided to Perkar—loudly.

Eruka shrugged. "Clearing land is hard work. I'll be happy enough to clear what I need."

"Or have your wife clear it," Apad said, an exaggerated sneer that was plainly meant good-naturedly—as opposed to as a deadly insult.

The Kapaka—up ahead with Ngangata and Atti, the older man with the thick red braids—cleared his throat. "It's a fine thing to plan," he cautioned. "Remember only that the Forest Lord may or may not give his word."

"Of course, of course," Apad replied. He winked at Perkar.

"You, Atti, will you take my bet?"

The braided man turned only slightly in his saddle. He had a habit of gazing all about him, all of the time—he never settled on looking at a single thing. "A useless sort of bet," he replied. "If we judge how much we have cleared by the end of our lives, what use will the winner have for a steer?"

"Well, fine, we can change the wager a bit. Let us say, then, whichever of us has the most pasture by the age of fifty."

Atti snorted. "That gives you many more years of chopping trees than I would have. Thirty to my ten. I might still win, though, against your soft valley hands."

Apad hooted. "We shall see, wild man from the hills! Will you use a broken stone to chop those trees, like your Alwat friends?"

Perkar saw the frown cross Atti's face before he turned forward again. Ngangata—had the jab actually been aimed at *him*?—reacted not at all. Eruka, though, shot Apad a cautioning look.

They don't like the halfbreed, either, Perkar realized. *Only Atti speaks to him. And with his wild braids and strange accent, he is like a wild man himself.* Something about that satisfied Perkar immensely. He had disliked Ngangata from the moment he met those insolent black eyes and that soft, rude tongue. He had also felt guilty about it—his father and the Kapaka clearly disap-

proved of such an attitude. But Apad and Eruka already knew
the Alwa-Man, and if they did not like him either, there must be
ample justification for feeling that way.

Still, that last remark by Apad had chilled the conversation;
apparently there were things that one should be cautious of joking about.

After a moment, though, the Kapaka broke the uneven stutter-
ing of hoofbeats. "Sing us something, Eruka. Something for
traveling."

"Ah, hmm," Eruka mused, and in a moment he hummed a
note and began. He had a clear, fine tenor, wavering wildly on
the final notes of phrases, an old style and difficult to do well.
Eruka did it well.

> Up to the hoof I come
> Lifting it up, taking it on
> Here is what I said I would do
> When the new people and their horses come
> But never did I promise
> Never did I swear to them
> That I would not have my fun
> Not make them ache where their butts meet the saddle
> Not make them wish for a woman and a bed
> I will have my own fun . . .

Apad chimed in now and then, on words like "fun" and
"woman," and he was a very *bad* singer. His "quavering"
sounded more like a child bawling or an injured man crying for
help. It made the song all that much more amusing, and Perkar
felt himself smiling, broadly and unreservedly, for the first time in
years. He was on the road, on the way out, to a world rich in
Piraku, a world that suddenly had possibilities he had never
dared imagine.

But for the rest of the day, imagine he did. And when they left
his father's lands, crossed into the wilderness where no axe had
been, his thoughts were not on goddesses, or mothers, or any

such sorrow, but on the gait of his horse and the sound of bois-terous voices.

The sun westered soon enough—the day seemed to fly by. The woods were as open as the inside of a hall, trees like wide-spaced pillars, leaves like the shingled roof of his father's house. Red dusty sunlight leaked through the roof, however, gathered here and there beneath the trees, as if swept into little piles. The bird-song had changed to an evening tune, and the little black frogs that lived in the thick leaf-litter of the open forest floor began throating their own weird melodies.

"We should travel faster," the Kapaka told them. "We can reach the damakuta of Bangaka before nightfall, I think. What do you say, Perkar?"

"We would *really* have to ride," Perkar said.

"Good enough," the king agreed, and he urged his red and brown piebald into a trot. The others followed. Soon enough they burst from the forest into rolling pasture; a few indignant cows ran from them as they fell into full gallop. The sky opened up, a tapestry, heavy purple clouds woven into an iron-gray sky. The clouds smelled wet, and far on the horizon crimson lightning silently lit one up, the glowing heart of an enormous ghost. The sky and the field were spacious, but the sounds of the travelers stayed close to them, as if the thudding of hooves and their voices feared to stray far into the coming night. They galloped on, and Perkar felt part of Mang, part of the great four-legged beast. He had heard that the Mang tribes believed that a horse and rider who died together lived on as one creature, half man, half horse. It seemed a wonderful dream.

Now the clouds were gray, and the heavens black, and the stars not hidden by thunderheads shone steady. The moon, red as a fire god's eye, rose, half lidded, sleepy.

So it was dark when at last they saw the watchfires of the damakuta, when the men came out to greet them.

Perkar knew Bangaka and his sons well enough; indeed, one of the women he had been urged to consider for marriage was a niece of Bangaka's and lived at his damakuta. Perkar resolved to avoid her, if possible. Bangaka himself met them at the gate; he was an old man, his back a bit stooped, hair as white and thin as thistledown. He had an old-age vagueness about his eyes that made Perkar uneasy. He had eight sons, but only the youngest three still lived with him.

There was not much celebration—the hour was late, and Bangaka had not been expecting visitors. The king retired with the old man, to discuss Piraku and so forth—but the rest of them were offered the barn, an open fire, and warm flasks of woti.

"Well," Apad commented. "The hospitality here is not of your father's quality, Perkar, but it will do." He gazed reflectively at the little knot of serving girls, peeking and giggling from behind an outbuilding. "Sit here, Perkar. Have some woti."

Perkar hesitated. "First I shall rub down Mang and Kutasapal," he said. "Then I will gladly join you."

"Let the wild men take care of that," Apad said.

"What?"

"We will brush down the horses," Ngangata remarked shortly.

"You aren't wearing a servant's livery," Perkar said. "I can rub down my own steeds."

Atti walked over to join the half Alwa. His braids were like rust in the firelight. Ngangata was frightening; his eyes were caves, holes sunken into his head deep, deep. His wide mouth looked less amusing now and more dangerous.

"Let them do it," Eruka called from across the fire. "They enjoy it."

Perkar tried to hold Ngangata's gaze, but there was nothing to hold, only blackness. Finally he shrugged and joined the other two at the fire.

Woti loosened Eruka's tongue.

"My clan—Kar Kushuta—is next to nothing," he said. "My grandfather lost half of our land in a wager, and that on top of a feud with the Kar Hakiru. We were always on the losing side of *that*. There was no land, and it was hard for my father to make a good marriage for any of us without land or daughters."

"No daughters?"

Eruka shook his head. "They say my mother was cursed by the goddess of our apple orchard, for something she did when she was young. She has never borne daughters."

Perkar understood the problem. Sons could only receive land as dowry, through their wives. A man was more likely to *give* a daughter and her dowry to a clan that had recently done the same for one of *his* sons. In this way the total lands of the clan remained roughly similar over time. A man with little land and no daughters was unlikely to find marriages for his sons.

"So I became a singer," Eruka concluded glumly. "There is some Piraku in that, though not much."

Apad, whose eyes were already beginning to glaze, slapped Eruka on the back. "Don' worry," he slurred. "Tha' will all change soon."

As Eruka had become more talkative, the garrulous Apad had been nearly muted by the strong drink. As Perkar watched, he downed another cup. He himself was drinking only lightly—his father and he having been drunk the night before.

Eruka nodded in response to the dark-haired man's promise. "If the Forest Lord wills," he muttered.

Apad's face grew dark. "And what if he doesn't?" he demanded tersely, softly. "What if he doesn't, Perkar?"

Perkar shrugged. "I don't know."

Apad took another drink, fixed his gaze on the dancing flames, perhaps searching for the little wild fire goddess there.

"Remember the 'Song of a Mad God'? About the mountain god who came down and devoured men?"

Eruka cleared his throat.

> And so I came down
> I came to the villages
> To the proud damakutat

> The holdings on the hills
> I wandered in the halls
> I wondered,
> How might a man taste?
> I drank the blood of mortal men
> Drank it but never quenched my thirst.

Eruka sang on, softly, as if afraid someone would hear. Sang about the hero Rutka, who put on the skin of a bear, posed as the brother of the Crazed God and learned his weakness.

> Only by the copper blade
> The axe beaten by the forge god
> The one in the hall of the Forest Lord
> Maker of death for gods

Rutka found the axe, after many adventures, and dispatched the blood-crazed god.

When the song was over, Apad was swaying, and Perkar feared he would fall into the fire. He wondered where Atti and Ngangata were; they should have been done with the horses by now.

"See, Perkar? They can be *killed*. What right has the Forest Lord to tell you and me what we may and may not have? We are Irut, true men—not like the Alwat, not like the little gods. Each of us is like Rutka. Strong! If the gods do not give us what we want, we will take it. Hey, Perkar? You're a good fellow, aren't you? Want what we want. We'll be heroes together, you and Eruka and I. We'll get what the king desires, even if the king doesn't like how we get it."

"What about Atti and Ngangata?" Perkar asked. His own head was swimming a bit now. The song made him proud, proud to be Human. He must have drunk more woti than he imagined, listening to Eruka sing.

"Heroes come only in threes and sevens," Apad snarled. "Never in fives." He reached for his cup of woti, but tipped it over with his hand. There was a giggle out in the darkness; the girls were still watching.

"Hah!" Apad muttered. "Let's see what *that* is!" He lurched off into the night. Grinning, Eruka followed.

Perkar watched them go. His elation was dimming, but there was something, something in the song . . .

Why had she slapped him? Called him a boy? Gods could be *killed*. If a mad god could die, so could a river. Of course they could, and the other men knew it! In the house of the Forest Lord there were things that could kill gods, surely.

The sky was clearing; tomorrow would be bright. Perkar found his way to standing, walked out across the bare ground. He waved at the tower guard as he went out the still open gate.

"Late," the man said. "I'll close the gate soon."

"I didn't want to soil the lord's yard," Perkar explained.

The shadowy figure didn't answer, but Perkar thought he saw his head incline. He walked on down the hill, relieved himself on the night-damp ground. Then he strolled a bit farther, to the willow-line he guessed marked a stream.

"And where do *you* go, god or goddess?" he inquired of it softly, but the stream—a rivulet, really—did not answer. Perkar thought he knew, though. They were up a neighboring valley, one that joined his own. Surely this little stream flowed down, eventually, to his father's pasture.

Perkar's head swirled, the warmth of the woti still coursing up from his belly. What could he send her, that she might know him? Know what he intended? What sacrifice could this tiny child of hers take to her?

He knew, of course. He fumbled out his little knife, the one he used for trimming leather laces. The cut went a little deeper than he intended—too much woti!—but it would not trouble him, there on the back of his hand. He washed the cut in the stream, gave it his blood. She understood blood; she would know his.

From back at the gate there was a whistle. Perkar let another drop or two fall into the water, then, satisfied and strangely happy, walked back up to the barn, and sleep.

INTERLUDE

Jik

A POLISHED deckplank creaked beneath Ghe's foot, and he froze, waiting to see if the slight sound had been heard. After a moment he relaxed, satisfied that the little creak had been folded neatly into the hundred other wooden complaints as the barge rocked gently in the River, into the frogs and nightbirds singing in the Yellow-Haired-Swamp just downstream. The sharp features of his shadowed face quirked in a sardonic smile at his own nervousness, and he reached with his thumb to rub the little scar at the point of his pointed chin. *I am a blade of silver; I am a sickle of ice,* he mouthed.

He moved on, slipping past a guard nodding at his post, mesmerized, perhaps, by the distant lights of the city, or the even more distant lights of stars. Dressed in blackest shadow, Ghe moved as effortlessly as smoke, through an ostentatious arch encased in gold leaf into a spacious cabin, onto the rich carpet woven in distant and exotic Lhe. Toward the great bed, and its sheets of finest linen.

Ghe had not the faintest idea why it was his task to kill the man who slumbered there; the priesthood would never make him privy to such details. He need only know whom to kill and where to find them; the why of it didn't matter to him. As a child, he had killed for nothing more than a few copper coins. Now his skills were for the priesthood, for the River himself.

He suddenly realized that no one was in the bed, and the hackles of his neck pricked up. The lights on the barge were extinguished; he had watched from the small boat that brought him until they had all gone out. That meant his target somehow suspected something, was hiding in the dark, waiting for his death to come looking for him and find a surprise instead. Ghe turned quickly on the balls of his feet, crouching at the same moment, searching with his eyes. After a moment of that, he sighed in exasperation and relief. He had overestimated this trader, this Dunuh, just as Dunuh had overestimated himself, somehow. For there he was, asleep in a chair, silhouetted against the lights of the city.

Ghe's relief faded as quickly as it came, for there loomed another shadow, standing near the sleeping one.

"Ah," the darkness whispered, "the much-vaunted Jik, I take it."

Ghe said nothing. If he should fail and die, there must be no proof that he was actually Jik. He carried no emblem, no sign of the priesthood. Unlike the other priestly sects, Jik were not castrated, so there would be no evidence of that sort. Only overconfident words could betray him, and though Ghe was *confident*, he was not overconfident.

His blade snicked out of its oiled scabbard, caught moonlight like a silver eel.

"Jik," the shadow went on, "I am Sin Turuk, from the ancient city of Kolem. You have heard of Kolem?"

Still Ghe did not answer. The man went on. "Kolem has many exports. The oil of the Kakla tree, textiles—and warriors. Warriors taught to fight from the moment we can hold a sword. Much-valued men." White teeth appeared, then, amidst the black skin of his face. A faint hiss was *his* sword clearing into the night air.

"My master is a drunken fool," Sin Turuk said. "But he is still my master."

Sin Turuk leapt, pantherlike, lighted on the tips of his toes an armspan from Ghe. Ghe darted his ribbon of sword for the man's heart, but his opponent stepped aside, the sword flickering by him. He saw his mistake in the instant he made it, that his lunge was what Sin wanted. Ghe had no time to recover his sword and parry. Instead, he dropped flat, and the foreigner's sword whirred above his head. Ghe lashed out expertly with his leg, caught his enemy at the ankles, who fell, and yet Ghe could feel that it was too easy, that Sin had anticipated this move, as well, shifted his weight so as to fall controlled. This insight saved Ghe's life, for instead of sprawling helplessly, Sin had somehow contrived to tumble over him, lashing out with the bright-edged crescent he held. Ghe dropped his own sword, lunged inside the blow, sweeping the strong arms on, delivered a *Tsehats* blow to Sin's neck. The man grunted dully, lashed out again. He should have been dead, but at least he was injured, slow enough that Ghe could snake-draw his dagger and plunge it straight into Sin Turuk's heart, jiggle it, and withdraw. Sin died silently, with the dignity a great warrior deserved.

"A sickle of ice," Ghe whispered to the man, as his eyes went from shocked to empty. "But you fought well."

The idiot out on deck had not even heard anything. Ghe sighed, slipped his knife into the sleeping man in three key places—heart, base of the skull, and temple. He left the other guards alive, to shame them, to let them see that a battle of Giants had transpired within their earshot and they had known *nothing*.

On the way back to shore, he saluted Sin Turuk by dripping a bit of blood in the River and by touching a dot of it to his own chin, to the first scar he ever received in combat. For his intended victim—who had merely exhaled upon dying, a breath stinking of expensive wine—Ghe did nothing.

VII

Ghosts and Wishes

"**Y**ou have ruined a five-hundred-year-old book," Ghan told her—rather matter-of-factly, without real heat.

"It was ruined already."

Ghan sighed. "No—it was damaged but repairable. *Now* it is ruined."

Hezhi looked up from what she was doing—pasting the fragments of a Second-Dynasty plate to a new backing—and met the old man's hard gaze.

"You don't pay attention, that's your whole problem. You don't pay attention to what you are doing, but to whatever happens to be running around in your silly little head."

One day, she thought, keeping her face neutral. *One day I shall be an adult, adult nobility, and you shall disappear in the night, Ghan. I will have Tsem take you and stuff you down a sewer pipe.*

"Like *that*!" Ghan snarled. "Like that, eyes gone all dreamy and stupid." He stepped swiftly up to the table. "*Here* is what

79

you are doing." He gestured at the plate. "*This.* Keep your fingers and your brain together, for once."

"I've been doing this for twenty days," Hezhi muttered, trying not to snap. "Couldn't I do something more interesting?"

"Like?"

"I don't know. You mentioned something called 'indexing.'"

"You can't do that, *Princess.* You cannot read well enough."

"Well, I'm tired of this."

"But you've yet to do it *well*," Ghan replied. "Why should I waste my energy teaching you another task when you have not demonstrated the ability to do even the simplest with proficiency? To teach you to index, for instance, I would first have to teach you to read, and I have *no* intention of wasting the kind of time *that* would take."

"But I can already read *some*," she began. Read? If the side effect of this bondage was that she would learn to read, it would be worth it.

"Be still. Add a little more water to that paste. When you can paste a simple page together without ugly, overlapped seams, then we can talk about you doing *something* else. Or . . ." Ghan looked sly for a moment, calculating. Then he leaned heavily on the desk, stooped forward, so that their eyes were quite close together. "Or you can leave here this afternoon. But you must not come back, ever. I have gotten poor work out of you, but you have not yet paid your debt. Being here, you do more and more damage each day. So I will report your bondage satisfied. Just don't come in tomorrow—or any day after." He smiled wanly, straightened, and walked off without a backward glance. That evening, when she finally unkinked her back, put her paste and thread away, he did not acknowledge her. She left in silence.

Qey met her at the door, anxious. "You must take a bath," she explained. Her fingers fluttered like butterflies lighting on her hands.

"I'm tired," Hezhi replied. She had no time for Qey's timid mothering.

"It matters not. Your father sends for you."

"My father?" What could he want?

Qey nodded vigorously. "You must attend court this evening."

Hezhi frowned. "*Must* I? Send Father my regrets."

"Oh, no, Hezhi, not this time," Qey sighed, shaking her head. She glanced past Hezhi, presumably at Tsem. Suspicious, Hezhi turned, as well. Tsem's face was carefully blank, but she could sense tension there. His neck muscles were drawn taut; he was grinding his teeth. "This time, little one, you must go. The messengers your father sent were very insistent."

She digested that silently. She had managed to avoid court for the better part of a year. But perhaps—just perhaps—if she went to court, she could actually speak to her father or mother. Convince them to take away Ghan's power over her. Just thinking about the old man made her furious. For two days after Ghan showed her the writ, Hezhi didn't go to the library at all. Four men in the dress of the palace guard came and got her, *forced* her to the library and Ghan. Hezhi had to restrain Tsem; she saw the dangerous look in his usually mild eyes. None of the guards ever knew how close they came to having their necks broken or long bones splintered. But if she had allowed Tsem to defend her, he would have been mutilated or killed later. She could not stand the thought of *that*.

Yes, perhaps she could reach her father's ear, if only for a moment—if he even knew who she was, at a glance. He had, after all, not spoken directly to her for something more than a year.

"What are the colors in court today, then?" she asked. Qey looked relieved, almost happy.

"They sent a dress along," she said.

"This is just the revival of a style from a century ago," Hezhi complained as Qey helped her struggle into the monstrous dress.

It had a laminated spine of rivershark cartilage that ran from the nape of a stiff collar down her back. The dress's backbone parted company with her own at the pelvis—there it lanced out and back, supporting a stiff but mercifully short train that resembled the tail of a crawfish. This "spine" had to be held on, of course, so the rest of the dress worked at concealing the tight straps beneath her breasts and across her abdomen. It was lime and gold, spangled with purple mother-of-pearl sequins.

"Was it considered as ugly a century ago?" Qey asked, and she actually giggled—as if it were years ago, before she became so *serious*. Suddenly a bit happier, Hezhi modeled the dress for Qey, walking smartly, lampooning the ladies at court. Qey watched her with eyes full of wonder.

"You may grow up into a woman yet," she said. "How did this happen so quickly?" Hezhi heard the obvious pride, caught the hidden sadness, the worry.

The dress finally on, Qey applied the thick, burgundy makeup presently popular in court, filling the hollows of Hezhi's eyes, drawing a fine line down her forehead to the bridge of her nose.

Looking at herself in the glass, Hezhi was mildly surprised. She looked like a princess—not like the bondservant of a bald old librarian, not like the dirty little girl skittering about the hallways of the abandoned wing. No, she looked like the other women at court. Like her elder sister, whom she had met once. A princess; something she was used to calling herself, but had no sense of how to *be*.

Qey was still watching her. "Certainly you will have suitors now, whether you want them or not," she remarked. Hezhi nodded glumly at the older woman, wished suddenly that she had Qey's worn square face and thick limbs. But even those would not ward *her* from suitors; she was the daughter of an emperor. Her ambiguous feelings over her appearance settled more certainly toward disapproval; the taunting voice of Ghan seemed just in her ear, dismissing her as some pretty palace creature.

But what did *she* care what Ghan thought, anyway? She sighed and followed Qey from her room, out into the courtyard. Tsem was there, waiting, and Hezhi smirked openly at him. He was lashed into a black cotton kilt, a lime shirt, and an open, brocaded vest. His hair was oiled and braided, the braids piled on his head and tucked beneath a little square felt hat. He was trying hard to maintain a dignified, nonchalant air.

"You look beautiful, Tsem," she remarked. "With your size and that vest, perhaps no one will notice *me*."

Tsem snorted. "Shall we go, Princess?"

"I don't want to."

"Neither do I," Tsem muttered fervently.

A ROOM should seem diminished when full, but the Great Leng Hall was as imposing as ever. Though its floor thronged with people—more people than she had been in the presence of in more than a year—it still seemed as vast as the sky. Indeed, its vaulted roof imitated the sky, deep azure at the rims, paler toward the meridian. The great buttresses seemed like the pillars holding up the heavens. She noticed a bird up there—a pigeon, a swallow? It was lost in the immensity, the apparent size of a mosquito.

And the noise! Drums were pattering somewhere, but that was nothing. It was the voices, chattering laughing voices that roared in Hezhi's tender ears, accustomed to the quietest corners of the palace. She felt buffeted by them, standing at the royal entry. When she was announced—*Princess Hezhi Yehd Cha'dune*—her name flew out into the din and was eaten, gone.

When her father came in, on the other hand, the voices dropped away, as if a hundred doors had been shut between her and them—one or two cackled on for a moment and then died, embarrassed.

The Chakunge of Nhol was an imposing man; Hezhi saw little resemblance to him in herself. He was tall, strikingly so, not thin or gangly. His shoulders were broad, his face sharp-boned but

with no hint of femininity. Power swirled about him, power beyond that conveyed by his rich robe of saffron and umber, his
turban and the golden circlet that held it in place. It was like the
wavy outline of a ghost, or the burning of air above the hot tile
roof in the summer. It made one's nape tingle just to look at him.
Sorcerer, king, child of the River—all of that one could see even
if he were naked. When he was announced, every person in the
room dropped to their knees. Those nearest the central fountain
reached for it, to wet their foreheads.

Hezhi's heart sank. She could never go near *him*, her father or
no. And she felt . . . ill. There was a tightness, a weirdness deep
in her stomach. It had been there before, all day, lurking, but
now it redoubled. What was wrong with her?

A little hiss went up from the crowd, surprise. The Chakunge
had not stopped at the dais upon which he usually sat; rather, he
descended the steps onto the courtyard floor itself. The crowd
parted away from him, like a mass of pigeons keeping well away
from the feet of a pedestrian. His two bodyguards, hulking full-
blooded Giants, walked ponderously on either side of him, massive gazes searching ceaselessly for any danger to their master.
They were dressed like Tsem, but they looked even more ridiculous; they were less manlike than Tsem, longer of arm, very hairy,
with brutal, flat faces and no chins.

Thus the floor emptied before the emperor until he stood at
the very base of the fountain. Hezhi watched him carefully, her
father, saw his sardonic face register some deeper, stranger sentiment as he approached the water.

It is the Blood Royal I need to understand, she reminded
herself.

He brushed the tips of his fingers through the cascading water;
that was all, and then he stepped back, eyes closed. The fountain
was a simple one, a single jet rising thirty feet into the air of the
hall and then roaring back down into a broad, alabaster basin.
Now the water began to shimmer, though. Hezhi was still watching her father, and *his* figure seemed blurred, as if he were some-

how vibrating like the plucked string of a lyre. The shimmering
in the water increased, and suddenly the column was soaring up,
up toward the vaulted roof of the hall. It grew like a great, watery palm, colors scintillating from it. Dark figures struggled in
the water—fish? They were carried up, up the waterspout. Near
the ceiling, the water suddenly ceased to shower down to its
source, but instead spread out in a pool, a pool floating in the air.
The pool quickly spread, shimmering and rippling, until the
dome of the ceiling was obscured by it. Then the most peculiar
thing of all; something about the water—not its wetness or its
density, but something else, like the *ghost* of water, shimmery,
feeling of depth—settled down upon the court. A little gasp went
around the floor; it was as if they were underneath the River,
staring up at the surface of the water. The dark things were still
there, but now they began to acquire a nimbus, black images
limned in glowing colors, jade, white, aquamarine, topaz. They
swam down from the ceiling, in and among the courtiers, brushing against them. Hezhi saw one swim *through* a woman near
her. Hezhi felt a terrible chill that started in her abdomen and
flashed out, and yet at the same time she was captivated. They
were lovely, these things. They were all creatures of the River;
some were weird fish, the length of a person, armored in plates
as if they were warriors. Some more resembled insects or crawfish, but were not the insects or crawfish Hezhi was familiar
with. No, these were the things that lurked as shadows in the waters of the River; ghosts of things that once lived and died in his
waters, however long ago. Now they swam and pirouetted at her
father's whim.

"Princess!" Tsem tugged at her, pointing. Three of the things
were "swimming" about her feet, gradually rising higher. One
was a fish; the other was like a scorpion built for swimming; the
third resembled a squid. These three were joined by four more,
and they swirled all around Hezhi, like a cloud. She heard those
nearest her gasp, and more than one whispered "Royal Blood."

Soon she could see nothing but the creatures enveloping her.

She should have been frightened, but instead she felt weirdly elated; the queasiness in her stomach seemed more like a glow now, as if there was something warm and strong in her. She laughed softly, reaching out her hands to touch the insubstantial fish. They seemed to suck at her, as if feeding, but she felt nothing.

Then they rose away, rushed back up to the watery pool above their heads, which was shrinking; with a sudden roar—the room had been nearly silent, save for awed whispers—the water began returning to the fountain, rushing down like torrential rain. The Riverghosts lost their shine, became shadows, less than that. In a matter of moments, the court was as it had been before her father came down. Save that now the people began to shout, shout her father's title. Chakunge!

The warm feeling in her gut had begun to feel "wrong" again by the time her father reached his dais. Hezhi noticed that during the strange performance, her mother and sisters had emerged from their rooms and were already seated on the benches. As the Chakunge joined them, he turned and clapped his hands briskly. The cleared place on the floor—where he had stood so recently—grew wider as many young boys in the dress of priestly acolytes ran about, ushering everyone back. Hezhi watched, interested despite herself. Her father had demonstrated his kinship with the River, shown that he could speak to it, bend it to his will—or more likely, beg its indulgence. What now?

The drums began again, a slow, powerful rhythm like a heartbeat. The dancers came out.

They seemed fragile creatures, men and women alike, until they began to move, to swirl to the ponderous drumbeats; then they became as strong as the drums, as supple as drumheads. This Hezhi had seen before; it was the more standard court performance. Still, the dancers were beautiful to behold, with their sleek muscles and their costumes of silk and feathers. The crowd around her began to squat, or sit cross-legged. Tsem rolled out a little mat for Hezhi—had he been carrying it all along?—and she sat, too.

The story was an ancient one; Hezhi knew it well. It was the story of the first Chakunge, the man born of water. Now the dancers portrayed his mother, Gau, bathing in the River, and now she was heavy with child. Others portrayed the People, harried by the terrible monsters who once inhabited the River valley. A monster under each stone, living in each tree. They were terrible, tyrannical. They captured the daughter of the headman, surrounded her with ugliness and pain.

Hezhi studied the woman portraying the daughter; she was slim, a slip of a girl no older than herself. Sad, she was, bereft of kin, surrounded by monsters. Without hope, for none of the People could save her or even themselves. Hezhi felt a little glimmer of identification. It was easy to guess how she might have felt: alone, threatened, unable to understand the monsters surrounding her.

Now came Chakunge, the Riverson, laughing, full of power. He was clad in the rainbow, in armor of shell and fishbone, in plates from the giant Rivercrabs. His weapons were wit and water, swords and spears formed of the very substance of the River. First he tricked a few of the monsters, one by one. He convinced the first of them—the Black-headed Ogre—that his power came from bathing four times a day in the waters of the River. The monster emulated him and was drowned.

Soon enough, Chakunge was done toying with his foes, however. He went among the monsters who held the chief's daughter and slew them all, turned them into stones and sharks, ground them into sand. He took the captive woman away, asked her to be his queen.

Who will take *me* away? Hezhi wondered. She had never considered such a thing. But it would be so *nice*, if a hero like Chakunge would come, free her from her problems, her worries. Perhaps that was where D'en was, off becoming a hero, so that he could come back and rescue her.

After the dance, the people in the hall lined up to file past the fountain; each drank from the water in their cupped hands, praying for their city, their emperor, themselves. Hezhi followed dutifully, and when she came to the fountain her mind was still picturing the dashing dancer portraying Chakunge, laughing, full of power. When she drank, she prayed silently. *Send me a hero,* she prayed. She felt weak, doing so. She felt as if she were betraying something. But at that moment, it was the foremost thought in her. *Send me a hero,* she beseeched, and she drank the water.

She had taken only a score of steps, and the water reached the hurtful place in her belly, and there it seemed to erupt, like pine knot thrown on a fire. She gasped and fell, saved only by the quick arms of Tsem from cracking her skull open on the hard marble floor. The water roared in her, rushed out into her veins, fiery. It made her skin feel like dough, like something soft and barely real; reality was the heat, the insides of her.

A hundred times she had taken sacred water, and it had always been just drinking. Now she thought she would die.

Her senses returned soon enough, though. No one but Tsem seemed to pay her much heed; *he* picked her up, carried her to a bench near the wall, and the two women occupying it leapt up hastily at the look he jabbed at them.

Perhaps Tsem is my hero, she thought, but no, Tsem was as surrounded by the monsters as she; he was like one of the men the chief sent who failed. But he was a comfort.

Tsem laid her on the bench, and after a few moments the flame became a tingle, an itch, was gone. But something was different, changed.

"I should take you back home now, Princess," Tsem whispered.

"No." Hezhi shook her head. "No, I'm better now. It was just the water . . . I'm better. I should stay for the rest of this."

"As you wish, Princess." Still, he made her remain on the bench long after she was capable of walking. When finally she wobbled to her feet, his face was filled with concern.

"I'm fine, Tsem," she assured him, but her feet felt like wood and she sat back down, as best she could, with her dress's tail hanging off the back of the bench and resting on the floor.

The ceremonies were over; now servants passed here and

there, bearing trays of steamed dumplings, fried fish cakes, strange foods that even Hezhi could not identify. She wasn't in the least hungry; she took a small cup of wine when it was offered, however, and the first few sips of it made her feel better.

She was taking another sip when she heard a polite cough.

"Princess? May I?"

It was the boy, Wezh Yehd Nu. He was dressed in as silly an outfit as anyone, a long robe of silk, green pantaloons, a shirt cut to look like a breastplate.

Hezhi reluctantly inclined her head in assent. The boy sat down. Tsem seemed to have withdrawn to some distance.

"You seem to be feeling unwell," Wezh remarked. "I thought I might ask if there was anything I can do."

"It's nothing," Hezhi said. "I felt a little faint, but I am much better now."

"I'm glad to hear that," Wezh said gravely. He moved his mouth as if to say more, but instead turned his attention back to the crowd. The two of them sat in awkward silence for a few moments.

"My father says these gatherings are the lifeblood of our society," Wezh said at last. "Don't you think that's true?"

Hezhi remembered her father, a blurred image with the River at his beck.

"I suppose," she replied.

There was another awkward silence, during which Hezhi began to feel well enough to be rude. Still, she held her peace. Perhaps those near her—Tsem, for instance—might be a little less annoying if she indulged their wishes just a bit. And of course, her father had probably been so insistent that she come for just this reason. Daughters were best married off early.

Wezh was not unkind or unpleasant looking. Perhaps, if not a hero, he could be a friend. She flinched at that thought—the thought of having another person as dear as D'en to lose—but it was no longer unbearable, as it had been a year or even a few days ago.

"I have a boat," Wezh said cautiously. "A little barge with a cabin on it. My father gave it to me for my fifteenth birthday. Do you like to go boating?"

Where had *that* come from? Hezhi wondered. From the life-blood of society to his boat?

"No, I have never been boating," she told him.

"Oh, it's great fun," Wezh told her enthusiastically. "You can imagine that you're one of those pirates from the Swamp King-doms, you know, like in the romantic plays? You *do* like the plays, don't you? Most girls do."

Hezhi had seen a few of the plays he spoke of. Pitiful, debased things compared to the great epics like the one they had just witnessed.

"I liked the dance just now," she told him. "It was a wonder-ful rendition of the Chakunge epic."

"I found it a little boring," Wezh said diffidently. "You know, old-fashioned. Now the other day I saw this drama about Ch'iih—he's a pirate, you know . . ."

"That means 'mosquito' in the old speech," Hezhi informed him.

Wezh glanced at her, his eyes a bit wider than before, if such were possible. "Indeed?" he said. "That might explain why his sword is so long and thin, mightn't it? Well, how illuminating! I'm sure that you would have many such observations, if you were to attend such a play. Ah, with *me* perhaps." He looked around the room nervously.

"Are you searching for pirates?" she asked with mild sarcasm. "I don't think my father would admit them, you know."

"Oh, no, of course he wouldn't," Wezh said. "No, I was . . ." He closed his eyes and cleared his throat.

"Umm . . . *Whither goes her brilliant beauty/My tongue can-not hold her name* . . ."

The words were so rushed they were nearly incoherent, and so it took Hezhi nearly two stanzas to realize that Wezh was reciting his—or more likely somebody else's—poetry to her.

"Oh," she interrupted, standing abruptly. "I'm sorry, Wezh Yehd Nu, but I must bid you good day."

Wezh stuttered off, looked a little puzzled and forlorn. "Are you feeling unwell again, Princess?"

"Yes, Wezh, that is it *precisely*."

She turned and gestured to Tsem, who shot her a small expression of chagrin. She turned once to survey the hall again, before she left. The fountain was in its normal state, the water rising no higher than usual. But among the sparkling droplets she thought she saw something dark rising, as well. With an involuntary shiver, she took her leave without another word to the anxious Wezh.

"That was *rude*, Princess," Tsem told her, when they were back in the Hall of Moments and out of earshot of anyone. The hall was lined with guards in armor today, and a lone priest was sweeping, smoke rising from his spirit-broom, a little acolyte behind him with a mundane broom and dustpan, gathering the ashes. None of them were close enough to hear what the princess and her bodyguard were saying.

Hezhi shrugged. "He is an idiot, Tsem, stupid and unlearned. What use do I have for a boy like that?"

"You will find a use for men someday, or you will live as a spinster—or more likely have a marriage imposed on you."

"I think marriages must *always* be imposed, if Wezh is the common sort of man."

Tsem shook his head, then bowed it, in respect, as they passed the old priest and his novice.

"Anyway, I'm really *not* feeling well. You know that."

Tsem was about to reply, but there was a strangled cry behind them; Hezhi felt the hackles rise on her neck, experienced yet another terrible shuddering. She stumbled and turned to confront the source.

Something had emerged from the hall. Its outline wavered, and so she knew it for a ghost, but it was like no ghost she had ever seen, save only in the fountain earlier that day. It was huge, twice Tsem's size. It had legs like a crab's, or a spider's, and its body was long, twisted, like a crushed centipede. A flared tail—horribly like the one on her dress—swept around frenetically behind it. Its head was a grotesque mass of chitin and tentacles, and yet there was something—its *eyes*—that seemed appallingly, undeniably Human. Human and *hungry*. She knew instinctively that it was hungering after *her*.

The guards seemed frozen, and for one terrible moment, Hezhi feared that no one could see the thing except her. Then it was in motion, a scuttling mass of limbs and tentacles. One of the soldiers leapt at it then, his curved sword finally flashing out, and he was in its path, a tiny creature compared to the ghost. His sword chopped but once, slicing unhindered through the thing, clanging with great force and noise onto the marbled floor. Then the ghost passed through the guard and he fell, writhing, clenched up in a little ball, a jabbering kind of noise issuing from him the like of which Hezhi never imagined a Human Being could make. The beast lunged forward, and another guard—attacking more hesitantly—went down. She had the dull realization that, like a ghost, the thing wasn't solid—but it could certainly cause harm to men. She saw the second guard die very clearly; his skin puffed and split, exuding vapor—as if the blood in his body were suddenly steam.

That was the last she saw of it. Tsem had her in both arms and was running. Her last glimpse was of the priest, broom blazing furiously, standing between them and the apparition. The rest was nightmare flashes of this corridor and that, of Tsem's pounding heart—and the images of what she had seen burning on the surface of her eyes. Tsem did not stop until they reached one of the far shrines, a place that no ghost would ever dare enter. Placing her inside, he waited at the door, fists clenched. After a long while—when nothing happened—Tsem pointed a finger at her.

"Stay here," he said simply, and then he was gone, loping back up the way they came.

"Tsem! No, Tsem!" she shrieked, but it was too late. The half Giant was gone.

It wanted me. And it would kill Tsem as easily as it would anyone; it had no neck to snap, no body to bludgeon. She recalled the first guard, so young and brave.

Frustrated, afraid, she sat with her knees drawn up to her chin. The tail on her dress was broken, she remembered not how.

Taking deep, slow breaths, she tried to calm herself. It was then that she noticed the blood.

Her first thought was that it was Tsem's, that he was injured somehow, for surely it couldn't be hers. But there it was, little smeared drops on the floor, on her dress. Not *much* blood. She touched some clinging to her legs. It was sticky, certainly blood.

She understood then. It *was* her blood, and she was not wounded. She had begun bleeding.

She was a woman.

PART TWO

≈≈≈≈≈≈≈≈≈≈≈≈≈≈≈≈≈≈≈≈≈≈≈≈≈≈≈≈≈≈≈≈≈≈≈≈

THE BLESSED AND THE CURSED

© Cherry '96

I

The Return of Steel

P ERKAR *stood amidst the waters of a great River. The current clutched at his ankles, touching him with more urgency but far less tenderness than the goddess of the stream. Beyond the thick water lay a settlement, and the word that formed in his mind was* city *though cities were only a rumor to him. It was a vast thing, this city, unimaginably huge, a white hive of blocky white buildings given scale only by their myriad, antlike inhabitants.*

The water swirled before him, and a girl arose. A girl, perhaps ten or twelve years old. Her dark skin, black hair, and tiny angular face bore no resemblance to his Anishu love, but she seemed to know him, to beckon for him. To whisper a name that was his own despite the fact that he did not recognize its sound. He shuddered, his feet shuffling toward her with a will of their own. Rather, the River moved them, pulling him toward the child. A panic seized Perkar, dream-panic that overwhelmed everything else, drove like a dagger between sleeping and waking, tore a rent

97

*in the wall of dream that he fell through, to lie blinking and
groaning on his blanket.*

"NEVER have I had such a dream," Perkar told Eruka. The two
of them were trudging along an animal track at the top of a
ridge, hoping to run across game—the expedition's supply of
meat was running low, and the Kapaka had ordered a halt for
hunting.

"The city you describe—I scarcely believe that such a place
exists."

Perkar shrugged. "It was a dream."

"But sometimes dreams have great potency, particularly if you
dream of something you have never seen. I once dreamed of my
father, niece, granduncle, and a bull, all naked save for hats,
dancing in a circle and singing. I think a dream of *that* sort
means little—tiny sprites turning things already in your head
inside-out. But the Great Songs speak of dreams in which heroes
see unknown lands, unforged swords—those things they *don't* already know. Dreams like that must come from more powerful
gods."

"Your niece—how did she *look*, naked?"

Eruka shouldered him good-naturedly. "My niece is more a
woman than the waif in your dream city of stone towers and
white streets. *Much* more. I can scarce reach my arms around her
waist."

Perkar grinned, but the dream image came back to him: a
black-haired slip of a girl with huge eyes and skin as dusky as a
Mang's. Certainly he had never seen *her*.

"Sst." Eruka motioned silence. "There is a deer!"

Perkar bobbed his head a bit, trying to see what Eruka saw. Indeed, there it was, a buck with spreading antlers.

Eruka motioned to their left and began padding that way,
drawing an arrow from the ornate quiver at his side. Perkar nodded and drew his own shaft, fitted it to the sinew cord on his
own bow.

Sapling, I
Bending in the hardest wind
Came along a Human man
His name was Raka
Sapling, said he
I know what you *might* be . . .

He whispered the little song the bow maker taught him under his breath; surely it would make his arrow fly more true.

The buck snapped up its head and began to run. Gasping, Perkar pulled back on the string, let the arrow fly. The shaft cut air and a few leaves—the buck was no longer to be seen.

A few moments later Eruka rejoined him, scowling. "I thought you had hunted before."

"I *have*," Perkar answered defensively. "But on horseback, with hounds running the beasts. With a spear, not a bow. And I've hunted mostly boar, not deer."

"Me, too," Eruka said, grinning sheepishly. "I thought it would be no harder on foot."

Perkar snorted. "We were lucky to even *see* that animal, I think. I doubt we will see another."

"If only I was a great heroic singer, like Iru Antu." Eruka sighed. "The kind of singer who can change the songs of things, make spirits obey his will. I could simply summon us a deer, have it stand still while we slew it."

"The other night you boasted of just such an ability," Perkar reminded him.

Eruka grinned back at that. "Woti talks for me, sometimes. I can do a few songs like that—a very few. But you have to know the ins and outs of the original song before you can change it, and I know none about deer."

"Rabbits? Elk?"

"None of those," Eruka allowed.

Perkar nodded glumly. "We go back empty-handed, then."

"So we do," Eruka agreed.

*   *   *

THEY were not the only ones empty-handed; Apad had had no success, either. Ngangata and Atti, however, had a fine buck hung up by its rear legs, skinning it. Atti was already offering blood to the local forest god and to the Lord of Deer, as well.

"Well shot," Eruka told Atti.

Atti shrugged. "Ngangata killed him; I was just there to drag him back."

"Just the same," Perkar said, "I'm glad *somebody* brought fresh meat back. Another day of bread . . ."

"How much more of this, anyway?" Apad asked, gesturing at the forest around them. "It's been six days since we left the last damakuta behind."

"And tomorrow it shall be seven," Atti replied. "And the day after, eight. This is no jaunt up to your summer pasture, Apad."

"I know that," Apad said testily. "I just want to know how much longer."

Atti glanced at Ngangata. The half Alwa turned steady eyes on Apad. "Another eight or nine days, depending upon the weather," he said.

"How long before we enter the territory of your kin?" Apad inquired, unable to resist a faint sneer on the word "kin."

"The Alwat don't count me as kin any more than you do," Ngangata retorted. "And we've been in their territory for five days now."

"Five days? Where are they?"

Ngangata shrugged. "If any are around here, they are avoiding us. The only signs I've seen have been many days old."

"Signs? What signs?"

"Footprints. Tools, a few shelters."

Apad frowned. "I've seen none of that."

Ngangata shrugged noncommittally, emphasizing his relative lack of neck. "I suppose you haven't."

"What does *that* mean?" snapped Apad.

"I just repeated what you said," Ngangata rejoined softly.

Apad scowled. He stalked over to the bloody deer carcass, examined it with his fists resting on his hips. "You probably talk to them while we are asleep, don't you? Did they kill this deer for you?"

Ngangata stopped skinning, looked down at his own feet for a moment. Then he walked over to his bundle of things, picked up his bowstave, and strung it.

"What will you do with *that*?" Apad asked. "That isn't a *man's* weapon." Perkar saw that his friend was trying to affect an easy, haughty attitude; but he also saw that his muscles were tight, corded—Apad was tense, worried, ready to reach for his sword or dash aside. He was afraid of the halfling. And why not? A warrior would not shoot another over an insult—challenge him to combat perhaps, but not simply murder him. But who could tell what this kinless creature might do?

"It isn't a warrior's weapon," Ngangata agreed. "I am not a warrior." With that, he snapped a black-feathered shaft onto his string; for him, the motion seemed as easy as stretching at daybreak. The bow bent and sang; the little man's body somehow bent, too, bow and arm and back together. Perkar wasn't sure exactly *how* it was so graceful—and certainly he could not do it himself.

Down came the arrow, a bird impaled upon it.

"If you are worried about where the deer came from," Ngangata told Apad, "there is *your* meat."

The Kapaka, sitting at some distance from the rest of the group, chose that moment to come and join them. He clapped Apad on the shoulder.

"Best we have a fire to roast this on, eh, Apad?" he said.

Apad stood a bit longer—to give the impression of reluctance, Perkar thought—and then left to gather wood. After a moment, Perkar followed to join him.

We all fear Ngangata, he mused. *We don't like him because we are afraid of him, afraid of what he might do.* He remembered a favorite saying of his father's:

There is little real hatred in the world
Only Fear prancing in a man's clothes

THE next day they left the rich lowlands behind, began ascending the hills. Ngangata led them through winding valleys, thick with laurel and hickory and, finally, higher up, white birch. The ways became steeper and steeper, but Perkar remained amazed that they made any progress at all, without trails and in such rugged country. The land pleased him, despite its wildness; he imagined how it would look in pasture, how well suited the ridge there on the right would be for a damakuta and its outbuildings. Oh, it would be far and far from his father's lands, but it would be *his*. It would be far from *her*, too, and that thought hung about him, a clinging mist of melancholy. He considered, once again, that perhaps it would be better, after all, to marry Bakume's daughter, if only so he could remain close to the goddess.

But no, he knew better than that. He could not have *her*. The best he could do was to give her a gift, a gift that she would remember in a thousand years, when he himself was the ash of a memory. His heart tightened on the thought of that gift, squeezing out other dreams, damakutat and pasture. Around him, the land lost its promise and luster, became merely trees and bushes.

His reverie was interrupted when the party halted. Knowing that he had missed something, Perkar glanced around him, searching for the cause of their delay. Nightfall was still some time away, and he saw no stream where they could water the horses.

"Who built *this*?" the Kapaka wondered, and it was then that the forest around Perkar came back into focus, reasserting its presence in his mind, if not his heart.

Near them stood the ruins of a damakuta. Perkar had ridden straight past the remaining timbers of its stockade, mistaking them for dead trees. The building itself had not been lived in for many years; the cedar shingles were nearly all gone, leaving the skeleton of the roof to bleach and wither in the sun and rain. The walls were collapsed, too, here and there, but whoever had built it had laid a firm foundation, for the frame still stood. The beams were entire trees, stripped of bark.

Inside, ferns and moss ran riot. The six dismounted and walked carefully through the ruin, searching for any sign of its inhabitants. Eruka began a little song to frighten off ghosts.

"What happened to them, do you think?" Apad asked of no one in particular, running his palm up the shaft of a support pillar.

"This wasn't their *place*, that's what happened," Ngangata answered. "They took from the Forest Lord without asking."

"How do you know that?" Eruka asked, interrupting his own song.

Ngangata shot the young man a clearly puzzled look. "Have you seen other damakutat? The Forest Lord has never granted Human Beings land this far into the forest. This is Alwat territory. The land is for them."

"To what end?" Apad growled. "I see no pasture, no fields, no fine houses. To what end do the Alwat use this land?"

Ngangata shook his head as if at a child. "That is no concern of ours. The Forest Lord does what he will with his land, gives it to whom he wishes."

Perkar frowned. "My great-grandfather bargained with a local god—not the Forest Lord. Perhaps these people did the same."

"Then where are they?" Atti asked, sweeping his hands around.

"They might have built elsewhere," Perkar suggested.

Atti shrugged. "Might. Might and a stone is just a stone."

"This once I agree with the half man," Eruka muttered. "This is no concern of ours. Let us be gone before the ghosts of these people waken."

The Kapaka was more stubborn than that, but not much. "We'll leave a cup of woti for the ghosts of men, burn incense for the women. This is the least we can do, for whoever they were."

Perkar helped the others make the preparations hurriedly, kindling a small fire to provide coals for the incense and to warm the woti so that it could be smelled by the ghosts. Eruka sang the "Thanking Ghost Song," but even his fine voice could not hide his worry—indeed, he fairly flew through the last seven stanzas. Much too quickly really. It was well past midday when they mounted back up. Atti was the last on his horse; he dug through the packs on his second animal and brought forth a chain-mail shirt.

"Why that?" Apad asked. "Afraid of the ghosts?"

"Not the ghosts," Atti said. "Just a feeling."

A little chill ran up Perkar's spine, and after a moment's hesitation, he shifted his weight into his left stirrup, preparing to dismount and don his own armor. A frown from Apad stopped him, though. It was as if the other man had simply said, "Show the hill man that *you* aren't afraid." And so he stayed in his saddle. But he made sure that his sword was within easy gripping reach; he tied it across his saddle horn, where it had been for the first week of their journey, when Perkar still entertained some notion that he might need it. Now he entertained that notion again.

The damakuta was still in sight, but just barely so, when Eruka whispered, "See? See there?" Perkar stood in the stirrups and looked back the way they had come. A little curl of smoke from the incense was still visible; it would go out soon. And there, near it, crouched four figures, or shadows of figures. Eruka, between Perkar and the apparitions, had his eyes shut now, was reciting something low and quick. Perkar nudged Mang into a trot.

"Hsst," the Kapaka said. "No. It would be rude to flee from them. Ride slowly, don't look back. They will not follow."

Nevertheless, as the shadows grew longer and deeper, Perkar felt uncomfortable about his back. His spine seemed to believe that it was turned toward something dangerous, something darker than the shadows and more sinister than ghosts. Perhaps the apparitions were not ghosts at all but tiskawal, perpetually starving spirits who hungered after Human spirit and blood. He didn't voice his fears, for they seemed silly. He had seen more than a few ghosts in his life, and those back at the abandoned damakuta had looked and behaved normally enough.

Mang and the other horses shared his disquiet, though, nickering and stamping, rolling their heads about. Ngangata and Atti seemed even more watchful than usual, their necks craning, gazing up into the trees and down to the steadily thickening underbrush.

"Someone cleared this once," the Kapaka observed of the dense growth. "See how there are no large trees, how closely the saplings grow? This was once pasture."

Ngangata agreed. "It will likely get thicker. We should circle around this; they can't have cleared much."

"*Too much. Far, far too much.*" Apad's voice sounded sharp and accusing. "They cleared and they burned. They killed my children and they never asked me if they could."

Perkar actually chuckled. Apad had pitched his voice so solemnly, so seriously, and yet the sentiments were not his at all. He was clearly mocking Ngangata's earlier remarks, speaking singsong, the way gods were supposed to, sometimes . . .

Perkar turned then and glimpsed the awful thing that spoke: a dark, hideous head perched atop a body something like a cat's, but much like a man's as well.

The real Apad gaped for an instant, then cursed and shrieked simultaneously. His horse reared and screamed horribly, as if imitating his master. The panicking roan crashed into Mang, smashing into Perkar's right leg. Pain lanced up through his thigh, and then Mang reared, dumping him beneath the roan's furiously pawing hooves. The ground came as a shock, like the slap in the face the goddess had given him before he left. His lungs sucked tight, and he could not draw air for a long, painful moment. He had barely the presence of mind to fold his arms around his head, seeking some protection against the iron-shod hooves.

Fortunately, for him, Apad brought himself and his beast into some semblance of control, and so Mang calmed in turn, despite the thing facing them, the thing that had spoken in Apad's voice. Gasping and moaning, Perkar struggled to a crouch.

His companions had all dismounted; their horses would not stand still enough to sit upon. Eruka and Apad brandished swords and Atti gripped his long-handled axe. The Kapaka had no weapon drawn, but his hand rested firmly on the hilt of his sword. Ngangata was just looping his bowstring into place.

"Steel," Apad's voice came from a rippling slit in a head like a black, rotten pumpkin. "You've come back. I just blink—take the merest nap—and there you are again, with your steel." The head seemed to grin; its eyes were knobs of deeper black, with no whites, pupils, or lids. Its teeth, Perkar thought, were much like a cat's and so indeed was its body; the monster squatted on a lion's rear legs, for certain. But the forearms, oddly thin for such a massive creature, looked very Human. Or Alwat. It was still, moving nothing but its mouth.

Eruka stammered at the god. *"A-Aniru,"* he began. "We have not met you before. We don't know your song, or how to honor you. If you could te . . . teach us . . ." He trailed off as the thing cocked its head speculatively at him.

Perkar felt his shock-induced calm begin to vanish; he was close to shaking, closer still to running as fast as he could. He knew of gods—they were all around, in each tree and stone—but all of the ones he had ever known were *tame*, and the only one he had ever *seen*, in manifest form, was *her*. This was a *Wild* God, and Perkar knew nothing of them. Or rather, he knew only one thing: that he feared them.

"If you dislike our steel, come no closer," Apad warned, but his words rang flat and unbelievable.

"Aniru," the Kapaka said. "We had no wish to trespass nor to do damage in your domain. We only pass along here, going to the home of the Forest Lord in the mountain. We have business with him."

The head quivered. It spoke, this time in Ngangata's voice. "I know of no Forest Lord. I know only of your kind, what you bring with you, steel. Now I think I will eat you, shit your steel out with your bones. Your ghosts may go on to see this 'Forest Lord.' "

The Kapaka reluctantly drew his sword, as well. "We mean no harm here."

"Like you meant no harm when you cut down my trees and built your wooden cave? Yes, I know what you mean by that."

"That wasn't *us*," Eruka complained. "Ngangata, speak to it!"

The halfling had an arrow nocked. "It is a mad god," he said. "Wild and mad. What would you have me say?"

"Tell it we are *leaving* here."

Strange words trickled from Ngangata's lips, weird short syllables, strangely songlike.

"I thought you had a different scent," the god remarked, when Ngangata was done. "Your kind respect me. You may go, if you wish."

The god leapt at them, springing from its haunches without warning. Perkar scrambled wildly to his feet, seeking Mang and his sword.

The Wild God reached Atti first, and one of Ngangata's arrows already stood in an opaque eye. Atti met the monster with a downstroke; his axe thudded into the bunching sinews between neck and shoulder. Then Atti went down beneath the thing's weight. Perkar reached Mang, who was rearing again. He had to take his eyes off the battle for an instant, long enough to grab the hilt of his sword and pull out the long, sweet blade. From the corner of his eye, Perkar saw Ngangata calmly launching another shaft. Eruka stood as if frozen.

When Perkar turned again, the god was in midleap, poised above Apad. Apad shrieked and stabbed, shielding his face with his left arm. The blade seemed to go in, but it made little difference to the black apparition, which scrambled on past him toward the Kapaka. Miraculously, before it could reach him, it staggered, an arrow impaling the roof of its mouth and exiting between its eyes. The Kapaka stepped sharply back, then hammered his sword *down*, cut into the melonlike head.

Perkar was surprised to find himself in motion, screaming, sword raised. A long, dark, Human-fingered hand darted at him, and he brought his sword down from his shoulder, crossing his chest with the blade. The steel met the black limb near the wrist; it was like chopping into a stone, and the hilt rang in his hand, numbing it. The Kapaka stepped in again, and again, his heavy sword carving slivers of god-flesh from the monster's neck and head. Behind, Atti struggled to his feet, chest smeared with red blood. Perkar recovered and stroked his sword onto the squirming backbone. Then Atti was there, axe descending in a blow better designed to split wood than for combat. It hewed into a rear leg and severed it.

Perkar would never hear another sound like that; he would later call it a howl, knowing that such was no description for a noise that burrowed all the way into his bones. The god flipped back toward Atti, who had fallen along with his axe. Still screaming, it thrashed about on the ground.

"Up!" Ngangata yelled, still loosing arrows. "Up and ride! We cannot kill it, we can only flee."

The Kapaka seemed to know the truth of that; he was already gripping his saddle, preparing to mount. Atti struggled to his feet again, leaving a snail-trail of blood on the leaves behind him. Eruka stood, blank-eyed, until Perkar grabbed him by the arm and shoved him toward his horse. Then he was scrambling onto Mang. Apad was already mounted. Ngangata stayed a moment longer than they, placing three more arrows in the god—Perkar saw shafts protruding neatly from each eye. Then they were all fleeing on the thunder of horses' hooves. Perkar leaned onto Mang's neck, urging the animal faster.

"He was sleepy," Ngangata howled, from behind them. "Sleepy and slow. But he is awake now!"

"The other horses! Our packs!" Apad yelled back.

"No!" the Kapaka returned. "I forbid it. Leave them!"

Leaves and branches lashed at them, as if by their own will. The six riders fought their way over one ridge, then a second. When would they leave this god's territory and enter another? Apad's words were finally penetrating. Kutasapal was still back there, back with that black monster. Perkar very nearly wheeled Mang around then. He only truly owned three things: his sword, Mang, and Kutasapal. If he left Kutasapal, he owned only two. And he had discovered something in himself, something he never knew he had. When his sword struck the god for the first time, when it reached for him—all of his hesitation, his fear had dwindled, replaced by something . . . large. Something like anger or fury but colder, harsher. Brighter. His desire had been to hit the god again and again, until it died or his sword broke. Now . . . why hadn't he?

Because if he died now, he could never kill the god he *really* wanted to kill. But now he *knew*. A god could be killed, and *he* could kill it, with the right weapon.

So they rode on, and night fell, and still they rode, for the moon was full. Perkar's hand tingled, and it felt good. He had struck a Wild God and lived. What could he not do?

Not much later, Atti fell from his saddle. Perkar had tucked away the memory of the blood he had seen, preferring not to think about it. But now he was nearest the flame-haired man, and he dismounted. Atti was already trying to regain his feet.

"Just wait a moment," Perkar told him. "Let us look at that."

"Get him back on his horse," Eruka called. "That thing might still be coming."

The Kapaka and Ngangata trotted their horses so that they stood between Perkar and Atti and the way that they had come.

"See to him," the Kapaka said. After an instant, Apad also moved up to join them.

"Some god was protecting *you*," Perkar told Atti. "Telling you to put on your mail." The tough steel links had torn in the Wild God's claws; three rips ran for the length of a forearm from sternum to crotch. The claws had dug deeper, and there was much bleeding, but so far as Perkar could tell, none of his organs were laid open to the air.

Atti swore copiously as Perkar got his mail and padded undershirt off of him.

"I have some long strips of colored linen here," the Kapaka said. "I brought it as a gift for the Forest Lord."

"Leave it then," Atti said.

"I have other gifts, still with me," the Kapaka replied. Perkar unpacked the linen and cut several lengths of it. Again to the sound of Atti's profanity, Perkar wrapped the cloth tightly about the hill man's chest and torso. Blood soaked it instantly, but even before the wrapping, Atti's blood had nearly ceased flowing of its own accord.

When Perkar was satisfied, he helped Atti back on his horse, handed him up a waterskin. Atti drank greedily.

"I think we need to go, if we can," the Kapaka said. Back behind them, the limbs of trees were beginning to wave to and fro. There was no wind.

"I can ride," Atti said. "I became dizzy for a moment only."

"This way," Ngangata said, spurring back to the front. He seemed to be examining something on the trees; Perkar thought, in the pale moonlight, that he saw marks there, tattoos on the trunks of the birches.

"THERE," Ngangata whispered. "See the firelight?"

The moon had set, and that had slowed them down considerably. Now Perkar saw the faint, pale flower of illumination Ngangata referred to. Left to himself, Perkar would never have seen it; fatigue sat on his forehead, pushing on his eyelids, gently, insistently. The Wild God seemed far away, a dream.

"Who can it be?" Eruka wondered. "I hope they have some woti."

"They do not," Ngangata replied.

They wound through the last few trees. There, in the flicker of the light, Perkar saw his first true Alwa.

Ngangata had seemed so strange to him when they met, but suddenly Perkar thought him very Human, compared to the Alwat. Five of them clustered near the fire, standing as upright as any human. They were slender-hipped and broad-shouldered, thickly muscled. Their arms and legs seemed almost normal, but their bodies were not quite right, too wedge-shaped. A fine, silvery hair lay over their pale skins. It was in their heads that they were most strange, however. Their faces were flat and broad, bones as coarse as stone showing through them. They possessed neither foreheads nor chins; above their thick eyebrows their skulls were plainly flat; thick white hair was pulled back into buns. Massive but receding lower jaws blended into thick necks. It was in their eyes that he saw the *most* strangeness; like deep pools of water, they were murky, unreadable. They glimmered and quickened, darted or remained fixed, but in ways that seemed all wrong, that hinted at odd thoughts that Perkar could not understand.

Ngangata said something to them, the same clucking language he had spoken to the Wild God. One of the Alwat clucked back at him. The others stood stock-still. Their mouths were huge; Perkar was further reminded of the Wild God. What was it the Stream Goddess had once told him? That many gods took their forms from Human breath and blood? If so, perhaps in Alwat lands the gods took of Alwat blood for their forms.

"What are they saying?" Apad asked irritably.

"They say that the god will not follow us here. They say that this is the place of another god, Hanazalhakabizn. Hanazal-hakabizn and V'fanaqrtinizd are old enemies."

"Banakartenis?" the Kapaka asked, trying to imitate the alien name. "Who?"

"V'fanaqrtinizd. The Wild God we just fought."

"But he will not follow us here. What about the local one—Hana-whatever?"

Ngangata and the Alwat conversed a moment; two of the others added something; Perkar realized with a start that one of them was female; though shaped much like the men, she was a bit smaller and had very obvious breasts. He was surprised he had not noticed earlier.

Ngangata listened and then relayed what he had been told.

"Human people are allowed to pass through on their way to the Forest Lord, but not to build or cut. V'fanaqrtinizd was driven insane by Human Beings who injured him and killed his trees. They say the sound of the trees dying drove him insane."

Perkar was just realizing something else; that beyond the fire there was a *building* of some sort. A number of limber saplings had been planted and bent and tied together to form a sort of longhouse—a rude and tiny imitation of a damakuta. It was covered in bark and mats woven of some material. The Alwat were house-builders. Strange that he had never heard that.

The Alwat seemed to be through talking. They all squatted down, resting comfortably on their haunches. One of them—the female, actually—waddled a few feet from the fire and, as Perkar watched, commenced to shit.

"What disgusting creatures," Eruka commented.

Ngangata regarded them darkly. "Yes. They have agreed to let us stay near here. Tomorrow they will guide us on toward the Forest Lord."

"What did you have to promise them for that?" Apad asked caustically. "Our heads?"

Ngangata shook his head. "No. They think Human Beings amusing. They like to tell stories about them. If they travel with us, they will have many stories to tell."

"And you? Do you tell them stories about us?"

"I do."

"I thought as much."

Ngangata ignored that. "They say we may make camp on the ridge above this place," he said. "They said we may take a small branch of their fire if we wish."

"Thank them for me," the Kapaka said.

"They have no such word," Ngangata told him. "I can tell them 'It is enough' or 'You can share our camp, too.' "

"Tell them it is enough, then."

Perkar was glad that they were sleeping at some distance from the Alwat camp, though he had no illusions about being safe from them, should they decide to attack. It was just good to be out of their sight, out of that strange regard, the kind a child or a very old man might hold upon you. As he closed his eyes, he wondered what an Alwa might dream about, if dream they did. He might ask Ngangata, who must surely have dreams of both kinds, Human and Alwat.

≈≈≈≈≈≈≈≈≈≈≈≈≈≈≈≈≈≈≈≈≈≈≈≈≈≈≈≈≈≈≈≈≈≈≈≈≈≈≈

In the Court of Black Willows

SHE'LU YEHD CHA'DUNE, Chakunge, Lord of Nhol, emperor of five domains and the desert hinterland, stared at Nyas—his vizier—with drooping eyes. The deep orange light slanting in through the chamber's high, narrow windows identified the hour as late, nearing sundown. He had been transacting the business of Empire since it had lanced through from the *other* side of the room at a similar angle. Soon, hopefully, he could snatch a moment of rest, some food in private. He need only focus his attention for a bit longer on the items of the day. Hard to do sometimes, when so many of them were so boring. For instance, Nyas was just finishing a tabulation of tribute received from the sixteen quarters of the down-River port of Wun Yang. She'lu hoped the next matter—whatever it was—would be a bit more interesting.

"Next, my lord, I have a somewhat personal item, a possibly

distasteful matter." Nyas peered around his nearly round nose with wide-set eyes, awaiting She'lu's leave to continue.

"Go on," She'lu said, his attention fully focused again.

"It concerns your daughter Hezhi."

"It isn't another complaint from the librarian, is it, Nyas? I thought we had settled that matter." He picked at his robe, frowning.

"Perhaps so, my lord. That is not what I must speak to you about."

"Good." She'lu frowned as Nyas actually looked around him—as if every person within earshot had not been Forbidden to speak anything they heard. As if anyone he did not know about could approach this throne. This must be a delicate matter indeed.

"You remember the incident in the Hall of Moments, just outside of the Leng Court."

"Of course. Three of my elite guardsmen and a priest were killed before they banished the thing. Apparently the priesthood has become complacent—more intent on playing politics than keeping dangerous ghosts out of the Hall of Moments." He aimed this remark, with a flash of his eyes, not at Nyas, but at the pale, pudgy man who occupied a lower seat to his right. The man—today's representative from the priesthood, one De Yehd Shen—colored visibly but did not respond verbally. Not here, anyway, and not without the support of a more eminent priest.

Nyas, of course, caught the exchange, and so shook his head. "Our records show that the hall was swept the day before, in preparation for court, and was being swept again when the attack occurred. It is hard to find any fault . . ."

"*Something* was not done right. I still feel the track of the damned thing whenever I walk there. It was *strong*, more demon than ghost. Almost like something summoned. But *I* did not summon it."

"Perhaps it slipped through or awoke when you called the

Riverghosts," the priest suggested, his little-boy voice clear and piping.

"I would have felt that," She'lu retorted, narrowing his eyes. "Do you think I have no more sense or control than to summon such a thing?"

"Perhaps if some other person took advantage of your summoning, however . . ."

"Stop," She'lu snapped. "Darken your mouth! I've been through this, and with members of the priesthood far more competent and knowledgeable than you. I don't wish to discuss this further. *And what does this have to do with my daughter?*" he demanded, suddenly realizing, to his chagrin, that he was somehow missing the point.

"Your daughter," Nyas said, "was seen in the Hall of Moments with her bodyguard at the time of the creature's appearance and attack." He looked meaningfully at She'lu.

The emperor glared back at him. "And?" he asked.

Nyas sighed. "If you remember, Lord, Hezhi is nearly of age—some twelve years old."

"Oh? *Oh.*"

"Indeed. It may be a coincidence, but it could be something more."

"Is my daughter being watched?" he asked. Was the priest actually hiding a smirk? She'lu trembled with the sudden exertion of *not* striking the simpering fool down. The urge to reach out, slap his soul a bit, was overwhelming. He was emperor, he reminded himself, because he could resist such temptations. His brother, after all, had been born with more *power*—but no self-control at all.

"She has been watched diffidently, my lord. There has been no formal assignation to her."

"I suppose we should make one then, just in case, though I find it inconceivable that *my* daughter . . ."

"Even *you* are not completely apprised of the River's will," his vizier reminded him.

"Yes, yes. Assign someone to watch her, then."

"My lord," the priest chirped. "That is the business of the priesthood."

"I suppose it is," She'lu grudgingly admitted.

"If you will permit me, I will bring this to the attention of the order."

She'lu drummed his fingers on the arm of his throne, looked tiredly around the chamber. The black columns that supported the roof and gave the court its name seemed to mock him, somehow. Like the priest; nothing he could overtly *do* anything about. Yet. "Very well," he said at last. "But I want to know *who* it is."

"I suspect I know who will be assigned, my lord, if you will permit me."

"Go on."

"A new Jik has recently been initiated. He shows enormous potential. He will be very discreet."

"Why a Jik?" She'lu asked irritably. "I see no reason for an assassin to watch my daughter."

"*Please*, my lord. The Jik are not assassins. They are priests."

"Yes. The sort of priests who assassinate people."

De darkened again. "It is common practice, my lord, when the child is a direct descendant of the Chakunge. You yourself were certainly watched over by a Jik."

She'lu aimed a smoky stare at his vizier. "Is this true, Nyas? You were my father's vizier."

Nyas nodded *yes*.

She'lu ceased tapping his fingers and glowered at the priest. "Very well. Send him to me, and tell him to have a care. I have high hopes for a good marriage for the girl."

"Very good, Lord," the priest acknowledged. "If you would but give me your leave . . ."

She'lu sighed heavily, drank some power from the River, felt it course and shimmer in his veins. He sent a finger of it out to the priest, touched his tiny, fragile soul. He stroked it a bit harder than necessary; the man shuddered and his eyes rolled up.

"You may speak of the matter of my daughter, and that *only*," he commanded. He held the command there for a moment, then pulled the touch away. The priest sagged in his chair, sweat beading on his forehead. She'lu smiled, feeling a bit better. He could have merely released his Forbidding entirely; it would have been less painful for the priest. Nothing that had been discussed was of any real importance, after all. But it pleased him to bring the man discomfort. Indeed, the fellow had been allowed to take notes on much of the court's business—the financial matters, for instance—and he would be allowed to keep those notes, so that the priesthood would not register a complaint. But leaving him Forbidden to *talk* about those same things would make the priesthood suspect he held unknowable secrets. It would keep them guessing.

"Now," She'lu snapped. "Is that all, Nyas?"

"No, my lord. There is still the matter of the Southtown Levee . . ."

Suppressing a snarl behind a courtly smile, She'lu settled back into his throne, resigned to an even longer day than usual.

II

The Alwat and the Gods

"THEY slow us down," Eruka complained. "Why did they have to bring *children*?"

"They would have slowed us down no matter what," Perkar pointed out. "They have no horses."

"We almost have none ourselves," Eruka reminded him. He felt a brief flash of anger at the flaxen-haired singer, but it quickly passed. They were in the same predicament—both had lost horses they could ill afford to lose. But Eruka was *trying* to keep in good spirits about it, as opposed to sulking; Perkar supposed he should do no less.

At least they were back on a trail now, though one that was clearly the result of Alwat feet and thus not comfortably broad enough for a horse. The branches sometimes grew low and that also made it difficult to ride, so they spent much time walking, anyway. The Alwat walked far, far in front. He only now and then caught a glimpse of them, as a matter of fact. He had been astonished when all seven of them came along as guides: two men, two women, an infant, an older child, and a gnarled creature Perkar guessed to be an old woman. For traveling they donned soft shoes of deerskin and long cloaks of the same substance, tanned white but with many odd figures and designs burned into them. It was the first thing like adornment Perkar had observed; they wore no jewelry that he could see. They did carry weapons, or at least tools, in little pouches slung over their shoulders on straps. Each adult bore a long cane-pole spear, sharpened and fire-hardened at the end. One of the women also carried a sharp stick. Now and then she would stop, dig some root out of the ground, and place it in a net on her back. She chattered to herself all the time that she did this. Usually she was through by the time the Humans had caught up to her, and she would scramble up and run back to the other Alwat, short legs pumping. Once, instead, she ran circles around the men with horses, chattering what almost seemed like a little song. The other Alwat were more aloof and sober, though when they took breaks to eat or rest they would come back down the trail and *watch* the Humans, muttering to one another now and then.

Eruka and Apad were proving poor company. He guessed that they were both shaken by the events of the previous day; Eruka by his paralysis, which no one had mentioned, and Apad—*his* eyes darted here and there, a shadow of fright over them. Given what had happened to Atti, even wearing armor, it was a miracle that Apad had survived unscathed, and that thought seemed to be lodged in his mind. Perkar had tried to congratulate him on his good fortune, only to be rebuffed by a scowl.

Both of his friends wore their armor today, he noted, and both cut fine, heroic figures; Apad in a mail coat of two layers, one steel and the other brass, brass greaves, and a hemispherical cap with a long, lozenge-shaped noseguard. Eruka wore black chain over a scarlet gambeson; rather than a shirt, his armor was a long coat divided into a split skirt that allowed him to straddle

his horse. They looked wonderful, warlike; but the air was thin
here, and he noticed them puffing and panting. For himself, he
had decided to trust the word of the Alwat, who said there was
no further danger of attack. As weird and disgusting as they
might be, they *lived* here, were as intimate with the spirits of the
land as he was with those of his father's pastures. If there was
real danger, they would tell Ngangata—after all, they must think
of him as one of their own—and Ngangata would tell them.

After a few more stabs at conversation with the sullen pair,
Perkar spurred Mang up ahead to where Atti rode.

"How is that today?" he asked the older man, gesturing at his
bandaged torso.

"Very stiff, very painful. But there is no fever in it, I think."

"Good. If you feel any, let us know. We can prepare a decoc-
tion of some sort."

Atti nodded. "The Alwat gave me something last night. It
helped me sleep, anyway."

"Doesn't that worry you?" Perkar asked. "No doubt their intentions are good. But medicine intended for a dog does not
work as well on a cow. Why should the potions of the Alwat not
poison *us*?"

Atti shook his head dismissively. "That isn't the way of it,
Perkar. Look; a cow and a dog cannot mate, cannot get offspring
from one another. Human and Alwa can; Ngangata proves that.
They are much like us, Perkar, much indeed. And I've had their
medicines before."

"They seem very different to me," Perkar admitted. Atti
shrugged. The two of them rode along in silence for a while. The
wind picked up a bit, and the sky began to hint at darkening as
a carpet of gray cloud slid in from the south. Atti shook his head
at that.

Ngangata had ridden ahead, apparently to converse with the
Alwat. Now he rode back. He said a few words to the Kapaka—
ahead, seemingly lost in his own thoughts—and then continued
on to join Atti and Perkar.

"The Alwat say there is shelter up this way, not too far. One of the stream gods told them it would be best to seek it."

Atti agreed. "Feels odd, doesn't it?"

Ngangata nodded.

"What feels odd?" Perkar asked, and then wished he hadn't, for they both looked at him blankly.

But after a moment Ngangata told him, "The wind. The wind feels odd. The gods are up to something strange, I think."

"Oh."

Above, a pair of squirrels chased one another, shaking leaves down upon the travelers. The branches crowded lower once more, forcing them to dismount yet again. Perkar considered waiting for Eruka and Apad, rejoining them despite their ill humor. He had thought to strike up some friendship with Atti, perhaps get some advice on hunting—but Ngangata made him very uncomfortable, though he grudgingly admitted that the little man was winning a sort of admiration from him. It was the admiration one had for a fine, sharp sword or a well-made fence. He glanced over at the half man, coughed to clear his throat.

"Without your bow, I think, the Wild God would have killed us," he said.

Ngangata frowned a bit. "I have had a lot of time to get used to my bow," he said. "It provides well for me. I thank the god from which it was made daily."

Perkar had seen that, the little man crouched over his stave, croaking the words of a song. Never loud enough for him to hear. He felt a twinge of guilt. How often did he offer to Ko, who had made his sword—or even to Ani Perkar, the oak spirit for whom he was named?

The wind gusted, and now Perkar thought that he, too, sensed something strange in it. A smell perhaps. A smell like flowers, or . . . something like that.

"Have you met these Alwat before?" Perkar asked. It seemed an inane question even as he said it; but he somehow wanted to talk to this Ngangata, this not-quite-man, wanted to understand his own fear and dislike of him.

"No," Ngangata replied.

"Do they all speak one language? It seems a strange tongue."

"All languages seem strange to me," Ngangata answered, and Perkar thought he saw the merest hint of a smile lift those wide lips. "Theirs no more than any other. It is a language more . . . fit for speaking to the forest gods than yours."

"But the forest gods speak *my* language," Perkar said. "Even the Wild God spoke it."

"He spoke what you speak because it is what you speak. He used your own voices, even," Ngangata reminded him. "But Human speech is ill-suited for speaking to the gods, in many ways. The Alwat have lived with the gods for much longer than your kind, have refined their communication with them."

"I suppose that's true," Perkar said, remembering the "Ekar Irusungan," the song telling of the world's beginning. When Human Beings came into the world, they found the forests and Alwat already there. "They are friendly with the gods, then?"

"As friendly as you are with those in your father's lands, I suppose. But the Alwat have reached a different accommodation. Their understanding of gods is different, I think."

"Do they ever . . ." Perkar felt himself flush hotly. "Do the Alwat and the gods ever have . . . ah, union . . . ?"

Ngangata was looking at him *very* strangely. "You mean sex?"

"I mean anything like that, touching, talking face-to-face, and sex, yes . . ."

"They live with them. They do not shut themselves up in dead walls . . ."

"My father's damakuta is not dead wood," Perkar said, a bit annoyed. "Father pleaded with the trees from which it was built; their spirits inhabit it still. As does the hearth god, and a little sprite or two—my house is not *dead*."

"No, no. But compare that to living in the wildwoods. There are two kinds of gods . . ."

"Every child knows that," Perkar said.

"Yes, but which is more common?"

"The Aniru, I suppose, the gods of places."

"And the Anishu, the gods who live *in* things—they are fewer?"

Perkar thought about that. In his father's lands, there was one pasture god, who had been the old forest god—he was Aniru because his life was not tied to a single tree, but to an area of land. The Anishu lived in things, *were* things—like Ani Perkar, who lived in the oak, like . . . *she*, for she *was* the Stream.

"Yes, I think so. In the whole of the pasture there is really only the one god, the old forest god."

"And the gods of the trees that once lived there, before your ancestor made his bargain with the old god of that land?"

"Gone, I suppose, or living as houses and fence rails."

"But here, look around you. A god in each tree, not just in a few. And rather than one huge place with one god—like your pasture—there are many little ones; the god of that hollow, of this ridge, of that rock outcropping. There are the gods of territory here, too—we fought one—but they are outnumbered. Some of these Aniru resent all of the smaller gods within their territory, I think. I think that is why some bargain with your kind, because you simplify things. Kill all the lesser gods and the gods *in* things. Then the Aniru, those who live *on* territories, large spaces of the earth—then they are alone, unchallenged."

"I never really thought about that," Perkar muttered. "I never really thought about the gods plotting against one another."

"Of course you have. Every child learns 'The Song of the Hawk God and the Raven.' "

"Yes, but that song is about *war.* There are many like *that.* What you speak of is much more subtle, much more devious."

"Yes."

"But the Alwat do not 'simplify' things for the Aniru?"

"The Alwat prefer the gods *in* things," Ngangata replied. "The trees, the little places. And yes, they are intimate with them. They consider themselves kin."

"As do we. I am kin to the pasture god."

"Yes. But did you ever stop to wonder how the kinship custom
came about? When Human Beings began moving into the forest,
seeking pasture, whence came the idea of becoming kin?"

Perkar stared at the little man. "The Alwat . . ."

"The Alwat did *not* give this idea to Human Beings. But the
gods knew how to create bonds with the Alwat, and they did the
same with your kind when you came along." Ngangata's wide
lips were *certainly* curved up at the corners now.

"How do you know this, Ngangata? Where does this knowledge of yours come from?"

"The Alwat sing songs about it."

"The Alwat could lie."

"The Alwat know about deception, and practice it often
enough. But lying in speech is an idea foreign to them. If they do
not want something known, they do not speak of it. Speech is
only for truth, to them. I don't think they can conceive of anything different."

Perkar laughed. "That is *very* odd." He looked speculatively at
the half Alwa. "And what of you, Ngangata? Do you share this
inability to lie?"

Atti—possibly bored by their philosophical discussion—had
been silent. Now he chuckled. "He lies half of the time, of
course."

"Just so," Ngangata agreed.

"You, Atti, do you know much of the gods?"

"More than I want to, I suppose," the red-haired man drawled
in his peculiar mountain accent.

"Has either of you ever been to the 'Great River'? The one the
Mang call Toh?"

The mountain man and the half Alwa exchanged a peculiar
glance.

"His headwaters are very near where we go," Atti told him
at last.

"What do the Alwat know of him?"

"They know him," Ngangata said. "They know better than to

approach him. They name him Klanahawakadn: 'The Swallower.' Also, they call him Ov'fanakaklahuzn: 'He Who Changed.' "

"Why? What does that mean? I understand the swallowing part—any big river would do that." *He eats me up,* she had told him. That meant more than he thought, he now realized.

"That River was once Anishu, like most rivers. He has become Aniru, the god of a place. A very, very long and large place. And he is very . . . simple."

"Simple." Perkar frowned. Simple. *He eats me up.*

Perkar rode along for a while in silence.

"I wonder how a god like that could be killed?" he whispered, just loud enough for Ngangata and Atti to hear.

Atti laughed, a loud, raucous belly laugh that must have hurt him, given his injuries. Indeed, he held his chest, tried to throttle his chortling. Ngangata reacted very differently; he scowled and shook his head. Perkar suspected the difference was that Ngangata realized he was serious, while Atti was picturing a flea arming itself to kill a horse.

P ERKAR was still pondering gods a while later, when the rains came. He was imagining a god who killed or caused to be killed every other god—the spirit of every tree, stone, little place in the world. It seemed to him—if there were only *one* huge god, like the pasture god but unimaginably bigger—it would be as if there were no gods at all.

The first few drops Perkar paid no mind, though behind him Apad and Eruka sent up a chorus of complaints and curses to the cloud gods, to the waters who fed them. But then the forest ceiling bent with the force of the rain, and sheets of water soaked them, as if the Stream Gods themselves had taken to the sky. Perkar was doubly glad now that he was not wearing armor, which would chafe painfully once the quilted clothing beneath it became wet. Apad and Eruka would soon have even more to complain about.

The rain carried that scent with it, that scent like flowers, and Perkar was suddenly, vividly reminded of *her*, of his sacrifice of roses. Of pale skin, so warm and Human, of the dark, musky smell of her as they lay together, her breasts pressed against him, her legs wrapped around him. The feelings were so bright-edged that he seemed to feel her fingers stroking his manhood, drawing the warmth in his belly into his groin and knotting it there. He groaned, listed in his saddle. The rain pounded on mercilessly, a shout from each raindrop coalescing into the roar of legions.

They caught up with the Alwat. The pale creatures stood waist-deep in a swollen stream, splashing one another. All but one, that is; the female that Perkar had begun to call "Digger" in his mind. She stood in the water, as well, but did not play. When they came close she gestured. Ngangata dismounted, bent close to her mouth as she spoke.

He turned after a moment and shouted back at them, "They say the cave is just up here. We can dry off."

That drew, if not elation, at least approval from the party.

Ngangata then sloshed over to Mang's flank, spoke to Perkar and only Perkar.

"This stream has a message for you," he said. "Sent by the rain from a goddess far away."

Perkar's heart filled his chest like an anvil and a blacksmith's hammer. He moved his lips, but no words emerged.

"She says you shouldn't have sent him your blood. She says he has a taste for you now. She says to stay away from him."

Ngangata's dark gaze held him for a moment, watched Perkar blink raindrops from his eyes. Then the halfblood waded out into the stream, tugging his horse behind him.

The rain still smelled of roses, but the scent was fading.

"WHAT a *stench*," Apad complained, wrinkling his nose in disgust. At first, Perkar thought Apad meant the soaked gambeson he had just shucked off—which *did* stink, noticeably, of sweat. But when Eruka added, "Worse than animals," he realized that they meant the Alwat.

Perkar wrinkled his own nose, but all that he could smell (save for Apad and Eruka) was the welcome scent of burning juniper and pine.

"At least they found us this cave," he noted.

"Oh, and a fine cave it is, too," Apad remarked. "Tight, narrow, smoky—and now it smells like animals, too."

"Better than being wet, I would say," Perkar said.

"He has you there," Eruka observed, gingerly touching the angry red skin where his armor had chafed through his quilted undergarment.

"Well, Perkar seems to be getting quite *friendly* with these Alwat," Apad noted, his eyes narrowed. "What did you find to talk about so long with our friend Ngangata, Perkar?"

Perkar shrugged, but he could also feel himself blush. "Things. This forest and its gods. We were nearly killed by one of them, so I thought I would learn what Atti and Ngangata could tell me."

"I don't trust those two," Eruka said, glancing sidewise at Apad—as if for approval.

Apad nodded. "Listen, Perkar. If they know so god-cursed much about this forest, why didn't they know about the Wild God?"

"It's a big forest," Perkar said, frowning. "Bigger than all of the Cattle-Lands put together. Who could know every inch of it?"

Apad smirked. "They don't have to know every inch of it. They have the Alwat to tell them what they need to know. Do you think these are the first Alwat our friends have spoken to since we entered the forest? Don't you ever hear Ngangata out in the woods, jabbering?"

He was offering to his bow, Perkar nearly protested—but he only had Ngangata's word on that. True, he had seen the halfling with the stave, but that could have been a ruse. Still, Apad's proclamation rankled Perkar enough to pursue the conversation for another step. "You aren't suggesting that Ngangata and Atti *knew* about the Wild God, led us there on purpose? Look at Atti; he's the only one who got injured."

"It went straight for the Kapaka," Eruka said. "Did you notice that? It went right over Atti. If Apad hadn't been between it and the king . . ."

Perkar remembered Apad shrieking and jabbing at the monster. It had not seemed to Perkar that Apad actually interposed himself between the king and the god, only that it had been his poor fortune to *be* there.

"True enough," Perkar said anyway. He *did* like Eruka and Apad; they were understandably upset. And he couldn't totally dismiss the possibility that they were right. After all, they knew Ngangata and Atti better than he. Ngangata had never entered the fray at all, had never really been in danger from the Wild God. Appearances could be deceiving, and Perkar thought it best to keep his mind open to possibilities. "True enough," he repeated. "They will bear watching."

Apad nodded. "I trust you told them nothing of our plans?"

"Shh," Eruka hissed. "Sound carries strangely in caves. Let us not speak of it here."

"I said nothing, of course," Perkar said, a bit annoyed.

"I knew you would not," Apad said. "You are a good fellow, Perkar. Like the oak they named you after."

Perkar nodded his thanks. "That reminds me," he said. "I think I'll make an offering to Ko, who made my sword." He clapped Apad on the shoulder as he stood, careful to avoid the tender strips of skin where the weight of the chain mail had pulled heaviest. He wondered if his friends would wear armor again the next day.

His offering to Ko was usually one of woti, but as far as Perkar knew, none was available. The king had a single flask left, but he had made clear to all of them that it was a gift for the Forest Lord. Still, Perkar had a bit of incense remaining. He would get a coal from the fire, then go a bit farther back in the cave.

The Kapaka, Atti, Ngangata, and the seven Alwat were huddled around the fire. Perkar did smell the Alwat now, but it was not a particularly unpleasant smell.

"Make room for some men," Eruka said from behind him, and Perkar realized that the two had followed him over to the fire. Perkar caught Ngangata's scowl.

"Ngangata," Apad asked softly. "Could you ask your kin to move and let us next to the fire?"

The Alwat were all watching Apad. It was impossible to tell what they were thinking.

"There is room around the fire," Ngangata observed.

"Sit down, join us," the Kapaka said.

"They smell," Apad said.

"Wait," Perkar said quickly. "Couldn't we build *another* fire, for the Alwat?"

Ngangata leveled his opaque gaze at Perkar and all but hissed, "Perhaps *you* should build a fire for you and *your* kin." Waving the back of his hand at the three of them.

Eruka gave a low whistle, and Apad made a little clicking noise. "Well, Perkar," he said. "Seems like you and the halfblood aren't such good friends after all."

Perkar was aware of the hot blood rushing into his face, and at first he wasn't even sure whom he was mad at. Then he was. He had tried to befriend the half man, hadn't he? Talked to him when the others would not. And this was how the little man repaid him, by insulting him when he was only trying to make things better.

"I think," Perkar said, "that you had better go get your sword."

Ngangata shot him a little sarcastic smirk. "Well," he said, "if I had a sword, perhaps I would."

"No," the Kapaka said. "Stop this, you two."

"If you don't have a sword, we can fight with our hands," Perkar said. Apad and Eruka, behind him, made encouraging noises.

An odd look settled over Ngangata's face then. It was a look of weary resignation, of boredom almost.

"Let's go, then," he said.

Eruka and Apad were hooting now, shouting Perkar's name. Perkar laid his sword carefully on a stone. He pointed to the widest, most open section of the cave. Ngangata nodded and strode there, turned to face Perkar with his knees flexed.

Perkar expected the king to stop them at any moment, but the older man, after his single injunction, had fallen silent.

Perkar wiped his hands on his trousers as he assessed his opponent. Ngangata was shorter than he by nearly a head, but more heavily muscled. Perkar remembered the half man's proficiency with the bow, wondered what other skills he might have.

Ngangata was waiting for him to make the first move; Perkar, to his astonishment, realized that the smaller man was reluctant to attack him.

Always keep your balance, Perkar's father had taught him. He did, stepping quickly but with his weight centered, and threw a punch at Ngangata's head. The half man jerked away from the blow, but the contact was still solid. Ngangata reeled away from him.

Perkar resumed his stance. He did not want to be tricked into a rash attack. He grinned despite himself—Apad and Eruka were applauding him.

He swung again, and this time Ngangata brought an arm up, actually caught the blow. Perkar, anticipating that possibility, stepped with his back leg and drove his left hand into his opponent's midsection. It was like punching stiff leather, though Ngangata responded with a *whoof.* The grip on Perkar's wrist was strong—*very* strong—and Perkar realized to his dismay that he had badly underestimated the strength of the little man. He twisted free but resumed his attack instantly. As when he confronted the Wild God, the fear in his belly was gone, a hard anger surfacing.

Ngangata slapped his punch aside and, like a sudden stroke of

lightning, launched his own attack; his fist darted out, so terribly
fast that Perkar barely had time to blink before a stinging slap
reddened his face. Perkar countered with a wild swing that lost
him his balance but landed solidly on Ngangata's chest; the
sound was as if he had punched a drum. Perkar's little anger was
suddenly a storm. Ngangata was playing with him; he had
opened the club of his fist into a mere slap; the attack that should
have sent him to the cave floor spitting out teeth had only come
as a reprimand. Twice the halfling had made him look foolish.
Two times too many.

He followed the punch to the chest with another to the chin,
and Ngangata's head snapped back, away from the blow, inhu-
manly fast. It must have looked like it hurt—the flagging enthusiasm of his friends' cheers picked up again—but he knew that
his fist had really only barely connected.

The next blow was solid, though, and this time Ngangata *really* staggered. Perkar drew back to hit him again. His opponent
looked at him enigmatically, and then—bizarrely—he smiled, a
mocking, contemptuous smile. Perkar hit that smile dead center,
and Ngangata fell, teeth smeared with his own blood. Slowly the
half man picked himself back up. Perkar hit him again, and again
he went down. Ngangata struggled to regain his feet once more,
paused to gather strength, swaying on his knees.

"Stop. Stop this, I demand it!" The Kapaka pushed roughly
between the two men. "Stop it. Ngangata is here under my protection, Perkar. If you strike him again, you must strike me."

"It is a fair fight," Apad protested. "They both agreed to it."

"Enough. This expedition is under *my* charge, whatever any of
you might think. *My* charge. I will not have you fighting amongst
yourselves."

Ngangata had regained his feet once more, though his legs
were shaking visibly. One eye was already nearly swollen shut
and his lip was bleeding copiously. His expression was completely unfathomable—puzzlement? scorn? Perkar did not know,
but he suddenly felt silly, stupid even. Hitting a man who was not

hitting him back. And now, the stupider he felt, the more angry he became.

"Why won't you fight?" he breathed, so low that probably only Ngangata and the Kapaka could hear him.

Ngangata shook his head as if a child should know the answer to *that* question. Perkar turned away in disgust. His fist was beginning to ache, and he vaguely wondered if he had cracked any bones in his knuckles.

Apad and Eruka clapped him on the shoulder as he walked away, back toward the fire. The Alwat were still there, watching, impassive. Atti sat somewhat apart from them, and he did not meet Perkar's gaze.

Perkar sat down, flicked his gaze angrily back toward Ngangata. The half man staggered out of the cave, out into the rain. Neither Atti nor any of the Alwat followed him.

III

The Light in the Labyrinth

Hezhi kicked back the embroidered coverlet and rolled across the bed to where the sheets were cooler. "Hot," she explained to Qey, who looked down at her with sympathy. "Hot."

Qey bent over, pressed a cool rag to her face. It was so cold as to be almost painful, and Hezhi winced away from it.

"I will send word to the library," Qey said. "Tsem will take it. Ghan cannot expect you to work when you are so ill."

"No," Hezhi insisted. "No, I have to go. He will send soldiers again . . ."

"Ssh, little one." Qey persevered with the rag, following her as she flinched from it. After a moment's contact, it began to feel better. "He won't," she assured Hezhi. "If he does, *they* will see you are not well."

Hezhi tried to protest once more, but Qey was right. She could not imagine standing up; her stomach lurched at the least motion, even on the bed. And she was so *hot.*

"Let me make you some tea," Qey suggested. She left the rag with Hezhi, who sponged it across her own face.

"What's wrong with me?" she wailed.

"It's your first bleeding," Qey replied. "It's harder on some than others."

Hezhi didn't believe her. There was some deeper worry in Qey's voice, and not a little fear. That, in turn, frightened Hezhi.

"Try to close your eyes, little one, get some rest. You hardly slept last night. Small wonder, with this and those horrible things that happened yesterday."

"It was after *me,*" Hezhi mumbled. "Why was it after *me?*"

"Quiet, child. It was just a ghost. It wasn't after anyone in particular. Get some sleep; I'll make some warm tea to help you, to soothe your stomach."

"I don't *want* to sleep." Hezhi groaned. "I don't like my dreams."

"They will fade," Qey promised.

"No," Hezhi said, but Qey had already gone to the next room. Hezhi wanted to explain that it wasn't the dreams of the ghost she was afraid of; those were bad enough, seeing that poor soldier die again, split open from inside. But that dream she understood, at least. It was the strange dreams, the weird ones, that kept her awake. And it wasn't what she *saw* in them; it was what they made her feel.

She heard Qey in the next room talking to Tsem, muffled noises she did not understand, heard the outside door open and then close again. After a while, Qey returned with a cup of tea. Hezhi managed to sit up enough to sip it. The tea was bitter, but good. It relaxed the terrible knots in her gut, made her feel a bit less nauseated.

"Hezhi," Qey said as she drank the last of her tea. "Hezhi, I don't want you to tell anyone that you began bleeding. Do you understand?"

"Why?" She was beginning to feel warm rather than hot, more comfortable. Perhaps she *could* go to the library after all.

"It would be for the best. You know how people are about such things."

Hezhi nodded, not really understanding but unwilling to argue about anything. Qey made to leave, but Hezhi grasped her hand. "Stay here with me," she asked.

Qey hesitated. "I have to go start some bread," she said. "I'll be back to check on you soon."

"Let me come to the kitchen then."

"You don't have the strength, you just think you do. It's the tea, little one." Qey patted her hand. "I'll be back soon."

Hezhi closed her eyes—for a moment only—and listened to Qey's footsteps recede. She really didn't feel hot anymore, just a bit warm.

H̲ᴇᴢʜɪ *was in a strange place. It seemed altogether too damp and green. Trees—trees the like of which she had never seen— surrounded her. They towered impossibly high, taller and thicker than even the largest cedar or olive tree, and they grew as profusely as wheat in a field. The sky above her was visible only as tiny blue slivers, the vast dome of it blotted from her sight by the vault of branches and leaves. Light glowed through the leaves, however, shone through them as if through paper so that she could see the delicate veins in those closest. She was reminded of the Hall of Moments, of the colored glass and the way it made the light play upon the marble floor. It was beautiful and a bit frightening because it was so alien; the smells were thick, pungent, unfamiliar. Worse was an awful awareness of something she had done wrong, some awful act she had committed. What have I done? she kept thinking, over and over.*

She awoke with a start; she blinked her eyes, for the images of the trees seemed to cling to them like the grit that formed in their corners at night. She rolled over onto her back, angry. Qey had tricked her into sleeping.

She tried to concentrate on what the dreams might mean. Royalty were said to live by dreams, to make them and understand them. But every dream she had ever heard of had to do with the River, with Nhol, with the Kingdoms. She had never even *heard* of a place with such large trees. Not in the desert, certainly, and not in the Swamp Kingdoms, though she had heard of thick stands of mangrove in the fens near the sea. But huge trees, like wooden castles . . .

When she got back to the library, she would steal a moment or two, when Ghan wasn't watching. She knew where to find at least one geography.

Something caught the corner of her vision, a small movement. Curious, she rolled her head that way. It was her little ghost, the one she had begun thinking of as a scribe. She smiled at the faint curdling in the air.

"Do *you* know?" she asked him. "Do you know where such a land is to be found?"

She was faintly astonished when he moved closer; in the past he had approached her only when she was asleep or when she was studying some writing she had copied. Now he came close for no apparent cause, though he seemed indecisive, now approaching, now retreating. She watched in fascination as he did this little dance, tried to recall his face as she had seen it once, years ago. Despite his vacillation, he sidled nearer and nearer, until, like a child stealing something behind an adult's back, a little appendage of distorted air resembling nothing so much as an arm reached out and *touched* her, down *there*, where she was bleeding. Outraged, she jerked away, but then paused, riveted by what happened.

The ghost was as a clear glass suddenly filled with dark wine. Color raced up the arm and poured into him, so that he was no longer a wavering in the air but a man, as sharp and distinct and real as any person she had ever seen. As distinct, in fact, as the monstrous ghost that had attacked her the day before. She shrieked, kicked away from him; from earliest childhood she knew the more solid-seeming a ghost was, the more power it had. The young man did not look powerful or terrible; he looked sad and rather frightened himself. He opened his mouth, as if trying to speak—and his color and form faded, became a wavery outline, vanished entirely.

Despite the fact that she was shaking with retreating fear, Hezhi bolted up to look at where he had been standing. There, on the floor, was a spattering of water, as if someone had spilled a small glass. One of the droplets held a spot of ruby red, expanding and fading to pink. It could only be a droplet of blood.

At that moment, Qey rushed into the room. "What is it?" she asked frantically.

Hezhi leaned back onto the mattress, studiously avoiding glancing at the damp place on the floor.

"Nothing," she told Qey. "Just a bad dream."

THE next day, she felt better and returned to the library. Ghan signaled her to halt as she walked in, and she did so, waiting impatiently near his desk. After ignoring her for a few moments, Ghan looked up from his writing board and nodded.

"Sit down," he said. Surprised, she did as he commanded, sat down on her calves with her dress tucked under. Ghan regarded her severely for a moment, then handed her a sheaf of paper and a thread-bound book. Next he shoved dry ink, a mixing stone, a little jar of water, and a pen across the desk.

"Copy the glyphs on the first seven pages," he said. "Memorize them. This evening I will test you, and I expect you to know them all. Do you understand?"

"I . . ." Hezhi began, but Ghan cut her off.

"I'm sorry," he said, his tone as insincere as his sudden smile. "That was really a rhetorical question. You *do* understand, and if you don't, I will know by this afternoon, won't I?" He returned his scrutiny to whatever it was he was working on. "You may use the table across the room," he concluded, not looking back up.

Puzzled, Hezhi retreated to the table with the things he had given her, but as she opened the book, a sudden elation swept her confusion out the door and away. Ghan was teaching her to read the old script! And to write it.

Excited, she bent to the task. Many of the characters were already familiar to her, but she copied them anyway. Still, it was daunting how many she *didn't* know; she wondered how she could possibly memorize them in such a short time. She wrote them carefully, repeating the names written to the sides of the glyphs in the modern syllabary. It was a bit frustrating; she could never quite draw them the way they were pictured. The ones in the book were elegant, flowing. Hers looked like little blobs of ink.

She blinked owlishly when she suddenly realized that Ghan was standing over her. Was it time already? She had scarcely noticed.

Ghan regarded her attempts at writing without comment, while Hezhi sat nervously, fingering the hem of her skirt. She knew he wouldn't be pleased—Ghan was never pleased with anything she did—but she hoped he would not be too *displeased*.

Finally he nodded and sat down across the table from her.

"Draw me *sungulh*," he said. Her heart sank. She could draw it—it was one of the easiest. But she was not so certain she could do them all. She had hoped he would point to them in the book and she would name them—but that was stupid, because they had their names written, right there, in the syllabary. Carefully, she traced out the open oval that meant "pot"; *sungulh* in the ancient tongue, *shengun* in the modern. He continued asking her the glyphs, and with each one she drew she became more and more uncertain. Her earlier happiness was beginning to evaporate; she suspected that for Ghan, this was merely another chance to humiliate her into quitting the library altogether. Yet she couldn't, especially now, when she had *so* many questions. Her quest had begun as one of several ways of finding D'en, but without ever finding the answer to that first question, she had inexorably been drawn into more and *more* questions. And she *felt* the answers were there, if she only knew how and where to look.

"Now draw *jwegh*," Ghan demanded. She merely stared at her paper, unable to remember that one at all.

"Well?" Ghan asked, after what seemed an eternity.

"May I speak?" she whispered.

"Go on."

"I'm sorry, Ghan. I tried—I *really* tried—but I couldn't remember them all." She kept her eyes averted; she knew Ghan hated for her to look at him.

Ghan sighed, gazed slowly around the library. Save for themselves it was empty. Hezhi silently braced herself.

"Nobody could," he said.

She gaped at him.

"Close your mouth and listen," Ghan admonished as he leaned across the table toward her. "What I meant to say is that no one could learn this script the way *you* have been doing it. Frankly, I'm astonished that you read as well as you do." He shook his head. "Digression after digression," he complained. "To teach you to index I must teach you to read. To teach you to read, I must teach you to *learn*." He straightened. "But you will not slip out of our bargain by being ignorant," he snapped. He took up the pen and handed it to her.

"Write *sungulh* again," he commanded.

Hezhi complied, more confused than ever. *Sungulh* was easy because it was the old word for *shengun*, or "pot." It *looked* like a pot, almost—oval, not closed at the top.

"Fine," said Ghan. "Now write *qwen*."

Hezhi knew that one, too. It meant "fire" and was also very simple: a curvy line going up and down, two other lines sprouting from its base and going off to the sides, at angles. Like the glyph for "pot," it looked something like what it meant.

"Now *wad*," Ghan continued. Hezhi marveled at how uncharacteristically patient he seemed to be, yet still felt fortunate that she knew this one, too. It meant "cook"; she had scribbled it on the doorway to the kitchen one day. Halfway through drawing it, she stopped, amazed.

"I . . . I never *noticed* that," she breathed.

"Noticed *what*?" Ghan demanded.

"*Wad* is made out of *qwen* and *sungulh*." It was, though the simpler characters were distorted; the oval of the "pot" was quashed way down, but now she could see that it was indeed *sungulh*. *Qwen*—the three wavy lines joined at the base—was quashed, too, and the center, straight line stuck right up through the middle of the pot. "Fire and a pot. Cooking!"

Ghan cleared his throat. "*Ngess'e'*," he demanded.

"I . . . I don't remember that one," Hezhi confessed.

"Look it up."

Hezhi did; this time, she understood from the start what she was copying; the glyph was made of "pot" again, this time combined with the symbol for "person." It took her a moment to understand.

"*Ngess'e'* is the old word for 'body,' " she mused. "Does this mean that a person's body is like a pot?"

Ghan nodded. "*Sungulh* really means 'vessel,' " he explained. "Anything that holds something."

"I see, I *see*!" she said, nearly forgetting herself and giggling. How could she have been so stupid? " 'Ship' is made from that, too, isn't it? And so is 'house'! A vessel with someone in it!" She doodled the two glyphs quickly, imperfectly—but legibly. Now that she could see that the lines weren't just random squiggles but other, simpler glyphs, they were easier to write.

Ghan watched her do that for a while, impassive. Then he reached over and stopped her with a touch on the wrist.

"Now," he said. "Now draw *su'*."

Su' was water, a little swirly coil. Hezhi put it down, but her mind was slipping ahead. Of course; ice had this in it, and so did weep—that was "water" and "face." She waited eagerly for Ghan's next command.

"Do the glyph for road," he said, using the modern—*not* the ancient—word for "road." That puzzled her but did not give her pause. She etched out the complex symbol. Then she stared at it, surprised. It looked like "water" and "land" mixed together.

"That should mean marsh, or island, or something, shouldn't it?"

"Why is that?"

"These are the glyphs for 'water' and 'land.' "

"Say what you *just* said slowly," he said, eyes intent on her face, watching as if he could *see* how she thought.

Hezhi complied. "These—are—the—glyphs—for—'water'—and—'land.' "

"Just the two words now."

"She', nyun," she said. "Water, land."

"Doesn't that sound like *shengu*, 'road'?"

Hezhi wrinkled her brow. "A little, but not very much."

"But what if you name those glyphs like that in the Old Language, with the old pronunciation?"

"Su'-ngan," she said carefully, then smiled. "I see! *Su'ngan* sounds like *sungu*, the old word for 'road.' "

"Indeed," Ghan said. "In those two ways, all complex glyphs are constructed." He smirked. "Rather than having to learn thousands of glyphs, you need only learn the hundred basic symbols."

Hezhi nodded, lost in the wonder of it. "How beautiful," she breathed.

"Now," Ghan asked softly, "do you think you can take these with you and know them by tomorrow?"

"I can take the book and the paper?"

"I want you to learn this quickly," Ghan explained. "I have no time to indulge you every day. You *must* work at home, as well."

"I'll know them tomorrow," she promised.

That afternoon, she had to restrain herself from dancing out into the hall where Tsem waited. He seemed puzzled by the happy look on her face.

"You seem to be feeling better, Princess," he observed.

"Yes, Tsem, I *do* feel better. Ghan is teaching me to *read.*"

"Ah. I can think of nothing that would make *me* feel better."

Hezhi noticed that, as he spoke, he kept glancing distractedly up and down the hall.

"Something wrong, Tsem?" she asked.

"No, Princess, nothing you need worry about."

"I don't like the sound of *that*," Hezhi remarked. "Whenever someone tells me that, it is almost certainly something I *should* worry about."

"No, not this time," Tsem said. "This is my own problem."

"Can I help?"

Tsem looked sharply at her, as if he thought she were joking. When he saw how earnest she was, though, he chuckled and tousled her hair. "No, Princess, but thank you for the offer. Shall we go on home now? Qey was making crescent-moons with cheese, I think."

"Fine," Hezhi said. "I have a lot to do, anyway. Come on, race me."

"Race you?"

"Like we used to do. Remember? I used to beat you all of the time."

"I remember letting you win so you wouldn't have a tantrum and order me beheaded," Tsem corrected.

Hezhi pretended to pout, then changed her expression to one of surprised discovery. She pointed up the corridor, where Tsem had been so nervously gazing. "Is that who you were looking for?" she asked.

Tsem turned to look, a flash of concern passing over his heavy features. When he turned back, puzzled—there was no one in the direction she pointed—it was just in time to see Hezhi's skirt vanishing around the corner. He rolled his eyes, bellowed, and gave pursuit.

HER servitude became joy after that. Each day her knowledge of the old script advanced, and, soon enough, Ghan began to teach her indexing. Indexing was actually simple enough; it involved reading—or at least skimming—a book and making a list of the subjects and important personages detailed or mentioned in it. There was a master index—a truly enormous book that Ghan kept hidden away—composed of entries under various subjects and persons. Under each heading could be found a list of the manuscripts that mentioned them and a set of numbers indicating where in the library the book was likely to be found. Hezhi was amazed—and a bit chagrined—to learn of this index. It would have made her earlier search much simpler. Books were shelved in the order that they were acquired, and as soon as they were placed on a shelf, that shelf was labeled with a number—the number following the one before it, naturally—and the same number was written on the inside cover or first page of the book, so that it could be reshelved. This meant there was no telling where a book on a particular subject was *without* the index.

Indexing was by turns boring and interesting, depending upon the book she was reading. Ghan seemed satisfied enough with her work, however, though he was gruff and even caustic when she made mistakes. As time went on, however, her mistakes became fewer and fewer; her eyes could dance through the glyphs, discerning their meanings, and, now that she could understand the complex play of metaphor and even outright punning that the script was based upon, she began to catch subtle shades of meaning she had never guessed at.

So absorbed was she in her work that she did not think much about the ghost that had attacked her in the hall or the strange forest she continued to dream of so often. Her mind had returned to the earlier question of D'en and her inescapable conclusion that she needed to better understand her own family if she was ever going to discover his fate—and her own possible fate, as well. So in the evenings, when she was done with whatever Ghan asked her to do, she would turn not to geographies of strange places or treatises on ghosts, but instead to Royal Chronicles. She *did* briefly glance at one rather recent geography that seemed to suggest that while there were no forests such as she dreamed of in the central part of the world, the distant reaches—north, west, east, south, and west of the sea—seemed to be *all* forest, occupied by monsters and subhuman creatures. Under such circumstances, locating *her* dream forest seemed unlikely at best.

She had almost as much trouble with her researches into the royal family.

"The index lists a number of books that are not on the shelves," she mentioned to Ghan one day.

"There are many books that need reshelving," Ghan observed. "You can do that this afternoon."

Hezhi did so, but the books she sought were not among them. She brought this to Ghan's attention.

"Tell me the titles," he said, and when she did, his eyes narrowed with anger.

"The priesthood took those," he practically snarled.

"Why?"

"Let me rather ask *you* why you want them."

"I am a princess, and I have an interest in the royal family."

Ghan shook his head. "Ah, no, Princess. You tell me the truth—so I will not punish you—but you omit much, as well. Your interest in the royal family seems very specific. The genealogies we have, and the *Book of the Waterborn*, which merely details the emperors and their deeds. But these—*Manifestations of Godhead in the Waterborn, The Origin and Uses of Royal Power, The She'Deng*—these are unusual books."

"Is that why the priesthood has them?"

"The priesthood has them for many reasons, not the least of which I think is the rare child like yourself." As he said this, he shuddered, and his eyes half closed.

"Well," he muttered, sitting down.

"They Forbid *you*?" Hezhi whispered.

"Hush," Ghan snapped. "Don't speak of it. And I advise you not to speak of those books anymore, either, to anyone."

"I . . . won't."

Ghan nodded. "The priesthood is singularly unimaginative," Ghan said, after he seemed recovered. "They take books from me in which puzzles are pieced together, but they leave the original pieces of the puzzle in the library."

"What do you mean?"

Ghan sighed. "The whole cloth is no longer here, but the

warp, the weft, and the loom may lie around." Another tremor ran through him, and Hezhi raised her fingers to her mouth.

"I'm sorry, Ghan. We won't talk about this again."

"No, I don't think we will," Ghan agreed, breathing heavily.

In the next few days, Hezhi read some of the texts on the royal family very closely—especially the histories. She turned up a number of rather cryptic references. One manuscript referred to the "River-Blessed," and at first she was certain that this meant people like her father, to whom the River gave powerful sorcery. Another mentioned a time when no suitable heir could be found who had reached the "age of investment," so that a vizier had to be appointed to rule until such time as someone reached that age. She discovered that many emperors had been no older than she when they ascended the throne—but none were much *younger*. On her paper, she wrote these two things down side by side. She returned briefly to a book on the history of the city's architecture, now that she could really read it. In it she found an oblique reference to a large portion of the palace being destroyed, not by flood or fire, but by a "River-Blessed unleashed." This "River-Blessed" was named: Ta'nganata Yehd Zha'dune. She looked him up in one of the genealogies and discovered that he had been placed on the throne as Chakunge at the age of ten—the youngest emperor ever to rule. The chronicle recorded that he ruled for just over a year. *This* work did not mention any general destruction of the palace; it merely mentioned that the *-nata* ghost suffix was added to his name at that time. This particularly intrigued her because it occurred at the very beginning of her own dynasty; *Zha'dune* was the old pronunciation of *Cha'dune*.

On her way home, rather than talking to Tsem—who seemed distracted anyway—she tried to piece together what she had learned. She could see clearly now what Ghan meant in his metaphor of the loom, warp, and weft. In no single book would she find *all* of the information about any person or event. The book on architecture had failed to note Ta'nganata's date of ascension and his untimely death, but the genealogy—which contained *that* fact—neglected the small detail that he had, in that year, destroyed much of the palace. These were threads she could weave together, threads that, she hoped, would form some tapestry with a picture she could comprehend. The loom, she guessed, was herself—no, that was wrong, she would be the weaver, wouldn't she? No matter. It *was* just an analogy.

Much of the evidence seemed to point to her own age—about twelve—as somehow critical in the royal family, at least for men who might be emperor. She suspected that it was somehow connected with her bleeding. If that technically made *her* a woman, there might be some similar change that made boys into men— though she knew for a fact that men did not bleed, had quite different organs than women. She decided that this would be the object of her research the next day. Whatever this change might be, it occurred at different times for different men, though within the same few years. This also fit with what she knew of women. The story she had reconstructed about Ta'nganata seemed especially important: a boy somehow raised to the role of emperor while still too young; at least that was *her* reading of it. Even in the genealogy there was a sense, though a *very* subtle one, that some mistake had been made in choosing him. She connected the fact that he had been the *youngest* emperor—she felt that this was emphasized in the text—revealed the nature of the mistake. And this boy—this eleven-year-old boy—had somehow destroyed a vast portion of the palace.

She was certain her father—and probably her mother—could do the same, if they wished. But there was no sane reason to do such a thing. That could be the source of the problem with Ta'nganata; eleven-year-olds, she knew from experience, were hardly sane. And yet, neither were many people, of any age. And why would someone incapable of suppressing awesome power at the age of eleven suddenly be able to at the age of twelve, thirteen, fourteen? The center of the riddle was in that question, Hezhi knew. This was the age at which royal children either went down the Hall of Moments to live with their parents or vanished, had the *-nata* suffix added to their names. Like D'en.

And inexorably, she was drawn back to the fact that she was

now D'en's age—or, rather, the age he had been when she last saw him. She was also Ta'nganata's age, for that matter.

Something wasn't right when she reached home. Qey met her at the door, twisting a dishrag mercilessly in both hands. Her eyes were red, and Hezhi abruptly realized that Qey had been crying. Next to her, Tsem stiffened. She felt his tension like a brittleness in the air itself.

"Hezhi," Qey said softly. "Some people have come to see you. I want you to do what they say, and not be worried."

Qey was clearly worried, but Hezhi did not say so. She caught the faint whiff of smoke; it was the same scent that the brooms of the priests gave off. She edged around Qey into the courtyard.

Four priests stood there, watching her entrance. They all wore cottonwood masks of a kind she had never seen before, blank-eyed, round-mouthed. They were fully robed, as if for some ceremony.

"Hezhi Yehd Cha'dune," one of them intoned, in a singsong voice as high and clear as a silver bell. "We have come to administer the rite of *Ngess'e'.*"

The name of the rite was in the old tongue, but Hezhi knew it: "body." She recalled the glyph for "body," a vessel affixed to a Human Being.

"What? I have never heard of this rite."

"It is one of the rites of passage into adulthood," the same priest explained. "One does not learn of it until the time comes."

"Sh-she has not begun bleeding yet," Qey stammered. One of the priests turned his masked face toward her rather sharply.

"That does not matter, whether it is true or not," he asserted implacably. "The rite may be repeated, if we do it when she is too young. But we must not wait until she is too *old*," he said, his smooth voice seeming to imply more than he said. Whatever the implication was, Qey shrank away from it.

This was it, Hezhi was certain. Events had caught up with her before she could understand them. This was the day she would vanish or join her parents. Tsem knew it, too. He was as immobile as a statue.

If they take me, she realized, *he will kill them. He will kill them all.* She remembered Tsem, hugging her to his breast as he bore her away from the demon ghost, pulling her from the water when she was younger, insisting that she would never disappear as D'en had.

She laid a hand on his arm. "Tsem," she whispered. "I wish some flowers from the west roof garden, the blue ones and the red ones. Go gather them for me." The west roof garden was the farthest of their old haunts, above the deserted wing of the old palace. It would take some time for him to go there and back.

Tsem suppressed a glare—only because he was in front of the priests. "Princess," he said, voice thick with anguish, "the priests may have need of me . . ."

"No. We have no need of you," the priest contradicted. "You may gather her flowers. The rite is brief but uncomfortable— she may want them to cheer her up afterward."

"Yes, Tsem," she said. "It cheers me to think of you picking flowers." *And alive,* she silently added.

"I'm sure it does, Princess," Tsem said, trying to sound like his normal, bantering self.

"Go on, Tsem," Qey murmured. "I'll look after Hezhi."

Tsem nodded and turned rather quickly. He closed the door behind him.

"What do I do?" Hezhi asked the priests.

They motioned her toward her room.

IV

The Forest Lord

T HE next day the rain was gone, the sky a cobalt dome unalloyed with clouds. Perkar trudged down the talus slope beneath the cave, rubbing his tired eyes. Sleep had not been kind to him; mostly it had eluded him, but when he did drop into its depths, weird frenzied dreams had allowed him no rest. In the clear light, he hoped to sort them out, to find their importance, if any. But his mind was dull, and a chill wind sweeping down from that bluest sky numbed his body, as well.

This is like autumn, he thought. Autumn, though the season stood midway through summer. Hubara, the North Wind, should be sleeping yet in her faraway mountain. But perhaps another cold wind lived in the mountain Perkar could now see, for certainly the wind came down from there, with its smell of wet cinders and falling leaves. The mountain itself was a wonder, a nearly symmetrical cone, slopes pale in the morning light, crowned with dazzling brightness. Perkar wondered if he should offer something to it, but he didn't know the Mountain God's song or even his name. But then he remembered that the Mountain God was also the Forest Lord, Balati.

So he burned some incense for Balati, though the wind took it in the wrong direction. Then he braided a little fishnet of horse-tail reeds and walked down to the stream, the one that had spoken to the Alwat. There he cast the fishnet in, softly sang a little song—a greeting, since he did not know its own song.

"Thank you for your words," he told it then. "If you speak to her again, tell her I only do what I must."

He sat by the swollen stream, knowing it would not answer him, and puzzled at his dreams. Some involved Ngangata, and those dreams were painful, embarrassing, almost like dreams of finding oneself inexplicably naked at some important gathering. Perkar perceived no clear reason why his dreams had that tenor; he was always clothed in them. The mere presence of the half man seemed to trigger the feelings. Others were of her, of course, of the smell of rose petals, of her pleading, of that sharp slap across his face. Those she had sent, with the rain; they were the only ones he understood. But mixed up with those dreams were the ones about the city and the girl. Houses and halls of white stone, a dry land and a river of unthinkable size. The River he knew, as certainly as he knew anything, though he had never seen it. In one dream the River was as red as blood, thick and sluggish. And the girl, standing at a fountain, saying his name. Asking for him.

"There you are." The Kapaka looked down at him from the trail to the cave. He was grizzled and unshaven, and he looked older than Perkar believed he was. *You didn't sleep well, either,* Perkar thought, and wondered what dreams might trouble a king.

The Kapaka cleared his throat and came on down to the stream. "You've made an offering? Good. That's good."

Perkar only nodded.

"Perkar," the old man began reluctantly, then with more force: "this expedition is an important one. If it weren't, I wouldn't have put my old bones in the saddle and come all the way out here. No Kapaka has done this in two generations, and I certainly never had any intention to. I would vastly prefer to be at home, telling my grandchildren stories. But younger sons are starting to fight among themselves, others are arming against the Mang. That is foolishness, Perkar; whatever the old songs may make of war, it is foolishness. Piraku is cattle, children, the love of family, giving gifts. War breaks things, tears them up, kills family, destroys cattle. Can you see that, as young as you are?"

Perkar nodded. "I think so. The great heroes were always the most generous ones. The ones who settled wars rather than starting them."

"Just so. And so this trip is important to me, to all of us, you see?"

"It's important to me, as well," Perkar told him.

"I wonder. You don't seem focused on our goal, Perkar. See, there it is, the mountain in the heart of Balat. But I think you see something else."

Perkar did not deny that. He merely shrugged. "It is important to me. And I hope to serve you, Kapaka."

The old man grimaced. "This business with Ngangata, Perkar—you have to let that go. You can't judge what he says as if he were a warrior, like the rest of us. He is not a part of the warrior's code, and it is wrong to hold him accountable to something that he never benefits from. And we *need* him, Perkar. Who will talk to the Alwat if something happens to him? Who will guide us to the Forest Lord? Apad and Eruka are loudmouths, but I thought better of you. Bear the halfling's company for this short few days of your life, for all of us. If that isn't good enough reason, then do it because I tell you to."

Perkar nodded. "I'm sorry I made trouble. Ngangata is safe from me."

"And you from him, I hope," the Kapaka answered. "Now we should get saddled and moving. We lost time yesterday, and the sooner we get done with this, the sooner I can get back to my grandchildren."

"Agreed," Perkar said.

The Kapaka turned to go, but he spared Perkar one more of his iron-gray gazes, this time one carrying approval rather than reproach. "You fought well against the Wild God. That was your first battle, was it not?"

"It was," Perkar admitted.

"Be proud of that," he said. "You defended your king, and I have never seen an unblooded man fight better his first time. Be proud of that, and not of last night." The gravel crunched softly beneath his boots as he walked back up to where the horses waited.

"You should be up in front," Eruka told him. "You should be vanguard instead of Ngangata, after last night."

Perkar shifted uncomfortably in his seat. "Ngangata rides in front because our Alwat guides are up there," he said. "Not because he is ranked ahead of all of us."

"We are heroes," Eruka said. "Heroes on a journey with our king. Don't you remember 'Ekar Kapaka Karak'? 'The Song of the Raven King'?"

Perkar was preparing to tell Eruka that it was too early for a song, but he wasn't quick enough; Eruka's voice rose up into the midmorning, mingled with the singing of birds and clopping of hooves.

> Arrayed behind me
> All of my bright-edged heroes
> All of my caparisoned heroes
> First in their ranks
> Rode Waluka my Wolf-Warrior
> My Warrior of most standing
> Trotting behind him
> Laga in his bronze-chased mail
> With his honey-colored axe
> Behind Laga's roan

The Stallion of white-maned Nika
Nika with his three-layered hauberk . . .

"This isn't an epic," Perkar reminded him. "We aren't going to
war."

"It *will* be an epic," Apad corrected. "And we *might* go to
war."

Perkar nearly wondered aloud who would fight in this war—
Eruka who had stood stock-still as a Wild God attacked his king,
or Apad, shrieking and jabbing wildly—but bit the comment
back. Eruka and Apad still planned to invade the Forest Lord's
home and search for god-slaying weapons; well, so did he. He
could use their help. And, after all, they were his friends, though
Apad especially was beginning to annoy him. What had the
Kapaka called the two of them—loudmouths?

They had goaded him into fighting Ngangata, too, and he was
beginning to resent that. Nothing good had come from that confrontation; Ngangata rode up front, as usual, except today one of
his eyes was swollen nearly shut and his lip was split and purple.
The worst thing about the fight was what it had really revealed
about Ngangata's position in the party. He had been thinking of
Ngangata, Atti, and the Alwat as a sort of faction, one which
the Kapaka nominally belonged to. Perkar had assumed that
Ngangata was the head of that group. But when the moment of
truth came—when a Human warrior beat a half Alwa nearly
senseless—Atti had made no move to interfere, nor to express his
compassion later. The Kapaka—in retrospect—had urged Perkar
to leave the feud aside but not because he liked the half man,
only because he thought him necessary. Even the Alwat plainly
did not think of Ngangata as any relative of theirs, for none of
them had made any overtures toward helping him, either.

That meant Ngangata was truly alone. It was something
Perkar had to think on.

The horses trudged steadily uphill now, through a forest
more evergreen than hardwood. Hemlock and spruce dominated,

spicing the air with their sharp scents. The sky seemed choked
with ravens, rushing about their domain on scything black wings,
and he remembered that Ani Karak, the Raven God, made his
home somewhere in Balat. Fitting enough that Eruka had begun
one of his songs.

Perkar struggled to recall what else he could about which gods
lived in the heart of the eternal forest, but nothing came to him.
He wished suddenly that he could speak to Ngangata, who
seemed to know much about gods, but the very thought reddened his face with shame. Why hadn't Ngangata fought back?
He could not ask him *that*, either.

The bones of the mountains showed themselves more and
more often now, outcrops and ridges of granite pushing through
the earth's thin hide. Now and then, Perkar thought he saw shadowy figures crouching on these stones, but only from the corners
of his vision—when he looked directly they vanished. The woods
were full of ghosts. Perkar wondered if they were the spirits of
past travelers or the ghosts of gods.

The rest of the day passed without much conversation, as did
the next. The pace of travel became nerve-rackingly slow, the
mountain hovering above them like a thunderhead, its shadow
pacing over them not long after the noon hour, as if the night
were rushing that much faster to meet them. When true night
came, a brittle-bone cold sank down upon them, enmired them
as if it were some sort of frigid syrup—the campfires they made
seemed little able to hold back that damp chill. As if that were
not enough, Perkar's dreams continued, growing more vivid and
tumultuous as the nights passed.

The next day they began descending into a deep, creased valley; the extent of it stole his breath, for it was morning, the great
mountain dreaming yellow in the rising sun, the depth below
them still shadowed but starting to glimmer in the sun's fixed eye.

"What a fine holding this would be," he could not help but
breathe. No matter that it would spend half the day in shadow
from the mountain, no matter that it was the deepest, most

haunted forest in the world. It was a valley such as a king might dream of for his children and their children.

"Put such thoughts away," the Kapaka told him. "This is our destination. This is where Balati, the Forest Lord, makes his dwelling."

Perkar nodded. It *was* a valley for a king.

After another moment's survey, they continued the descent. The slope was steep, and the conifers of the upper ridges were soon replaced by mixed hardwoods, the heady fragrance of the mountains becoming the more familiar smell of decaying leaves and wet moss. The moss, indeed, was thick, and here and there they crossed what seemed like meadows of it, shaded from the sun by branches that steepled above them like the rafters and roof beams of a vast damakuta. Ferns grew so high and thick that the hooves and legs of their horses vanished into them; there was no path visible to *his* eyes, and yet the Alwat never seemed to doubt where they were going.

As they neared the valley floor, but before the land grew level, the Alwat halted, and after a few exchanges, Ngangata tersely explained that the party must wait there.

"The Alwat must call another guide," he told them.

Perkar dismounted heavily. After days in the high reaches of foothills, the thicker air of the valley felt like water in his lungs. He sat down, rested his back against the frayed trunk of a cedar, and watched the Alwat.

At first, he thought that they were building a fire. They gathered branches, sorting them according to size. But then Digger, the young female, brought in hoops of grapevines and long, slender willow branches. The Alwat clustered around these things, chattering in low voices; one began striking a pair of sticks together—rather arrhythmically, Perkar thought—and chanting a song of two notes.

"Keep watch, Perkar," Apad said, nudging him. "We could be in danger." Apad was nervously fingering the hilt of his sword.

"What do you mean?"

"Do you think Ngangata and his kin will let your fight go unavenged?"

Perkar frowned, watched the stocky man-creatures continue their ritual. They had lashed the willow branches into a small tower, of sorts, the base ends of the shafts thrust into the moist earth, the tops tied together. Now they were weaving more of the grapevines in and out of the frame thus formed. The branches of various sizes went into this, as well.

One of the Alwat spat some gibberish at Ngangata, who nodded and walked over to the Kapaka; the two conversed in tones too low for the others to make out. After a moment, however, the king joined the Alwat, tentatively adding branches to the bizarre construction.

When the Alwat finally came away from the thing, gently tugging the Kapaka with them, it was the size and shape of a tall man. Twin branches projecting from the crown of the structure resembled the antlers of a stag.

"I don't like it," Eruka muttered, and Perkar silently agreed.

The oldest Alwa was still singing; the two notes had become three, and though Perkar certainly could not understand them, he could tell that what she was singing were words and not merely syllables. Now, more than ever, he wished that he could ask Ngangata what was happening, and he gritted his teeth at his self-imposed ignorance.

Leaves stirred on the forest floor, took tentatively, then joyfully, to the air, swirling around the Alwat creation as if it were the center of a whirlwind. The woven saplings began to quiver. A god was coming, Perkar could see that easily enough; the air began to tremble, blurring the image of the Alwat standing behind their construction.

When it happened, it was rather sudden, as in the moment when something hidden is recognized. Perkar had experienced such a feeling before, staring at a tangled maze of branches and tree trunks that did not so much hide as camouflage a deer. Once the deer was seen, you realized it had always been there, wondered why you hadn't seen it before. It was in this manner that the goddess appeared; Perkar suddenly saw that she had been there all along, amongst the Alwat-woven branches.

In form, she was much like a rather tall Alwa, but her limbs and torso were covered more thickly and evenly by coarse black hair. The hair on her face was even more pronounced, black but with faint gray markings. From her head, antlers spread proudly. And yet Perkar could see that the antlers were still wooden rather than horn. That this was a goddess was more than clear; she was unclothed—though she bore a sheaf of arrows and a bow—and obviously female. She smiled a wide, enigmatic Alwat smile.

"Welcome, Kapaka, Prince of the Human People," she said. Her voice was a burring kind of sound, filled with vibration and resonance.

"Thank you, Goddess," the Kapaka said. "I have brought gifts for you, and for the Lord of the Forest."

"Our Lord will distribute whatever gifts you bring," the goddess said. "As for me, this form you have provided me is a fine gift—rare that I am incarnate in this fashion, and it pleases."

"You are more than welcome," the Kapaka said. "But still, I would offer you something, if you are to guide us to . . ."

"I shall take you to him," she interrupted, seeming amused. "Worry not. The Alwat know to call upon me, and not some more feckless god."

"I regret," the Kapaka told her, "that I know not your name nor any song of yours. But I have brought a singer along." He indicated Eruka, who might have shrunk back just a bit. "He can learn one, if you will teach him, and we will sing it in our damakutat through the winter months."

"You may call me Paker," she said, and now there was certainly humor in her expression; her generous lips parted to reveal a row of sharp, shining teeth. "You may call me Apa, Bari, Ngati. Or you may call me Huntress. I care not."

"Those are other names for the Forest Lord," Eruka whispered, so that Perkar—but surely not she—could hear. Even so, her smile broadened.

"And here," she said, stepping away from the Kapaka and toward the other Humans. "What is this? What scent is this?" She walked to Perkar, growing taller, it seemed, as she came. She reached out with one furred, long-fingered hand and very, very lightly touched his cheek.

"How sweet," she said. "How very sweet." But her grin was carnivore, a tiger sizing up a meal. Stepping away from Perkar, she seemed, for an instant, lost in thought, until her head snapped back up and around, black eyes flashing suddenly yellow and green, iridescent.

"Come now," she said.

The rest of the journey was dreamlike; Perkar remembered striding over chasms on the woven backs of branches, groves parting for them, dark hollows that seemed more like cists beneath the earth than anyplace aboveground. At last they descended farther still, into what amounted to a huge bowl-shaped depression, a valley within a valley. The walls were of crumbling stone, and the dark mouths of caves gaped at them as they passed.

"Are these the dwellings of the Forest Lord?" Perkar asked.

The Huntress shrugged. "I suppose. He dwells in them at times."

"Damp, dank places," another voice said. Startled, Perkar turned toward it.

It was a raven that spoke, a raven the size of a large dog. He sat, grinning, on a low branch, eyes glittering like jewels in deep water.

"Huntress, what do you bring me?" the Raven asked their guide.

"Pretty things," she said. "Pretty little things to line your nest with, to show the other gods when you come to the feasts."

The Raven lifted one leg nervously from his branch, clenched his claws closed, then flexed them open, renewed his grip on the limb.

"I see no pretty things," he complained. "Nothing pretty at all."

"As you say, then," the Huntress said. "And so we shall bid you good day."

"Wait," the Raven croaked, cocking his head suspiciously. "Perhaps they have pretty things *with* them."

The Huntress sighed and turned to the Kapaka. "Best give him something, I think. He can be childish at times."

The Kapaka nodded and opened his treasure bag, felted and embroidered with clouds and feathers. He searched about for a moment.

"Here is this," he said at last. He held up a sparkling brooch, silver with a blood red garnet.

"Pretty," said the Raven. "Yes, pretty. Perhaps you have more."

"I know you," Eruka interrupted. The Raven looked puzzled— he tried to shift his glance to Eruka but at the same time seemed unwilling to take his regard from the jewelry.

"Know me?" the Raven asked.

"Yes," Eruka told him. He coughed and then sang:

> I swallowed the Sun
> A pretty light
> Thus I was, thus I am
> I brought up land
> And spread it out
> Thus I was, thus I am
> I carry Lightning
> To glitter at night
> Thus I was, thus I am
> I painted the birds
> Who sing in flight
> Thus I was, thus I am . . .

"Thus I was, thus I am," the Raven repeated. "An old song, sung long ago. Almost I have forgotten it."

"You are Karak, the Crow God," Eruka said.

"I know who I am," the bird replied testily.

"Yes, and I know who you are, as well," the Huntress put in. "And if you do not cease your prattling and let us be on our way, I will add another feather to you—on the end of a hard, straight shaft."

"Give me the pretty thing," Karak grumbled pettishly.

The Kapaka stretched up, offered the coal-dark bird the silver brooch. The Raven took it in his beak.

"I swallowed the sun," he muttered. "You would think people would remember that."

"Oh, we remember," the Huntress said. "We remember that we had to slit you open before you would give it up."

"How rude," Karak said crossly, and, lifting his great wings, flew off into the forest. Perkar could hear the heavy beat of his wings long after losing sight of him.

"Is that true?" Perkar asked. "Did he really do those things?"

The Huntress smiled. "The world was much different in those days. Perhaps they never really happened at all."

"What do you mean?"

"The only difference between a story and the truth is how often the story is told," she replied.

Perkar didn't understand that, either, but he didn't say so. He was used to gods; they lived everywhere. He was not used to gods who claimed to have created the world or swallowed the sun. That seemed ridiculous, beyond the power of anything. Yet these were the old gods, the gods of the mountain, rarely spoken of, rarely sung about. After all, better to sing about the god of your pasture who would hear you, consider your requests.

These Mountain Gods frightened him, but they fanned a flagging spark, as well. His dreams were not just fantasy. Gods who could swallow the sun would have weapons to match their power. Such weapons could slay other gods, could they not?

The Huntress led them down the steep trail, and eventually to a meadow, nestled deep in the mountainside. The moss there was a carpet; Perkar's feet sprang upon it as they walked. In the center of the meadow was a tree, its girth greater than that of his father's damakuta. The tree—it looked like an oak—soared upward, enormous, shadowing out the sun entirely.

"Here," the Huntress said. "Here we wait."

Wait they did. Once or twice, Apad made overtures to a conversation, but the words died, eaten by the silence the magnificent tree seemed to cast about itself. Birdsong rang out, but it was far away, the memory of song. The tree seemed to be the still point of the world. So still it was that, despite himself, Perkar began drifting in and out of dozing, his head lolling over onto one shoulder, then jerking awake. Attempting to remain alert, he contemplated the tree, walking over to its spreading base, and gazing up its trunk, trying to count the layers of branches he could see, guess those he could not. Soon enough, however, he returned to sitting, and his eyelids began to droop once more.

All of his companions seemed to be having similar troubles; only the Huntress seemed alert, crouched in the clearing, unmoving as a statue, bright quick eyes darting here and there. The Alwat, Perkar suddenly realized, were nowhere to be seen.

A moment arrived, and Perkar no longer felt sleepy. The tree, the moss, everything around them suddenly unfocused, blurred into colors without much form and no detail. At first he believed the trouble was with his eyes, blurring vision to trick him into sleep; but then he heard the gasps around him. The world had gone strange, had faded. Perkar wondered if it would return. His mind turned over a conversation his father had had, long ago, with a shamaness who came to visit them, a relative of his mother's. She said something that reminded Perkar of this blurring. "The world of gods and the world of Humans is the same world," she said. "They are both like a damakuta; but the world of gods is like the whole damakuta and the world of Humans is the paint on the outside of it. We live in that paint, see only what is painted there. The gods are visible to us sometimes—they are like carvings on the beams of the damakuta, and if the painter painted those carvings we know that they are there. Of course, the gods may choose to paint and then unpaint themselves, when it suits them . . ."

A god was painting himself, and in doing so he was smearing the paint already present.

This went on for longer than was comfortable, but finally the greens and browns congealed into what they were before: the great tree, the meadow, the surrounding forest and cliffs.

Save that now Balati, the Forest Lord, was among them. He stood where the Huntress had been crouching; she was gone.

At first glance, the Forest Lord was mostly Bear, an enormous shaggy mass reared up on hind legs. But Perkar quickly realized that he was not a bear, but something older than bears or men or Alwat, something that they were all dim reflections of. Huge, furred, with legs and paws like the boles of trees. Like the Huntress he was horned, but these were not horns of wood; they were great elk antlers, that measured, from tip to tip, more than Mang's body length. A powerful smell of black soil and beast permeated the air, nearly overpowered him with its intensity. Equally overpowering was the Forest Lord's single eye. It was bird and panther, deer and snake, flashing, changeable. Compelling and frightening. Its companion was a dark and empty socket.

"Lord Balati," the Kapaka said, and he bowed. The towering figure regarded him impassively.

"Balati," the Kapaka continued, after a suitable interval, in which Perkar found himself on his knees, as well. "We sing songs of you, down in the pasturelands, in the valleys, in our hill holdings. We remember you well, and the ancient pacts you made with our fathers and their fathers."

Balati shifted back his shoulders, and a low growl issued from him, so profound that it was more a rumbling in the earth than a real sound. And yet there was sense in it; there were words.

"It is good," Balati said. "It is good that you remember. Tell me of something. Tell me something you remember."

There was silence; Perkar saw that all of his companions were bowed down, Eruka on both knees, Apad, grim-faced, on only one. Both looked as frightened as he felt.

"Eruka!" the Kapaka prompted, after a moment. "Sing an *Ekar*!"

Eruka looked up slowly, as if he were having difficulty understanding his king's command. Perkar feared he would not sing—that his voice would be as frozen as his body had been when the Wild God spoke to them. But after a moment, Eruka cleared his throat.

> Among roots and branches
> On and on I dreamed
> One day like the next
> In the tall birches
> In the white rustling aspen
> In the deep bottoms
> In bright pools
> On and on
> One day like the next . . .

Eruka's voice shook at first, uncertain. But the songs of birds seemed closer now, seemed to fly beneath and between his song, supporting it, lifting it higher. He gathered confidence.

> Ages passing, on I dreamed
> Hooves and claws
> Coming and going
> In the hard wind from the ice
> Dreaming in the sweet southern wind
> Age to age
> One age like the next . . .

It was a song that Perkar had never heard, and it was beautiful, captivating. Eruka sang of Balati in the endless forest, walking about his mountain, of the legions of gods in the forest who were both a part and not a part of him. The song went on like that for many, many stanzas. For hours, it seemed. Then, finally, the words became more familiar, as it told of the coming of the

Alwat and finally of Human Beings. After that, Eruka sang of the first meeting of Humans and the Forest Lord, of trees chopped down for pasture, of bargains made. When Eruka finally finished, Perkar found himself still listening, still waiting for an ending. But there was not one, of course. There was no ending. But one verse—a brief, minor thing in the course of the Forest Lord's Epic—one verse glittered to Perkar like silver to the Crow God. It stayed there, shining, repeating itself:

> Dreaming on and on
> I watched my brother grow bitter
> Grow gluttonous
> Humans fed his appetite
> Fed his dark, voracious desire
> Flowing from the root of our mountain
> Our cradle, our birthplace
> Bitter my brother, Rivergod, Changeling
> Took his hunger seaward
> Dreaming on and on
> Growing and changing
> Each day more ravenous
> Than the last
> Dreaming on and on
> Even I feared him
> And so armed myself . . .

Brother, thought Perkar. But a brother not trusted, a brother to arm against. Perkar felt something in his grasp, for who could this brother be but the dreadful River, the one that ate her? There was a weapon, and it must be nigh. His enemy and the weapon, here together.

He was scarcely aware when the earth began to rumble with the Forest Lord's speech.

"It is good," Balati intoned. "We can add another verse to this song. What will that verse be about?"

The Kapaka stood, spoke a trifle too loudly, a king of instants confronting a lord of epochs. "In the Human lands, more and

more sons go landless. We begin to turn on ourselves, and I fear
troubled times. The local gods tell us that you have asked them
not to bargain, as in days of old. They tell us that we must petition you for new lands and holdings to cherish and worship. So
here we have come."

The Forest Lord seemed to swell larger, like a shadow moving farther from the sun. Above them, the sky darkened with
twilight.

"It is good that you heeded my word," Balati said. "It is good.
Many valleys and hills, many gods have I given into your care,
and you into theirs. It has been well enough, but Balat is smaller
than it was, and I will only give so much. You understand this;
you are a lord of your kind."

"Yes. I understand. But I must request it."

"You have respect, you honor the memories of your fathers,"
Balati said. "We will talk, you and I. We will talk here, tonight,
and we will decide. But I will tell you, I cannot give you much.
Not much."

He hunched down, became a hillock of darkness, horned, single eye of flickering foxfire. A nighthawk cried, somewhere.

"Come," a voice whispered, and a gentle tug at his sleeve.
"Come, Ngangata says we must leave them." It was Atti. The
Alwat were visible again, at the edge of the clearing; they seemed
to be waiting. Ngangata was already walking toward them, leading his horse.

"Come," Atti repeated.

"And leave the Kapaka with *that*?" Apad demanded.

But the Kapaka was waving them away, as well. Perkar rose
up reluctantly, went to recover Mang. He let Atti go ahead,
lagged back to make sure Apad and Eruka would follow. Behind
them, neither the Kapaka nor the Forest Lord spoke; it was clear
now that they were waiting for the others to leave.

"I don't care for this at all," Eruka said.

"It doesn't sound good," Apad said. "Did you hear him? He
won't give us anything. We'll have to fight, as we planned."

"Shhh." Eruka gasped. "We might be overheard. Who knows what gods might lurk here? Or even Ngangata and the Alwat."

Apad nodded tersely, in agreement, acknowledging his mistake.

But Perkar leaned very close to Apad's ear. "The caves, Apad. We must look in the caves. We have the time, and we must take it."

Apad did not meet Perkar's eager gaze. "Yes," he answered. "I suppose . . ."

"Hurry," Eruka urged. "The Alwat will lose us here if we don't keep up."

Perkar nodded and quickened his pace, but he marked everything in his mind, tried to paint a map as they moved away from the clearing. He must find the trail up to the caves, in the dark. With or without his friends.

V

Blindness

THE Alwat did not lead them very far from the clearing, only to the base of the valley wall, where the trees climbed steeply up the slope. There, on the gentle rise clinging to the base of the precipitous one, a little fire was burning, a cheerful sight in this web of gods and power. The Fire Goddess was always friendly to Human Beings, always on their side.

The Alwat had also erected shelters, simple lean-tos roughly covered in sheets of birch bark.

"Do they expect rain tonight?" Perkar asked Atti, gesturing at the huts.

"Not *tonight*," he answered

"Not tonight? What other night? How long will this take, this negotiation?"

To his surprise, it was Ngangata who answered him. The two of them had not spoken since their fight, and Perkar did not expect to speak to him ever again.

"The Forest Lord has little sense of time," he said. "It could take a night or many nights. There is no way of knowing."

168

"Why did the Forest Lord send us away, then? Why can't we attend our king?"

Irritation flashed across Ngangata's broad features, as if his answer to Perkar was meant to be singular, a gift to be accepted but not a precedent to be taken for granted. Perkar felt his face burn, but not with anger. He stepped back from the fire lest it show.

"The Forest Lord doesn't really understand Human Beings or even Alwat, I think," he said. "He believes we are like the Huntress, like Karak."

"He thinks we are gods?" Perkar asked, unwilling to stop now that the half man was speaking

"No. The Raven and the Huntress are gods in their own rights, but they are also aspects of Balati, parts of him. As leaves are parts of a tree. Better yet, they are like aspen trees. Each aspen is a tree itself, but all of the aspen in a forest are part of the same root."

"And he thinks we are like that? All aspects of the Kapaka?"

"It is his habit to think that way," Ngangata answered. "Besides," he went on, "the king is wise, and he has been schooled in this kind of negotiation. We will be allowed to fetch him water and food when need be; Balati will not notice our presence."

"You say that the king is wise," Apad said, his voice low and flat. "Do you mean to imply that we are not?"

"I mean only to imply that you are not as wise as the Kapaka," Ngangata said softly. "That is no insult, only a fact."

"Who can dispute that?" Atti added, a little too quickly.

Apad's expression said that *he* might, but he kept his peace. For days, Apad had been trying to goad Ngangata into a fight, following Perkar's example, but with no success. Ngangata's answers to him were always couched in words just short of insulting, and Perkar realized now that when Ngangata openly insulted someone, he *meant* to do so. The fight at the cave had been no accident, no slip of the tongue. The half man had invited Perkar to fight him and then let himself be beaten. Apad and Eruka would never see this—but they had not felt the strength behind Ngangata's half-hearted blows. What Perkar still didn't understand was what the little man was up to. What shamed him was the suspicion that it had been some sort of test, one he had failed.

And why did he care about that? Ngangata was not a warrior, had no Piraku. Having his respect gained one nothing.

But he did know one thing; he would rather have Ngangata with him tonight than Apad or Eruka, though he liked the two Human men better.

"I'll make my offerings now," he told them. He gave a little incense to the Fire Goddess, then moved off into the shadows crouching about the camp. There he offered to his sword, to Ko who made it. He offered to his armor, too, unfolding it as he did so. To the gods of the mountain, he made no offerings at all; he did not want to attract their attention.

His oblations were hurried, as he began to feel a nagging urgency. If he was going into the caves of the Forest Lord, he must do so now; for all he knew the Kapaka and the Balati were even now concluding an agreement. Best, in fact, not to go back to the fire at all. Ngangata and Atti might become suspicious; if he left now, they would think that he was displaying more piety than usual. It would be a good while before they actually began to look for him, and then it would be too late. Or perhaps they would go to sleep and not realize he had been gone at all. Part of him wanted Apad and Eruka along, but he was forced to conclude that he might be better off without them; after all, *he* had no intention of seeking battle, save with the Rivergod himself. He had no quarrel with the Forest Lord nor any god in his domain. Nor, he realized, did he really seek glory or a place in some epic. All of that was just his friends talking. It sounded good at the time, but growing fear and apprehension was stripping it away. After all, he had *seen* the Forest Lord, knew something of the being from whom he intended to steal; and at the moment, he felt like little Perkar, not like some Giant from one of Eruka's songs.

He donned his hauberk, and as it settled over his shoulders, a terrible cold fear settled with it. The steel felt hard and unforgiving against his body, too heavy. Almost he took it back off, returned to the fire to wait for the Kapaka. He did not. This was his only chance; if he did not go tonight, he would never go, no matter how long the Forest Lord and the Kapaka negotiated. Because as his fear was stripping away his reasons—Piraku, heroics—it also gnawed at his most basic cause. How often had she told him that there was nothing he could do? How often had she begged him to forget? She was a goddess; she knew so much more of these things than he did.

A goddess, but not a warrior. She did not know what a man with the right weapon might accomplish.

And so he settled the hauberk, donned his steel cap with its plume of horsehair, strapped on his greaves. Then, with a single backward glance, he set off along the base of the valley wall, searching for the trail up, the one that went past the caves.

It soon became terribly dark, though a glimpse now and then showed the Pale Queen to be full. The forest was, fortunately, open and expansive, so that he did not become hopelessly tangled. His progress was anything but the silent stealth he had imagined, however; everywhere there were branches to step on, snags to stumble over, and his armor protested in a metallic chorus each time he tripped. Worse, it seemed impossible to keep his bearings, and he worried that he was traveling in entirely the wrong direction. He thought seriously about lighting a torch, but that would attract the attention of everyone around him—and every*thing*—and so he decided to muddle on without one.

He did not find the trail, and the moon set. Balat became darker than the inside of a coffin, darker than any cave could be. Perkar *did* try to start a torch then, but could find nothing suitable from which to make one, nothing that would catch fire. Finally, blind, he sank to the cool earth, rested against an unseen tree. He thought he heard people calling his name, after a time, but could not be certain. In any event, he did not call out himself. It would be too humiliating, too stupid, and he could already imagine the condescending expression on Ngangata's face. His back to the rough trunk, Perkar cursed himself until he dozed.

He awoke with a start, but there was no clear indication of what had awakened him; the woods were still dark. Nightbirds were calling, but not close or loud. He rubbed the grit from his eyes and strained them at the darkness, realized that it was not entirely dark, after all; he could just make out the enormous bole of an ash, to his left, the suggestion of a fern frond, there. It must be, he thought, the earliest glimmerings of dawn. Soon it would be light enough to find the camp. He would tell them that he had gone off in search of solitude, he supposed, that he needed to be alone. They would think it odd—Apad and Eruka would know it to be a lie and Ngangata, at least, would suspect some more foolish motive. But it would be better than admitting the truth. Perkar realized that he felt relieved, unburdened. The knots tied in his gut were loosened and gone. The decision had been taken from him by the forest itself; he had *tried* to find the caves, the magical weapon—if it existed. He had failed; not because he wasn't strong or brave, but because the forest would not let him find the way. It was simple, a relief. *Be a man,* she had told him. *Dream of the possible.*

The light was a bit grayer, more details were coming clear. He studied the earth near his feet, trying to puzzle out details, occupy himself until it was really light. He made out one of his bootprints, pressed into a worn, muddy place. There, another.

He frowned. One of his prints crossed another. Not his. He found more as he searched; many men in boots, walking one behind another. And the prints of horses. Perkar drew a tight breath, and his heart pounded. It was the trail.

THE songs often spoke of caves as mouths or doorways, but to Perkar they seemed like eyes, slitted and unblinking eyes of some enormous creature. He panted as he regarded them and tried to decide which to enter. The path up was harder than the one down, as his grandfather used to say. Especially in full armor, without a horse. His clothes were already soaked with sweat, though the morning was cool. The first true rays of the sun were yet to be seen.

He had no time to dither, he knew. Ngangata and Atti might not know what he was about, but they would certainly come looking for him, follow his bumbling trail through the woods. He understood that he could yet turn back, and that nagged at him. Once he entered the caves he was committed to his course of action. He was telling himself that for the fifth time when he heard muttering voices coming up the trail, the rattle of armor.

Suddenly his choices narrowed. There was only one cave close enough to reach before Ngangata and Atti came into view, and he found himself scrambling upslope toward it. It was not the largest cave, nor the smallest; but part of its floor had collapsed and the rubble formed a ramp leading up to it, like the wrinkled folds beneath the eye of an old man. He levered himself from one broken chunk of rock to the next, fingers fumbling desperately for purchase on the moss-covered stone. He was almost to the opening when he heard his name called. Reluctantly—and yet *still* a bit relieved—he turned toward the voice.

It was neither Ngangata nor Atti; it was a red-faced, puffing Apad, Eruka trailing not far behind him.

"Wait!" Apad called. The two of them straggled over to the talus slope and started up it—somewhat more cautiously than Perkar.

"Where are Ngangata and Atti?" Perkar called.

"They went to take food and water to the Kapaka. We said we would look for you," Apad explained, through his wheezing. He and Eruka were both clad in their armor, as well, and had probably been running or at least trotting since they left camp.

"What are you doing here, alone?" Apad demanded as he drew abreast of Perkar. "We agreed to go together."

Perkar shrugged. "I guess I thought . . ." He trailed off, unwilling to say what he had really thought.

"You thought you would have the glory to yourself," Apad

finished for him. "But heroes come in threes, remember?" He glanced upslope, at the cave. "Is this the right one?"

Perkar raised his eyebrows. "I don't know. It was the closest."

"You don't know?"

Perkar shook his head.

"Eruka," Apad said to their companion. "Can you find out? Is there a song?"

Eruka pursed his lips, an uneasy expression on his face. "There is a song," he admitted reluctantly. "I *think* it would help with this."

"Well?"

"What do we want to know exactly?"

Apad looked heavenward in exasperation. "We want to know which of these caves leads to the Forest Lord's armory," Apad said.

"I know a song that might help," Eruka repeated. "But it could be dangerous."

"How so?"

"Any spirit I call here might tell the Forest Lord."

"The Forest Lord is busy," Apad said. "And heroes must take risks."

"Why don't we risk entering the wrong cave, then?" Eruka suggested.

The conversation had given Perkar time to think. He vividly remembered being lost in the forest at night. One could just as easily become lost in a dark cave.

"We need light to find our way in there," he said. "At the very least we need torches."

Apad considered that. "Do whatever it is you can do, Eruka," he said. "Perkar and I will make some torches."

Perkar hesitantly followed Apad back down. The two of them started searching for branches.

"Look for heart pine," Apad said. "That should burn brightly and long."

Perkar had his doubts about that; his father usually made torches from bundles of dried reeds—but he also usually coated them in tar or fat. Behind them, Eruka began singing, but Perkar was already far enough out of earshot that he could not make out the words.

Perkar found a long piece of heart pine in a rotting tree—but he also chanced upon some dry reeds, which he collected into a bundle, binding them together with some greener, less brittle stems. When he got back to the trail, Eruka was no longer singing. He and Apad were sitting in the nearest cave, feet dangling out. Eruka was holding something that looked suspiciously like a flask of woti.

"I thought we had no more of that," Perkar said as he climbed up to join them.

"I thought we might need it," Eruka said. "Some gods only respond to woti or wine."

"You lied to the Kapaka?"

Eruka shrugged. "I just didn't mention it." He took a drink of the woti and passed the flask to Apad. The air near the cave seemed drenched with the rich, sweet scent; Eruka had poured a libation into a small bowl, probably while singing.

"Did your song work?"

"I don't know," Eruka admitted.

Apad offered the flask of woti to Perkar. "Woti makes you brave," he said.

Perkar grinned crookedly. "You aren't a Wotiru, are you? You chew your shield?"

"I don't know. Perhaps I am," Apad said, taking another drink. Perkar didn't think Apad was a Wotiru; he had met them, at his father's house. They drank copious amounts of woti to fill them with battle-fever, but even when there was no battle they carried an air of recklessness—even madness—about them that Perkar had never noticed in Apad.

"We should move farther back in the cave," Perkar said. "If Ngangata and Atti come looking for us, I don't want them to see us."

"Pfah!" Apad sneered. "We can deal with them, if they oppose us. You know *that*."

"I know that if Ngangata chooses to use his bow against us, we are all dead men, armor or no."

"He's right," Eruka said, plucking at Apad's shoulder.

"And where is your spirit? The god you called?" Apad asked Eruka, brushing the hand away.

"I don't know," Eruka said. "Gods are capricious. Or perhaps I phrased the song all wrong."

"No," a voice said from behind them. "No, your song was sufficiently irritating that I came looking for you. Now give me that woti you promised."

The three of them whirled as one, and Perkar scrambled to his feet, as well. The speaker was an Alwa, to all appearances, though a stunted, extraordinarily thick-muscled one. And whereas the Alwat were pale, this creature was *white*, and devoid of all fur. His eyes were white, too, though the pupils were black.

"Well?" he demanded.

Apad carefully set the bottle of woti down near the bowl. The Alwa ambled over, picked up the bowl, and drank its contents. Then he turned his attention to the bottle.

"This *is* good," he said at last. "The only decent thing that ever came from Human Beings. Now. Who called me?" He turned his blind-looking eyes to them, seemed to search them out. Perkar was reminded of Ngangata.

"What god are you?" Perkar asked.

The Alwa grinned wide. "Don't know me? I guess your friend does."

Eruka cleared his throat. "He is a . . . ah, he is one of the Lemeyi."

Perkar gaped. "A Lemeyi," he repeated. The white creature laughed, a loud, raucous sound.

"Why . . ." Perkar began, but could not finish. Not with the creature standing right there. Why would Eruka call such a creature? When he was a child, his mother had frightened him with promises that the Lemeyi would come to steal him away. At least one child he knew *had* been devoured by the strange creatures.

"Yes, why me?" the Lemeyi said. "What do you want? Why shouldn't I eat you here and now?"

"We called you in good faith," Eruka protested.

"Answer your friend's question," the Lemeyi growled.

"I . . ." Eruka turned to face Perkar. He was sweating. "I couldn't call any of the normal gods," he said. "They would just tell the Forest Lord—or he would know without being told. So I . . ." He trailed off miserably.

"So you called a bastard," the Lemeyi finished. "A bastard, that's me! My father was an Alwa and my mother was a stone!" He laughed, so loudly that Perkar feared the Forest Lord would hear.

"And so now," the Lemeyi said, when he had done laughing, "what do you want of the bastard?"

Apad and Eruka were just staring at the creature. Perkar found his voice. "We want to see the armory of the Forest Lord."

"The armory?"

"Where he keeps his weapons."

"You want to see the Forest Lord's treasures?" the Lemeyi asked. He seemed amused by this, as he did by everything.

"If that's where the weapons are."

"And you just want to see them?"

Perkar hesitated. He answered carefully. "We want to see them. Can you take us there?"

"Well," the Lemeyi mused. "Well. I can take you anywhere in the mountain. Anywhere you want to go. But when you get there, you might not like it."

"Why?" Apad asked.

"You just might not. Humans are funny that way. Never really like what they desire."

"Well, we desire this," Perkar said. "Let us worry about whether we like it."

"Oh, I wasn't worried," the Lemeyi explained, spreading his hands generously. "No, I wasn't worried. If that's where you want to go, I've nothing better to do. Follow me."

"This is the right cave?" Perkar asked.

"Any of them is the right cave, if you know where you are going," the Lemeyi replied. He frowned, looked back over his shoulder. "You can't see in the dark, can you?"

"We have torches," Apad said.

The Lemeyi shook his head. "The Fire Goddess would arouse notice. Just follow close to me." He turned and started down into the cavern.

Perkar shrugged and followed, his friends a few paces behind. They followed the Lemeyi down the dark, constricting tunnel. Perkar prepared himself for blindness, but as they progressed farther and farther from the entrance, his eyesight did not seem to dim; indeed, it improved somewhat, though the *distance* he could see was limited. The Lemeyi, in front of him, was distinct, as were the floor and walls of the cave. But up ahead, beyond their guide, it was as if a fog obscured his vision. Rather than dwelling on this feat the Lemeyi was clearly performing, Perkar instead concentrated on memorizing the path through the cavern. Always they seemed to be going down, and the way was usually rough; they picked their way over jagged swords of stone that pointed always up, toward the roof—a roof that Perkar could not usually see. At other times, however, the ceiling descended to their very heads; twice they had to crawl on their bellies through narrow clefts in the rock. His armor no longer seemed hot; though he perspired freely from the exertion of wearing it, he felt cool, almost cold, and the motionless air was colder still. When anyone spoke—the Lemeyi spoke often—the voice seemed to fill the space around them like water in a jug, and it seemed to Perkar that all of the underdark must know their whereabouts. He himself kept his mouth tightly shut whenever possible.

They crossed a swiftly coursing stream, flowing roughly in their direction of travel.

"She used to flow through here," the Lemeyi said, indicating the way they were going. "But that was many years ago. She still talks about it—constantly. I think she regrets cutting her new channel."

"What?" Eruka asked.

"Well, before, she flowed down through here and finally south," the Lemeyi explained. "But she cut through to a lower fissure, worked that all up into a tunnel. Some of the little mountain gods down there were angry about that! They still resent it, even though they should pity her instead."

"Pity her?" Eruka queried.

"Oh yes, for of course she flows *north* now. Into the Ani Pendu, the Changeling."

Ani Pendu, Perkar thought. *Changeling.*

"What if we meet one of the gods?" Apad whispered.

"What if you do, mortal man?" the Lemeyi shot back.

"How are they best fought?"

The Lemeyi, of course, laughed. "From far away, by someone else."

IT was too late, of course, to regret his decision, but just the right time for Perkar's apprehension to grow. By now they must be deep in the mountain, and his sense of that profundity made his magical ability to see in the dark seem a lie. In fact, he reflected, it might *be* a lie. The Lemeyi were said to be capable of such things. Perhaps even now they were still at the cave mouth, and this was all a dream in the white creature's head. If so, it was a lengthy dream. Perkar had not the faintest idea how long they had been traveling. Three times his throat had grown dry enough to wet with water from his skin, twice he had relieved himself while the Lemeyi waited impatiently. None of that told him much, only that time was indeed passing—something he might otherwise doubt. The dark tunnels all looked the same; they crossed a few more streams, had to wade in one for a while. The streams all seemed to flow in the direction they were going—which meant down, of course. That might be a help, should the Lemeyi choose to abandon them, something Perkar considered a distinct possibility.

Thinking along those lines, nagged by worry, Perkar at last decided to speak to the godling again.

"May I ask why you're doing this?" he asked.

"Me?" The Lemeyi sounded genuinely astonished. "Doing what?"

"Leading us. Taking us to the Forest Lord's treasure."

"Why, you called me."

"That doesn't compel you, does it? I thought Eruka's song was only to get your attention. I didn't realize it obligated you in some way."

"Why, I hadn't thought of that," the Lemeyi said, scratching his head. "I guess I'm not compelled to do this at all. Thank you for bringing that to my attention, mortal man." He smiled broadly and vanished. Or, rather, the entire tunnel vanished into darkness as if Perkar had been struck blind. Which, of course, he had been in a sense. Perkar heard a double sharp intake of breath behind him, a curse.

"Well, that was clever, Perkar," Apad drawled, behind him.

Somewhere, the Lemeyi began to laugh.

VI

The Rite of the Vessel

THEY made her undress. She burned with embarrassment and outrage as she did so. Her body had begun to change in ways that bothered her; in private ways that only Qey should share, and sometimes not even she. No man—with the exception of Tsem, and he not in years—had ever seen her unclothed. It was an insult, a terrible insult, to have to stand exposed to their masked faces. And yet, though it should have, it did not make her angry; instead it made her feel helpless and more than a little sick.

"Lie down," one of the priests told her; his voice was also high and clear, and she remembered that priests weren't technically men; they were made into eunuchs at an early age—or so she had heard—to better serve the priesthood. She tried to think about that, about how that fit into the whole question of age and "investment," tried to flee their staring masks into the puzzle within her mind. It didn't work; they were too real, the experience was too personal.

181

Two of the priests lit bundles of herbs, the same ones used in their brooms, and the rich but acrid scent of the smoke permeated Hezhi's room quickly. The third priest began to chant in words that she did not recognize, and the fourth—the one who had done all of the speaking up until that point—unwrapped a cloth from a brass vessel, a stout cylinder the size of a man's head, closed on the bottom, almost closed on the top. A brass tube projected from the midpoint of the cylinder and rose upward at an angle to the level of the top of the can. There it ended in a perforated ball, the holes many and small. Though much more ornate, the design was essentially that of the watering can Qey used to care for her potted plants.

The priest set the watering can aside and opened a pouch dangling on his belt. From this, he produced a wad of damp herbs.

"Open your mouth," he said.

She complied, trying not to hesitate, not to let on that she was worried or afraid. The herbs were bitter, and nearly filled her mouth.

"Swallow whenever you wish, but keep them in your mouth," the priest cautioned sternly. Hezhi nodded, unable to speak.

The man joined his brethren in chanting, which seemed to go on forever. She began to wonder if the rite consisted of nothing more than chanting. She had to swallow repeatedly as her mouth filled with acrid saliva. Once again she tried to concentrate on what was happening, to force the facts together so that they made perfect sense. To *understand* before her fate caught up with her. After all, there might still be something she could do.

That thought struck her as funny, somehow, and the more she thought about it, the funnier it got. Her thoughts began to echo strangely in her head, like beans rattling around and around in a jar.

When the ceiling began to swirl, she realized that something had been done to her. She could feel her heart, thudding away like something not connected to her at all, and suddenly her unnatural amusement faded, replaced by a cold terror the like of which she had never felt before. It was already over, she suddenly understood. Whatever they sought to know about her, they already knew from seeing her naked body. She was poisoned and dying. Soon her heart would explode, and that would be the end of it. She struggled to rise, but two of the priests were suddenly there, forcing her back down. She tried to cry out, but the herbs choked her, seemed to swell and fill her whole head. Why had she sent Tsem away? He could save her, kill the priests, take her away . . .

The hands of the priests were cold, hard, but soon the impression of being held down vanished, as well. Her body was gone, already a ghost, and all that remained were the frightened, skittering thoughts in her head. Even they refused to come together, to organize themselves.

Let me die, then, she thought, resigned.

Now one of the priests came forward, holding the watering can. Hezhi realized suddenly that the other men had released her, and she tried to struggle again, but her body did not respond at all—her desires were no longer wedded to her muscles. There was nothing there.

But then, in that vacuum of sensation—where her toes had been—she experienced a tingling. She studied them, trying to understand. The priest was sprinkling water on her feet; it seemed to fall very slowly, sink into her nonexistent limbs, and that was where it tingled, *inside* rather than upon the skin. He moved up her body, sprinkling the water, and where it fell, the sensation persisted.

As the priest moved beyond her legs and pelvis, as the water showered on her belly, something began to *arise*. It felt the way she imagined a plant might feel, bursting from its seed, reaching up toward the light. It began small, then expanded, carrying her thoughts up with it but also pushing *through* them, a strange, alien thing that was part of her and *not* part of her. All of her scattered, panicky thoughts suddenly converged, melded, drew around the rising thing like sycophants about a king.

This is it, she knew. *This is what they want to see, this thing ascending.* Her helplessness at being naked seemed as nothing now. The fear that she had already been poisoned faded as she understood what she should really fear. This thing was *hers.* If they saw it, if it grew large enough for them to see . . . She closed her eyes, searching, searching for some way to push the thing back down. At first it had seemed inexorable, beyond her control, but now she saw that it wasn't. It was pushing, trying to come up out of her so the priests could see it, but in growing it was stretching thin, becoming weaker. If she helped it—and part of her wanted to—it would escape, become a virtual tree, blooming and unmistakable. Now that she knew that, she realized that it drew much of its strength from her wish to release it.

Somewhere, floating in her mind, she found a tendril, pushed down upon it. It was a slight pressure, but she could feel the tendril more clearly as it resisted. She found more such tendrils, knitted them into a string and then a rope, hardened that into a hand and an arm, pressing *down.* For a moment, the two forces stood in equilibrium, and then slowly, ever so slowly, the expanding force—the *thing* inside her—began to contract, to dwindle, become denser but smaller, a tree pushed back into its seed. Hidden. After that, her thoughts lost their coherence again, swam away from each other like frightened fish.

"Keep her in bed for the rest of the day," she heard a voice command, and then nothing.

When she awoke, the odor of smoke had been replaced by the perfume of flowers, a great huge bunch of them, blue and red, in a vase near her bed. Tsem was crouched in the corner of the room, head on his knees.

She shook her head to clear it, found that it wouldn't clear entirely; the herbs had not completely run their course. She was able to feel her body again, however, and swung her legs around experimentally. Her mouth was dry and tasted bad, but at least the herbs were gone. Outside, the courtyard was dark, the crickets chirping. A few fireflies rose sparking, so she knew it had been dark for only a short while. She tried to stand up.

Tsem came alert at her motion.

"Stay in bed, Princess," Tsem cautioned. "I can bring you whatever you need."

"I need to *pee*, Tsem," she replied, reaching beneath her bed for the bucket there. Tsem blushed and looked away. Hezhi realized she was still naked.

"You can get me a gown," she conceded, and Tsem hurried off to find one.

"They didn't take me," she said, when he got back.

"No," Tsem replied.

"Why?"

"I don't know. They usu—" Tsem's head jerked violently and he convulsed for a long moment. Tears started in Hezhi's eyes as she watched, helpless again.

"Never mind," she got out. "Forget it. Forget I asked."

Qey entered the room, glanced at Tsem, who was just regaining his composure.

"Hello, Qey."

"Are you hungry, little one?" Qey asked.

"Not at all," she replied. "But some water would be nice."

Qey nodded and went to get it.

They hadn't taken her, so their test had not turned up any results. But it should have, one way or the other, decided her fate, should it not? If the "thing" in her had shown itself or if it hadn't, one result should have led to her disappearance and the other to her graduation to the royal wing.

"Qey," she asked when the woman returned. "Qey, will I be moving down the Hall of Moments now?"

Qey shook her head. "No, little one. According to the priests it is not yet time. You will stay here a bit longer."

So the test wasn't a yes-or-no test, she realized. The priests *had* wanted to see the force in her. It was somehow the nature—*not* the mere presence—of that *thing* that decided her fate. A negative result—which the priests must have gotten—*that* only allowed her to remain where she was—remain a child, in essence.

That meant, as the priest had implied, that more "rites" would

follow. She knew, knew very deeply, that she would never be able
to suppress the force in her again. Next time it would show itself,
and she would be either saved or damned.

She dozed again after a time and awoke to the morning sun,
feeling much better. There still seemed to be a sort of shroud
about her, muffling sight and sound, but it was shredding away
now, like the dead skin from a snake. The sausages Qey fried for
breakfast were good, the huzh with cream and pomegranate
sauce better. It was, in fact, Hezhi's favorite breakfast, and she
loved Qey for fixing it.

"I'll be fine," she told the worried-looking woman. "I feel
much better."

"I was afraid . . ." Qey's words stumbled over her tongue and
she stopped, tried unsuccessfully to smile. "I'm glad you feel better," she said at last.

"You lied about my bleeding, Qey. You mustn't do that
again."

"Hezhi, there are things you don't understand . . ."

"I understand more than you think," she responded. "And I
know that you can't tell me the rest, so you mustn't feel bad."

"Oh. You were always a very bright child, Hezhi. Even when
you were very young, in your cradle, you used to *look* at me in
this way, this strange way . . ." She trailed off.

"Anyway," Hezhi went on, after an embarrassed pause. "I
don't want you to lie that way again. Next time they test me, I
think that they will discover I have begun bleeding. Do you see?
I don't want you to get in trouble for lying."

Qey nodded numbly.

"Qey . . ." Hezhi took another mouthful of bread, sopped up
some cream and jelly with it. "Qey, if you are forbidden to speak
of this, don't. But will I be able to see you, after I move over to
the royal wing?"

"Well, I . . . Well, Hezhi, it's not *forbidden*. You can come see
me anytime you like, and of course Tsem will go with you. But
I don't think you will *want* to come back here. There will be *so*

much for you to do, you will have so many new friends . . ." Qey patted her leg indulgently. "You would just be bored, coming to see an old woman."

"What will you do, Qey? After I am gone?"

"Oh . . . I don't know. Probably raise another little girl—or a boy. It's what I like to do."

"Really? Did you raise any before me?"

Qey ceased eating, stared down at her plate. She seemed intent on something, something halfway between the plate and her eyes. Hezhi wondered what it might be. A face, perhaps?

"Why, yes," she said, again failing to smile. "Yes, I . . . raised a little boy."

"Do I know him? What was his name?"

Qey pursed her lips for a moment, sighed deeply, and then stood, a little shakily. "I have wash to do," she said vaguely. "Hezhi, dear, you rest some more."

She watched Qey cross the courtyard to the linen room. Then she went back to her own room, selected a comfortable dress, and changed from her gown into it. She arranged her hair as best she could without Qey's help. Then she found Tsem and started out for the library.

INDEXING was a little beyond her that day, and she told Ghan so. He nodded, didn't ask for an explanation or become angry—at her anyway.

"A band of fops came in here this morning," he grumbled. "Boys looking for poetry. Not *real* poetry, mind you, but the doggerel that passes for it in the court these days. They had a writ, so I couldn't stop them, and they unshelved half of the library before I found a pretense to send them on their way."

"It might have been easier just to show them where what they wanted was," Hezhi told him.

Ghan snorted. "What they wanted is not here. They should have been looking in the private libraries of older fops, not in the

Royal Archive. Idiots." He scratched out a few more characters from the book he was copying. "Anyway, you can reshelve those for me."

"I *can* do that," Hezhi told him.

"And Hezhi . . ." She turned. It still surprised her when he called her by her name, rather than "you" or a sarcastic "Princess." "After today I will no longer require your labor."

"What?" she choked out. "Ghan, what did I do? I'm sorry, whatever it was."

"Yes, I'm sure you are. If you must know, what you *did* was to satisfy the terms of your servitude. I feel that you have repaid the debt you owed me."

"But . . ."

"Your father was very specific in the writ. I will be held accountable if I require you to work after today. The debt is paid, Hezhi."

"But there is so much to do," she argued. "More than you have time for. Who would copy that manuscript if you had to shelve these books?"

"I managed long before you were born, Princess, and I will do quite well tomorrow, and the day after."

He was still copying the book, not looking up at her. Hezhi stood there, not quite sure what to say. Finally Ghan stopped, leaned back on his stool. "Is there something else?" he asked mildly.

"Just this," Hezhi replied. She bent over the desk, took a page of the old book Ghan was copying and yanked it sharply, so that a thumbnail-size tear suddenly appeared. Ghan gaped at her, and then, for the first time since she had known him, he chuckled. Not an outright laugh, but a real, genuine chuckle.

"Well," he said. "Shelve those books, and I *will* see you here tomorrow."

SHE had shelved all but three of the books when she caught the *ah-hem* of a throat clearing behind her. She turned to face a young man—he was perhaps twenty. He was tall, his face thin and pleasantly tapered to fit a delicate aquiline nose. He was clothed in a plain gray tunic, not of royal cut. Still, Hezhi thought he looked elegant in it.

"Pardon me, my lady," he said, bowing slightly, "but you seem to know something of this place."

"The library? You want Ghan, I think. He is the master here."

"Ah . . . yes. I have spoken to him. He allowed me in because I have a writ from the priesthood, but he said—how did he put it?—'I won't go so far as to be of any help to you,' he told me."

She smiled. "That's Ghan. Which probably means I shouldn't help you, either." She cast a speculative glance at her mentor, but he seemed consumed by his copying task. Hezhi shrugged. Despite the lingering effects of the drug—or perhaps because of them—she felt giddy. This man had a pleasant way about him. "What sort of help do you need?" she inquired.

"I have recently joined the ranks of the Royal Engineers . . ."

"That's part of the priesthood?" she asked.

"Yes, in a roundabout way. Sort of caught between the priesthood and the emperor. I think that's their unofficial motto, in fact."

"Sorry," Hezhi said. "Go on."

"Well, you understand that my father is a merchant, not in the royal family at all, but many engineers are hired from the merchant class, despite our mean birth. I tell you this so that you will understand I have absolutely no knowledge of the old script. It is a total mystery to me."

Hezhi rolled her eyes. "You think most nobles know it? Most men your age are considered brilliant if they can puzzle through the syllabary."

"Well, that makes me feel a bit better," the young man admitted. "But it really does nothing to solve my problem."

"Which is?"

"Well, my first assignment is to design a system of sewer ducts to go from the New Palace to the annex we begin building in a few months. It's a minor sort of thing, really, but I can't do it without knowing all about the old system I'll be adding on to, and frankly, I don't know all that *much* about underground construction or sewers at all." He spread out his hands, his voice dropping to a low whisper. "If I fail, I think I will be shunted back to my father and end up having to pilot one of his scows. *That* I would not enjoy doing, my lady. So I'm appealing to you . . ."

Hezhi nodded, captivated by the man's motivation. Few who came into the library showed much interest or incentive to do *anything*. Most were scribes checking old trade agreements, genealogists tracing family relationships. Their research was carried out laconically, without ambition or zeal. This young man had a real *need* to learn. She could identify with that.

"Well," she began, "much of what you want will be written in the syllabary, so there is a lot you can do without knowing the glyphs. Most of the New Palace was constructed after the syllabary was adopted, you see, and surely engineering texts have been written since then."

The young man shook his head. "Fascinating. I *knew* you had the look of someone with intelligence. But how do I find these books? There seems to be no rhyme or reason here, and there are so many books . . ."

"Let me explain to you about the index," she said. "Follow me as I replace these books."

She showed him the numbers on the shelves and those in the books that matched them. With some pride, she even took him to volumes that she herself had indexed and shelved. He appeared suitably impressed. She explained the index and how to use it, which he seemed to comprehend. He was also gracious, thanking her and departing before she grew tired of his questions.

That afternoon there were still a few moments for her own research, but her thoughts kept returning to the man, his questions. Something he had mentioned . . .

Then she had it. *Sewers*. The First Dynasty had not built any, but the Second Dynasty *had*, and extensively. Even with the flooding, some of the ancient sewers might have survived. After all, unlike the buried building she and Tsem had explored, sewers were *designed* to be underground. Add to that the fact that all of the palace had not been buried—parts of the western extension dated to the Second Dynasty—and the young man's assertion that new sewers had to be articulated with the older ones, and her mind began piecing a kind of map together. It was baroque, that map, a brocade of ducts and tunnels lying across old buildings or even through them, those attached to newer ones, and newer still. This added an entirely new set of possible pathways to the ones she had already discovered—the ducts that piped water *in* to the palace. If she had maps of all of those things, then surely she could find a way to D'en. In fact, she could do some of the young man's research for him, and earn a bit of his gratitude, as well, something she had to admit did not exactly displease her.

Sewers! She went to ask Ghan for the index.

A FEW days later she had the beginnings of a map. She worked on it back in the "tangle," away from prying eyes. Ghan reluctantly gave her three colors of ink, so she was able to sketch the old, ruined palace in black, the ancient water ducts in blue, and the sewer system in red. She made a separate map of the palace as it was now, matching it to points on her hypothetical map of the buried city with numbers and notations. She worked on this in the evenings, of course, and at lunch. Ghan told her he had renewed his petition for her indenture, based upon the newly damaged book. Though the writ had not yet come back from her father, she attended to shelving, indexing, and repair just as she had for the past few months.

She was busy at the index when the young man—the engineer—came back in.

"Hello," he said.

She nodded at him.

"You know, I forgot to ask you your name when I was here last," he continued, a bit embarrassed.

"Hezhi," she told him. "Hezhi Yehd . . . Hezhi." For some reason it seemed important to her that the young man not call her "princess." That seemed absurd, really, considering his mean birth, but part of her enjoyed keeping him in the dark about exactly who she was. Later, when she moved down to the Hall of Moments, perhaps she would tell him *then*, and he would be surprised. Perhaps he would tell his friends of how casually he and the princess had spoken together.

"Ah," he said. "And I am Yen, son of Chwen. I wanted to thank you for your help—though I haven't had time to look at this index yet."

"Well, this is it," Hezhi told him. "But, actually, I had a few moments the other day, and I wrote down some of the books you may want to look at. These first three are all in the syllabary, so you won't have any trouble with those. This last is in the old script, but that really shouldn't matter because it contains the diagrams you will want to see."

"Well," Yen said, blinking down at the paper she handed him. "This is more than thoughtful of you, my lady . . ."

"You may call me Hezhi," she informed him, in the "gracious" tone the ladies used at court. He smiled at that, and she realized that he thought she was lampooning those ladies. Her ears burned a bit, because she had actually been trying to sound grown-up, adult.

"Hezhi," he began again, "I have no way to repay you for this kindness."

She waved it off. "It only took me a few moments, really. Please don't think anything about it."

"Well," he said, bowing a bit. "Thanks again." He went off with the paper and began searching for the numbers and titles she had listed, and was soon poring over the books, lost in concentration. She noticed that he made notes, now and then, on a roll of paper he had brought with him.

On their way home that evening, Tsem asked Hezhi about Yen.

"Yen *son* of Chwen? Not a noble, then."

"No," Hezhi replied. "He's with the engineers. I've been helping him find some books he needs."

"He smiles a lot," Tsem noted. "Too much."

"You would smile a lot, too, if you were in the palace for the first time. You would be worried about who you might offend if you did not smile."

Tsem shrugged. "I suppose. You talk to him a lot, I think."

"Twice, Tsem. That isn't a *lot.*"

Tsem was silent, and she realized that she might have hurt him, a little. She and Tsem hadn't spoken that much lately, and since D'en's disappearance he had been her best friend. He had never been quite like D'en, of course—Tsem was always reminding her that he was her servant, and that was somehow different from a friend even if you *liked* each other. Still, she had taken him for granted lately.

"Let's go to the fountain on the roof, Tsem. I want to look out over the city."

"Qey said we should come home early . . ." Tsem began, but Hezhi rolled her eyes at that.

"Come on, Tsem," she said, and changed their route. Soon they were winding through the abandoned wing.

"This could be dangerous," Tsem remarked. "If a ghost can attack you in the Hall of Moments, it can surely happen here, where the priests rarely come."

That gave Hezhi pause, but only for an instant. "We've been coming here for years, Tsem. It's never happened before."

"Things are different now, Princess."

They came to the foot of the stairway and started up. "I trust you to protect me," she told him.

"Is that why you sent me away when the priests came?" he asked. His voice was mild, but she heard bitterness there.

She looked down the stairs at him. "They were priests," she said. "I don't need protection from priests, do I?"

The line of Tsem's mouth was tight and flat; he had nothing to say to that.

Dusk painted Nhol in rust and pollen; the River flowed molten copper, painfully beautiful. Hezhi gazed out at the wonder of it.

"You go out into the city, don't you, Tsem?" she asked.

"Often, Princess. Qey sends me to buy spices and meat sometimes."

"Would it be possible for me to go with you, next time?"

Tsem shook his head. "Not outside of the walls. Not yet."

"When? When I move down the Hall of Moments?"

"Yes, then," Tsem said.

Hezhi nodded. It was what she suspected. She traced around the city with her finger, over the great ziggurat and its perpetual flow of water, along the thousands of tiny cabins that crowded the levee. "Will you take me down there, when I'm old enough?"

"Of course, if you wish it."

"Good."

She gazed off down the River and then up it, trying to imagine where he came from, how many leagues he flowed across before reaching Nhol. Were the forests in her dreams up there, up along the River? Desert, first, of course, more miles of it than she could imagine. The geography she had skimmed said the River was born in some mountain, far away, but it did not say what the mountain was like. It was named merely She'leng, "The Water Flows Out," and figured in many of the ancient legends. She had always pictured it as perfect, austere, a great bare stone, pointed like the mountains on the maps. She had of course never seen *any* mountain.

"Tsem," she explained quietly, "I sent you away because I don't want anything to happen to you. You're the only friend I have."

"My duty is to protect you, Princess," he replied.

"I know that. And you always have. But not against *priests*, Tsem. If you hurt a priest—if you even touched one without permission—they would torture you to death in the Leng Court and *still* they would do to me whatever they wanted."

"But they would pay," Tsem muttered. "By the River, you would cost them a high price."

"By the River? Do you think the River cares for *me*, Tsem? Whatever happens to me, it will be because the River makes it so. I am part of him, the way my father is, the way the priests are. Whatever comes to Nhol, the River brings it, does it not?"

Tsem did not respond, but he joined her at the parapet. The River had faded with the sun, gone from copper to mud, and soon enough he would catch the stars and moon, hold them in his turbid grasp. Hezhi wondered, idly, where the merchants lived, where Yen's house might be. Perhaps there, near where the ships clustered; houses stood there—not noble, but comfortably large. She almost asked Tsem if he knew, but refrained when she saw the reflective look on his face.

A moment later, Tsem's massive hand stroked her hair, a gentle movement. "Come, Princess," he said. "Supper will be cold and Qey will be colder."

"It's over, isn't it, Tsem?" she asked, surprised to find herself so near tears for no clear reason.

"What's over, Princess?"

"Childhood. I'm no longer a child, am I?"

Tsem smiled, as faintly as the sun's last rays. "You never were a child, Princess." He stroked her hair again. Her tears stayed where they were, back of her eyes. She and Tsem walked back home, together, as behind them the River faded to gray.

VII

The Monster in the Raven's Belly

PERKAR revised his opinion of the previous night's darkness. A cave *could* be darker and most certainly was. He thought briefly of the bugs he had drowned in tar as a boy, wondered if having tar poured all over him would be this dark. But of course, the tar would be very *hot*, and any darkness it brought would be the least of his worries. Which was, in fact, their current situation. Lack of sight was discomforting—frightening—but they had other, more serious problems. It did not seem like the time or place to voice such thoughts.

"We'll have to light a torch," Apad muttered. "Piss, Perkar, why did you have to open your mouth?"

A cackle of laughter erupted right in Perkar's ear, and he could see again. The Lemeyi was crumpling against the wall, holding his belly.

"We'll *have* to light a torch," he shrieked gleefully, his voice pitched high and shrill. "We'll *have* to!" He howled on.

196

"Dung-eater!" Apad snarled, yanking his sword free. "Laugh at *this*!"

"Laugh at *this*!" the Lemeyi roared, waggling a finger at Apad. Apad growled inarticulately and sprang forward, his sword swinging high and overhand. Perkar stood as if frozen, a protest trying to get from his numbed brain to his lips. Apad was not joking or making a threat; murder was plain on his face.

He miscalculated his attack badly, however; doubtless he had never practiced swordplay in a narrow cave. The blade screeched in protest as it met with the low ceiling of the tunnel; sparks spattered onto the floor. Apad dropped the weapon; it clattered to the stone and he staggered, holding his wrist. The attack nearly killed the Lemeyi anyway; his chuckling became convulsions of hysteria, and Perkar thought that perhaps the creature had swallowed its own tongue; he watched incredulously as the Lemeyi's face changed from red to purple. Apad glowered, still nursing his wrist. Grimly he stepped to pick up his sword.

"No!" Perkar snapped at him. "No, we need him!"

"It's true, Apad," Eruka agreed.

Apad watched the Lemeyi—who was actually wiping tears from his eyes—disgust and hatred plain on his face. Nevertheless he nodded, retrieved his weapon, and after glaring at the nicked and dulled blade, returned it to its appliquéd scabbard.

"You ask why I do this," the Lemeyi said, when he was able to speak. "There is your answer." He shook his head gleefully. "And now, if you great warriors would like to continue on . . ." He gestured down the tunnel.

PERKAR forbore asking the Lemeyi any other questions. They continued their passage into the mountain, the Lemeyi chortling every now and then, remembering his joke.

At last the passage widened and then opened into an enormous glittering chamber. It was like the vault of heaven, shimmering with a million more stars than the real night sky. Every surface of the cavern was encrusted with jewels, radiant in their unnatural vision. For a long moment he could only stare, gape-mouthed at the wonder of it, at the cascades of shimmering crystals. The only sound was their breathing and the faint dripping of water somewhere.

"Well," the Lemeyi remarked. "Here we are. Karakasa Ngorna."

"Kadakasa Ngorna," Perkar corrected, thinking that the Lemeyi had mispronounced "Belly of the Mountain."

"No, no," the Lemeyi said, a bit crossly. "Karakasa. The *Raven's* Belly. When he swallowed the sun that time, this is where it rested."

Perkar studied the Lemeyi's face. Surely, as always, he was joking. And yet, Perkar knew so little of these gods. The claims they made . . . and the Crow God liked pretty, shiny things. Like the sun, or these crystals. Was it possible that this cavern was, also, in some way, some part of Karak? Better not to know for sure, Perkar decided.

"The weapons?" Apad asked nervously. "Where are they?"

The Lemeyi snorted. "You only demonstrate your mortality with such impatience," he muttered.

"We're in a hurry," Perkar explained.

"Of course," the Lemeyi replied, more than a hint of condescension and sarcasm in his tone. "This way."

He conducted them across the cavern floor. "This is his feasting hall, you know," the Lemeyi confided.

"Feasting hall?" Apad asked. "Where are the tables, the benches?"

"Can you not see them?"

Perkar, to his astonishment, thought he could. To his eyes, the cave seemed to flutter, like the wings of a bird; now an empty cave, now a hall more glorious than that of any damakuta, replete with tables and benches, all unoccupied, awaiting occupants.

"I do not," Apad muttered.

"Then you are entirely mortal," the Lemeyi retorted. "Is there *no* godblood in you?"

"No," Apad said. "There is *not*. And that pleases me."

"Of course it does," the Lemeyi replied, and Perkar put a hand on Apad's shoulder as it bunched, as he reached again for his sword. His friend shot him an angry look, but the sword remained in its scabbard. They continued on, Perkar stepping around a table, Apad walking through it.

"Ah," the Lemeyi noticed, observing Perkar. "But *you* have a tiny bit of the golden blood in you, do you not?"

Perkar did not answer. The surprise was that Apad had *none*. What family had no god anywhere in its lineage? Apad's, apparently, and he was proud of it. From the corner of his eye, Perkar saw Eruka avoid the table, as well.

They reached the far end of the gallery, and the Lemeyi stopped. "This is as far as I go," he said. "I may wait for you here, if it pleases me—and I suspect, somehow, it will. The treasures are just down there." He indicated a small side chamber; Perkar could just see it, adjoining the larger one.

"You may speak to the guardian about seeing the treasures."

"Guardian?" Apad asked.

"Yes, well, of course there is a guardian. Some gods are greedy, and wealth must be protected."

"What sort of guardian?" he persisted.

"Just go see," the Lemeyi answered, taking another drink from the woti flask. "She and I don't get along, so I'll wait here."

Perkar drew a deep breath. He had come this far; he was in the heart of the mountain at the heart of the world; he could all but feel his enemy to the north, the Changeling. He could not come so close to victory and walk away empty-handed. Without another word, he crossed into the adjoining cavern.

It was much like the Raven's Belly, though smaller. This meant that the shimmering walls were closer, in a sense more splendid. Yet Perkar would not let himself be distracted; his scrutiny was fixed on the guardian from the moment he saw her.

Perkar was not sure what he had imagined—a dragon, perhaps, like the one encountered by Iru Antu in the "Ekar Iru

Antu." But this was no dragon, no one-eyed Giant. The guardian was a middle-aged woman, black hair shot with silver framing a careworn but handsome face. She wore a simple black shift, and across her lap lay an elaborate gown that she seemed to be embroidering.

"Hello," she said, hardly looking up. Behind her, weapons rested on a shelf of stone. Swords, straight and sickle-curved, promised edges finer than glass. Hammers, spears, sheaves of arrows lay carelessly about. Around the weapons, other treasures vied for his attention: golden circlets, flasks of woti, all sorts of Human-made adornment.

"Grandmother," Perkar said carefully.

"Who are you?" For the first time her gaze really fastened upon him; her eyes were gray, faraway—mist in the distance.

"My clan is Kar Barku," he told her. "My own name is Perkar."

The woman smiled a thin little smile. "Perkar—so you are an oak tree, are you?"

"That is my name."

"A god named you?" she asked.

"Of course. The god of our household named me for her friend, the oak tree."

The woman nodded, held up her needlework to contemplate it more closely. "Are your friends back there coming in?"

Perkar shrugged. "I don't know."

"You keep bad company, you know."

"You mean our guide?" Perkar asked.

"I mean the Lemeyi. If he brought you here, he must think you mean mischief. What mischief do you intend here, Oak-Tree Boy?"

"I am no longer a boy," Perkar said softly.

"So you say. You have yet to prove that to me, however. What do you want here?"

Perkar fidgeted. He had expected a fight, perhaps, but not this interrogation.

"I told you my name," he said. "It would be polite if you would tell me yours."

"What good would that do you?" she asked.

"I might know a song about you," Perkar said. "So that I could honor you. Or my friend, Eruka, who is a singer . . ."

She cut him off with a wave of her hand. "There are no songs about me, Oak-Boy. At least none you would have heard. Now, tell me what you want. Or can I guess?"

"I want to see the weapons of the Forest Lord."

"Well, there they are," she said. "You see them. Would you like to examine them more closely?"

"Yes, Goddess, I would."

She frowned in irritation. "Don't call me that," she said.

"You haven't given me a name to call you," he pointed out.

"Don't call me anything, then." She quit her needlework, crossed her hands over it. "What do you want the weapons for, Oak-Boy? To win glory in battle? To kill someone and take his damakuta? You could do that with the sword you have."

"I didn't say I wanted to take them," Perkar replied.

"You didn't deny it, either, and that's a good thing, too, or you would have lied," the woman replied. "Do you think the Lemeyi would have even brought you down here if he did not believe you would steal one of them? What do you want them for?"

"I wish to kill a god," Perkar said.

She nodded. "Of course. And what did this god do, that you hate him so?"

"I don't want to tell you that," Perkar said. "Not unless it will convince you to give them to me."

She smiled wanly. "I have nothing to give you, Perkar. The treasure will not leave this room while I am alive."

"What?" Perkar was distracted by a furious spate of whispering out in the big cave. Apad and Eruka were still out there, discussing something with the Lemeyi. Something Perkar should know about, no doubt, for it seemed the moment of truth was approaching.

"I must fight you then?" he asked.

"I can't fight," she said. "I'm just an old woman."

"You said the weapons would not leave while you are alive."

"That is what I said. I never said I would fight you. Here." She reached over and grasped one of the smaller swords. Holding the blade gingerly, she held it out to him.

"Take it. Take it and leave."

Puzzled, Perkar took the brass-wound hilt of the sword. It tingled against his palm, and the blade shivered, like a god appearing. As if the blade, too, was just a "painting" over something deeper and more real.

"Leave," she repeated.

Perkar took a deep breath and began to back out of the cave. He kept the blade in guard position, ready at any moment if the old woman should transform into some fierce beast. She did not; rather, she sighed and shook her head.

Near the entrance to the treasure cave, Perkar laid the sword down and walked out. After only a step or two he frowned, then turned furiously. He bent to pick the weapon up again, but as soon as he did he set it back down. Seven times he tried to carry the sword from the room; each time he ended by depositing it back where it rested.

"How are you doing that?" he demanded, finally.

"I'm *not* doing it," she said. "The weapons are bound to my blood. They will not leave me."

"That is a lie," Apad hissed from behind him. "Perkar, she is a sorceress. Can't you feel the spell on you?"

Perkar certainly knew the spell was there; the overwhelming compulsion to lay the sword down did not come from any part of himself, that was certain. But it somehow seemed wrong to suspect the woman of *casting* the spell.

"You try to take it," Perkar told Apad. He watched the woman closely as Apad tried, without success, to remove the sword from the room. She made no move at all. Frustrated, Perkar picked up the sword and strode toward—rather than away from—the woman. He thought he saw something in her eyes then—fear? Resignation?

"You are going to kill me," she said. "You will kill me for your vendetta against this god?"

"I have no quarrel with you, lady," Perkar maintained. "If you will just tell me how I might take these weapons, I will leave you in peace."

She sighed. "You would have to kill me," she said.

"I don't want to do that."

"Perkar!" Apad warned, from behind him. "Watch yourself! Watch her witchery!"

Perkar turned to Apad. "I think the witchery here is from the Forest Lord, not her."

"Do not mistake her for a Human Being, Perkar," Eruka called from outside. Apad was edging farther into the room. "The Lemeyi has warned us of her illusions."

"Are you a Human woman?" Perkar demanded. "Or are you a goddess?"

"Which answer will save my life?" she asked.

"Perkar!" Apad cautioned again, as Perkar moved closer.

"I've said I mean you no harm," Perkar said, anger mounting in his chest. "But I do want the weapons. With which of these did the Forest Lord arm himself against his Brother?"

"His Brother?" she said, staring at Perkar in horror. It was the most passion Perkar had seen in her. "The *Changeling*?"

"Which sword?"

Apad was at the weapons now, touching this one, that one. It made Perkar nervous. "What are you talking about, Perkar? We care nothing for any brother. We need weapons that will harm the Forest Lord himself. Ask her about *that*."

"You think he would keep his own death here?" the woman asked mockingly. "Who is your stupid friend, Oak-Boy?"

Apad turned slowly from the weapons, eyes revealing dangerous fires in his heart. "What do you want from us, witch-goddess? We are losing patience."

"I am not a goddess," she said, her voice low, betraying a hint of concern. "Don't kill me."

"I warn you," Apad cried. "We have fought gods before, and without such swords as *these*, eh, Perkar?"

"Wait. Just wait a moment, Apad."

"Wait for what? What's wrong with you, Perkar? Can't you see her for what she is? She is toying with us, waiting for her friends to come, waiting to pounce."

"I would give you the weapons if I could," the woman swore. "Please. I have only a short time to go—a few more months. I have been here for so *long*." She blinked, and to Perkar's vast surprise, a small tear formed in the corner of one eye and ran slowly down her face.

"No," Perkar said, stepping forward. "There is no need to cry." He reached to touch her shoulder.

"Perkar!" Apad shrieked. Perkar felt a hard, desperate shove from behind. It threw him off balance, and with the unaccustomed weight of his armor he toppled awkwardly, dropping the godsword and throwing out his hands to break the fall. He was half successful, managed to get one hand under him and take most of the impact on his other shoulder. Puzzled and angry, he scrambled back to his knees, a demand for an explanation already on his lips. Something spattered onto his face, his chest, his armor. It was red, salty, tasted of iron.

Apad was swaying above him, likewise spattered with blood. His eyes were wide, shocked. He dropped the sword he had been wielding and backed away, his mouth working. None of this made any sense to Perkar. It was all too fast, too strange.

The lady had blood on her, too. She trembled in her chair. He was kneeling almost at her knees, and as he watched, blood drizzled off the end of her shift, began pooling on the floor.

"I thought . . . I . . ." Apad mumbled, behind him.

Suddenly it *did* all make sense. The woman's neck was half severed, blood gushing from the gash in it. The slash ran between clavicle and throat, down through her chest nearly to the sternum. Her eyes were glazed, her mouth working wordlessly as she slumped forward into Perkar's arms. The blood was red, bright Human red, not gold or black like the blood of gods.

"Don't," she said in his ear. "Don't."

Outside, the Lemeyi began to snicker.

"Why? Apad?" Perkar gasped in anguish. He felt warm blood completely soaking the upper half of his gambeson. He wondered wildly what they could do for her, what sort of bandage might suffice. He tried to lay her back, and her head all but fell off, lolling to the side so that the cut in her neck and breast yawned open. Perkar began vomiting then, great heaving retches, and he ground his head against the cave floor. When he was done, she was dead. Apad was still backed against the cave wall.

"I didn't know ... I thought she ..." he mumbled. The Lemeyi was hooting and gibbering.

"There is no need to *cry*," he screeched, imitating Perkar's low country accent. It was suddenly too much for Perkar. He snatched up the godsword.

"You did this, you stinking beast," he snarled, and leapt out toward the half god, hardly noticing how easily the sword left the chamber now. The Lemeyi may not have expected him to move so quickly. He knew he saw a flicker of fear in the Lemeyi's eye as the sword cut at him. Still, the Lemeyi had more than enough time to avoid the blow, dancing backward, if a bit clumsy from haste.

"Now, now," the Lemeyi chided. "After all, you got what you wanted."

That only made Perkar angrier. He chased after the halfling. Abruptly he was chasing it in total darkness.

"If you were to hit me with that thing, I wouldn't like it," the Lemeyi informed him reasonably, from somewhere out in the black.

"Apad! Eruka!" Perkar yelled. "Light your torches!" He took a few more swings with the blade, but the Lemeyi was certainly somewhere out of reach. He gave that up and knelt, putting his knees on the sword, took out one of his reed torches, flint, and steel, and a few shards of lighter knot. He began striking sparks.

He almost had the tinder going when sudden brightness flared behind him.

"There," he heard Eruka say.

"Good," Perkar replied. He looked quickly around, hoping to see the Lemeyi, but he was not within the torch's small circle of illumination.

"Here, light yours, too," Eruka said.

"No. Just one going at a time; we may need them all to get out of here."

"Oh," Eruka said. "Good thinking."

Apad was still in the treasure room, head between his knees, retching as Perkar had been only moments before. His vomit reeked of woti.

"Get up, Apad," Perkar growled. "Thanks to you, we have no more time for this. We have to get out of here *now*!" He shouted the last word, and it seemed to sink through to Apad's consciousness. He staggered to his feet.

Trying not to look at the corpse, Perkar strode over to the weapons. "Bring the torch, Eruka," he commanded, and the singer obeyed.

"Which one?" Perkar muttered. Perhaps any would do, even the one he held. He gnawed his lip, knowing he had no time.

"Each of you take one," he enjoined. "Leave your own weapons here. We'll have to run, I'm sure." He made his own decision, took up a long, slender weapon with a blade the color of jade. It reminded him of water. As soon as he touched the hilt, he felt a tingle, as when he grasped the last, but this felt stronger, somehow. He hesitated, when he unbuckled the sword Ko had made, the sword his father had given him to make him a man. He hesitated but left it, anyway. It would be too heavy to carry both of them, and his own sword could not slay gods, of that he was certain. Perhaps this one could. He dropped the sword and its scabbard, only after he did so realizing that he had dropped it into the slowly spreading pool of blood. In an instant, the scabbard was stained, the appliqué pattern his mother had made ruined. Near it lay the woman's needlework, doubly red with blood and torchlight. Perkar was transfixed for an instant, understanding in a sudden flash how deep the roots of ruin could burrow, once a single seed was germinated, began growing. The instant passed; he would outrun what ruin he could.

Eruka selected a weapon without much dithering, and when Apad just stared blankly, Perkar thrust one into his hands. Apad nodded numbly and took it. He kept looking at the dead woman, a puzzled expression on his face.

"We go," Perkar said, shaking him roughly. "We *go*." He belted on the new sword, thrust his unlit torch into his belt, took the burning one from Eruka. A significant portion of it was already gone. Without waiting to see if his companions were following, Perkar left the treasure room, retracing their steps. In the torchlight, the cavern winked at him with bloody eyes, a million ruby accusations.

THE first torch was burned down nearly to Perkar's hand; he lit his reed bundle without stopping.

"We have to move faster," he told Apad and Eruka. "If we run out of torches, we might as well start our death chants."

"Is this the right way? Are you sure?" Eruka asked.

"As sure as I can be," Perkar admitted. "I think I remember how we came."

"If we get lost . . ."

"Then that will be that," Perkar said. "Save your strength for running."

They could not, in fact, actually run. The tunnel floor was too uneven. In the tightest places, crawling seemed nightmarishly slow, and Perkar feared that at any moment the Lemeyi would reappear to work further mischief. He was certain that he occasionally heard the half god cackling, but the way sound traveled ı the caves, the creature could be almost anywhere. Worse things than the Lemeyi could find them, as well, things bent on vengeance rather than cruel amusement. Perkar had no idea whether the woman had any relatives here—it seemed plain enough now that she was a Human Being or at least mostly Human. Perkar clenched his teeth on another eruption of bile; he had no time to be sick; let that come later. He swore silently that he would burn offerings to the woman's spirit, but he knew this was empty, for he did not even know her name, much less her lineage. The memory of her dull, glazed eyes and that terrible wound stayed with him, mocking him, and he understood that even if his offerings found her spirit, she would know them for what they were: a pale attempt to appease his own guilt. And though he was angry with Apad, Perkar knew the fault *did* lie with himself. Apad and Eruka, for all of their talk, would never have entered the cave at all if he had not forced the issue by running off to do it alone; he had challenged their manhood, allowed their fear of missing out on fame and glory to overcome their growing reluctance to implement their grandiose scheme to wrestle land from Balati. And it was fear—fear, not rage or anger or even greed—that had killed the old woman. How many songs told of seemingly harmless creatures discovered by the hero to be dragons or monsters in disguise? Apad's failure in the fight with the Wild God must have gnawed at him; he must have planned night and day what he would do next time they encountered danger. And then the evil Lemeyi whispering in his ear, cajoling him.

But he wouldn't have come in without me. If I had paid more attention to him, I could have stopped him.

Of course, then they would not have the weapons, the jadelike sword that rattled and flapped on his thigh.

I will avenge her, too. When I slay the Changeling, I will make her death worth something, turn it into Piraku for the whole world.

But that rang hollow, too. He had a vivid vision of the Stream Goddess, fury in her eyes—or weeping—knowing the things he was doing in her name.

The reed torch seemed to last longer than the heart pine, but it constantly threatened to go out, guttering to almost an ember at times. Perkar had to nurse it as they went along, and that slowed them further. When he lit the third torch, it was with a growing sense of despair. He did not know how far they had to go, but he knew it was much farther than their torches would light the way for them. After that it would be fumbling at the walls, the darkness surrounding them, the Lemeyi standing an arm's breadth away, laughing, fully able to see them but invisible to the Humans.

The blood beneath his armor was beginning to dry, to stiffen, and the gambeson began to rub his skin raw. It stank, too, a thick, sweet scent that the smoke from the torch could not cover. To that unpleasantness was added another; behind them, to their sides, the Humans began to hear noises. Slithering and scraping, faint chittering, a clicking like a hundred hard rods rapping against stone. In the larger spaces, the ones that the torch did not fully illumine, they caught glimpses of things just at the edge of the torchlight. Eyes, mostly, blinking green, yellow, or red. Once Perkar saw something *large*, irregular, shaped nothing like a man, retreating from the light on many spidery black legs. Perkar remembered that the Lemeyi had warned them that light in the tunnels would be noticed. Perkar could only hope that the unaccustomed glare would also deter whatever lurked about them—followed them.

Soon, though, it was the last torch that was nearly scorching his hand. He wondered wildly if there was anything else to burn; the noises—especially those behind them—were growing in volume; they could not be dismissed as imagination, and fear took hold in their minds. Perkar wondered how long they would last, fighting in the dark.

"My father will never know what happened to me," Apad groaned—the first coherent words he had uttered since their flight began.

"Our spirits will wander here without gifts, without even woti. I have killed us all."

"There's plenty of blame to go around," Perkar said. "If it hadn't been for me, we wouldn't have even come in here. Without Eruka, that thrice-damned Lemeyi would not have been our guide and we would have neither found the weapons nor been tricked into slaying their keeper. We've all been fools, but we can't make up for that dead."

"It was like cutting butter," Apad said, his voice rising hysterically. "These swords are terrible things. It just slid through. I thought it would be like fighting the Wild God, hacking and hacking almost without cutting at all. I thought I had to attack first, before she could change ... *Her blood was red!*"

"Shut up. Shut up, Apad!" Perkar shrieked, and from behind them there was not a single laugh, but a chorus of them, and one clear voice, high and joyful.

"Her blood was *red!*"

The torch was singeing Perkar's hand now, and if he thought his fingers might burst into flame and light their way for another few moments, he would have held it still. Instead he set it down. In the few flickers of light that remained for them, he motioned his companions against the wall.

"Apad," he said, "you get in the center, against the wall. Feel our way for us. Eruka, you go in front of him, I'll be rearguard. If anything touches you, anything at all, strike it. But don't panic, Eruka. Keep one hand on Apad. We have to stay together!"

The two arranged themselves as he said. The tunnel was narrow here, and it was easy enough to do. Perkar drew the godsword as the torch went out. They stood for a moment, waiting, and for an instant there was total, calm silence. Then the noises began again, the sounds of a summer evening made harsh and strange, a susurrus of little sounds, each menacing but together utterly terrifying.

"Go. Apad, Eruka, go!" Perkar commanded. And slowly they commenced moving up the tunnel, blind.

Something scuttled up to Perkar, a sound like many legs with small, naked feet of bone. He thrust grimly with his sword and was rewarded by the shock of contact with something that wriggled away. He brought the sword back, rapidly sliced at the same spot—the sword scraped the cave floor and struck sparks. Eruka, ahead of him, suddenly shrieked, and there was a similar clang.

"Keep your head," Perkar yelled. Something feathery brushed his face. A jolt of surprise and disgust raced from his heart to his arm, and he cut out flat with a weapon, a stroke horizontal to the ground and about waist high. He hit something thin, like a piece of cane, and it seemed to sever easily. Something else hissed, and then a paralyzing pain stabbed him in the shoulder—a long thin weapon—like a needle—piercing him.

As with the Wild God, his fear was suddenly gone. Furious, he leapt at the darkness, hacking out a downstroke that would have cut into a man's neck and cleaved groinward. He hit something, hit it again, felt fluid spurt onto him.

"Come on!" he shrieked. "Come all of you, stinking demons! Fight the blind man, if you have the courage!" He swung twice more, encountered nothing but the cave wall. He panted into the silence that followed—but of course, the chittering began again.

"You wish to see?" someone asked. Perkar's rage mounted higher. It was the Lemeyi taunting him.

"Come here, you stinking beast," Perkar shouted. "I don't need to see to kill you!"

"If you wish to see, you may," the voice calmly responded. Perkar suddenly did not believe it to be the Lemeyi at all. The voice seemed to be just inside of his ear—it did not echo through the cave like his own, or the Lemeyi's laughter.

"Yes, yes, of course I wish to see," he muttered.

And then he could, see well enough to hack the mottled, leprous arm from a skeletonlike ghoul, bring the weapon around to threaten something that was part spider and part worm. See well enough to make out the Lemeyi, capering, back at the last turning, with several other creatures that resembled him. It was much like the magical vision the Lemeyi had granted him, but it was something more. He could *see* danger—his eyes were drawn to it, without his will. The black, scorpionlike thing that was menacing Eruka was *behind* him, yet his head seemed to turn of its own volition and *make* him see it. Snarling, he took two quick steps and sent the point of the blade plunging into what he guessed to be its head. He then suddenly realized that Eruka, still blind, unaware of the thing, was swinging wildly at *him*, and so he ducked away.

"Apad, Eruka," Perkar said, keeping his voice steady. "I can see. I think there is some god in my sword. It asked if I wanted to see, and now I can."

Apad and Eruka promptly began petitioning their own weapons, but their eyes remained terrified, sightless.

"We'll go slowly," Perkar said. "The monsters have retreated a bit; I hurt some of them. I think they are cowards, like the Lemeyi. I think I can keep them back and lead us out of here at the same time."

"I hope so," Eruka whispered. "I don't like this."

"Sing us a song," Perkar said. "Sing us a song, to show them we have no fear."

"I . . . I don't think I can sing."

"Do it," Apad groaned. "Please, Eruka. I can't stand the sound of them. Drown them out."

"Perkar," Eruka asked plaintively. "Can you really see?"

"Yes," Perkar told him, clapping him firmly on the shoulder. "I can see. Now sing us something."

"What?"

"I don't know. Something about light and green valleys."

"Ah." Eruka sighed. Perkar took his hand and placed it in Apad's. Then he took Eruka's other hand in his own, moved to the front.

"Come on."

The monsters were still behind them. They seemed to know how far his vision extended and were staying just at the edge of it. That was fine with Perkar. He led his companions up the tunnel. Eruka began to sing, a childhood song, a song about hunting crawfish and tadpoles with bows of willow. Perkar did not smile, but it made him feel a bit better.

Not much later, they saw light up ahead. Eruka broke off his singing to cheer hoarsely. Perkar joined him; the darkdwellers seemed to be gathering courage, bracing themselves for an over-whelming attack that Perkar—even with a godsword—did not think himself able to repel, despite his encouraging words to Apad and Eruka. Even as they quickened their pace, Perkar glanced back as much as he glanced forward.

The nearer they came to the light, the more his own unnatural vision faded. That was probably a good sign, as well. It might mean that the demons following him were losing their vision also, though the Lemeyi, of course, would be undeterred. Per-kar was just wondering if it was the strange transition in vision that made the outside light seem orange when Eruka gasped something.

"What?" Perkar asked. "What did you say?"

"It looks like sunset out there."

For a moment that didn't sink in, but then Perkar caught Eruka's meaning. If it was growing dark outside, the demons might not be deterred at all, might follow them from the caves.

"At least we'll be outside," Apad remarked. "At least we won't die in *here*."

"We aren't going to die," Perkar snapped. Then he halted, al-most stumbling as the source of the light came clearly into view and his dark vision was entirely dispelled. It was not sunlight at all, but a torch.

VIII

The Huntress

NGANGATA'S normally pale face was flushed with fury so bright that it showed nearly purple in the torchlight. Behind him, Atti looked equally dour.

"You *fools*," Ngangata grated. "You stupid, dung-eating *fools*! What have you done to us? What were you *doing*?"

Perkar gestured behind them. "Time enough to explain that later on. Right now we have more to worry about than our stupidity."

Ngangata scowled as he looked around the three, peering out at the edge of the torchlight. There was nothing there to see, but the noises were still plain enough, without Human voices to cover them.

"I see," Ngangata said, voice still flat with anger. "Perkar, you are bleeding. Is anyone else injured?"

"It isn't all my blood," Perkar said. Indeed, the wound in his shoulder was nearly closed, though it still ached worse than any pain Perkar had ever experienced. It was as if an icicle had been imbedded in him.

"Let's go then," Ngangata said, when the others had not brought any injury to his attention. "We still have some distance to travel."

The torches Ngangata and Atti carried were good ones, slow-burning and bright. The demons stayed at bay, and at last they saw true daylight grinning at them from around a bend in the tunnel. When they finally stepped back out into the sunlight—it looked like morning—Eruka fell to his knees and began to sing the Sun Woman Epic. Atti yanked him roughly to his feet.

"Not now. Not now. Now you explain where you've been to the Forest Lord, and you had better be convincing. You fools may have doomed us all." Eruka seemed more than taken aback by this; he seemed on the verge of tears. Apad, covered with dried blood, seemed hardly alive, and Perkar took one glance at the assorted colors of blood staining his own clothes.

"We should take off our armor, shouldn't we?" he said. "I mean . . ."

"It doesn't matter," Ngangata said. "Whatever you did— whatever you *fools* did—the Forest Lord already knows."

Atti gave Apad a push, to get him going down the slope toward the trail. "Hurry," he said.

"Don't push me!" Apad shrieked, suddenly coming alive. His new sword came out, danced in the sunlight. It seemed to Perkar that the sword was moving Apad's wrist, rather than the other way around. The tip flicked dangerously near Atti, whose hand went to his own blade.

"Apad!" Perkar bellowed. Then more softly, "Apad. Put that away. You don't want to kill anyone else."

Apad's eyes seemed mad, but as they focused on Perkar, they softened. A bit of puzzlement replaced the wildness there.

"Perkar? Tell them not to push me. I can't stand it."

"No one will push you, Apad. Put that sword away. It looks like it wants to kill something." He noticed, startled, that the sword had blood on it. He must have handed Apad the selfsame blade he had killed the woman with. He didn't remember doing that. In fact, he thought he remembered a different weapon, straight-bladed rather than curved. Apad had always held that curved swords were "just for butchering" while straight ones were for warriors. It seemed that he was right. Nevertheless, slowly, reluctantly, Apad put the blade away.

"Those are godswords you have," Ngangata declared, astonishment as plain as the chagrin. "Gods of heaven and mountain, what have you done?"

"Nothing good, I think." Perkar sighed.

The trip back down into the lower valley was nearly silent. Perkar wanted desperately to stop and rest, if only for a moment. They had plainly been underneath the mountain for a full day and a night. He had hardly slept the previous night. The pain in his shoulder seemed worse, and his legs were beginning to wobble beneath him. So numb did all of this make him that, try as he might, he could not conjure up any image of the coming confrontation, had no idea what he would tell the Forest Lord. When at last they came before him, it was all he could do to stay on his feet.

The Kapaka, seated on a stone, rose as the party approached. He was ashen, his face paler than his beard. Perkar almost thought he swayed when he saw them in their armor, with all the bloodstains. He closed his eyes for a long moment.

The Forest Lord loomed larger than before; he seemed, somehow, to have become a part of the enormous tree, his huge bearlike body merging imperceptibly into bark and wood. His eye, now a wide black orb, seemed as sightless as they had been in the underneath. Perkar was vividly reminded of the Wild God. So low was Balati's voice that he almost didn't understand it.

"So you see," Balati told the Kapaka, "you *have* lied to me. I smell the blood of a mortal woman on them. They have slain her and stolen from my treasure."

The Kapaka bowed his head. When he finally spoke, it was with a semblance of conviction, but Perkar sensed the despair behind the seeming. "Lord, these men are young. They act foolishly. We will return your things and make restitution for the woman."

Balati may have considered that and he may not have; his head turned from side to side with glacial slowness.

"I will give no more land to Human Beings," he said finally. "And you must leave now, before I lose patience. That is the best I can do for you. No more words from you. Take your steel out of my realm. Take the things you have stained; I care nothing for them."

Apad was suddenly in motion, sword whipping out, a mad, inarticulate shriek on his lips. What then happened Perkar had to sort out later. He remembered Ngangata seeming just to *appear* in Apad's path, the godsword cutting bright ribbons of light around him. Then Apad was lying on the ground, spitting blood from his mouth. Ngangata bent and carefully took the sword from where it had fallen. He seemed unscathed.

"I think I'll keep this for the moment," he said.

The Forest Lord, apparently unimpressed by any of this, turned and moved off into the forest. His bulk seemed to shiver, to break apart like a pile of leaves blown about by the wind. Each shard became a crow, a cloud of them, and they rose into the sky like a whirlwind of ashes.

Perkar flinched away from the Kapaka's gaze. The old man sat back down on his stone, lips pressed tight.

"He had agreed to give us three more valleys, boys. Three more." He closed his eyes again, put a hand to his temple.

"Kapaka," Ngangata said. "Kapaka, we had best go now."

Perkar could see the Alwat. They all looked agitated, kept glancing around themselves nervously.

"*Now,*" the half man said.

Atti touched Ngangata's shoulder. "Couldn't we wait a moment? Until the king recovers his strength?"

Ngangata shook his head. "We are already too late, I think. The Huntress and the Raven will waken by morning if not sooner. If we are not far, far away by then, we will certainly die."

"But . . ." Eruka began, trailed off.

"He told us to leave," Perkar finished for him.

"Yes. But I know these gods, and I know the Forest Lord. He is never of one mind. The Huntress and the Raven will want blood for this, and they will want to hunt. Thus we should go, now, be the best prey we can be. If we are very clever and very fast we may reach someplace beyond their power before they catch us."

The Kapaka looked up at that, his eyes watery and tired. "Then we die. No place is beyond their reach, I think."

Ngangata shook his head. "No," he stated. "There is *one*."

PERKAR patted Mang's neck sympathetically. The horse's flank heaved with exhaustion and his normally beautiful coat was foamy with sweat.

"The horses can't take much more of this," he complained.

"They *have* to," Ngangata called back to him.

The worst part of it was, despite the valiant exertion of the animals, they seemed to be making little progress. The hill country had no trails, and the ridges ran in the wrong direction. They spent all of their time climbing up and running down hills, picking their way around fierce thickets of brambles. Mang's coat was crisscrossed with bleeding scratches, and none of the other horses was faring any better. Miraculously the Alwat, on foot, somehow managed to keep pace with them, though the eldest rode up behind Ngangata. Perkar tried to offer Digger a ride as well, but she seemed afraid to approach Mang closely, and, after all, she might not have really understood his offer. Unaccustomed as he was to reading Alwat expressions, it seemed to him that they understood their plight better than he; even the normally frolicsome Digger seemed grim, pushing through thorns and clambering over rocky ground with little regard for the countless wounds on *her* body.

"Why must the Alwat flee?" Perkar asked. "Surely Balati knows they had no part in our folly."

"No. Are you deaf? I told you how the Forest Lord thinks. We were all with the Kapaka; he thinks of us all as the Kapaka. Whatever crime one of us commits, he sees that as the fault of all of us, even the Alwat. I *told* you this, and still you went ahead with your insane scheme."

"I didn't *understand*," Perkar said.

"Well, you will," Ngangata said. "And let's leave this off. We have no time to fight amongst ourselves."

"What if we split up, went our own ways? Mightn't they hunt only those of us who are actually guilty then?"

"No. They would kill us all, alone, individually. Our only hope, together or alone, is to reach the Changeling. They will not follow us there; the Forest Lord fears his Brother."

"But what of the Changeling?" Atti asked. "Will he treat us any better?"

"I have no idea. But I *know* for certain what will happen to us if we dally here."

They crossed over a ridge, and Perkar saw another line of hills in the distance. Between them and those ridges stretched a vast bottomland.

"We can make better time down there, perhaps," the Kapaka said hopefully.

Perkar couldn't answer. More than anything, he wanted rest. His clothes and armor felt like a skin of scabs, and he could not think clearly. His eyes were wooden balls, rattling aimlessly about in their sockets, his fingers continually slipping from the reins.

"We need rest, Mang," he muttered, patting the great beast's neck again, leaning his forehead down upon his mane. The rich, warm scent of the horse seemed the only real thing in the world, a smell from home, the scent of the barn. Everything else was a dream, a fumbling, nightmarish dream in which he ran and ran and never got anywhere. He kicked Mang's flanks, regretted it even as he did so, as the great heart under him strained to go just a little faster. Perkar felt his eyes blink closed, open reluctantly, blink closed again.

He was standing near the city of white stone, ankle deep in water. The water sucked and pulled at his feet. He looked down at them, saw the angry, brilliant reflection of the sun there. Immensely tired, he stripped off his armor and clothes, crouched down in the water, and then, with a sigh, lay back in it, relaxed in its insistent tugging.

When he opened his eyes again, there was the little girl, gazing at him with large, expressive black eyes. As he watched, she began to weep, and with a growing horror, he realized that her tears were red, like blood. Rivulets of it collected on her chin, cascaded down her chest, thickening, so that sheets of blood were pouring into the river at her feet. It was then that he realized that the entire river was blood, and the stench of it filled his head. He leapt up out of it, but the blood clung to him, even when he wiped at it frantically with his hands. He began to cry, but his own tears were blood, too. He began to shriek.

Perkar jerked awake, gasping, his heart hammering in his chest. It took a long moment to remember where he was, what was happening. The dream had been *so* vivid that it seemed more concrete than waking. A miracle that he had not fallen off of his horse. The others were ahead; Mang had taken his dozing for a break. Reluctantly Perkar urged him on.

When he caught up with the others, Apad was talking to Eruka. Perkar was a bit surprised; after recovering from Ngangata's blow, Apad had been sullen and completely silent.

"Perkar," Apad said as he trotted up. "We thought we had lost you for a moment."

"I fell asleep. I need rest."

"We all do," Apad said.

"How are you, Apad? We've been worried about you."

"I'd be better with some rest, I think," he said. "I was mad there for a while, wasn't I?"

Perkar shrugged.

"I've never killed anyone before," Apad admitted.

"Nor have I," said Perkar.

"I just can't believe . . ." Apad trailed off, his eyes becoming distant.

"Later," Perkar told him. "Think about it later. Right now we have to see that the Kapaka lives to reach the River."

Eruka nodded, but worry lay on his face, slumped on his shoulders. "Do you think Ngangata is right? Will the Huntress come after us?"

"I think so," Perkar said. "Ngangata knows this land, these gods. It was stupid of us to doubt him."

"I know," Apad said. "Much as I hate to admit it. If we live through this, I suppose we have him to thank for it." The tightness of Apad's mouth suggested that this observation was not one he enjoyed making. "He should give me my sword back, though. If he's right, we're going to need it."

"If any of them will listen to any of us," Perkar said. "But when the time comes, I will ask for you."

"Thank you, Perkar," Apad said. "I'm sorry for what happened. I'm sorry I killed her. It's just that I thought . . ."

"The Lemeyi set you to it," Eruka said. "He told us she was the Tiger Goddess, just waiting for her chance."

"The Lemeyi," Apad said dully. "It *is* his fault. Why did he do that?"

"I don't think the Lemeyi needs a rational reason for doing things," Perkar said, and then, after a moment: "Any more than we do."

AFTER noon, the sky began to darken. A thunderhead gathered above the mountain, and cold, wet wind began to bluster down, bending the trees. Leaves flapped their pale undersides, and it seemed to Perkar as if they weren't leaves at all, but thousands of white moths, clinging to dead branches. Ravens flew above, croaking their dire songs, ebony harbingers of the storm.

"The hunt has begun," Ngangata said grimly. "We still have far to go."

They redoubled their speed, and Perkar was again surprised at what Mang was willing to give him; though he could feel the animal shuddering, he broke from canter to gallop as they beat recklessly across the open floor of the bottomland. Perkar tried to calculate how far they had to go to the next line of hills. Engaged in that, he heard the first, faint howling. Wolves, and many of them, singing their hunger.

Thunder cracked above, but to Perkar's ear it sounded more like the croak of a giant raven.

By the time they reached the hills, the howling of the wolves had taken on an exultant tone, a fierce anticipation.

"Maybe we should just stop, make a stand," Perkar shouted up to Ngangata. "After all, we have the godswords."

"That is the Forest Lord's hunt," Ngangata bellowed. "He can call every god and beast in this land. You cannot slay them all, Perkar. It would only give them sport."

"They will catch us anyway!"

"Over these hills is the basin where the Changeling flows. We *must* cross those hills."

Perkar set his teeth. Eruka was pale, frightened. Apad—Apad looked grim.

They forded a stream, stopped just long enough for the horses to wet their mouths. Ngangata reached back to the bundle on his saddle. He took his bow and strung it; Atti did the same. Perkar watched helplessly. He could string his bow, of course, but if he tried to fire it from horseback he would certainly fall off.

Ngangata slid the godsword he had taken from Apad from his saddle. He scowled at it.

"Apad," he called, and tossed the sheathed weapon to the man. Apad caught it, bowed his head in acknowledgment and thanks.

"Piraku around and about you, Ngangata," he said softly.

Ngangata nodded back. "Don't let the horses fill their bellies," he told them all. "They won't be able to run."

Mang stumbled often as they hurried up the steep slope. Once both front legs collapsed, and he nearly rolled over Perkar trying to get back up. Perkar dismounted and ran holding the reins of the trembling beast. Slower, that put him back with the Alwat, who were at last beginning to straggle. They were running in a tight little group, the slightly larger males on the outside, cane spears in hand. Perkar got a glance at their feet; their deerskin shoes were in tatters, and the flesh within was bruised and bleeding.

The ground steepened a bit more and, worse, became gravelly. The horses slipped on it, and for that matter so did Perkar. The wolves were close now; Mang shivered nervously at their scent, but was otherwise brave. Glancing back down the slope, Perkar made out a gray shape coursing toward the base of the hills—and then another and another. And then, through a break in the trees, the hunt itself.

More wolves than he could count swarmed through the forest, but they suddenly seemed the least of their worries, for with them came the Huntress. Her face was too small to read at this distance, but Perkar could see her eyes flashing green fire. Her antlers were black, and in one hand she carried a recurved bow of bone. She was seated atop a lion, but it must have been the Lion Master, for it was three times the size of any lion Perkar had ever seen, golden but striped with black. It was female, maneless, a Huntress, too.

Karak, the Raven God, sat on the shoulder of the Huntress. In their train came more beasts: tigers with long fangs, boars the size of cattle. Many of these creatures also had riders, feral-looking men who were surely not men. They wore the skins of bears, and Perkar suspected that they were more of the Mountain Gods, ones he did not know.

Perkar realized that he had been staring, paralyzed. It was Digger, tugging frantically at his sleeve, who broke the spell.

The hill sloped more gently, after that, and he remounted. Wolves were actually loping on their flanks now, but they seemed only to be pacing them, herding them perhaps. Ngangata stood in his saddle; now and then, he loosed an arrow. Each shot was rewarded by an animal howl of pain.

Perkar drew his sword. "You gave me vision when I needed it," he said to it. "What can you give me now?"

"*I tend your wounds,*" the voice in his ear said. Perkar reached up to his shoulder. Indeed, the pain had gone out of it, and to his astonishment the skin had already closed in a little pucker over the puncture. Only the hole in his armor assured him that he had not been dreaming when the demon stabbed him.

"*I took the poison from you, too,*" the sword assured him.

"Poison?"

"*The wound was full of poison.*"

"Can you kill gods? Can you kill the Huntress and the Raven?"

"*I am a weapon. Of my own volition I can kill nothing. Wielded by the right hand I can certainly kill a god. But I make you no quicker or stronger than you ever were, no more skillful.*"

"You did something to my vision, made me see danger . . ."

"*There is that. I can draw your gaze to where it needs to be.*"

"Can you draw my gaze to where I must strike, to kill a god?"

"*Yes. But a god cannot be killed with one blow. You must sever the cords that hold their hearts, and that is not easily done. Gods have heartstrings like metal, and they must be severed one stroke at a time.*"

"How many of these strings?"

"*Seven is the usual number.*"

Perkar wondered if the sword could close his wounds fast enough to allow him to fight the Huntress. He asked it that.

"*I heal your wounds by strengthening the mortal strings of your heart with my own. A god will see this and begin severing mine. When I am cut away from your heart, I can no longer heal you and you will die.*"

"You make me equal to a god?"

The voice in his ear clucked, and Perkar realized that it was *laughing.*

"Not equal to a Mountain Goddess. She would always be faster than you and stronger than you, cut your heartstrings like horsehair. Perhaps if you came upon her asleep . . ."

"She is not asleep. She has the hunt with her."

"Well, then, I wonder who shall carry me next."

Ahead, Ngangata and Atti both loosed arrows nearly simultaneously. One final scramble and they reached the top of the ridge, Perkar and the Alwat last. He looked back, the way they had come. The hillside was not heavily forested; the rocks gave purchase only to tough, scrubby plants. Perkar could see the hunt as a vast rustling, like an ant bed stirred up. The Huntress was in sight below them. Atti fitted an arrow to his bow and loosed it.

Perkar held his breath as the shaft arced down. Ngangata fired, as well. The goddess jerked as Atti's arrow slid into her chest, nearly fell from her mount when Ngangata's took her in the shoulder. Perkar saw her teeth flash in a horrible, predatory smile, and then her own bow was bending.

The next instant Atti reeled from his saddle, his throat neatly pierced by a black-feathered shaft. Perkar watched in horror as the red-haired man thrashed about on the ground.

"Over!" Ngangata howled. "Over the ridge!"

"Get Atti!" the Kapaka ordered.

"He is already dead!" Ngangata answered. Indeed, Atti still seemed alive, though his thrashing was already feeble. The shaft had passed through the great artery in his neck, and his blood was a fountain. Perkar urged Mang on, over the ridge. Ngangata, Eruka, and the Kapaka had already crossed.

A vast basin spread out below them, the hollow into which all of the surrounding hills and mountains bled their waters. In the crease of it was a gorge, the bottom of which they could not see at this angle. Nevertheless, there could be no doubt that it was the River, the Changeling. There was also no doubt that it was too far away. Perkar had once had a nightmare about being deep underwater, holding his breath, able to see the surface but with the sure knowledge he would never reach it. It was the same here. The slopes and floor of the basin were mostly bare, smooth stone, open ground that their horses could traverse quickly. But their horses were tired, and the hunt was strong, was gaining on them too quickly. It might be a close chase, but the certainty that they would not make it clenched Perkar's heart like a fist.

Sunlight leaked through the clouds, casting mottled golden light on the gorge. He was not too tired to see the irony in the situation—his first view of his great enemy, and yet at the moment the Changeling represented salvation.

All of the party except Apad and the Alwat were already ahead of him, threading down the slope. He looked back, fearing to see Apad shot. He wasn't; he was close behind Perkar. The Alwat, however, had halted. They were gathered in a little clump, their spears bristling out like the quills of a hedgehog.

"What are they doing?" Perkar asked—rhetorically, for Ngangata was too far ahead to hear.

"Picking where they are going to die," Apad said. He grinned, suddenly, fiercely, the first such expression Perkar had seen on his face for some time. He held up the sword Perkar had chosen him, the one that had slain the woman. It was shimmering, colored like a rainbow. Perkar hadn't seen it do that before.

"There was a trick to it," Apad confided. "I'm glad I didn't learn it earlier, or I would have killed Ngangata. I was wrong about him."

"We all were," Perkar said. "Come on."

Apad glanced back at the Alwat. Digger was watching them, her expression unreadable.

"Good-bye, Perkar," Apad said. "Remember me to my family." He turned his horse and in an instant plunged back over the crest of the hill, back the way they had come.

For a second Perkar was paralyzed; then, with a shriek, he, too, wheeled his horse. With their weapons, he and Apad could make a fight of it, could slow the Huntress for an instant or two at least; give the Kapaka more time to reach the River. This mess was his fault as much as Apad's. He felt a brief flare of guilt, for he was probably dooming Mang, as well, but that was as it must be.

He plunged down the slope behind Apad, heedless. It seemed almost as if their horses were falling rather than running, so great was their speed. When he whooped, Apad turned once and grinned at him. About that time, Perkar felt a terrific flash of pain in his chest. He looked down, gape-mouthed, at the arrow standing there.

"*One heartstring gone,*" the sword told him. Perkar slumped forward in the saddle, spit blood out of his mouth. It hurt terribly to breathe. Mang continued his plummet, however, and they tore through a slash of scrub; there, just below the steepest part of the cliff, the Huntress was following their progress with the tip of another arrow.

Apad did not slow his horse or take it down the switchback trail they had made coming up. Instead, shrieking like a madman, he urged his horse straight down, so that the poor beast bolted out into space. He seemed poised there for an instant; the shaft loosed by the Huntress seemed to float lazily up at him, before it lodged in the airborne horse. Then Apad and his mount slammed into the Huntress and the lion she rode, the horse shrieking piteously. Karak squawked and took to the air, just as the Huntress went down beneath Apad and his horse.

Perkar had too little strength to challenge Mang to the same feat, though the pain in his chest was already fading somewhat. Mang charged down the switchback; when Perkar reached the fray he could see that Apad had not only rolled clear of the tangle of horse and lion, but was setting about him among the feral-looking riders. He was shivering like his sword, dancing wildly with more skill than Apad had ever before demonstrated. Even as Perkar watched, one of the Bear-Men sank to his knees, decapitated, his blood a golden spray from his neck.

"*He's carrying Madedge,*" the voice said in Perkar's ears. It sounded jubilant. "*Madedge can fight!*"

Perkar wasn't paying attention anymore. Mang died underneath him, sprouting a dozen arrows. Perkar took another in the ribs and two more glanced from his hauberk, but now his anger was on him. Even as Mang stumbled he was leaping from his saddle. A wolf died instantly, cloven by the jade blade, and Perkar let the weapon guide his eyes, prioritize his attacks. Next was one of the Bear-Men. Perkar parried a spear thrust and impaled him. Wrenching the sword out, he pushed on.

"That didn't kill him," the sword informed him.

Perkar didn't care. "Huntress!" he shrieked. "Fight me!" He slashed at wolves, fighting toward the Huntress. She had regained her feet, wielding a long, bright-pointed spear. Her smile was one of satisfaction, even of joy.

Perkar saw Apad die; Karak, the Crow God, lighted on him, one black claw on each shoulder, slashed down with his razor-sharp beak. Apad's head split like a seed.

Perkar stumbled as a wolf bit into his leg; he cut it, but it did not let go, and then his head snapped around to face the greater danger: the lion. It was favoring one leg, probably from the impact of Apad's horse. Still, it leapt, snarling, and Perkar sheared into its skull even as the weight of the beast hit him. Distantly he felt his belly split open, heard the mail tear. More pain followed, from too many places to keep track of. The last thing he saw was the Huntress standing over him, her spear flashing down toward his throat.

IX

≈≈≈≈≈≈≈≈≈≈≈≈≈≈≈≈≈≈≈≈≈≈≈≈≈≈≈≈≈≈≈≈≈≈≈≈

A Gift of Bronze
and Hope

FOR the next few days, Hezhi worked diligently on her map; she hoped to have it done before she started bleeding again, before the priests came back. Despite what she had told Tsem, she had no wish to have her fate decided without even knowing what was happening. D'en and the others were taken down the Darkness Stair. It was clear to her now that, as she had suspected, the stair descended into a part of the buried palace. She found evidence that the central portion of the palace had its foundation reinforced with thick pillars of basalt—so that it would not collapse into the underpalace. It seemed to her that it would have been simpler merely to fill the old rooms with sand, as had been done in most other places—unless there was some *use* for the rooms. The extra foundations suggested that the rooms down there were still open, perhaps even maintained. A sort of secret palace, where people like D'en were whisked off to for some reason connected with puberty. With power, she suspected. With being "River-Blessed." Her hypothetical "underpalace" could be quite large, she realized. Her earlier explorations actually might have taken her very near it.

Thinking about it further, she concluded that the Darkness Stair could not be the only way in, either. If there were people down there, there must be water—and, of course, a sewer system. For the first time in a year, her thoughts returned to actually going down, beneath the city again. But she wanted a map first, some idea of where she was going. It would be easy and embarrassing to get lost, and probably fatal to Tsem.

She stopped work about midmorning and began her tasks for Ghan. He had ceased to watch her closely, these past days, and she realized gradually that he *trusted* her. Though he seldom complimented her work, he rarely denigrated it, either. For Ghan, this was a rare show of kindness. She suspected—only suspected, and she would never mention it to him—that he had torn the book and indentured her because it was the only way he could *teach* her. He was a stern, hard man, without much love for anyone, no children that she knew of, no wife. He never gave anything away, at least ostensibly, and yet it seemed to her that he had given her the most valuable gift she could imagine.

Yen came into the library about noon. He had been there, working, almost every day, though they had not spoken for the past several, only nodded at one another from across the room. Today, however, he approached her, rather shyly, she thought.

"Hello, my la . . . ah, Hezhi."

"Good day, Yen," she returned, again hoping she sounded a bit older, more mature.

He nodded nervously. "I wanted to thank you . . ." he began.

"You did that already," she told him.

"Yes, but it appears that thanks to you I will keep my position with the engineers, at least for a while. I . . ." Still embarrassed, he produced a little cloth package. "I wanted to give you something. To show my appreciation."

Hezhi's eyes widened, and she reached hesitantly for the small packet.

"Please don't misunderstand," he added quickly. "It's just . . . well, it's only a present because you helped me. I'm not . . ." He stuttered off, unable to finish, his dark eyes appealing for her to understand what he was trying to say.

"Thank you," she said. "I understand; there isn't any need to explain. Here in the palace we give presents often." *But no one other than my servants ever gave one to me,* she finished, in her head. Not even the annoying Wezh, who had been trying to get her attention more and more lately.

"Ah, well, see if you like it," Yen suggested. "If not, I could bring you something else."

She fumbled at the cloth, simultaneously eager to open it but aware that she should not seem *too* eager. When the wrapping came away, she grinned in delight. It was a little bronze figurine of exotic workmanship, quite unlike anything in the palace. It was a horse in full gallop, but instead of a horse's neck and head, the slender torso of a woman rose up, naked. Her hair was feathering behind her, as if in the wind, and in one hand she carried a spear. Her expression was fierce, barbaric, joyful.

"It's beautiful," she breathed. "I've never seen anything like this."

"It is Mang," he informed her.

"Mang?"

"My father trades with them, sometimes, with the southern ones, anyway. They follow the River down from the north to the port at Wun."

"The Mang are half horse?"

Yen smiled. "No. This is part of their legend. The Mang live on horseback, you see. They believe that horses are their kin. The horses are even members of their clans, if you can believe that."

"It seems very strange," Hezhi murmured, turning the statuette over and over in her palms.

"They are very barbaric," Yen confided. "I met one once. They always carry swords and spears and never take their armor off, even to sleep or . . . uh, even to sleep." He reddened a bit and then went on. "Anyway, they believe that horse and rider who die together are reunited like this, after death. They even say that there is a place, far to the east, where these creatures dwell."

"I like this," Hezhi said. "I like the story, too. Thank you for both of them."

He grinned happily, bowed. "My lady," he said, and then backed away toward his books.

Hezhi examined the figurine again. When she looked back up, she caught Ghan staring at her, a look of pure disgust on his face. She purpled, knowing what he was thinking. He would believe that his prediction was coming true, that all of his time with her would be wasted when she ran off with some "young fop."

Hezhi went back to shelving, trying to look *very* busy. Ghan was wrong if he thought that, wrong in *many* ways. First of all, Yen was no "fop." He was thoughtful and intelligent, totally un-like the courtiers whom Ghan so hated. Second of all, he was not courting her and she was not interested in him. Such a thing wasn't even conceivable; she was the daughter of the Chakunge. Of course, she had never told Yen that, and very tenuous nobil-ity sometimes married younger daughters into the merchant class . . .

But that was ridiculous. He was *much* older than she, and while political marriages could create such unions, they did not happen out of attraction. Such a good-looking young man as Yen was certainly not attracted to a twelve-year-old without visible breasts or hips. She had heard Tsem and some of the guards often enough, talking about what attracted men to women, and it didn't seem to be wit or good manners.

So Ghan was wrong, and he should know better. The more she thought about it, the more angry she got, and after Yen left, when it was nearly time to go, she marched up to his desk.

"He *isn't* courting me," she hissed at him.

Ghan looked up at her, his face registering puzzlement.

"What?" he asked mildly.

"I saw you look at us . . . at me."

The shadow of a smile fell across his lips. "I was angry because you were helping him," he said. "I have no great love for the priesthood, and *they* sent him here."

"Oh," she said, her voice suddenly very small.

"But now that you mention it, you do seem to *watch* him a lot . . ." Ghan observed thoughtfully.

"Well," Hezhi said, perhaps a bit defensively, "he just seems brighter than most people who come in here."

"*That's* true enough," Ghan remarked dryly, "though that is by no means an endorsement."

"No, I guess it isn't," she replied.

Ghan pursed his lips. "This Yen is not a bad sort, I suppose. The priesthood has always been a sore in my mouth, that's all, and anyone connected with them . . ."

"Like nobility?" Hezhi asked.

Ghan stopped, stared at her for an instant. "I suppose I am too obvious," he said. "One of these days I will go too far, and they will punish me."

"Ghan, I've never asked. What clan are you?"

Ghan puffed out a breath and regarded her for a long moment.

"Yehd Hekes," he said finally.

Hezhi frowned. "Yehd Hekes?"

"I don't have to repeat myself."

"I thought all of you were . . ."

Ghan rolled his eyes. "You know *everything*, don't you? Yes, they were all banished—but me. I had only to renounce my claim to nobility—*in* writing, *in* blood. So actually, I have no clan. No clan at all."

"Why? Why did you stay? As I understand it they were given estates in the south."

"Estates? Oh, yes," Ghan muttered. "A hundred leagues of cotton and not more than ten books *made* from it on the whole place. I couldn't leave this, girl."

"I'm sorry. Sorry I asked."

Ghan took up a blotting rag, patted at the sweat standing out on his forehead. He pursed his lips again and then shrugged, composed again. "You ask questions. That's what you do," he said. "That's not a bad thing." He leaned toward her, his voice suddenly low, conspiratorial. "Just be *very* careful what questions you ask of whom. Very careful, Hezhi. Royal Blood is no protection against Royal Blood." He settled back on his stool.

"Now," he said sternly, index finger extended. "I don't want to see you flirting in here again. This is a library, not a court. Now go home. I want to lock up, go to my rooms, and pour a glass of wine."

A FEW days later, she started bleeding again. She had cramps beforehand, and the experience was generally unpleasant, but the fever and sickness did not return. She was also depressed; Qey informed her that this was normal, but that didn't mean she had to like it. She also knew that her depression was not so simple as Qey might think. The return of her bleeding brought all of the questions she had—which now seemed so close to being answered—back to mock her, to frighten her. Her most terrible fear was that the priests would somehow know and return to examine her again. Though she still did not actually understand what they were trying to determine, a persistent logic—one that dated to D'en's disappearance—argued that she was in danger each time the priests examined her. She thought, now and then, about questioning someone who was not a servant, who might not have been Forbidden. Her sister, for instance, or her mother. Unfortunately, that seemed too dangerous, both to herself and to whomever she spoke with. Instead, she just thought a lot—and that depressed her. Once she even found herself standing on the roof of the Great Hall, contemplating the flagstones far below, as she had when she was younger. The temptation to jump was not very great, though she remembered that it once had been. It seemed like a long time since thoughts of suicide had crowded about in her head. Once they had seemed very real, insistent. But since her quest for D'en began, she rarely had time to indulge herself in such moods. For nearly three years she had devoted almost every waking moment to her inquiry, and perhaps that had saved her. It felt almost good now to stare down at the tiny people below, to think of a short, hurried flight to join them, of oblivion and peace. Nostalgic, indulgent, a waste of time, yet somehow satisfying. She did not jump, of course, and even Tsem—whom she knew was somewhere near, despite her halfhearted attempt to escape him for a moment—even Tsem did not seriously believe she would kill herself. It was just a game, a fantasy she had outgrown.

But still an option, she reminded herself. An alternative to D'en's fate, should it prove to be her own and as terrible as she imagined it. Rather fly from the roof than suffer passively whatever the priests might consign her to.

Tsem began going home a bit ahead of her, to make sure that the priests were not waiting for her again. It became their standard practice, her in the shadows of an abandoned hall, Tsem looking in and then coming back out to stretch if things inside were normal. It made her feel a bit better; at least she could decide whether she would submit to the demeaning, disgusting ritual again. She also began preparing for another trip beneath the palace. She squirreled away a bit of rope, made sure the lantern had oil in, got Tsem to find her some "suitable" clothes. Nothing he brought back satisfied until he returned with a little boy's work clothes from the docks: long pants spotted and gummed with tar and a matching shirt. They fit well enough, they were easy to move in, and they would protect her from abrasions and so forth. Nothing worn by the nobility would do that, since men and women both tended to wear skirts, kilts, or gowns. Hezhi would never have even thought of *pants*—very odd clothing, twin tubes made to cover the legs loosely—had it not been for Yen. Eager to know more about her gift, she had checked the index under "Mang" and found a small but fairly thorough treatise on them. They wore these "pants" because they were better suited to life in the saddle than anything that exposed the leg. Indeed, the word in Nholish for "pants" had been borrowed from Mang, she discovered.

She tried the clothes on at night, after Qey was asleep. Bad enough that she had involved Tsem in her madness, she would *not* have Qey know of it. They felt very odd on, snug in places clothing should not be snug. She tried to imagine herself astride a horse, the same wild expression on her face that the little horse-woman bore. She ended by giggling at herself, doffing the clothes and hiding them beneath her mattress, and going to sleep.

She dreamed, of course, the same dreams of forest. But in this one, for the first time, she saw a man. He was very strange in appearance, pale as linen, his hair a peculiar, impossible shade of brown. His eyes were stranger yet, gray, like the River in very early morning. She wondered if he was some sort of River-man, filled up with water. Her feeling that she had done something wrong redoubled, and for an instant, in her dream, she was standing in the Leng Hall, drinking the sacred water from the fountain, wishing for some hero to come and save her . . .

"I was sick," she found herself explaining to someone. "I didn't *mean* it."

"Well," a voice answered. "*Now* he is awake." And then she was, too, sweating in her bedclothes. It took her a long while to get back to sleep.

The next morning she rose, cross. She spoke barely a word to Qey or Tsem, set out for the library more than a little later than she wanted to. It was Wezh's misfortune that he chose that morning to meet her outside of the archive hall.

She clenched her teeth when she saw him, leaning against the wall, his lips moving.

"Probably reminding himself to breathe," she muttered to Tsem.

"The princess isn't feeling very *nice* this morning," Tsem observed from the corner of his mouth.

Hezhi tried to ignore Wezh, but he actually interposed himself, grinning his vacuous little grin.

"Good morning, Princess," he remarked brightly. "You look radiant this morning."

"Well, so do you," Hezhi answered, surveying his jaunty red hat, felted orange vest, and flower-stippled kilt. "Positively lovely."

"*Thank* you," he said, pretending to wave her compliment off. "I wonder if I could speak with you for just a moment. Ah, alone," he finished, eyeing Tsem significantly.

Hezhi sighed. "Could you give us a moment, Tsem?"

The half Giant shrugged his massive shoulders and moved off down the hall a short distance.

"My father—" Wezh began, stopped to dab his lips with a kerchief. "My father asked me to invite you to our rooms for dinner this evening," he said.

Hezhi blinked at him. "I'm afraid I can't do that," she replied, trying to be polite.

"Oh," Wezh said, a little perplexed frown on his face. "My man went to see your nurse—what's her name, Hay?—anyway, she said you should be free."

Hezhi trembled with sudden fury. This idiot had sent someone to talk to Qey? He had conspired to see her? She was suddenly sick to death of people arranging her life, planning it, plotting about it. It was as if something broke loose inside her, something red and hot scrambling up her from her gut and into her tongue.

"Darken your mouth!" she hissed. "Leave me alone, do you hear? *Do you hear?*" She felt a sort of shudder run along her bones, and though her clenched fists never left her sides, she had a sudden dizzying sensation that felt almost as if she had reached out and *slapped* the little fool. The most startling thing was that Wezh reacted exactly as if he *had* been slapped. He reeled into the wall, his eyes suddenly glazed, unfocused. Spit drooled down his chin.

"Leave me alone!" she repeated. Wezh sagged against the plastered stone, almost fell, and then suddenly ran, unsteadily at first but then with great enthusiasm. In an instant he was out of sight.

Hezhi stood there, astonished. Her body seemed to hum, to vibrate for just a bit longer, and then it was quiet, normal. But she had just done something, she knew. She had *done* something to Wezh, something more than simply yell at him.

She caught a motion from the corner of her eye and half turned. Tsem was goggling at her, and so was Yen, who must have just come around the corner. Yen averted his staring eyes, then looked back at her.

"What did you say to *him*?" he asked.

"I . . ." Hezhi looked back up the corridor, the way Wezh had run. "I guess it was the *way* I said it," she concluded.

X

The Heart of Water

Hezhi nudged Tsem with her toe; somewhere outside in the night a peacock called, half threat, half plaintive complaint.

"Tsem," she hissed. "I'm going."

The dark bulk rolled over, and large, sleepy eyes caught a ray of moonlight. "I thought we were done with this fumbling around in the darkness, Princess," he grumbled.

"Quiet. I don't want to wake Qey."

"I wish you could extend *me* the same courtesy," Tsem groused further. He rose, mountainous in the dark.

"I have everything right here," she assured him. "Just get dressed."

Tsem nodded and groped around a bit behind his bed. She couldn't make him out clearly, but the rustle of fabric suggested that he was complying with her command. When he stood up, she handed him the bundle in her hands. "Keep that upright," she warned. "The lantern is in there."

Tsem didn't answer, but shuffled quietly toward the door.

Once outside, he unpacked the lantern and lit it; it would be madness to try to trace even these familiar halls in total darkness. There were no fancy skylights or stained glass here in the old wing. The night sky entered this part of the palace only through the roofless courtyards, and the illumination of star- and moonlight did not diffuse far into the plastered halls.

Tsem's face appeared suddenly in the lamplight, thickened with shadows into the bust of some ancient monster. The monster grimaced and bared its teeth, and it took an instant or two for Hezhi to recognize the expression as a smile.

"Well, don't you look *fine*," Tsem whispered, squinting at her.

"I thought I would change before we went," she answered back.

Tsem nodded. "Well, you wanted to look like a boat caulker, and so you do."

"I need no advice on dressing from *you*," she replied loftily. "And we should go, before you have to explain to some soldier why you sneaked a little peasant girl into the palace."

"Never fear," Tsem replied. "They would never take you for a girl."

"Huh. Go!"

They threaded through the deserted halls. Hezhi knew where the guards would be, and fortunately they did not have to pass near any. Most, of course, were patrolling the roof, since that was the only sensible way a thief or assassin could break in from the city—should one manage to scale the palace wall, that is, no small feat in itself. Padding softly past a second and then a third suite of apartments, they came at last to the point she had marked on her map. Each major suite—such as her own—had its own courtyard and fountain to provide fresh water. Suites were arranged into compounds—there were seven suites in hers—and most compounds were built generally around a still larger courtyard. These larger courtyards were slightly downhill from the suites, so that waste water could flow through stone trenches to the "sink," a large opening in the center of the yard. Housekeepers brought other things to throw into the sink by hand: kitchen garbage, the contents of toilets, and so on. Hezhi's map showed the sink emptying into the sewers, where the sacred water recirculated, eventually to rejoin the River.

"Princess," Tsem began to protest, but she hissed him into silence.

"It's the best way," she explained.

"I shudder to think what the worst might be," Tsem glumly retorted.

"Hush. I'm a princess, and *I'm* going into it."

"Not if I don't *let* you," Tsem replied, a bit of the iron he was named for in his voice.

"Tsem. We *have* to do this. I have to know what the priests plan for me, and *you* can't tell me. So I have to see. Unless you know a better way, *this* is what we are going to do. Or I'll do it alone, if need be, one night while you're asleep. I thought our bargain was still good, or I wouldn't have awakened you."

Tsem was silent for a moment. "It's still good," he admitted.

"Then who goes first?"

"*I* will. What shall we fasten the rope to?"

"I thought of that," she replied proudly. She held up a poker stolen from near Qey's stove. "We'll tie the rope in the middle of this, brace it over the sink. Then we can pull it in after us, so no one will know."

"And does your plan explain how we'll get back up?"

Hezhi shrugged. "Throw it back up until it catches again."

Tsem sighed. "That will make a lot of noise. What if someone comes to investigate?"

"Then they do."

"Princess, *you* will not be the one flayed alive in the Great Hall."

"I'll tell them I thought some of my jewelry was thrown down here, accidentally, that I *made* you go after it. That should sound like something a princess might do."

Tsem heaved another sigh. "Unfortunately, it does," he agreed. "Hand me that thing." He passed her the lamp in trade.

The waste-water trenches were flagged over in the courtyard

itself, and they entered the drain just below the level of the yard. The sink, however, had a raised wall around it, to prevent young children from falling in. After placing the poker across the width of the opening, Tsem pulled himself up onto the wall, then, with another dubious glance at the forged iron, swung himself over the lip. Hezhi watched his head disappear, then leaned over the edge of the sink, holding the lantern out to give Tsem light to see by. She noticed that he didn't much trust the rope; he was descending more by bracing himself against the walls of the sink than by lowering himself. His body more or less blocked the shaft; she couldn't see around him to his eventual destination, though she had of course looked down it in the daytime. It hadn't seemed that deep then, but now Tsem seemed to be going down and down. As if night conspired with darkness to make the depth more profound.

Finally she heard a pair of splashes, and Tsem looked up, huge white teeth gleaming orange in the lamplight. "Lower the lantern." His voice floated up.

She grimaced. She hadn't thought of that. Impatiently she pulled up the rope, tied the lantern to it, and then lowered it back down to Tsem. She glanced around anxiously, worried that someone might have noticed them by now, but she saw no one in the faint moonlight. She climbed up onto the lip of the sink. Light flickered up from below. It was a weird sight, the deep, yellow hole with Tsem's shadowed face at the bottom of it. Taking a deep breath and a hold on the rope, she let her weight drag her over the edge.

The breath turned out to be a mistake, and she gagged audibly at the stench surrounding her. The smell at the lip of the sink was bad, but somehow the effect was different when one was suspended in its maw. And soon she would be wading in the source of that fetor! Nevertheless, she let herself down, depending, unlike Tsem, entirely upon the good intentions of the rope. True to her trust, the braided hemp did not fail, and Tsem's thick hands received her, lowered her gently into the noisome muck at his feet. She stared down, appalled, at the viscous liquid that stood up to her ankles. It was barely moving. That meant that the overflow from the fountains was not feeding this part of the sewer—confirming what her map said. Despite the horrible smell, Hezhi felt a little spark of elation. It was real; the things she had worked out on paper, in the library—they were *real*.

"Move up the tunnel a bit, Princess, so I can pull the rope down."

She complied, taking the lamp back from Tsem and stepping out from under the sink, farther down the sewer duct itself. Behind her she heard Tsem cursing as he yanked this way and that trying to dislodge the bar braced across the opening. Meanwhile, she examined the sewer.

It was not as large as she expected. She had to stoop a bit in it, which meant that Tsem would have to go on all fours. It was plenty wide enough for either of them, however. Tsem would not get lodged in it, like a stopper in a bottle.

Behind her, Tsem's low curses were punctuated by a sharper one, as the poker finally fell and presumably hit him.

"Tsem? Are you all right?"

"Oh, I *will* be, Princess, as soon as I'm down on my knees in this muck."

Hezhi stifled a giggle. "Sorry, Tsem."

"You carry the lantern, Princess," he replied dolefully. She nodded and began making her way down the low passage, in the direction of the water flow.

Fortunately for Tsem, it wasn't long before they joined a larger tunnel. They passed beneath another sink, and after that the duct sloped more steeply downward, flowing into a central passage. This was vaulted, easily rising high enough for Tsem to stand upright. Hezhi had read that these larger tunnels were designed to return vast amounts of water to the river in the event of a flood. The passage seemed capable of that to her, being easily as wide as one of the halls in the palace. Better yet, the edges of the passage were raised above the channel of the sewer itself, making it possible to avoid actually being in the water. This was fortunate; she couldn't tell how deep the channel was, but she suspected that it would be over her head. A constant sound of trickling water surrounded them, fountain overflow joining the stream. Unlike the first, narrow shaft, here the water was actually flowing with some force.

"Which way now?" Tsem asked from behind her.

"Left," she replied. She had memorized as much of her map as possible to avoid having to consult it constantly.

The ledge was comfortably broad, even for Tsem. At his insistence, he went first. Hezhi began to protest, but at the limits of the lantern light she noticed something that changed her mind: a plethora of minuscule lights, the shining eyes of rats staring at the lantern. She relinquished the light to her bodyguard, and they continued on.

The larger tunnels were less noisome than their entryway. The air moved a bit more readily here, helped by the sinks and storm drains they occasionally passed beneath. Twice they heard people near these openings, conversing about this or that, and she felt a little thrill of excitement. It was like being invisible, able to see and hear others but not noticeable herself. In fact, however, she realized that they were in a great deal of danger of being detected, if anyone happened to be glancing down one of the shafts when the light of the lantern passed beneath them. But this didn't happen, and her fantasy of invisibility remained intact.

"We'll enter the Second-Dynasty sewers soon," she whispered excitedly to Tsem. "They are below these and lie atop the buried city."

"Second-Dynasty sewers," Tsem grumbled. "My heart is filled with joy."

Up ahead, water muttered angrily, cascading more loudly than the constant background gurgle of inflow through the small ducts. The crashing increased as they approached it, and soon the two stood peering down into the depths of yet another hole. This one was very large, white limestone blocks set along its rim. The stone below it was limestone, as well, but it was a different color, seemed older somehow.

"See?" Hezhi commented. "This hole was cut down to the old system. Everything below this is Second Dynasty or older."

Tsem just sighed and uncoiled the rope, keeping any further comments to himself. The cataracts fell downward perhaps fifteen feet. There was nothing to brace their trusty poker against— the hole was much too wide. Tsem cast about for something to tie the rope to. He stopped when Hezhi tapped him on the arm.

"What?" he asked. She pointed.

"Engineers have to come down here periodically to make sure nothing important has collapsed," she explained. "We don't need a rope."

A series of steel spikes were driven into the side wall of the shaft. They were almost certainly intended to be used as a ladder.

"Ah," Tsem replied. He approached the spikes, reached down, and grasped one. He pushed hard on it, gradually shifting his full weight to bear upon it. The spike remained firm.

"Seems sturdy enough," he commented, and after a slight hesitation, he began clambering down the questionable ladder. He yelped when the fifth spike down tore from the stone under his enormous weight, but maintained his hold.

"Several of them are loose now," he called back up, when he had reached the landing at the base of the wall. "The stone is more rotten the farther down you go."

"I'll be careful," Hezhi promised. In a few moments she stood on the landing next to the half Giant.

"Well," she said, scanning what she could see in the lamplight. "Second-Dynasty sewers look remarkably like Third-Dynasty sewers."

"I have no opinion," Tsem commented, "lacking your informed judgment."

The lower tunnels were a bit narrower than the upper, and now and then the two were forced to leap crumbled places in the ledge. More often, they were forced to step over side passages en-

tering the channel. Many of these seemed absolutely still and
stagnant. Hezhi gave out a little gasp when she saw something up
one of them, something large, moving beneath the surface, visible
only by its ripples.

After that they saw ghosts, many of them. Most were as insubstantial as the one in her room, points in the atmosphere that
caught the lamplight and twisted it up. The majority fled from
their lamp, though a few more curious ones actually approached.
There was one, however, that seemed quite solid. It was a man—
she could tell *that* much—and he stayed just ahead of them, at
the fringes of illumination. The dark hollows of his eyes were unreadable, but Hezhi still had the impression of intense concentration, as if the ghost were studying them in some way.

"If we meet a *real* ghost down here," Tsem muttered, "like the
one in the Hall of Moments . . ." He did not finish.

"I have part of a broom," Hezhi whispered.

"What?" Tsem turned to face her, his eyes wide, shocked.

"I took part of an old broom from one of the shrines," she
explained.

"You *stole* from the priesthood?"

"Well," she considered, "I don't know that *stealing* is the right
word."

"I don't believe this." Tsem sighed. "My days are certainly
numbered."

"Hush, Tsem. Besides, I did a bit of research on ghosts. Monsters like the one in the Hall of Moments are rare and usually
asleep. Hopefully we won't wake any."

"Hopefully." Tsem snorted.

Whatever strange, dead thoughts their onlooker might enter-
tain, he continued to back away from them, made no move to
attack.

Not much farther along, the passage suddenly widened, and
they found themselves crossing a room. The channel cut on
through, and they could easily see, across the room, that the tunnel continued on. Above them the roof rose perhaps a span more

than the roof of the sewer, and it was vaulted. In the dirty stone they could see numerous cracks, and a dense mass of gnarled and groping tendrils punched through the fractures.

"Roots," Hezhi remarked. "We must be beneath one of the gardens."

"What is this? This looks like some of the buried rooms we used to explore under the old palace."

"It's the same architecture," she replied.

"I thought the buried city—First Dynasty—was still below us."

"This is an upper story," she answered smugly. She indicated a stairway in the corner of the room, leading down. "That's how we'll get down to the buried palace."

"Right here?"

"No, this isn't the right place. At least, I don't think it is." She took out her map and unfurled it in the lamplight.

"No," she said. "I've been counting side passages. We have to cross six more."

"Did you count the one that was filled in?" Tsem asked.

"Yes." Hezhi nodded.

They went on, counting six more tributary ducts. Their companion remained with them, gazing hollowly from the shadows.

"The next room, then," she whispered. Her skin was beginning to tingle with a strange sort of exhilarating fear. A few more paces, and they passed into another upper-story room.

She located the stairway easily enough, splashing across the water standing on the floor.

"This is it," she breathed.

"I will go first here," Tsem stated. It was not a question.

"Good enough, Tsem," she agreed.

The stair was slick, with a fine coating of mud, but unlike the rooms under the abandoned wing, it was clear of substantial debris. Water stood in the room, as well, but they discovered it to be only a few feet deep—to Tsem's knees and Hezhi's waist.

Even Tsem recognized the place, despite the outdated architecture.

"This is a shrine," he muttered, taking in the thin, decorative columns, the inoperative fountain choked with stagnant water, the faded glyphs on the walls.

"Yes," she confirmed. "A First-Dynasty shrine. You see? That is the royal seal of the Chakunge."

"The seal is much larger here. I've never seen it so prominent in the shrines above."

"Back then the Chakunge was the First Priest, as well," Hezhi explained.

"I thought he still was."

She shook her head. "Only symbolically. In the First Dynasty, there was no Priestfather. Everything flowed from the Chakunge. After the war of priests, the priesthood and the emperor became divided."

"I've never heard of any 'war of priests,' " Tsem said.

"No. It isn't much talked about," she told him.

"So now where to? I don't see any exits."

Indeed, the exits from the room had been walled up, precisely similar to many of the chambers they had encountered a few years before.

"Oh," Hezhi said. "This won't get us where we are going. I needed to see this shrine to mark my place and to learn a bit more."

"About what?"

"I think the glyphs in here may tell me some things I need to know."

"Ah."

"Here, let me have the lantern." She took the light source over near the sacred pool and began studying the glyphs there.

"Tsem," she said after a moment, "go count the number of treads in the stairway for me."

"What? Why, Princess?"

"It's important."

Tsem sighed and began sloshing toward the stair. Hezhi took

her opportunity, knowing she had to hurry before Tsem caught on. The lip of the sacred well was above the waterline; she set the lantern down on that and scrambled onto it herself. From there she was able to reach the narrow duct that once fed the pool. Heart pounding, she grasped the slippery lip of the tube and began pulling herself up. Her arms seemed absurdly weak—she had only managed to get her elbows inside the duct before Tsem cried out behind her.

"Princess!" he yelped, and she heard a great splashing as he slogged across the room toward her. She wriggled desperately, abdominal muscles clenched, heaving herself into the tube. Everything in it was slimy, offering no purchase. In one frantic heave she got inside up to her belly, braced her arms, and wriggled farther in. Strong fingers clutched at her foot. She kicked wildly, worming away from Tsem's grip and farther into the dark shaft.

"Princess," Tsem repeated, the sound of his voice muffled by her body. The tube was narrow enough that she could not quite get to her knees, and so she effectively blocked it.

"I'm sorry, Tsem," she called back, hoping he could hear. Her voice rang weirdly, right in her ears but also humming down the endless duct. "I'm sorry, but you can't fit in here, and it's the only way. I knew you wouldn't let me go alone."

"Nonsense," she heard him say. "But come back out here for the light."

In response, she drew out the tiny oil lamp she had concealed in her bag. Calmly she checked the wick to make certain it was still soaked with oil. Resting on her elbows, she also drew out a small packet of four matches, sealed in waxed paper. She struck one match against another and lit the lamp.

"You *knew* about this," Tsem howled, stamping about in the water. "You *planned* it."

"I *had* to, Tsem," she called back.

"Princess, *please*," Tsem begged.

"Wait for me, Tsem," she said. "I'll be back." Holding the little lamp in front of her, she began to crawl with her elbows.

The shaft was not exactly dry, but it was at least not full of water, either. She was grateful, once again, for the clothing Tsem had acquired for her; her elbows hurt already but she could imagine how badly they would be scraped if they were bare. Too, she could comfort herself with the thought that the slime that now darkened almost every inch of her was not, for the most part, on her skin. She sighed as Tsem continued to yell after her. The tube had the unfortunate quality of conducting sound undiminished. In fact, she remembered reading of priests using the tubes to talk to one another, communicating between shrines without need of actually sending a messenger.

Though she fought the sensation, Hezhi quickly felt hemmed in. The realization that she could not rise up, even to a crouch, was accompanied by the overwhelming desire to *do* so. Her breath became rapid, and she tried to move along more quickly, as if racing with her lungs. Images of the tube being blocked at the other end kept coming into her mind. Then she would be forced to *back* out, something she was not certain was possible. She began to tremble. What was she doing? This was insane! The shaft was becoming smaller as she went along!

The air seemed bad, too, thick, and her lungs had no room to fill completely.

Hezhi was close—*very* close—to screaming when she finally saw the end of the duct. She scrambled toward it so frantically that she extinguished the lamp. She did not stop to relight it, but wriggled on and on, until at last her head emerged into a larger space. There she gasped, drawing deep, full breaths, trying to calm down. She relit the lamp with her last two matches.

She knew where she should be, but this was another instance of paper not preparing one for reality.

The ancient Grand Hall was still magnificent. Even with water standing deep on its floor, even with piles of rubble sloping down from the walls, it was awesome. The ceiling arched up, its roof unreachable by her tiny light. Thick, ornate pillars rose to help the buttresses in the corner support that vast midnight, strips of gold and lapis here and there glittering dully beneath coats of muck. The Chakunge's dais was a many-tiered pyramid, rising above the water, still impressive in ruin. At each corner of each step crested an alabaster wave, frozen forever in the act of curling back down to the River. The tube opened above the first step emerging from the unrippling *real* water that filled the cavern. Carefully, quietly, she lowered herself onto the dais. She took up her little lamp.

"I'm here, D'en," she whispered. "Where are you?"

Her voice trembled in the magnificent abyss.

XI

~~~~~~

The Cursed

PERKAR awoke to morning light. He had been dreaming of the city and the girl, of the River. He was cold.

A chill mist was settling down from the hills; a few birds were chattering in the trees. Perkar was thirsty, his mouth as dry as cotton. He felt for his waterskin and found it, drained what remained there. The water burned terribly going down, and then he remembered his throat, reached up to feel for the hole. There was much blood there, clotted and congealed, but the wound had closed.

"One heartstring left. You are a lucky man."

"I don't feel lucky," he tried to mutter, but only a strangling noise emerged from his throat. The dead lioness lay across most of his body, and she was heavy. It took much wriggling and squirming to extract himself. Her weight had shoved the arrow in his chest all the way through, and so saved him the effort of doing it himself. He reached back and grasped it on the shaft below the protruding head and pulled it on out. The one in his ribs he was able to extract more easily; the hauberk had all but stopped it.

Removing his armor was actually more painful than extracting the arrows; many of the bright rings were crusted to his rapidly healing wounds, which began bleeding afresh as he removed the ruined hauberk. Freed of that, he felt a bit better; lighter anyway. One heartstring left.

"Surely she knew," he gasped, managing a faint whisper this time.

"Who knows? Gods can be fully as careless as mortals. Perhaps she did not know me."

"Should she have?"

"She has never wielded me or met me in battle."

Grimacing with a hundred pains, Perkar staggered to his feet, leaned against a scrubby tree for support. Mang—or what the wolves had left of Mang—lay not far away. He wondered why they had not eaten him, as well. Apad had not been spared that fate; Perkar could see his savaged body a few strides away, along with the two Bear-Men he had killed. Three dead wolves and the lioness were the only other testimony to their battle.

The sword Apad had been wielding lay near him, quiet now. For a moment, Perkar considered taking it; it seemed in many ways more powerful than the one he bore. But it hadn't saved Apad, and the jade sword had saved him, for better or worse. He arranged the curved blade on Apad's chest and left it there, regretting he had no time to bury his friend. He had to go, though. He might still be of some use to the Kapaka. He did spare the time to sing the "Ghost Homecoming Song" for Apad. He burned the last of his incense while singing; some for Apad, some for Mang, and after a moment's hesitation, some for his slain enemies.

> Return to Your Mountain
> Ani Waluka, Rutkirul,
> Lioness.
> Don new armor

Walk forth anew
We may meet again
As friends . . .

Feeling a bit stronger, he turned and, for the second time, began
ascending the last ridge before the River, following the tracks of
the hunt.

Perkar found the Alwat at the top of the hill where he had left
them. They had acquitted themselves well, armed only with cane
spears. He wished he could have seen them fight. Five dead
wolves were mute testimony to their determination. Digger lay
curled around her torn throat, one hand still grasping her spear;
the other end of it was fixed in the mouth of a wolf; the point
emerged at the base of its skull. Inexplicably, tears started in his
eyes, though years later he could not explain why he chose *that*
moment to cry and not one earlier or later. He sank to his knees,
sobbing. For himself, he supposed, for Digger, for Apad, for the
nameless woman back in the cave.

Still blinking back tears, Perkar started down the slope. Gravel
and scrub soon gave way to sloping expanses of red, sandy rock.
It was, in fact, a plateau of solid stone, though soil filled low
places and creases in it, giving tenuous purchase to the roots of
short thick pines and cedars. Occasional deeper depressions held
horsetails and willow, small wet islands of green amidst the rust.

Even on stone, the tracks of the hunt were clear, scratches in
the rock, the shed hair of beasts, a stray arrow here and there.
He strained his senses for some audible sign of the hunt or his
companions, but, try as he might, he heard nothing save the
wind; the world seemed all silence and blue sky, the clouds and
thunder that rode with the hunt now flown far away.

At least he had seen no other Human bodies. The rest of the
expedition had made it this far. He suddenly wondered if he had
lain as dead for a single night or many. He asked the sword.

"Two nights. This is the third day since your battle."

Then his remaining companions were dead or escaped, probably the former. But surely he would find their bodies; the Huntress had not made trophies of Apad or himself.

It took longer than he thought it would to reach the gorge, and there he found Eruka. The flaxen-haired singer stared up at the sky with empty eye sockets, his mouth slack. The godsword was still clutched in his hand. There were two dead wolves nearby, and much blood on the stones. Tracks led to the edge of the gorge.

The Changeling had cut deep into the stone, deep indeed, and the striated walls of the ravine were sheer and unforgiving. There was no path down that he could see, only the precipice. Steeling himself, Perkar gazed over the rim and thus saw the Changeling for the first time outside of a dream.

It both did and did not resemble his visions. Even in the sunlight, the River appeared cold, shadowed, the color of a killer's gray-eyed glance. Fast-flowing, gnawing eternally at the stone, he hissed hungrily between close walls. He was not huge or wide here—not the horizon-spanning monster of Perkar's nightmares—but for being this close to his *source*, the Changeling was broad indeed, a faint but certain promise of the River by the white city.

How had his companions gotten down? The hunt *must* have stopped here, and Ngangata and the Kapaka were yet unaccounted for. They had to have descended to the River. He peered over the edge, puzzled. There were no hidden paths there, no switchback trails in the absolute verticality of the walls.

Then he saw it, on a sandbar, his explanation. The carcass of a horse. He shook his head, trying to deny what should have been obvious. A slight ticking on the stone alerted him, and he turned at the sound.

A man stood there, naked save for a long cloak of black feathers that fell from about his shoulders to midcalf. His skin was whiter than bone, where it showed. Luminous black eyes watched Perkar from beneath beetled, ebony brows and an unruly mop of hair, also black.

"I know you," Perkar whispered, drawing his sword.

"And I know you," Karak answered, his thin lips parting in a grin. "The Huntress believed you dead, but I knew better."

"Why?"

"Why, why? Mortals and gods alike ask that question more often than I care to hear it. I let you live because I like pretty things."

"You think me pretty?" Perkar asked incredulously. He tried to imagine what he might look like now, encrusted in ten kinds of gore, the blanched puckers and slashes of unnaturally healing wounds, his matted and stinking hair.

Karak smirked. "No. But that fight—you and that other Human, charging down on the hunt, killing the Huntress' own mount—*that* was a *very* pretty thing. A shame if no one survived to polish such a gem."

"I don't know that I believe you," Perkar said, keeping the sword up and steady. A hard gust of wind enfolded them, flapping Karak's long Crow-feather cloak, bathing Perkar's bare torso in coolness. "I saw you kill Apad."

"So I did. After all, you couldn't be allowed to *win*. But you— you should have been dead, little mortal. Even now I see your one heartstring—such a thin little thing. I'm afraid the Changeling will eat even that, if you go down to him."

"What happened to my friends?"

"The other Humans? They flew into his clutches. That was a pretty thing, too; I came to tell you about it."

"Did any of them live?"

"All but this one," Karak said, indicating Eruka, and Perkar's heart soared for an instant, until the Crow God's meaning came clear.

"All but this one; he did not fly. He stood here on the edge and waited for us. He was frightened, but less frightened of us than the edge."

"The others?"

Karak cocked his head, pointed to the base of a tree. A broken rope was tied to it.

"He stretched that rope between these trees; we did not see it, for his sword was blazing. Two wolves and a huntsman we lost, for they tripped on the rope and tumbled over the edge."

"I'm proud of him. I wish he had killed more. But what of my other friends?"

"They flew over the edge when we approached."

"They jumped, you mean."

"That isn't as pretty."

"Are they dead? All dead?" It seemed incredible that anyone could survive such a fall.

Karak shrugged, a slight movement. "I don't know. Shall we see?"

"What do you mean?"

"I can take you to the bottom of the gorge; no farther. Even I fear the Brother."

"You? Who swallowed the sun?" Perkar asked sarcastically.

"The Changeling can swallow much more than that," Karak replied softly.

Karak drew the cloak more tightly about himself, as if he were cold, and shivered in the way of gods. In an instant he was a Raven again, huge, his gleaming beak a reminder of Apad's fate. Perkar considered trying to avenge his friend, but it was a thin thought, an obligatory one that sank away into his confusion and weariness. After all, he had already died for honor once, more or less, and killed for it, too. If Karak wanted to help him, no matter how whimsical his reason, Perkar would be a fool to spurn him.

Karak flapped into the air, took a hold on Perkar's shoulders in precisely the way he had taken on Apad, before pecking into his brains.

"Best that you grip my legs," Karak said, "else I will have to dig into your shoulders too hard with my claws."

Perkar acknowledged with a nod, reached around the scaly bird legs, wrapping his arms so that both his hands and the crook of his elbow held him there. Nevertheless, when the Crow God flapped again and they took to the air, his claws bit uncomfortably into Perkar's flesh.

They floated lazily down into the gorge, Karak's wings popping and snapping in the air. The Raven hugged close to the sheer stone, intent, it seemed, on not flying over the surface of the River. He deposited Perkar on a narrow shingle of gravel and fallen stone.

"I don't see your friends," he said. "But perhaps they are here. I can see nothing, this close to the River."

Indeed, Karak seemed somehow paler, his feathers less lustrous. As Perkar watched, a few actually faded to a dull gray.

"You see? This is what you wanted to battle, Perkar. Even asleep, he already begins to eat at *me*." The Crow hesitated and cocked his head to the side. "But a battle *is* coming, Perkar," he hissed softly. "A war of gods and men. You would be wise to choose the right side."

"A war?" Perkar grunted. "I'll have no more of that."

"You have no choice, pretty thing." Karak stretched his wings and beat once more at the air. His flight seemed labored, but the higher he flew, the more dextrous he became.

Perkar frowned at his retreating form. "Thank you," he called out. "But how did you know my plan to fight the Changeling?"

Karak uttered a short, harsh laugh. "With which of these did the Forest Lord arm himself against his *Brother*?" he called, in the mocking voice of the Lemeyi.

For an instant, Perkar's dulled brain did not understand, then fury stabbed through the fog.

"You!" he shrieked. "That was *you*."

"Indeed," came the diminishing voice of the Raven. "And you have everything you desired. Your enemy at hand and a weapon to kill him with. Good luck to you, Perkar. I will send you one last gift . . ."

And, despite Perkar's curses and imprecations, he was gone and did not return.

P ERKAR sat on the shingle until the sun westered and the long shadow of the gorge consumed him. Then, not knowing what else to do, he rose stiffly to his feet and began to walk along the narrow shore, downstream. He passed the sandbar, where the corpse of the horse lay, bloated and covered with flies. He recognized it, of course; the Kapaka's horse. Reluctantly Perkar waded out to it, sinking up to his waist. The water felt like any water he had ever been in, save for a faint cold tingling that might have been the result of his exhaustion. Two days' sleep, it seemed, were not enough to heal such grievous wounds as his without cost.

The horse stank terribly, but Perkar managed to free the packs that still remained upon it. He found full waterskins (he did not trust the River) and some food, the latter miraculously still dry in its resin-impregnated sack. These he took, along with a single bar of incense and a flask of woti, presumably one of the gifts the Kapaka had been saving for the Forest Lord. He trembled as he took them, remembering the dream he had shattered, the misfortune he had brought to his people, grandchildren who would not see their grandfather again. The Kapaka was dead at heart before the hunt came after them, dead the moment the Forest Lord revoked his offer of new lands.

My king is dead, he realized, and his knees buckled, betrayed him into the cold River water. This was what it had all come to. A strange, new kind of panic came over him, a lucid surge of horror. Since Apad had killed the guardian, everything had seemed a terrible dream, the sort one could never run fast enough in. Now the running was done, the nightmare over, and he awoke to find it all true, morning without light or comfort.

He had not merely led his friends to their deaths, not merely thwarted his king's wishes; he had destroyed the Kapaka, *killed* him.

For the first time since leaving his father's valley, he felt the eyes of his people fasten on him, accusing. He had felt them before, but then they looked upon him with amusement, with disdain at worst, seeing a "man" without a wife, without lands, without Piraku.

Now they saw a monster. His father, his mother, his brother, his grandfather, his honored ancestors—even they saw him so, the man who had killed the king, and more. For in killing the Kapaka, he might have killed his people. If the Forest Lord was now their enemy . . .

They had been fools. *He* had been so much worse than a fool. No weapon could cut the Forest Lord, no host could stand before the hunt. If his people marched against Balati—for revenge, for territory—they would be swept away like autumn leaves before a whirlwind.

Because of me.

He thrashed about in the shallows, searching for the king's body, for anything. For something to *save*. But he knew, even as he thrust numb fingers against the rocky bottom, knew that the Changeling had taken *his* share, too, taken the Kapaka to make pebbles of his bones and fish of his flesh. Taken even that.

So Perkar continued on, stumbling, almost blind with remorse.

It was nearly dark when he saw the spark of flame ahead, and the only hope he had felt since meeting Karak quickened his pace. The wind shifted his way, and he smelled burning juniper. It seemed delicious to him, more desirable than any food. When he got closer, he could see a Human form huddled near the fire, eyes reflecting the flames as they watched him approach.

"Ngangata!" Perkar called. An arm raised weakly, waving.

"I THINK you *did* slow them down," Ngangata told him, his voice scratchy and weak. "For what it was worth. It is good that Apad died well." He seemed genuine.

"I should have died, too."

Ngangata did not respond to that. "The Huntress was dismounted," he said, after coughing a bit. "You must have killed her lion."

Perkar twitched his lip. "My sword did."

Ngangata nodded. "Well. We could have all had swords like that, and it would have made no difference. You and Apad did

well. It was *my* mistake. I meant to bring us out farther upstream, where the river-wall is lower."

"*Your* fault?" Perkar declared incredulously. "Apad and Eruka
and I broke the trust. *We* stole the weapons, killed their guardian.
You have done nothing but try to salvage something from the tatters we left you. Nothing here is *your* fault, Ngangata. I only wish
you had killed me, back in that cave where we fought."

Ngangata coughed raggedly. "That might have been best," he
agreed. "Apad and Eruka would have never had the courage to
enter the mountain by themselves."

"I know that. Why *didn't* you beat me when we fought? You
could have, and I deserved it."

Ngangata looked dully up at Perkar. "Do you know how
many times I have had to fight because of what I am? Seven days
haven't gone by since childhood without some loudmouth chal-
lenging me. In my youth, I always fought to win, and I usually
did." He gazed out across the River. "I believed that someday
men would respect me, if not *like* me. But when I beat them, it
was never said that I was fast, or strong, or brave. Always it was
said I won because I was not Human, a beast. When men say
things like that, they talk themselves into doing things they
wouldn't ordinarily do."

"What do you mean?"

"Years ago, a man—never mind his name—I fought him,
much as I fought you. But I beat him, in front of his friends.
Later that night they all came for me, battered me senseless. I
was lucky to survive."

Even in his present state, Perkar was shocked. "No warrior
would ever do such a cowardly thing." He gasped. "Piraku . . ."

"Does *not* apply to one such as myself," Ngangata said dryly.

Perkar, ready to continue his protest, stopped. The Kapaka
had said nearly the same thing. And if Perkar had been humili-
ated by Ngangata, what would Apad have said? He would have
asserted precisely what Ngangata claimed—that the half Alwa
had an unfair advantage over Humans.

"I see," Perkar said instead. "Yes, I can see that."

Ngangata waved his hand. "It's an old story," he said, dismissing the matter.

Darkness fell complete, though after a time the Pale Queen peeped over the canyon rim. Frogs sang in the River, and the two men huddled closer to the fire as mosquitoes tried to drain what was left of their blood.

"I'm glad you lived," Perkar said, after a time. "But the king . . . ?"

"The Kapaka is dead," Ngangata replied. "He hit the rocks and the River took him. I think he was dead even as we jumped; one of the Huntress' arrows pierced him."

"I found his horse," Perkar told him, feeling his throat tighten as he said it. "I've got some water and food."

"Good. We'll need those."

"The Kapaka . . ." Perkar gasped, choking back a groan, his odd panic suddenly intensified.

"Many died," Ngangata answered him. "We survived. That is a fact."

"He was not *your* king," Perkar hissed.

"No. He was much more than that to me," Ngangata shot back wearily.

Perkar stared at the glimmer in Ngangata's eyes and wondered what he meant, what lay there behind the black orbs.

"I'm sorry," he said finally. "I don't know you at all, Ngangata." He shifted, peered more closely at his companion. "What wounds do *you* have?"

Reluctantly the half man pulled his shift aside. A bloody bandage covered his ribs. "An arrow there," he said. "And my right leg is broken. Not bad for an encounter with the Huntress and a fall down a canyon."

A sudden inspiration struck Perkar. "Take this sword," he said. "It can heal you."

"*No,*" said the voice in his ear. "*Saving you bound our heart-strings together. I explained that. No one else can bear me unless those strings are severed, and that, of course, would kill you.*"

Ngangata saw the look of consternation cross his face.

"What is it?" he asked.

"My sword speaks to me," Perkar told him hesitantly. "It says it can heal only *me*."

Ngangata lifted his shoulders, attempting a shrug. "No matter," he said. "I will heal. My leg is splinted already, and the bleeding from the arrow has stopped."

Perkar doubted that last; he had seen the flecks of blood when Ngangata coughed. He did not mention this, however.

"Tomorrow I will hunt for us, or fish perhaps," Perkar told him. "When you can walk, we will strike off down-River."

"If you are hunting, we will certainly starve," Ngangata replied, but he smiled a bit.

"An insult!" Perkar returned, with a forced playfulness no more real than the love of a corpse. "Now we shall have to fight again." He tried to grin.

"This time I *will* kill you," Ngangata replied, in kind.

His smile was cruelly painful, and so Perkar relinquished it. "You were the best of us, Ngangata. We shall never fight again." He reached over and grasped the other man's hand. Ngangata returned the grip; it was still surprisingly strong. The strength seemed to leak out of it, though, and the pale man sank back onto his rough pallet of reeds, eyes closing gently. Perkar's heart caught in his throat.

"Ngangata!" he cried, reaching for the man's neck to seek his pulse.

"Let me sleep," Ngangata whispered. "I need some sleep."

Perkar sat with him, occasionally touching the body to make sure it was still warm. "I want you to live," he told the sleeping man.

T HE gorge walls kept the sun from waking Perkar until late morning. He rubbed his eyes and wondered where he was. The swiftly flowing River reminded him, and he turned anxiously to Ngangata. His companion was still asleep, but a brief touch was enough to assure him that Ngangata was still alive. He rose and stretched in the sunlight, feeling better than he had in some time. Surprisingly, his sleep had been untroubled by dreams. Perhaps the Changeling ate those, too.

Waking was more painful; the Changeling apparently feasted neither on memory nor on guilt.

He set about trying to make good on his promise to find food. He was ravenous, and yet the hunger was pleasing, as if he were a shell filled only with air and light.

He fashioned a gig with his boot-knife and the slender branch of a willow, lashing the knife on with a length of leather lace. Crouched by the River, he waited for a fish to come by. He waited a long time before he saw something moving along, something broad and fish-shaped. He set his mouth in anticipation, and when the creature swam beneath his spear, he stabbed downward with it, felt the point plunge into flesh. With a flourish and a cry, he heaved the fish up onto the bank, where it flopped about wildly.

It was a strange fish, the like of which he had never seen, plated with armor. Still, it would certainly be edible . . . Perkar watched in shocked wonder as the fish suddenly collapsed in upon itself, became a stream of water, and flowed back into the River. A tingle ran up the nape of his neck as he fully recalled where he was. This was the Changeling, and nothing was what it seemed here, where water could dream of being a fish.

He speared five of the ghost fish before finally skewering one that fell out on the bank and stayed there. Unlike the others— which had all been unfamiliar in appearance—this was a trout, and a large one. Disquieted by the new revelation regarding the River, but still happy to have caught something to eat, he stirred up their small fire, added a few branches to it, and gutted the fish. He was just propping their soon-to-be meal above the flames when something on the River caught his peripheral vision.

There was a boat coming downstream. Perkar blinked at it for a moment and then, with a wild cry, plunged into the water. In

an instant he was over his head, and he thanked the Stream Goddess that he had learned to swim as a child. Stroking frantically,
he strained to intercept the craft before it whisked past him. He
needn't have worried; the boat nudged into him, as if by a will
of its own. Throwing his arms up over the sides, he pulled himself in.

It was a fine craft, shallow draft, a dugout that must have been
hewn from an outrageously large tree, so broad and steady it
was. Perkar scrambled back to the tiller, took hold of it, and
pointed the bow toward shore. The boat responded as if it were
being paddled, actually cutting a wave across the current as it
glided sedately to the rocky beach. Perkar remembered Karak's
parting words, his promise of a last gift. This was certainly it.
Perkar doubted that god-made boats were often found wandering
masterless, even on the Changeling.

He secured the boat as best he could to one of the few willows
on the shore, then walked back upstream. He found Ngangata
awake—probably roused by his frantic cries—and tending the
fish.

"I take back what I said," Ngangata confessed. "You have
caught two fish today."

Perkar smiled weakly, indicating the boat. "A gift from the
Crow God, I think."

"From the Raven," Ngangata corrected. "The Crow God gives
nothing away."

"There are two of them? Two Karakal?"

Ngangata snorted. "No."

Perkar thought he understood, but he was weary of gods, sick
to death of them, and did not feel like perfecting his knowledge
of them any more.

"Are the walls of the canyon lower farther down?"

"Lower and more sloped, perhaps a day or so downstream,"
Ngangata acknowledged. "There will be rapids between here and
there."

"Should we wait until you are stronger?"

Ngangata shook his head. "We should go now. If the Raven knows we are here, the Crow does, as well, and one can never be sure where which Karak will be at any moment. Better to leave Balat behind."

"I agree with *that*," Perkar conceded. "We'll eat, and then we'll go."

As it turned out, it was nearly dark before they set out; Ngangata's dressing needed changing; Perkar went back upstream to salvage the leather from the harness and saddle of the dead horse. Ngangata claimed that it would be many days before they reached any Human settlements, and they would need everything they could carry with them. Perkar wished desperately that he had taken more from Mang, but his own pack was all he had; there were some useful things in it: sinew, whetstone, a firemaking kit, but no food. Perkar wondered aloud what would happen to them if they had to drink River water. Ngangata pointed out that they could drink from streams that fed the Changeling, for they would be innocent of weirdness until they joined him.

Like the goddess, Perkar thought.

When they did put out into the River, Perkar felt a return of his earlier depression. Ngangata, exhausted by even a little labor, fell asleep quickly, leaving him alone with the slowly appearing stars, with the lapping of water at the bow. The lapping of his enemy. It was a quiet moment, even within him. The terrible raging of his mind was calmer, replaced by melancholy, by reflection. It occurred to Perkar that he had ruined the Kapaka's expedition and gotten everyone but Ngangata killed so that he could reach this River and challenge it. Now that he was here, probably less than a day from the Changeling's source, he was timidly *fleeing* it. If it weren't for Ngangata . . .

Then what? Perhaps better to perish at least attempting that for which he had sacrificed so much than to return with the shame that would follow him home. He had killed his king and perhaps ruined his people. His only hope was to die well, like Apad and Eruka.

But he would not have Ngangata killed, not him, too. No one else should suffer for his destiny. Idly, Perkar drew his sword, laid it across his knees.

"Can you see the Changeling's heartstrings?" he asked it.

"They are faint, far upstream. I can see them."

"Are they many?"

"Seven times seven," the sword replied.

"But he sleeps. How many could I sever before he awakens?"

"Many, perhaps. Not enough."

Perkar knit his brows in frustration. Would he ever be this close again? How often did the River sleep, present this opportunity? He brooded, and in the next few moments, a plan came to him. He would take Ngangata to the first Human settlement, see that he was cared for, and then come back, if he could. The boat was magical, steering itself, cutting easily across even this swift current. Would it sail *upstream*?

Perkar felt a bit of elation. He could test *that* now. He would not go far upstream; but if it could be done, then he would not feel so helpless, so cowardly. He would *know* that return was possible.

Checking to make certain that he would not run them aground, Perkar pulled the tiller half and then all the way around. The boat responded instantly, turning on the rushing water as if it were a placid lake. In no time, their prow was aimed upstream, back at the mountain, the heart of Balati. Not only pointed that way, but moving *upstream*. Perkar tightened his grip on the tiller, jubilant. He would take Ngangata on down-River and then come *back*, to die perhaps, but at least to have an *ending*. Triumphant, he let the boat keep its nose for just a bit longer.

The craft suddenly shuddered, the tiller wrenched from his hand. A wave from nowhere slapped the prow, and then, as if the wave were a great hand, turned the boat about and bore them back downstream. Perkar yanked at the tiller, but it was like straining upon a rod of steel forged to steel; it would not move in his grip at all. Around them, the River was abruptly different, somehow. It took him a moment to place the difference, but soon he understood it. The moonlight, formerly broken by the River into a million softly glowing shards, was gone from the water. The stream flowed as dark and silent as a night without any light at all. But above them, in the sky, the Pale Queen was glorious still, almost full.

"*Well,*" the voice in his ear remarked. "*Now he is awake.*"

XII

~~~~~~

The Blessed

THE Grand Chamber, she knew, was at the locus of four great halls. The ground plan of the original palace was a series of rectangles, one within the other. This court was the center of that concentricity. She could see that all of the halls were intact—not filled in here. They were, however, sealed by huge iron grates. The dais was built in the corner of the room, reflecting a First-Dynasty preference for angles as focal points. The corner was considered the most prominent part of a rectangle. The halls were thus in the midpoints of the long walls. To reach most of them she would have to swim—something she had learned a bit about but which she wished to avoid—or wade, perhaps, if she was lucky and the water not as deep as it appeared. The gate immediately to the right of the dais, however, could be reached more easily; a dark bar of debris butted up against the wall and stretched nearly to the hall itself. After a moment, Hezhi chose this path. She might have to swim once she reached the hall, but the longer she could put that off the better;

she doubted that she could stay afloat and keep the lamp lit at the same time.

Stepping down toward the debris, she slipped on the alabaster steps, flailed with one arm wildly to keep from falling or dropping the lamp. One of her feet sank into the water at the foot of the dais. Pain erupted instantly, like flame lapping straight up her leg, into her belly, flaring toward her head. Choking off a little cry, she jerked her foot out; her vision blurred and swam, and she quickly sat down on the stepped dais for fear that she would collapse if she didn't. She reached down to stroke her foot, but already the strange sensation was fading. Though more intense and brief, she recognized the sensations, the taste of the water on her skin. It was the same as that when the priests sprinkled her during the Test of the Body.

"The River," she muttered. The ruined court was *not* filled with water from the storm drains and sewers. This was the River, crept up under the palace. The lower palace had sunk down into him. This was where sacred water was drawn.

Her foot wasn't even wet. The court was flooded not merely with water, but with *She'ned*, Smokewater, the lifeblood of the River. As ghosts were the spirits of Human Beings, *She'ned* was the ghost of water, the spirit remaining when the substance departed.

The burning passed, but a deep, involuntary shudder rippled through Hezhi's body, and the *thing* in her—what the priests had tried to force into revealing itself—stirred. Unmistakably. Overcome, she remained on the steps, weeping.

SHE stopped her weeping when she heard a soft whispering. At least, she believed it to be whispering; she could not make out any words; it was merely the hiss one hears at a distance when people confide secrets.

I have to do something, she resolved. *I have to try to find D'en.* .

The map had taken her this far, but now she had no clear idea of where to search. Her research had discovered the center of the old palace as the place to which the Darkness Stair descended. It had found her a path by which she might reach it. But her map did not have a point marked "D'en" on it.

Not that it mattered anymore. Hezhi now believed that she would not find him. It seemed to her that immersion in the Smokewater would dissolve a body, draw the spirit essence from it. Perhaps that was where ghosts came from. Those ghosts her father had summoned—the fish and the other things—they had all died in the River. It must be that when royalty died—no, when they were *killed*—it must be done in the River, so that he could reclaim their essence, the part of them that was *him*. That was what she felt inside of her, she realized. Part of her was River. She suddenly recalled her conversation with Tsem, nearly three years before. She had said something about the "Royal Blood" working in her, and Tsem had become absolutely solemn, almost fearful, had told her to never say such a thing. Perhaps that had been as much as he could say, Forbidden. To warn her about her blood.

That was it! It was all coming clear, deadly clear. If the Royal Blood worked *right*, if the River surfaced in one in the *right* way—whatever that was—then the child became like her father, her mother. Powerful, able to summon the River's puissance to do sorcery. A ruler. By using the part of the River that was *in* them. But if it went wrong, somehow, if it was . . . she still didn't know that, how it went awry. But it *could* go wrong, that was clear, and when it did those so "Blessed" were brought here and executed, returned to the River. Here, in the dark, where the people of the Empire would not know, would never see nobles die.

She reflected that many—like Wezh, for instance—might have noble blood but no waking power in them at all, destined neither to rule nor to die. Hezhi understood that she was not one of *those*.

Still she heard the whispering. She stood again and, more carefully this time, stepped out onto the rubble. She was vaguely sur-

prised that it did not crunch beneath her feet; it must have settled
through the centuries, become compacted. Moving as quietly as
possible, she worked her way toward the gate.

She reached it easily enough and was soon peering through the
steel bars. Beyond, the hall extended farther than she could see.
There was something odd about the corridor, though she could
not place for certain what it was for an instant. Then she understood. The water in it was moving—not flowing, but stirring
about, as if something were swimming in it. The whispering was
down that hall; it was a bit clearer now, and she could almost
make out a word, now and then.

She knelt on the pile, set her little lamp down, and, shading
her eyes from the flame, tried to see as far as she could; the
brightness of the flame itself tended to blind her.

She wobbled on her haunches and put down one hand to
steady herself. Doing so, she realized that whatever she was
squatting on, it was neither rubble nor sand. Puzzled, she studied
it more closely. She believed, at first, that the stone or whatever
was covered with moss or even fungus, but the texture was unlike that, as well. It was actually rather smooth, slick but not
slimy, *bumpy*. Like the skin of her mother's salamander.

As she was thinking that, an eye blinked open, no more than
an armspan from her. It wasn't there and then it was, an eye staring at her, a perfectly Human eye. Beneath her, whatever she was
squatting on tremored. It moved, shifted in place.

Hezhi tried to suppress her shriek of terror, but it leapt free of
her throat and soared away, a bright bird of sound in a dark
place, flapping around and around before the underpalace ate it
up. She crouched, shuddering, not knowing what to do. The eye
stared at her, then slowly closed again.

Shaking, she looked up and down the length and breadth of
the thing with entirely new eyes. She was on the back of something alive. It might be, she realized, rather like those fish in her
father's summoning. Or like the ghost that had come after her.
Yet this was no ghost; this thing was substantial in a way that a

ghost could never be, at least according to everything she had read—which was admittedly not that much, when it came to ghosts. It was real, alive, sleeping, even though she was on its back.

She noticed other things, now that she was looking. It helped her to study, detached her from her fear, from the fact that she was on the back of some alien *thing*. A stubby projection on the "bar" was some sort of fin. Or tentacle. And there, that lump . . . She shuddered and closed her eyes, detachment failing, not wanting to see more, wanting only to be somewhere else, alone, with Qey, with anyone, but *very* far from where she was. Because the lump was not a lump. Pale, like a fingered mushroom, a Human hand sprouted from the creature's back.

I have to open my eyes, she thought crazily. *I can't leave unless I open them.* But as much as she wanted at that moment to be gone, the thought of looking at the thing, of discovering some new horror was too terrible to face. Even less did she want to move. What if she woke it up?

"How did you get here?"

Her heart stopped for a moment, restarted with a painful jerk. She snapped her eyes open. The voice was strange, watery, tortured sounding. It came from beyond the grating.

"Who . . . ?" she began, and then stopped, still afraid of waking the monster she sat upon. She heard water stirring.

"Whoever you are, you are in a very bad place," the voice told her. A shadow was gliding in the ebon pool, beyond the light of her lamp.

"And where did you get that *light*?" it snarled. "Put that out. You'll have no need of that."

"Who are you?" Hezhi asked, holding the lamp higher, trying to see.

"Put that *down*, I say."

She set the lamp down but made no move to put it out. Nevertheless, the shadow swam closer. She caught a glimpse of it then: coils of scales glittering in the light, bony plates, a host of centipede legs—they did not congeal, form anything unified in her head.

"Who are you?" she repeated, her voice close to shrieking again.

"I don't understand how you got from the Darkness Stair to here without my seeing you," the thing complained. "But if you hadn't been so intent on slipping by me, I would have warned you about old Nu there. If she wakes up, you'll warm her belly."

"I didn't come down the Darkness Stair," she whispered, trying to keep her voice steady. "I came in through the ducts."

"The ducts? The ducts?" The thing swirled about crazily in the water. "You weren't *brought* down here, were you?"

"Let me see you," Hezhi pleaded. "What are you?"

A head suddenly moved into her circle of vision. It was Human, basically, though gills branched like feathery horns from its neck. It had no hair, either. The back of its head devolved into a rubbery, spiky mass that seemed to be constantly writhing.

"What am I?" the abomination repeated. "Why, my dear, don't you recognize a prince when you see one?"

"Prince? Prince?"

"Prince L'ekezh Yehd Cha'dune, at your service."

"That isn't possible," she managed to choke out, though she already knew that it was. "Who was your father?"

"Why, the Great Lord Yuzhnata, of course."

"Oh, oh," Hezhi gasped, still not quite able to grasp; but the puzzle was solving itself in her head *again*, the pieces rearranging themselves.

"That makes you my father's brother," she quavered faintly.

There was a moment of silence from the thing.

"Well," it said. "Well, I have a niece. Welcome, niece, to the Chambers of the Blessed. Now, you should trust your uncle and do what he says. Climb off Nu and swim through the grate. I'll protect you."

"I don't want to get in the water," she moaned.

"Well, you don't have much choice about that," L'ekezh replied. "Embrace it, let it fill you up. Become accustomed to it."

"Why?"

"Because you will never leave here, that's why."

"I will," Hezhi insisted.

"You say you came here by the ducts. On purpose. Why did you do that?" L'ekezh seemed to be becoming more accustomed to the light. He swam nearer, put his in-Human face up to the grating. She saw that his teeth were sharp and long, ivory needles.

"I wanted to know . . . where we *go* when they take us off."

L'ekezh laughed with a kind of bubbling delight, though it sounded more like someone choking.

"How bright you must be!" he remarked. "That's too bad for you, though I'll doubtless enjoy our conversations. Then again, the bright ones go mad the most quickly. I think I've stayed sane for so long because I'm a bit thick. Tell me . . ." His voice dropped low, became an exaggeration of the "conspiratorial" tone used in theater. "Tell me. Do the priests know yet? Have you begun to manifest?"

"Manifest?"

"With me," L'ekezh offered, "the power came first. She'lu— your father—was *so* jealous. Even when his power came, mine was always stronger. The Blessed are strong, girl. But then the priests came and they found—it's always a little thing, something you haven't really noticed—one of my toes had changed color. So, of course, they brought me here."

"I don't . . . *why*?"

"Why? Why? *Look* at me. Look at Nu, there. Could anyone stand to see us on the throne? Dancing about the court, with lords and ladies on our arms? And, of course, there is our power. They fear that the most."

"Power," she repeated dully.

"We are the Blessed," L'ekezh snarled. "I have more power in one of my eyes than the Chakunge and all of his court."

"Then why do you stay down here?" Hezhi asked.

"Because," L'ekezh began, and then stopped, his eyes staring at her with awful intensity. "Are you real?" he whispered. "Did I create you?"

"I am real," Hezhi assured him.

"I will go mad, one day, you know," L'ekezh confided.

"Why don't you leave?" she asked once again. "If you have such power?"

"Because the River drinks it," he replied woodenly. "When they first put me here, I raged. I tried to pull down the foundations of the damned palace around me, kill them all. I could have *done* it up there, but they drugged me, of course. Down here, when the drug wore off—well, however powerful the Blessed are, nothing is as powerful as the River. Nothing. Nothing. *Nothing!*" He finished by shrieking. Then he stared at her silently, his face writhing like a nest of stinging worms.

"You really shouldn't be on her back," he said again, after a time.

"How many . . . how many of you are there?"

"How many Blessed?"

"Yes."

"Alive? Still in flesh?"

Hezhi nodded.

"Oh, just a few. Five."

"Where are they?"

"Oh . . . around here somewhere. Your light frightens them. Anyway, I'm lord here, now that Nu sleeps most of the time. It's my responsibility to welcome the new ones. I still don't see how I didn't notice them bringing you down the stair."

"I told you, I didn't come that way."

"Well. So you did," L'ekezh muttered, perhaps more to himself than to her.

"I wonder . . ." she began. "Is there one named D'en among you?"

"D'en? Of course, D'en," the once-prince answered.

"I came to see him," Hezhi said.

"Oh? Came all the way to see D'en. Well. Wait here."

The head ducked beneath the black water and ripples marked his passage away.

SHE waited a long while, and it began to occur to her that she had been forgotten. L'ekezh seemed to have trouble *remembering* things. But just as she was despairing, as the fear of the sleeping thing upon which she sat began to overwhelm her, the water stirred again.

It was not L'ekezh. It was, to her eyes, a Human man, with long stringy black hair. His eyes, however, protruded on stalks and the hands that came up to grip the steel bars were clawlike, chitinous. One still possessed five fingers but the other had become like a pincer, the thumb grossly exaggerated and the other fingers melted together.

"D'en," she whispered. "Oh, D'en."

The thing looked at her with its crablike eyes. It croaked, like a frog. It croaked again, more insistently, and Hezhi thought she recognized her name.

"D'en? Can you talk?" She suddenly knew that she was going to be sick. Her stomach expelled the bread she had eaten before waking Tsem and continued heaving long after nothing remained in it. D'en watched her impassively.

"D'en doesn't talk much," L'ekezh told her, surfacing a few spans away. "He did at first, talked all the time. Usually our bodies change the fastest, then our heads. D'en—he changed inside first."

"Why . . . why do you change?" she managed, faintly. As if knowing would help.

L'ekezh smiled, a rubbery arc that might have been amusing to a madman. "He fills us up," he said, voice confidential. "A mere Human body cannot contain his full power."

She tried to understand, while D'en—or what D'en had become—cocked his head, as if regarding her from another angle would offer him something new. It may have, for slowly, tentatively, he reached the hand that was most Human through the bars.

She reached over and, after hesitating briefly, touched the hand. The fingers flexed but made no other movement. It felt cold, hard, not at all like the hand she remembered, the one she had held as they ran, laughing, across the rooftops. Now that hand clutched vaguely, not remembering how to hold another. It was a mercy when D'en suddenly snatched his hand away, croaked once again. His horrible eyes swayed on their stalks, and then he sank, quickly, beneath the water.

"He recognized you," L'ekezh told her. "I can tell. That was more than I expected."

"D'en," Hezhi mouthed softly. Beneath her, the rubbery flesh trembled again.

"Quickly," L'ekezh cried. "If you care for your life. Nu is awaking. If you really came through the ducts, go now. The River might yet let you."

Hezhi rose shakily to her feet.

"Good-bye," she said.

"I'll see you again soon enough," L'ekezh said. "See if they will let you bring me some wine. Though, of course, they won't."

He sank away, vanished. She took up her lamp and stumbled across Nu's back. As she reached the dais, the monster was beginning to twitch and, before she had mounted it, began heaving. She hurried to the shaft, spared a glance back and saw Nu rising up. There was nothing recognizably Human about Nu at all; she was all fish and scorpion, her long, pointed tail lashing now at the water. More quickly than Hezhi could have ever imagined, the creature turned and lunged up onto the dais, flopped there, heaved and flopped again. Reflexively, she hurled her lamp; it shattered on the damp stone, and fire splattered among the shards. Nu hesitated at that, faceted, insect eyes flinching away from the light. Hezhi scrambled into the dark tube and began to crawl frantically, gasping with fear. She clawed at the stone, trying to propel herself more quickly into the darkness, tore nails to the quick without even noticing the pain. She didn't even *begin* to calm down until she saw the pale illumination up ahead of her, where Tsem was waiting.

She was sobbing uncontrollably when the half Giant lifted her gently from the tube. He cradled her tenderly in his massive arms, stroking her wet, slimy hair, and made soft, comforting noises. Then, carrying her in the crook of one arm and the lantern in his other hand, he waded across the room and began ascending the stairs, back toward light and home.

≈≈≈≈≈≈≈≈≈≈≈≈≈≈≈≈≈≈≈≈≈≈≈≈≈≈≈≈≈≈≈

On Red Gar Street

GHE fingered the scar on his chin and breathed deeply, filling his lungs and nostrils with the smells of his childhood. Savory meat grilling at streetside stands, carts of fish just beginning to stink in the afternoon sun, the sharp, prickly scent of *J'ewe* incense; those were the best of them. When the wind shifted, shifted up from Southtown on the River, he got the worst. Garbage, mostly. The excrement of people and dogs, half-rotted food, stagnant, marshy pools where the River crept in. Here, on Red Gar Street, there was no trash to be seen, of course, but Red Gar cut the line between the sparkling center of Nhol, where the prosperous classes—the store owners, the boat captains, the merchants, the relatives of the relatives of nobility—met the much vaster realm of Southtown, where lived the *Hwe-gangyu*, the lowest of the low.

Ghe remembered well which side of the street he had come from. He would never cross there again save to kill someone at the command of the priesthood, and it was singularly unlikely that anyone in Southtown could possibly attract the attention of the priesthood. No, he would never willingly enter Southtown again, for he had risen above it and it was wrong ever to step backward. Here, though, on Red Gar Street, he had spent the best moments of his youth. Here, the child he had been could briefly forget the squalid hut he lived in, the mother he had killed by being born, the aunt who beat him and made him sleep with the dogs. On the street, he could see the best Nhol had to offer side by side with the worst, and he could plan his escape from Southtown. An escape he had now accomplished.

Ghe idly flipped a coin toward a boy watching the crowd with hawklike eyes. The boy snatched the glittering treasure from the very air, grinning and nodding at Ghe. Ghe nodded back and went on down the street, humming to himself. The wind shifted again, blew down from the palace and the clean side of town. A flock of Rivergulls went chattering overhead.

Ghe found Li just at the edge of Two Cottonwood Square. The old woman sat, as always, with her back as rigid as a board, her bone dice carefully arranged in front of her on a worn velvet cloth. The same cloth, indeed, as the one she had spread those years ago, when Ghe first met her.

"What do the dice say of me, ancient Li?" he asked. Her head turned up sharply at the sound of his voice.

"Ghe!" she crowed delightedly. "The bones *told* me that you would come see an old woman again!"

"You didn't need the bones for *that*," he whispered, bending down to place a kiss on her withered cheek.

Li's eyes sparkled. "Sit down, *duh*, my little one, and tell me of the priesthood!"

"There isn't a lot I *can* tell," Ghe said apologetically. "But it is a good life. Everything that *can* be available to someone not of noble birth *is* there for me. Good food, wine, books . . ."

"Women," Li interjected.

"Them, too," Ghe agreed, unembarrassed.

Li nodded. "I haven't seen you in two years, little *duh*. What have they been doing with you?"

Could he tell her? If there was anyone in the world he could trust, it was Li. And yet, though she had once won his trust—and even his love—there was still in him the boy who trusted no one. So he chuckled and clapped Li on the shoulder and told her a truth that was a lie.

"I pray a lot," he told her, and she nodded.

"And look, I brought you something," he went on hurriedly. He pulled a bundle from inside his shirt, carefully laid it near Li's feet so that she might open it. She did so and clucked with amazement at the contents.

"I thought your old cloth might be a bit worn," he explained. "And you've always needed a hat, to mark you out from these other so-called soothsayers. Now, here is a hat that will tell everyone that *you* see *true* futures."

"It's beautiful," she said. "The moons and stars on it seem to shimmer. Is the thread gold?"

Ghe shrugged. "I don't know; I only knew that you would like it."

"You're very sweet to an old woman."

"Without this old woman, I'd still be slitting throats for copper soldiers on Lung Street," he replied.

"So now you slit them for the priesthood, eh?" Li's eyes sparkled dangerously, revealing the hardness sleeping in her. He didn't blush, but he did touch her hand. The two had once dispensed with hardness between them, and seeing it again in her eyes felt like a little knife in his ribs.

"I'm sorry, Li," he said. "I meant to tell you."

She softened. "That's all right, *duh*. It's a difficult thing the priests have chosen for you."

Ghe shrugged. "It was that or nothing, I think. They were only interested in me because of certain . . . *skills* I have. And, Li, I *have* learned much. I can use a sword—a sword!—better than any soldier you will ever meet. They taught me tricks of fighting with my hands that I never imagined."

"Have you yet been set to a task?"

He nodded. "I can't talk about that, Li, not in any detail. I have been Forbidden. But twice now I have been sent out, and twice returned with blood on my hands. The priesthood is most pleased with me."

"As they should be." Li smiled, squeezed his hand. "And the enemies of Nhol will fear you, though they know not your name. Didn't I tell you that, those many years ago?"

"You did. But I think the prophecy came true through the prophet. You helped me when I needed help, taught me how to speak to the priests, introduced me to the admittance council."

Li shook her head in disagreement. "You were never meant to rot in Southtown, fathering brats and eating shit. You were meant for better things, and anyone with a brain in their skull could see that. I knew the priests would understand it as soon as they met you."

"You saw it first," he reminded her.

"So I did," she agreed. "But tell me, how is life in the palace?"

"Very good, as I said."

"And the Riverborn? What is it like living amongst them?"

The two of them had been conversing in low tones amidst the babble of the street; Ghe felt perfectly comfortable speaking secrets here, for no word would travel more than an armspan farther than Li's ear. Still, he lowered his voice even more. "They are idiots," he confided. "I would never have imagined it. If it weren't for the priesthood, the city would collapse under their stupidity."

"So I've often suspected," Li said.

"Oh, the Riverborn have *power*, there is no doubt of that. But their minds are like the minds of very young children. Even some of the priests are like that, I suppose. But many of the priests are like me, not of noble birth."

"Are none of the Riverborn capable?" Li asked.

"There *are* a few," Ghe replied thoughtfully. "There is one girl I have been watching. *She* seems very bright indeed." He smiled and cracked his knuckles. "It will be a shame if I have to kill her."

PART THREE

CHANGELING

© Cherry '96

I

~~~~~~

On the Hungry Water

Perkar had long since relinquished the troublesome task of numbering days and their dark complements. Singly or bundled together like so many reeds, they held no sense for him; his sense was all the River. Not that the River was outside of time, for he remembered earlier and later times upon it. Earlier, when the boat thrashed through the rapids in clouds of argent spray, pitching like a child's toy. He remembered the sickening grinding of stone against wood, the vague wonder that even a godboat did not splinter and join the spume in ecstatic flight up and away from the rocks. Still early, after the frantic water, when he had made his first real attempt to bring the boat aground on an inviting shore in a gentle, forested valley, he recalled the bitter helplessness as the willful boat continued on in the channel, despite exertion at the tiller that left him with blistered palms and aching muscles. He knew that even if his arms had been stronger he could have pulled until his heart burst with no more effect.

"The River has us," Ngangata told him once, when he was free of fever. "He will never let us go."

Perkar had ceased doubting that. Twice the boat had allowed them to make landfall, both times on islands in the channel. In each instance, he attempted to swim to shore, and always the current seized him and brought him, exhausted, back to the boat. On those occasions he had carried a rope with him, tied to the bow; he had no intention of leaving Ngangata.

It was *later* now. The mountains and even the hills were far behind them. They were more days than he could number—if he still counted them—from his home. A few times he had seen Human Beings; not his own folk, but dark, hard-faced men and women astride horses worth killing for. Many of the steeds were marked like his poor, dead Mang, striped with the hue of dried blood. The dark people and their horses watched him curiously as he drifted by. That had been *later*, when the River was no longer hurried, no longer gnashing through soil and stone with invisible teeth. Grassland rolled gently away from level banks thick with willow, tamarisk, and cottonwood. The sun was harsh, inescapable, burning their skin and then stripping it from them. Warning them to return to their softer land and then punishing them for not heeding the warning. Ngangata suffered the most. Though Perkar eventually stopped burning, his skin tanning a light coppery brown, Ngangata continued to be seared. His worst wounds had healed, and yet he never seemed much improved; he was weak, listless, spent much of his time in fevered sleep.

Perkar watched the halfling now as he turned uneasily, eyes closed but in constant motion behind swollen lids.

"*It is the River eating him,*" Perkar's sword told him.

"Why doesn't it eat me?" he asked.

"*It does. I heal you, though not so much as I could if we were away from him. I have restored all but two of your heartstrings, but it is a struggle. He is trying to eat me, as well, but that is one advantage to being enclosed in this form. It is like a seed too hard for him to digest. If you were to drop me into him, he could consume me, but even that would take time.*" The sword seemed to hesitate, then went on. "*There is something else. The River seems to know you, somehow. Not the way you would know a person, or even understand something. He knows you as you might know a taste, a scent. I think even without me, he would not eat you yet."*

He nodded dumbly. The goddess had tried to warn him of this, told him that the River knew him, through her. He wondered if the blood he had loosed into the rivulet at Bangaka's damakuta had also gone to him, but of course it had. For the first time, he realized that his dreams—the dreams that now made it nearly impossible to sleep—the dreams had begun a handful of days after his sacrifice. Had they begun when his blood reached the River? It seemed likely.

Almost from habit, Perkar examined his crimes. They had hardened in his time on the River. They no longer raged in him, diffuse, but lay sharp and cruel, like odd crystals that he could turn over and over in the palm of his mind, seeing each terrible, glittering surface, each stupid mistake. He could easily see the first blunder, the root from which all the others grew. From the moment he had loosed that blood, he had not done a single right thing. Even killing the Kapaka had not been enough for him, had not nearly been the end of it. Now he had doomed even Ngangata.

Doomed the only one who knows what you did, the most evil part of him whispered, now and then.

Ngangata awoke that evening, his eyes bleary. Perkar gave him a bit of water and some raw fish. Obtaining food—so long as it was fish—was not a problem. A hook cast into the water, baited or not, was soon heavy with their next meal. They had no way of cooking it, of course, but one could become accustomed to raw fish easily enough. On the islands, Ngangata recovered enough strength to set snares, and they had eaten rabbit, squirrel, and even deer once. The longer they remained on the islands, however, the more vivid and constant Perkar's dreams became. Ngangata, though healthier on land, always returned them to the boat when Perkar became incapable of doing anything from lack of sleep. He begged the halfling to leave him, but Ngangata refused.

Today Ngangata was lucid, propped against the side of the boat. He drew a deep, weary breath.

"My fever is gone again," he remarked.

"Good," Perkar said.

"I'm not much company."

Perkar frowned at him. "I've been thinking," he muttered.

Ngangata tried to smile. "That has been a dangerous thing for you to do, in the past."

He nodded his head in agreement. "Yes. But I've been thinking about you."

"Even worse," Ngangata pointed out.

"I've been wondering if you couldn't stay on one of the islands—if we ever see another. You would get stronger, perhaps strong enough to swim. He might let *you* swim to shore."

Ngangata nodded. "I've thought of that. More likely he would eat me up right away. The River has no love at all for Alwat, and he would probably mistake me for one."

"Ngangata, we've seen people bathing in the water, remember? They didn't seem to be in danger. It's me, only me he wants. It might not even be the River that abducts us; it might be this boat. It was, after all, a gift from Karak, not the most trust-worthy of gods."

"It is the River," Ngangata replied. "I can feel it. And I believe he will not let me go."

"You could *try*. Otherwise, I'm afraid you will die. I don't want you to die, Ngangata."

"Very good of you," the Alwa-Man replied. "But if I am to die, I doubt that you can do much about it. Tell me about your dreams again."

Perkar was frustrated by this sudden change in topic. He wanted to argue longer, to convince Ngangata to try to leave the boat.

"I've told you already," he answered shortly.

"Yes. But I've been thinking about them since. Tell me again."

He sighed. "I dream about this River. But farther down, much

farther down. As wide as he is now, there he is so broad that one
bank cannot be seen from the other. And there is a city there, a
city with more people than in all of the Cattle-Lands, in all of the
valleys."

"You see them, these people?"

"Yes, I see them, massed along the bank, fishing in boats,
bathing, *so* many of them."

"But the one girl you dream about?"

"She looks to be about twelve years old. Dark skin, very black
hair, black eyes. Pretty, in a foreign sort of way. She seems . . ."
He knit his brow together in concentration. "She is sad, worried.
Frightened, I think. In my dream I always want to help her. I hear
her call my name, but in some language I don't comprehend.
Does that make sense?"

"It makes sense," Ngangata replied. "Of course it makes
sense. It is a dream."

"Yes," Perkar muttered. "Her language, though, lately I have
begun to understand it, or . . . I don't know, this part is very
strange. It makes me sick, because it happens when I am awake,
as well."

"What?"

He drew in a steadying breath, wished for the thousandth time
that he had a flask of hot woti.

"I see a cottonwood," he said, gesturing out at the bank. "But
I do not *think* 'cottonwood.' I think '*hekes.*' " The strange word
slipped off of his tongue and left a bad taste behind. "I see the
sky, and I think '*ya.*' It is as if the dreams are swallowing me up
and leaving themselves in my place."

Ngangata looked evenly at him. "I'll tell you what I think. I
think the River wants you to do something, something involving
this girl. Or maybe it is the girl herself; maybe she is a goddess
or some powerful sorceress. I think you have been compelled to
go to this city down-River, summoned the way a shamaness summons a familiar or a god. I think I am caught up in this with you
because the River is very, very powerful but not all that wakeful

or discerning. Like the Forest Lord, he makes no great distinction between you and me. We entered the River together, that is all *he* knows. And then you woke him up by trying to go upstream, made him notice us."

"I'm sorry." Perkar sighed.

"You've said that so often that it is just a sound to me," Ngangata replied. "But, Perkar, I hold no ill will toward you— not anymore, at least. The River drew you to this, somehow, guided you."

"No," Perkar disagreed. "No, my stupidity was my own. Even if the damned River chose me somehow, that was my fault, too." He explained, then, for the first time, about the goddess, his love for her, her warning, his blood and seed loosed into the stream. Ngangata listened patiently, and when Perkar was done, he slowly nodded his head.

"I see," he said ruefully. "I have had the ill fortune to meet a hero, a lover of goddesses. Now everything comes clear. Had you told me this when we met, I would have ridden far away, avoided you for the rest of my life." He grinned sardonically. "It is my firm policy to avoid heroes," he confided.

"I'm not a hero," Perkar snapped. "I'm a fool."

"There is no difference," Ngangata answered. "A hero is merely a fool glorified in song. A hero is words woven around mistakes and tragedy to make them seem fine."

"I don't . . ."

Ngangata sighed. "Believe it or not, I heard the great songs as a boy, too. At first I loved them, imagined myself as the great hero Iru Antu or Rutka. But as I grew older, I knew myself. Knew that I would never be a hero; heroes are always Human, and whatever I am, I am not that. When I realized this truth, I began to hear the same songs in a different way, Perkar. I began imagining that I was not the hero, but one of his friends or companions. Or even an enemy." He glanced at Perkar meaningfully, to make sure he understood. He was beginning to, and though he had thought himself numb, Ngangata's words struck pain in him.

"What happens to the hero's companions, Perkar? Destiny

cares little for them. They die so that he can avenge them, or they
betray him so that he can punish them. The ground where a hero
passes is littered with the bodies of his friends and enemies."

Perkar closed his eyes, remembering the dead faces of Eruka,
Apad, the old woman in the cave whose name he had never
known. The Kapaka without even the dignity of a burial. Ngangata, suffering from day to day, barely alive. And, of course, the
goddess, who tried to stop him, save him from destiny.

"She wanted me to be a man rather than a hero," Perkar said,
and to his horror discovered a tear trickling down his face. "She
tried to make me into a man."

"Then she is a rare goddess," Ngangata replied. "The gods
love making men into heroes. It is their nature. They do it without even meaning to, most of the time. It is in the nature of their
relationship with us."

"This takes none of the blame from me," Perkar muttered.

"No. But if a song is ever made from this, it *will* take all your
blame, place it on the shoulders of the gods."

Perkar looked up fiercely, though more tears were starting.
"Such a song would be a *lie*," he snarled.

Ngangata snorted. "Songs are lies. That is *their* nature."

Night came, and Perkar lay on his back, studying the stars,
lulled by the gentle motion of the boat but not yet willing to
sleep, to turn himself over to River dreams. Ngangata was undoubtedly right. The city downstream, the girl, the River—
something was pulling him there, against his will. When he got
there, did whatever they wanted, would he be released? At the
moment the only release he could conceive of that would give
him peace was death. What he wanted more than anything was
to see Ngangata escape, cut loose from him, no longer the companion of a hero. Ngangata did not deserve such a fate. If the
"Ekar Perkar" were to be sung one day, it must not contain a
stanza about Ngangata dying in his arms.

Perkar took out his sword, lay with it across his chest.

"What is your name?" he asked it.

"*I'm not sure I remember,*" the sword responded.

"I have a question for you, no-name sword."

"*Yes.*"

"Will you permit me to die? Cut my own heartstrings, here, now?"

"*No, I cannot do that. I know you desire it, but that is not how I am made.*"

"What if I throw you in the River, as you suggested?"

"*That was hypothetical. I would never let you do that.*"

"You are cruel, then, nameless. It would be best for us all."

"*Perhaps not. Perhaps you are called to do something wonderful.*"

"I don't believe that," he countered. "I don't believe that there is anything wonderful *to* do."

The sword didn't answer right away. Above, a cloud drifted across the stars. *Ya'ned*, sighed the dream in his head. Cloud.

"*Harka,*" said the sword.

"What?"

"*That was my name, long ago. I have been called many things, as a sword. Jade, Sliver, Fang. But my name was Harka. I was a very young god . . . I barely remember it. I went out into the world clothed as an eagle, and was killed. The people who killed me were kind enough; they sent me back to be reborn on the mountain. The Forest Lord caught me, and I was born as this sword.*"

"Harka. A fine name. Harka, please let me die. I'm tired of being dragged this way and that, of having no will of my own."

If a sword could snort in contempt, it did. "*You know nothing of that,*" it replied.

He lapsed back into silence, wondering if he would ever learn not to shame himself.

He closed his eyes only briefly but dreamed much. Dawn opened his lids back up. Harka was still across his chest.

"*You wake just in time,*" the sword informed him. "*Someone wants to speak to you.*"

Puzzled, Perkar sat up. The sun was a mountain of red light directly before their bow. He blinked at it. Ngangata was still asleep. What could the sword mean?

Something on the bank caught in the sunlight, pulled his eyes that way. The Riverbank was thick with reeds and bamboo, a virtual forest denser than any he had seen in many days. They were just passing the mouth of a small river; a bar of sand extended toward them like a tongue, deposited there by the incoming stream.

A woman stood on the bar, watching them. It was she, of course, slim, beautiful, shining in the morning. She was weeping, her eyes fixed on him. As he watched, she walked toward him. He could see her reluctance, see the muscles in her legs bunching, as if she were being dragged by some force he could not discern. Her foot stepped off the bar, touched the water, and she melted. When that happened he heard, as clearly as a silver bell, a little gasp of pain, of horror, and even worse, of submission.

She appeared again, stepping from the mouth of the stream, stepping Riverward.

"I told you," he heard her say, her voice just audible. "I warned you, my love! But you can escape him, as I cannot . . ." Then she was gone again, eaten by the River.

Always, he thought. Every moment. He had known that she was in pain. Only now was he beginning to understand it. He had promised to rid her of this pain as if she were a young girl with a cruel father or a nagging aunt. How she must have hated him for promising that, for mocking her agony with his youthful stupidity.

Far behind now, she appeared again, still watching him, replaying her ancient fate.

Live, Perkar, he thought she called, but her voice was very faint.

II

Dread and the Living

Hᴇᴢʜɪ stretched back on the bench, let sunlight drench her, seep through her skin and down into her bones. A breeze sighed through the ancient cottonwood in the center of the courtyard, stirred the white yarrow, and enfolded her in its fragrance. Her face felt transparent, the fine little bones beneath her dark skin like brittle glass. Here, in the courtyard, she could close her eyes and yet the light shone through; there was no darkness to be found even if one sought it. Her eyes were weary from avoiding darkness, and closing them was an extravagant luxury.

"Too much sun can burn you, Princess," Tsem's great voice informed her gently.

"I'll stay here awhile longer, I think," she told him.

"Princess, what of Ghan? You don't want to anger him, do you?"

"I don't care," she said. "I don't care if he is angry. I want to be out here." Away from the darkness, away from the image of D'en that darkness always awoke.

"Princess, you haven't been to the library in days. This isn't like you."

"It doesn't matter, Tsem," she said. "It doesn't matter anymore, don't you see? I found him. I found D'en. *D'enata.*" Her voice trembled on his name; she had never said it aloud as a ghost name, ever. But she said it now and knew it for the truth, though his body—or what it had become—was yet living.

"You and Qey, you were right all along. It was better that I didn't know."

"You would have learned eventually," Tsem pointed out.

"Eventually, when it's all over, when I either join them or join my father. And I wouldn't have had to *see* him, then. You don't *know*, Tsem."

"I know I don't, Princess."

"I would have been happier, Tsem, if I had never tried to find out."

"Really?" Tsem said. "What's the point of that sort of speculation? I might have been happier if I'd been born free, among my mother's people. But I might not have. I'll never know."

"It's not the same thing," she snapped.

"You am right," Tsem pronounced thickly. "Tsem not understand what Princess feel."

She fought to be angry at that. Tsem only used his stupid voice with her when he was questioning *her* perceptiveness. She couldn't find her anger, though. She found sadness instead, and fear, fear of what she would do without her huge friend.

"You're always good to me, Tsem. I'm sorry. Maybe our situations are similar, in *that* way."

Tsem stroked her head. "No," he said. "I think you're right about that. I only meant that wondering what might have been is not as productive as planning what might be."

"Where does a slave learn this kind of wisdom, Tsem?"

Tsem coughed out a short, humorless laugh. "It is the kind of wisdom slaves *have*, Princess, if they have any at all."

She pushed thoughtfully at her dress. "I wish I knew when the priests will test me again."

"What good would that do?"

She lifted one hand in an I-don't-know sort of gesture. "In the meantime . . ." she began.

"Yes, Princess?"

"In the meantime I want you to deliver a message for me."

Tsem raised his eyebrows. "A message?"

"Yes. Please inform Wezh Yehd Nu that I would like to meet him in the Onyx Courtyard this evening, if it is to his liking."

"Princess?"

Hezhi sighed. "I have to go on as if I will have a life," she told him. "Else I will go mad."

Tsem nodded solemnly. "If you will be safe here, I will go inform him at once."

"I think I will sit here a bit longer, but then I will go to the library. You can meet me there this afternoon to escort me to meet Wezh."

"Very good, Princess."

"And thanks, Tsem," she said earnestly.

"You are quite welcome, Princess." He heaved to his feet and lumbered off. She watched him go, let the sun saturate her a bit more. Reaching into the pocket of her skirt, she pulled forth the little statuette, the horse-woman, turned it over and over in her hand. Did the strange, pale man in her dreams ride a horse? She decided that he probably did. Lately, she had come to welcome the dreams of forest and the strange man—they kept away the nightmares about D'en and L'ekezh. Ironically, those dreams of faraway had become less frequent, less forceful. The forest was almost faded entirely, though the man, when she dreamed of him, was more vivid than ever. Reluctantly she rose and set her feet in the direction of the library.

"I'm not complaining, mind you," Qey insisted. "It's just that I thought you didn't *like* this Wezh fellow."

"Well," Hezhi explained, biting into a plum, "it doesn't really matter whether I like him or not, does it? There are worse men to be courted by, and to hear Tsem tell it, they are queuing up to do so."

"Well, they should be. You are very beautiful, Hezhi."

"Pfah. I could be a sack of grain, for all they care. As long as I was a sack of grain whose father was Emperor."

"That may be true," Qey admitted, "but there are many noble daughters. In you, the young men can see a lovely woman, and in a few years a stunning one. If one must marry, it is better to marry someone pleasant looking."

"They don't see that in *me*," she protested.

Qey shook her head. "You'll see. You'll have your mother's face and figure, I can already tell that. Even if you inherit from your father's side—his sisters are all quite pretty."

"Not so pretty as his brother," Hezhi muttered.

Qey turned an astonished face away from the stove. "What did you say?"

"Nothing," she quickly amended. "Nothing, just a joke."

"Your father's brother is dead, Hezhi. It isn't something to joke about."

"I know." She wiped the plum juice from her mouth with the back of her hand.

"Anyway," Qey remarked, changing the subject, "how was your meeting with Wezh Yehd Nu?"

"He tried to be pleasant, and succeeded well enough, I suppose." She smiled. "I think he was very surprised to hear from me. He told me he had given up."

"Did he bring a present, then?"

"Oh, yes. I think his mother picked it out." She reached into her bag to show Qey her present, feeling a brief, inexplicable sadness when her hand brushed the statuette. She drew out Wezh's gift and set it on the table.

"Oh, that's a nice perfume," Qey said, examining the crystal bottle.

"So I hear. I'll wear it next time I meet him."

"You'll be meeting him again?" Qey asked, a bit surprised.

"Yes. He's taking me to a drama tomorrow."

"Which one?"

Hezhi cleared her throat. "*The Eel and the Lion* it's called. A romance, I think." She half sang the title, the way Wezh did. He was quite excited about taking her to it.

"Will you like that?" Qey asked, doubtfully.

"Almost certainly not," Hezhi said. "But I have to learn to tolerate such things. After all, I can't spend the rest of my life in the library, like Ghan."

"Well, but I never expected to hear *you* say that, little one."

"Everything changes," she philosophized, biting into another plum.

"Yes," Qey agreed. "If there is any truth in the world it is that."

The next day Hezhi went into the library early. Ghan raised an eyebrow and his face puckered into a frown.

"Will I be graced with your presence for the *entire* day today?" he asked sarcastically.

She blushed. "I'm sorry, Ghan. I've been . . . I don't know. I'm sorry."

"It's nothing less than I expected," he remarked sourly.

"I'm here now. What do you want me to do?"

"Do what you like. I shelved yesterday. And by the way,"—he frowned up briefly at her before continuing—"a 'friend' of yours came by this morning. One 'Wezh,' I believe. Since you weren't here, he asked if I might deliver a message pertaining to the drama you will be attending tonight."

Hezhi felt her face burning furiously as Ghan went on. "He said you should wear something 'frip' with lots of 'lacies.' It's the style for this show."

"Ah . . . thanks," she stuttered. Ghan glowered at her.

"You have better uses for your time than that, don't you? Do you even know what 'frip' means?"

"No," she replied. "He says it a lot."

"Does he?" Ghan sneered.

Hezhi felt a surge of anger swarm up through her embarrassment. "This isn't your affair, Ghan."

"Isn't it? I've wasted too much time on you to have you running off with boys who say 'frip' and 'lacies'! By the River and Sky, you can do better than that!"

"What would you have me do, Ghan? I have to make a life here! Soon I will no longer be a child, and people will expect things of me. Maybe it's fine for you, buried here with these books, but *my* clan isn't banished away somewhere! They're right here, watching me, wondering what to do with me when I come of age. I've denied reality long enough, don't you think?"

Ghan gaped for just a moment, but he quickly shut his mouth so he could form a reply. "Who are you?" His voice was suddenly mild. "Who is this?" he asked the air. "Is this the same girl who lied to me just to get in here? Who taught herself to read—however poorly—in the ancient script? Who came in here, day after day with *no* help and *no* encouragement at all, who fell asleep with her nose in my books because she wasn't even sleeping at night but *thinking* about what she had been reading all day?" Ghan rose off of his stool, and as he did, his voice rose as well. "What have you done with her?" he demanded.

That stung, much more than she was willing to admit. "Everything is different now," she told him, fighting back tears.

Ghan regarded her for a long moment before answering.

"It *must* be," he finally said, and returned to his work.

She waited for him to say something else—*anything* else—but he did not. He kept to his pen and paper. Glumly, Hezhi trudged over to the new books, produced her pen—the new one Ghan had given her—and began to make notes for the index. She looked up at Ghan now and then, but he was studiously ignoring her. Unable to bear it, she took her things and went back into the tangle.

She had been working only a moment when someone coughed quietly behind her. Briefly she thought it was Ghan, and she turned, ready to try to explain. It wasn't Ghan, though, but Yen, a gentle smile on his face.

"I guess he isn't in a very good mood today," he commented.

"It isn't his fault," Hezhi replied.

Yen shook his head. "He shouldn't have snapped at you like that. He should understand."

"No," she disagreed. "He can't understand. No one can."

"I'm willing to try," Yen said softly. "If you want to talk."

She gazed up into Yen's kind eyes. "It's nothing I can talk about," she explained apologetically. "It's just that . . . have you ever discovered that your life wasn't at all what you thought it was?"

Yen frowned, tapped his chin with his thumb. "No," he finally said. "No, I've always known what my life is. I've had some nice surprises, and some unfortunate ones, but I've always known myself."

"You're fortunate, then," she said. "When you grow up in the palace, you never know. Ever. There's just one betrayal after another, and you never know where you stand. But you *think* you do anyway, and then . . ." She trailed off. "I'm sorry, Yen. It's very kind of you to listen, but nothing I can tell you will help me, and it might be bad for you."

"It can't be *that* bad," Yen soothed.

"My life is like the River," she said. "It flows one way, always downstream, inevitable. I never faced that before. I guess I always believed that I could somehow remain a child, stay in the cracks of the palace—here, in the library, where no one would ever notice me."

Yen sat down across the table from her. "When *I* was a child, I always wanted to be my father, always wanted to be older than I was. I was impatient to grow up, to captain a boat, to sail up-River and see strange sights. Not at all like you, I guess. You always wanted to be yourself, and I wanted to be someone else." He sighed. "But it was my father who encouraged me to join the priesthood. I joke about him, but he really wants me to succeed at this, to be a great engineer and have my name go down as the one who designed such-and-such a shrine. 'Don't be a sailor like me, boy,' he told me. 'You were cut out for finer things.' "

Hezhi shook her head ruefully. "I was always told what to be. I've never been offered a choice, but I was too stupid to realize that." She attempted a smile. "I should like to meet your father one day. He sounds like a nice man."

"He is," Yen assured her. "Perhaps one day you will meet him."

"Maybe," she doubtfully allowed, but then brightened a bit. "But when I am a woman, when I join my family, then I will be allowed to leave the palace. Perhaps then. I should like to sail in a boat."

"Well." Yen chuckled. "I know more about *that* than I care to admit. But you will have royal barges at your disposal, won't you? No battered trading scows for you."

"Yes," she said, suddenly feeling very shy. "But royal barges never sail up the River, never visit the Mang or any other strange lands. I envy your father that, even if you do not."

Yen shrugged. "Well. Perhaps someday . . ."

She shook her head. "No. That's a silly thought. Nobility on a trading boat—that couldn't happen."

Yen ticked his finger against the wood of the table. "No, I suppose not," he admitted. "But if you dream of it . . ."

She held up her hand. "You have no idea how tired I am of dreams," she said ironically.

Yen nodded as if he understood. "Anyway," he went on, "I hope you find happiness of some kind. And if you ever want to talk about these things, I'm willing. I won't tell anyone." He grinned. "Not that I have anyone here to tell. You're the only person I really know here. Everyone else ignores me."

"You don't have any friends with the engineers?"

"No." He sighed. "It's notoriously hard to become liked among them. The ones who have been here longer delude themselves into believing they are royalty, and of course some of them—the overseers—are. If I make it a year, two years, then some of them will deign to talk to me."

"That's too bad," Hezhi empathized.

"Not too bad. I can still go see my father, now and then."

Hezhi nodded. "That's how Tsem and Qey are to me. They are my only friends."

"Tsem is the big fellow?"

"Yes. He's half Giant. My father ordered his mother to mate with one of his Human guardsmen. He was curious as to what would result."

"Ah," Yen replied. "But what about this Wezh person? The one who came in here earlier, the one the old man was scolding you about? Isn't he a friend?"

She snorted and shook her head. "No. He's just courting me. People are rarely friends with those who court them."

"A shame," Yen remarked. "I don't see that you could enjoy courting much if you don't like the person."

"That's right," Hezhi confirmed.

"Well." Yen coughed. "Well, I should get back to what I was doing. But . . . if you want to count me a friend, too, I would like that."

She blinked at him. "Thank you," she responded, not knowing what else to say.

Yen nodded and then hurried off.

She returned to indexing, though she remained distracted for the rest of the day, wondering why the only people she could seem to count on were those not related to her.

III

Brother Horse

THE transition from tall grass to short to none at all was seamless, and yet one day Perkar was watching the wind's footsteps bending waist-deep prairie and not many mornings later he realized that the River was surrounded by desert. Desert, he could see, was more aggressive than prairie. The plains had crept up to the banks of the River often enough, but more often a thick screen of willow, cottonwood, oak, and bamboo buffered the two from one another. Now, however, the screen of trees was a thin green shadow, a billowy olive veil easily penetrated by vision. The distance that beckoned was vast and empty, and seemed to Perkar like another vision of hunger, perhaps as great as that of the River. He wondered how bitterly the two gods of water and sand might hate one another, or whether they might be allies. Or even two shadows of the same presence, like the Huntress and Karak.

Bludgeoned though he was, Perkar felt a spark of wonder, still. Wonder that any land could be so very different from his own.

The River had actually contracted a bit. Perkar suspected that the fierce sun was drinking thirstily from the god, and it pleased him slightly to think that something was capable of causing the River pain. Of course, the sun was not particular, and drank greedily from Perkar and Ngangata, as well.

Ngangata lay in the meager shade of a deerskin Perkar had finally had the sense to stretch as a sunscreen between some willow saplings he lashed to the sides of the boat. The Alwa-Man was consequently improving, though he still hovered near the edge of fever. Perkar forced him to drink as often as he could, though the River water had a bitter, even salty taste. Almost like blood, Perkar reflected, remembering his dream of the River flowing red.

Near noon one day, he saw that they were approaching an island. He took hold of the tiller, and, as usual, it allowed him to steer just that much, so that they ran aground on the sandy strip. Once the island had been merely a bend in the River, but he had eaten right through the land, so that the channel now flowed on both sides.

He dragged the boat up into the thick reeds, starting involuntarily when he nearly stepped on a snake as long as he was tall. Without even thinking, he began a little chant to the Snake Lord—to beg pardon for frightening one of his people—and then he remembered: Here, there was only the River. Harka, his sword, was certain about that.

"At first," Harka had told him, one day, "I could at least hear the gods in the distance. They did not crowd to his banks, but they were there, just beyond. Even in the grassland I could sense them watching from afar. Now I don't know how far you would have to go to even hear a whisper. It's true what they say about the Changeling. He eats them."

As if he had any doubt of that, after seeing her.

He lifted Ngangata out of the prow and sloshed farther inland, hoping that the entire island was not marsh. After fifteen steps or so he was relieved to feel his feet on firmer ground. Barefoot, he winced a bit at the barbed burrs that assailed his tender feet. Still, he sought the middle part of the island; *Nu*, said his dream voice. There he could make out the odd swaying trees that resembled—as much as they resembled anything familiar—tall ferns.

Ngangata stirred awake in his arms, looked muzzily around him. "Oh," he said. "Let me try to walk, Perkar."

Perkar set him on his feet, caught his companion when his knees buckled. But then, with teeth gritted, Ngangata took one and then two trembling steps without leaning on him. He continued to walk, slow and wobbly, until they reached the trees.

Perkar was astonished at what they found there. The thick, brushy undergrowth of the island had been cleared back to form a yard of bare, sandy soil. At the far edge of the clearing stood a house made of what appeared to be bundled reeds lashed to a willow framework. Fish were drying on a raised stage, beneath which a faint wisp of smoke timorously sought the sky. An old man and a dog watched their arrival with apparent interest.

"*Dubu? Du' yugaanudiin, shiheen?*" the old man croaked. His dog—a yellow mutt spotted brown—cocked its head at him as if listening.

Perkar held out his palms, to show that they were empty. "I don't understand you," he said. This wasn't his dream language, and it certainly wasn't the language of his own people.

"Oh," the man replied, in a heavily accented version of Perkar's tongue. "I was just asking my dog who you were."

"*Huuzho, shutsebe,*" Ngangata said weakly.

"*Huuzho, shizhbee,*" the old man replied, smiling. "So you, at least, know the *real* speech."

"My name is Perkar, Clan Barku," Perkar told him. "My companion is Ngangata."

The old man shook his head in bemusement. "Such names!" he mused. "I was never able to keep them straight!" He came to his feet—it seemed quite a struggle—and gestured for them to join him. "I forget myself," he said cheerfully. "Join Heen and me. I will make us some tea."

Perkar was uncertain, but Ngangata nodded. The two of them

crossed the clearing, Perkar walking, Ngangata stubbornly stumbling along. The old man, meanwhile, disappeared into his strange hut and emerged with a copper kettle. He filled it with water from a rainbarrel at one side of the house, and after adding some herbs to the pot and a bit of wood to the flagging fire, came back to join them. He walked bow-legged, on limbs as spindly as those of a spider.

"Now," he said, as he returned to his seat. "Please sit down."

Perkar and Ngangata folded their legs beneath them. The old yellow dog appraised them briefly with half-lidded eyes, then returned to sleep.

"My name is *Yushnene*, or at least it was when I was younger. That means 'Wolf-Minded.' They called me that because I was such a terror in battle." He chuckled to himself, as if at some small joke. "After that, they called me *Gaan*, because I was a shaman—that's what that means—but now, when I see anybody they just call me Old Man or something like that. But when I used to go up into your country, to trade, up there your people called me Brother Horse. You can call me whatever you want."

Despite himself, Perkar felt a smile drawn from him by the old man's manner. "Any of your other names would make me sound as if I were sneezing," he admitted. "May I call you Brother Horse?"

"That's fine with me. I always used to laugh when they called me that, because it had to do with a misunderstanding. I didn't speak your language very well, and someone asked me my horse's name. I didn't know how to say 'He is Dog-Chaser, my second cross-cousin on my father's side,' and so I just tried to tell them he was my cousin. What came out, though, was 'brother.' By the time I realized my mistake, the name was stuck to me. Anyway, I like it well enough, and I thought of Dog-Chaser as a brother anyway."

"You are Mang then?" Perkar blurted. "I've heard you share lineage with your mounts."

"Mang? Yes, that's what you people call us. My own tribe is

really the Sh'en Dune, the South People, but foreigners always call us Mang."

"The Mang are the chief tribe in their confederacy," Ngangata explained. "The ones your people are usually at war with."

The old man nodded. "Yes. I've never been to war against you Cattle People, though, so I hope there are no grudges."

Perkar shook his head. "No. Mang attacked my father's damakuta many years ago, but I hold no enmity against brave warriors."

"Well, that's good," Brother Horse replied. "It would be a shame if Heen and I were forced to kill you both." His eyes crinkled merrily in his square, dark face. His hair still had some black amongst the white, but Perkar thought he must be older than any other man he had ever met.

"How long have you been on this island?" Perkar asked, not wanting to speak any further about warriors or battle.

"Heen and I have been here for five winters. But what you *mean* to ask is *why* I'm out on this island, don't you?"

"He marked you," Ngangata observed. Perkar nodded sheepishly.

"Well, it's a tragic story," Brother Horse told them. "If I did not mention it, I will tell you that I am quite an old man. Did I mention that?"

"I'm not sure," Perkar replied.

"Well, I am," Brother Horse stated carefully. "I have outlived my sons and daughters, and all of the horses of my line. My grandchildren and great-grandchildren are fond enough of me, of course, but they don't want to have to look after an old man like me. They would, of course, but they wouldn't like that and I'd know it. My last wife died a good while ago, too, and so I thought I might find me a new wife—to look after me, you know. I even thought I might find one, for a change, who could outlive me, and a pretty one hopefully. I heard about this girl Ch'an De'en—that's 'Pretty Leaf'—up in the north foothills. She was supposed to be daughter of Nuchiinuh, the Woodpecker Goddess—ah, wait a moment." He

rose back up and took the kettle off the flames; the water in it was
boiling. He ambled back into the house and returned with three
porcelain cups. "Got these from a down-River trader," he confided.
He poured a bit of the tea into each cup and handed one to
Ngangata, one to Perkar, and kept one for himself.

"There. Where was I?"

"You were going after this girl."

Brother Horse nodded. "I took along presents, of course, the
kinds of things gods like—beer, wine, incense—"

"You were going to marry a goddess?" Perkar interrupted.

"Her *mother* was a goddess. Her father was some Tiger People
man. So, I went up there, and the old woman said no."

"The goddess?"

"Right. She said I was too old for her sweet daughter. And she
was sweet, very beautiful, just past sixteen and never seen a man
before. So, well, I knew this little song that I thought would
make Nuchiinuh sleep, and after I sang that, I thought I would
convince the girl to go with me. She was willing enough—it must
have been boring for her up there in the mountains. We were just
'trying each other out'—she thought I might be too old, you
know, for marriage. So we were doing that when Nuchiinuh
woke up. She wasn't too happy about things. I managed to hide
myself with another song and get back home, but when I got
there I found the Woodpecker Goddess had been there before me,
looking for me. There aren't too many places you can be safe
from a goddess like that, but out here in the River is one of
them," he finished. "None of them dares come within sight of
him. So here I sit, wondering how long she'll stay mad. A few
more years, maybe." He took a long sip of his tea. "People come
out here, now and then, and bring me presents. I told everyone
that I had decided to become a hermit and meditate, so they
come out here to ask me questions about things. I guess I can tell
you the truth, though, since you aren't Mang." He smiled crookedly, raised his cup, and took another drink.

Ngangata seemed to be regaining some of his strength, as he

usually did when they were on land. He finished his tea and then asked if he might get more. The old man nodded at the kettle.

"Well," Brother Horse said after a time. "My people always considered me a little too talkative, and I've only gotten more garrulous and nosy since I've been living alone. Heen is a slow talker, you see. But Heen was wondering what brings the two of you so far from your forests, pastures, and cattle."

Perkar noticed that Heen seemed to be snoring, but didn't feel it was politic to mention that fact.

"Well," Ngangata said, before Perkar could respond. "To explain that, I would have to tell you the tale of Perkar, and that would be too long in the telling. I think Heen would be bored."

"Heen can suffer through almost any tale, the more long-winded the better," the old man responded.

Perkar shifted uncomfortably, remembering his conversation with Ngangata about heroes and songs. Ngangata patted his shoulder and continued.

"Like your story," Ngangata began, "this begins with the wooing of a goddess . . ."

If the story had been sung, the way Eruka had done it, he wouldn't have been able to stand it. But Ngangata told their adventures plainly yet with great elegance. He was true to his word about songs, however. Somehow Perkar's most terrible mistakes became tests put forth by the gods. Even the fight between the two of them became a magical moment in which they became fast friends. Ngangata shifted the blame of the old woman's death entirely onto Apad, without ever making Apad seem bad. Perkar remembered that killing as vividly as if it were yesterday, how frightened and nervous they all were, Apad half mad with tension and self-doubt. In Ngangata's words he was a true champion, beguiled by the illusions of the evil Lemeyi into his action. Somehow, this made Perkar feel a bit better, though he was unsure why. He had avoided thinking about his dead companions as much as possible, and Ngangata was offering him a way to think about them stripped of their faults. He also pared away

Perkar's shortcomings—the parts about himself in Ngangata's story rang hopelessly flat in Perkar's ears, twisted his stomach. But hearing Eruka and Apad turned into characters from a song seemed better. The fact that it was Ngangata doing it was an act of generosity almost beyond comprehension, and it was this more than anything that prevented Perkar from shrieking "That isn't how it happened at all!" The story was both Ngangata's forgiveness and the punishment he exacted from Perkar, and Perkar felt compelled to accept both of them, the grace and the pain.

"So now we go down-River, trapped by the will of the River-god," Ngangata concluded, "not knowing our destiny, the meaning of Perkar's strange dreams, but ready to meet fate."

Brother Horse seemed rapt, nodding here and there with enthusiasm and dismay, but utterly taken by the story. Only toward the end did he seem troubled.

"That city you dream about," he said a bit later, after they had eaten some fish soup. "I have *been* there, you know."

"So it *is* real, then?" Perkar wondered. It wasn't something he *really* questioned, more a prompt to keep the old man on the subject.

"Oh, yes, Nhol is real. It is the greatest city in the world. I went down there once, when I was very young, with a party of warriors. We had some very unrealistic ideas about raiding the city." He laughed at the memory. "In any event, when we got there, we saw how hopeless it was, how pointless. Instead we got drunk in one of the portside taverns, gambling with boatmen. They took everything we had, including our swords. But it was a wonderful sight, that city. It was also frightening."

"My dreams of it frighten me."

"The city is wholly of the River," Brother Horse went on. "There is nothing else. There are no little gods in the houses, no Fire Goddess in the flame, no spirits in the trees. They have killed them all. Even the River doesn't have that kind of power, not by himself. He can eat what comes near him. But for scores of leagues on either side of the River, in the whole empire Nhol rules, there is not one god but the River." He shook his head dolefully. "It's beautiful, but it's dead, haunted by ghosts from the River and his children."

"What do you mean, his children?" Ngangata asked.

"I say there are no gods," Brother Horse said. "I can *see* them, you know—I was given the *sight* by my totem god Yush very early on. In Nhol, I could see only the River, except—except there were certain people, the rulers of the city. They looked to me something like gods."

"They killed the gods in the land and on the land," Ngangata declared, "and the River made gods of the Human Beings who helped him." He turned to Perkar. "As I told you once," he reminded him. "The River *simplifies* things."

Perkar shook his head. "They pray to these half gods?"

Brother Horse nodded. "The Waterborn, they are called."

"In my dream, there is a girl," Perkar said thoughtfully. "I am supposed to do something for her—or *to* her, perhaps. The farther down-River we go, the more clear that seems."

Brother Horse grimaced. "I don't know about these matters," he grumbled. "If it were not Nhol you were being called to, I would suspect that your dreams were sent by a goddess. But there are no goddesses in Nhol."

"But what of these Waterborn? You say they are like gods."

"*Like* gods. They resemble gods as anger resembles love. Both are strong emotions, both can make you kill, but they are very different, with different ends. I think the Waterborn are just walking, talking aspects of the River. He sleeps, you know. He is more wakeful now than I have ever known him to be—this may be the result of your adventures. But I think it is really through those Waterborn that he is wakeful."

"Do you know this?" Perkar inquired.

"No. It is only a feeling. I was only there once, long ago. It is just that I have been thinking about the River and Nhol a lot lately."

"Since you've been on the island."

"No, only in the past few months. Your story makes me think."

"Makes you think?"

Brother Horse dusted off his bandy little legs, stood, and stretched. "Makes me think of a god so huge that his head doesn't always know what his feet are doing. Of messages traveling up and down the River, like an old, old man talking to himself, do you see? And me, sitting here with Heen, hearing just a little bit of that senile mumbling."

"And what is he talking about, this old man?"

Brother Horse fixed Perkar with a strange gaze. "You, perhaps."

Perkar shifted the bundle of firewood in his arms, wondering how far upstream the branches had drifted from. Above him, the familiar stars were dwarfed by the splendor of the Pale Queen, and for the first time in many days, he was struck almost physically by a longing for his native pastures. How long had it been since he departed them? Months, but he didn't even know how many. Already that life of his was gone, become the story Ngangata had told today. He felt prepared to add another observation to Ngangata's pondering on songs. They were lies, yes, but they were also corpses, dressed in finer clothes than they had ever worn in life.

Preparing to return to the camp, Perkar's gaze was suddenly drawn up-River by something odd. Caught from the corner of his eye, it took a moment before his strained vision could make out what it was.

Shafts of moonlight, walking on the water. *Walking.* The surface seemed dimpled, an amorphous constellation of stars winking on and off, coming slowly and deliberately downstream. Perkar wondered if it might be some school of fish—or ghost-fish—that glowed beneath the waves, swimming toward him, for the River had held no moonlight since that moment in which he awoke. Was he sleeping again?

Perkar watched, the single eerie call of a whippoorwill the only companion to the rasp of his breath. He could see the texture of the lights now, and they were clearly *on* the River's surface, not beneath it. Concavities appearing and vanishing in the current, cups of moonlight first here and then gone. It was nothing he had seen before, but it was familiar . . .

"Do you want to see?" Harka asked as he furrowed his brow in concentration.

"See?"

"I can show you, if you want."

"Show me," he breathed. And his vision changed, blood running tingling up his back, stroking his heart and lungs with shock.

The dimples were hoofprints. There were horses, walking upon the water. *Formed* of water, flanks of glistening moonlight, whirlpools of darkness for eyes. Nevertheless, he knew them instantly. Ngangata's old mount, and Bear, the Kapaka's stallion.

The Kapaka sat astride Bear. His face was a hollow, featureless, but Perkar could not mistake him, the way he sat his horse, the relaxed hold on the reins. The nothing beneath the helm turned to Perkar, and suddenly he was cold beyond belief, cocooned in water. All of his pain and fear chilled dull, faded, the sharp angles of his crimes coated in layers of muck and sand. For that instant, he was a tree made of ice, motionless, without passion, watching the ghost of his king as if it were nothing more unusual than a flight of geese.

The head turned from him, and fire rushed back into Perkar's belly. Everything: pain, remorse, hatred. He groaned hoarsely, flung himself savagely into the trunk of a willow, the firewood he had gathered flying about him. He reeled but did not fall, spun to look again upon his king. But the image was gone, the faint spackle of moonlight fading even as he watched. Snarling, he drew Harka, dashing at the line of trees, hacking at the branches clumsily until finally he dropped the sword and began hitting the trunks with his bare knuckles, pounding until bones cracked and blood smeared up to his wrists. At last, clumsily embracing the trunk of an oak, he slid down to the ground, sobbing.

"I hate you!" he cried, out at the water, but it was unclear even to him whether he meant the River or himself—or both.

Why? Why had the River shown him those ghosts? It could not be an accident, not with everyone and everything the River had swallowed in his time. The bones of a hundred kings must lie in his depths, a thousand steeds.

His hands were aching now, balls of flame, but he forced himself to think, to confront. What did the River want of him?

"What?" he shouted, but no answer came save the distant sound of the nightbird.

"Father, help me," he sighed. "Mother!" He reached up to finger the little charm his mother had given him, and he felt a familiar spark there, the same life that had entered him at birth. Touching it, he touched the place where his caul was buried, and for the beat of a bee's wing he saw that place: a mighty oak, limbs spread like a big man yawning and stretching, and near its roots a silver stream, laughing and lovely. In that instant, the distance between him and his father's damakuta dissolved; it stood just beyond the star-flecked horizon. There sat his father and mother, wondering what had become of him. A day's travel from there was Apad's family, and not much more distant, Eruka's. At his masterless damakuta in Morawta, the grandchildren of the Kapaka might be wondering where the old man was, why he hadn't returned.

What would his father tell him to do? What would he say?

Finish what you begin, he would say. *Piraku is more than having, it is doing.*

But do what? He had believed that there was nothing good he could do now but die. Anger surged again, and he spat out into the River, glared across his now-quiet waters.

"Yes!" he hissed. "Yes, take me where you wish. I will *go* with you. Do you hear me, Changeling? I resist you no more."

Damn Ngangata for reminding him, for making it all clear. He had begun a story and resisted ending it. There was still a chance to redeem his failures, make the saga come out right. It didn't matter that he wasn't worthy. It didn't matter that he hadn't *un-*

derstood where his actions would lead him. He had no choice, that much was clear. Piraku demanded that he go on, and if he had betrayed his people in *everything* else, he could at least not betray them in that.

"I warn you," he told the water, voice flat. "I warn you that if you let the bit slip from my teeth—if you give me the *slightest* opportunity—you will rue the day that you set me on this task. If it is this girl I am to seek—what do you want of *her*? But if you want her alive, I will kill her. If you want her dead, she shall live." He shook his fists, and droplets of blood made rain-circles in the stream. "Take more of my blood," he said, almost without volume. "Take all of me you want, but one day we will reckon things, you and I."

Harka tingled as he took the sword in his hand.

"I was beginning to wonder about you," he said. *"Wonder if there was anything in you besides remorse and self-pity."*

"Oh, yes," Perkar told his blade. "I just found it."

H ᴇ gathered up the firewood and took it back to the clearing, where Brother Horse sat braiding his long gray and black hair. His eyes lingered an instant on Perkar's bloody knuckles, but he made no comment about them.

"I can see your sword," he remarked instead. "If it weren't for that, I might almost doubt your story."

"What does it look like?" Perkar asked curiously, his anger diffused, cooling.

"Well, I see the two of you together. You're tied up somehow. But together you look like a bird. An eagle, I think."

"The sword's name is Harka," Perkar confirmed. "That means Eagle."

"Of course," the old man answered. Nearby, Ngangata stirred in his sleep.

"Your friend is badly hurt," Brother Horse apprised him. "If he continues with you, he will die."

"Yes, I know that," Perkar responded. "That is why I want to leave him with you. Can you see what would happen if I leave him?"

Brother Horse nodded. "Yes. I see him getting stronger, I see you weakening. He is the last, the last of your companions, is he not? The last thing tying you to your homeland and the strength you draw from it."

"I tell you the truth, Grandfather," Perkar whispered. "At first I hated this man. I feared him, and I hate what I fear. I have come to hate myself, because I fear the things I have done. But Ngangata has given me one present after another, even when I couldn't recognize them. He does not deserve to die for me, and I don't deserve to die *with* him—in such good company." He let his gaze drift over to the fire, which seemed pale and sad without a goddess dancing in it. "Brother Horse, will you watch him? When he is stronger, I know he will repay the debt."

Brother Horse reached down and scratched his dog behind the ear and sighed. "If Heen doesn't mind, I won't object," he said.

"Thank you," Perkar replied.

"There's some dried meat in the house. Take some of that. And listen," he said, leaning a bit closer. "If you meet any of my people, tell them I said to let you be. Tell them the old man on the island, who was once Yushnene, who was once Gaan, told them to take care of you."

"That's very kind," Perkar replied, by way of thanks.

"Oh, well," Brother Horse said. "It won't cost *me* anything; I'll be here with this man fetching and serving." He paused, and his eyes twinkled. "Too bad you couldn't have had a sick *woman* with you. But nothing's perfect." He took a drink of tea and then cocked his head to the side. "Listen," he said. "I remembered something else about the River."

"Yes?" Perkar answered.

"You remember that we were talking about him being awake?"

"Yes."

"There is an old song, a legend. I remember that it says one day the River will come fully awake, find two feet to walk on."

"What does that mean?"

Brother Horse shrugged. "Bad things. Maybe the end of the world. It is an old song, and I don't remember much of it."

Later that night, after Brother Horse had finally faded into sleep, Perkar went back to the shore, dragged the boat into the water, and let the current take him on. For the first time in clear memory he felt alive, ready to face the future. Not happy, not content—but at least no longer numb. For thirty days or more, with every fingerspan of water they had crossed he had been resisting, as surely and as stupidly as a man paddling against a current far too strong to fight. Karak's boat had learned its lesson immediately. He had not, and the struggle had worn him out. Yet it was not too late for him to absorb this truth. If he *had* to meet fate, best not do it trying to retreat, back turned, weary to the bone. Better to meet it flying on the balls of his feet, sword drawn.

"I wonder who *will* bear you next, Harka?" he remarked, with more irony than resignation.

IV

Transformations

"Have you ever seen such a wonderful story?" Wezh exclaimed, his fingers fluttering enthusiastically. "The way he arrived *just* as the pirates were going to kill her! And such swordplay! That man should be the head of the imperial guard!"

"That would be fine," Hezhi replied, "if he actually existed."

Wezh blinked at her uncomprehendingly, then blew a little shower of spit from his mouth as he suddenly laughed. "You are so *witty*, Princess," he howled, dabbing at his eyes. "Of course I meant the actor who portrayed Ts'ih. The way he handled that sword. Did you enjoy it? Were you inspired?"

"I *was*," she agreed, though she reflected that what the drama had inspired in her was almost certainly not what it had evoked in Wezh.

"Well," Wezh said, still visibly recovering from mirth, "I wonder where we should walk tonight? The Forest Courtyard is said to be lovely this time of year."

"I was actually feeling a bit tired," she told him, again not lying.

"Nonsense. A breath of fresh air will restore your recalcitrance!"

Hezhi went back over Wezh's last sentence in her mind, trying—as she often found herself doing—to imagine what word the young noble *meant* to use. It didn't really matter though; it was clear that he was insisting on at least a short walk together. She was preparing to reinforce her stated lack of interest in such a stroll when she caught Qa Lung's expression. She hadn't realized that Wezh's bodyguard was near enough to hear her.

Qa Lung made her uncomfortable. Not a slave like Tsem, Qa Lung was actually a member of the Yehd Nu Clan—Wezh's uncle, in fact. As such he had full power to oversee a courtship and offer the terms of marriage. He was also, she knew, one of the small herd of sycophants who had her father's ear, and worse still, he had connections with the priesthood. She felt certain that he was carefully watching her every move, and that many ears would hear what he observed. So rather than loosing the rather pungent reply she had been forming to give Wezh, she smiled sweetly, if a bit painfully, and said, "The Forest Courtyard sounds wonderful." From the corner of her eye she caught her chaperon—Tsem, naturally—suppressing a grin.

A number of the other drama-goers also had a notion to visit the Forest Courtyard. She noted that the vast majority of them were young couples and their chaperons. The balance seemed to be married women without their husbands. These latter were clustered together, discussing the relative merits of the drama and cooing a bit over the protagonist. Their enthusiasm was no doubt heightened by nende'ng, the intoxicating black snuff currently in favor with the court. Their overhappy, glazed expressions and the black stains around their mouths and noses testified amply to that.

The Forest Courtyard was one of the largest, so called because of the eighteen trees that were planted in it and the numerous shrubs, all carefully sculpted to appear wild. It was deemed one of the more romantic spots for courting and for extramarital affairs because it was designed with privacy in mind; the shrubs and screens of climbing plants created numerous small alcoves.

Couples ahead of them slipped off into the "private" places, their bodyguards lagging discreetly behind. This and a bit of prescience inspired in her a distinct drowning sensation, sinking and out of breath all at once. When, as she feared, Wezh took her hand and guided *her* toward one of the grottoes, she shot Tsem a silent appeal. He shrugged slightly as if to ask "What can I do?"

"Alone at last," Wezh said smartly. He hadn't thought of that himself—it was a quote from the drama, probably supposed to evoke in her the same tender feelings it had in the play's heroine. Instead, she wondered how Wezh would react if she were to become ill. Oblivious to her growing dismay, Wezh led her to a little stone bench. She craned her neck; Tsem was no longer visible to her.

Wezh had undergone a disquieting transformation since they had been seeing one another. His shy, tentative nature had slipped aside, and behind it lurked an arrogant self-confidence. Whenever they went anywhere, he made a great show of being *with* her, the Chakunge's daughter. He liked to be noticed. Worse, he believed that he knew her feelings, sensed what she wanted, because, he bragged, he "understood women." *Asking* her what she wanted never seemed to enter into this understanding of his, and indeed, he seemed to feel that doing that would be cheating. Ts'ih, the dashing pirate, would of course *never* have to ask; he would *know*. The only thing that ever dented Wezh's impervious armor of self-delusion was any visible show of anger on Hezhi's part. While he clearly had no recollection of whatever it was she had *done* to him that time, there was some distant corner of his mind that recognized danger when it was *very* near. Unfortunately, she was afraid to show her anger; Qa Lung would see it, see its effect on Wezh, and then he might wonder—wonder and talk.

Therefore, when Wezh leaned over and kissed her—on the *mouth*—she let him. It was peculiar, she thought, that people made so much of kissing. When Wezh kissed her, it felt as if someone were pressing wet liver against her lips—except that liver tasted better. Qey said that one got used to it, but she felt that it was all she could do not to pull away from him. She reminded herself that it was, after all, only the second time Wezh had kissed her. Perhaps it *would* get better.

He moved his attentions from her lips to her neck, and now it felt as if the wet liver were being sponged on her *there*. This was actually more pleasant than the lip kiss—it tickled a bit, and that wasn't bad—but it also meant that Wezh's head with its stink of half-rancid olive oil was right under her nose. She sighed in resignation.

Wezh, of course, took the sigh for one of passion and, thus emboldened, moved his hand up her thigh, toward the juncture of her legs. That was quite enough for *her*, Qa Lung or no Qa Lung. She reached down and firmly removed Wezh's hand from her body.

"Don't be frightened," Wezh soothed. "You'll like it, you'll see."

Hezhi disengaged herself entirely, slid toward the nether end of the bench. "I am Hezhi Yehd Cha'dune," she hissed fiercely, "and I know what I do and do not like."

"No you don't," Wezh assured her. "You know only books and old paper. You have never been awakened by the caress of a man."

She felt certain that he was quoting most of *that*, as well, though she didn't know from where. She fixed him with an angry stare. "I wish to return to my rooms now. The afternoon has been a lovely one." Now *she* was quoting—the lines of the heroine to an unwanted suitor, the villain of the piece.

Wezh nearly purpled. "You little snake," he growled. "*You* let me *bring* you here."

That was so outrageous, she had no reply at all. She merely stood up and narrowed her eyes.

"Sit back down," Wezh said in a reasonable tone.

"If you don't take me home *now*," Hezhi said, firmly and evenly, "you will never see me again save at my wedding to someone else. Further, I will embarrass you right here, right now, in the Forest Courtyard. If you wish to leave this place with any dignity, you will do so now, and no one will know what happened or didn't happen back here. You can *say* whatever you wish. But you will not touch me in that manner."

Wezh actually grinned at that, and, too late, Hezhi realized that her little speech must resemble yet some other drama, for Wezh suddenly grabbed at her. "You resist," he said dramatically, "yet in your eyes I see submission!"

Wezh was much stronger than he looked. Hezhi could not break the grip on her arm, and then he was holding her, grappling her, forcing her down. She found herself suddenly out of breath, heart pounding with fear. He was *strong*! As Wezh pushed her down onto the bench, he let one of his hands free to grope at her barely existent breast. Hezhi's hand, given a life of its own by sheer panic, shot out as if to embrace him and snatched a full firm handful of his oiled hair. She wrenched at it, and Wezh's head snapped back up, a look of utter surprise mingled with pain distorting his features.

"That *hurts*!" He groaned.

She yanked harder; he brought both hands up in an attempt to disengage her fingers, but at that moment she felt a sudden surge of strength from the *place* inside of her. Still jerking his hair, she wriggled out from beneath him.

"Let go!" Wezh all but shrieked.

"I want to go to my rooms," Hezhi hissed into his ear, keeping his head pulled back as he swung his balled fists ineffectually back at her. He twisted wildly, gathered his own feet under him, and lifted his fist again, preparing a more accurate jab. She let go of his hair and stepped back. Wezh lost his balance and tumbled to the ground, crawled back up with murder in his eyes.

For a moment, she thought he *would* hit her, but then his hands dropped, fingers uncurling.

"I don't hit women," he sneered.

She felt herself trembling, whether from fear or fury it was difficult to tell. "Why not?" she snapped. "You seem perfectly willing to *wrestle* them."

Wezh brushed at his clothes. "I'm going to forget this happened," he said, then added sulkily, "You don't appreciate romance at *all*."

"Just take me home," she demanded, voice dripping with as much venom as she could manage—which was quite a bit.

"With pleasure."

The return to her rooms took place in utter, sullen silence. She caught Qa Lung eyeing her, but Tsem had noticed her mussed clothes and angry expression, too. He placed himself at her side, rather than walking behind, a clear message to all that, for the night at least, courting was over.

"Is this how it's going to be?" Hezhi asked Qey, when she was safely back in her rooms.

"No, little one," Qey assured her, placing Hezhi's gown, neatly folded, before her. "You mustn't think that all men are like that."

"I see no reason to doubt it," Hezhi returned, her lips tight.

"Things will seem better, later on. One day you will laugh about this, tell your girlfriends at court."

Hezhi glowered back at Qey. "I doubt this will ever seem funny to me, even if my face is smeared with nende'ng. He *attacked* me, Qey."

"I'm sure he didn't see it that way," Qey responded carefully.

"That makes it worse," she snapped. "How can someone not know he is attacking you? Must I be courted by men who don't even know the difference between romance and *fighting*?"

"Ssh, little one. No one is to say you must marry Wezh. Soon you will have many suitors. Some are reluctant now because you haven't ascended yet. Wezh is merely the most eager, trying to gain an advantage by courting you before you are certain to join the court. When you go up the Hall of Moments, suitors will follow you like the train of your dress. Many of them will respect you, will understand your wishes."

"Many will be like Wezh, and I won't know it until *after* they attack me. How much of that must I endure? He *frightened* me,

Qey, and I have seen things that should make him seem silly, unable to frighten a child . . ." She trailed off, suddenly realizing that Qey was looking at her worriedly. What did Qey suspect?

When she stopped, Qey regarded her for a moment, then took her hand.

"It isn't easy to believe this," she said at last, "but I was young once, too, and not even a princess. This seems very difficult now, I know. But it will get better, if you endure. One day, believe it or not, a man will put his hand on your leg and you won't *want* him to move it. You will want him to hold you and kiss you."

"He didn't *hold* me," Hezhi said softly. "He *grabbed* me. Isn't there a difference?"

"Usually." Qey sighed. "Usually."

SLEEP came with some difficulty. She kept reliving the evening's experience over and over in her head, thinking of all the things she *should* have done. She had felt the thing in her—the *River* part of her. She could have struck at him, just as she had done before, and yet she felt instinctively that using that power was very dangerous right now. Even so, without her even asking, it had made her stronger, filled her arm with enough might to best Wezh; the muscles still tingled, even itched a bit. Actually, that arm had been itching for a few days, now that she thought of it.

Over and over, she reviewed the scene, her anger staying alive and keeping her awake. Finally, deep in the night, an odd thought struck her. She imagined the situation again, but this time, in place of Wezh, she imagined that *Yen* was her suitor. A ridiculous thought—he was much too far beneath her station. And yet, when she imagined the scene with Yen, it came out differently, somehow. When *he* placed his hand on her leg, she stopped him, as well. But *Yen* just smiled kindly, his offending hand gripping hers briefly, and he leaned forward to kiss her forehead. Then the two of them rose and walked, hand in hand, back to her apartments where he bid her good night.

She ran it through her head like *that* a few times and finally drifted off to sleep.

She awoke to a gray dawn, just drizzling in from the courtyard. Something had awakened her, something annoying, but it took a moment for the sleep-fog to lift from her senses enough to localize it. It was her arm, itching furiously. Sleepy and annoyed, she reached to scratch it. That felt better, in the way that scratching does. In the same way, when she stopped, it itched more than before. Grunting, she scratched even harder.

Her nail caught on something, like the edge of a scab. Picking at it again, she wondered when she had injured her arm. Had Wezh wounded her? Curious, she stood up. The apartments were quite silent, and cloaked in that stillness she padded effortlessly out into the courtyard. The sky was slate, with a promise of coral just appearing eastward. A little mouse, surprised at her early entry into its night domain, scuttled into the patch of sage. A cool wind paused in its flight above the palace, just long enough to drop into the courtyard, swirl about her once, and set back on his way.

There, in early light, her life changed once again. No scab on her arm, no injury, no rash. Instead, just above the crook of her elbow, tiny but perfectly formed, grew a scale. Blue, with a hint of iridescence.

V

The Bit Slips

DAYS began to matter again. Perkar first noticed it a short time after he left Ngangata. Impatience was the root of it. It wasn't so much that he cared about days themselves, but that there seemed to be too many of them, too many between him and his destiny. He began marking them, each passing sun a score in the tough wood of the boat.

"*What I cannot do,*" Harka explained to him, "*is cut through days as if they were curtains. I cannot cut them open and let you walk on through to where you want to be, not even I. You must brush each drape aside, one at a time, just as anyone would.*"

Perkar snorted. "What good are you then?"

"*Without me, you would be long dead, piles of shit in a cave.*"

He didn't reply; he still wished sometimes that he *had* died. He clung now to what the goddess told him long ago. Live with what *may* be, what is possible, and not what you childishly wish. He was *not* dead, that was a fact. The goddess was right; remorse and guilt were indulgences, candy to console a troubled

328

child. A man who could not rise above self-pity was useless in any capacity.

He could tell himself that, anyway. But if he had learned that lesson long ago, then his king would still be alive. Apad and Eruka . . . he still saw their faces each morning. Apad's ruined features, Eruka's sightless eyes—the Kapaka as Perkar had last known him alive, ashen, his dreams dead and his own ghost yearning for oblivion. Or worse, the cold, faceless spirit in the moonlight. But he could *tell* himself that grief was pointless, get on with things. He had a purpose now, though it was vague. He had something more to do.

If only he could do it soon, before he lost this new resolve, before the memories and the dreams dragged him into madness. The wounds on his knuckles were already merely scars, and the tedium of the boat trip made it difficult to sustain his anger. Still, it was there, waiting, at least for the moment.

Five days after he began counting suns again, he passed by the city of Wun. He knew that it was Wun because Brother Horse had told him that Wun was the first city he would encounter. He knew that it was a city because he had never seen anything like it save in dreams. There was nothing astonishing about the first cluster of houses he went by. Though the dwellings were willow and reed rather than of stout planks with shake roofs, in size and number they were much like the village near any damakuta. The people, despite their dark skin and exotic features, were familiar, too, seemed to go about life the way villagers did. A woman filling a water jug, boys swimming in the River, waving at him as he passed, a man watering his sheep. But as he drifted along, the houses grew denser and denser, larger, and the people more numerous. Some young women, bathing in the River, giggled and pointed at him, and one even motioned him toward them, to the mock dismay of her companions. Perkar waved and drifted on, eventually passing houses made of stone, wooden docks thick with ships, some larger than any he had ever imagined, clustered at the planked walkways like fish feeding at the edge of a stream.

Men and women in colorful clothes watched him go by curiously, perhaps wondering if the stranger in his little boat could really be as pale as he seemed from a distance. He laid hard on the rudder, though he suspected the uselessness of it, was rewarded only by warmed muscles as Wun slid along beside him, shrank to small clusters of houses again, was gone, leaving him to wonder, from his brief glimpses of color and life, what the people might be like, what they might hope and dream, consider good food, teach their children.

Paradoxically, though he had never seen more people or buildings in one place—perhaps in his entire life—Wun still seemed small to him. His vision of "city" was a dream one, dominated by buildings that dwarfed even the largest in Wun.

Passing Wun, he crossed the mouth of a river flowing down from the north. He surveyed it curiously, speculating about from whence he or she flowed, whether it suffered as much as the Stream Goddess did, where she entered the Changeling. It almost seemed that the tributary spoke to him, not in words or even like Harka, but in signs. In its thick turbid waters, swollen by some far-off rain, Perkar seemed to catch evanescent images of distant mountains, storm clouds, raven black, encasing bones of silent lightning. Rain falling for days on end. The mud the tributary brought fanned out into the Changeling, trailed darkly along his northern edge, thinner with each downstream moment but still visible. Perkar considered the tributary's resistance, its unwillingness to immediately die, and a vague hope gathered courage and became an idea. Once more he put his weight on the tiller, hoping to enter the fading brown stream, to reach a place where the hold of the Changeling might not be absolute. When that failed, he lifted up his pack and sword and prepared to jump.

"Don't," Harka warned him. He ignored the sword and leapt anyway.

He believed, briefly, that he had succeeded. His strokes took him cleanly toward the bank, and the current, while mightily strong, was not swift. Almost he reached the brown streak and its promise, the gift of some storm cloud far away, but then the current

took him like an immense fist, and his pitiful Human strength was
nothing. Exhausted, he soon found himself back against the boat.

"It was worth a try," he told Harka later, his shirt drying in
the sun.

"*I thought you had resigned yourself to this,*" the sword
chided him.

"I have," he told it, and did not further explain himself.

A day passed, and a night, and then a new morning. The River
in the past few days had swollen to an enormous size, so huge
that, even in the center of the channel, Perkar had to strain to see
that southern shore, a fine line of green against the yellow haze
of endless desert. The Changeling was still meandering east, but
the sunrise was still farther to his left each morning, and so he
knew they—the boat, the River and he—were gradually turning
more southward, toward an ocean he had only heard the vaguest
rumors of and could not imagine at all. Surely the River held all
of the water there was in the world. How could the "ocean" be
larger? His own language did not even have a word for such a
thing; he could only call it the Big Lake. But the language in his
head, with its strange vowels and clattering short consonants, *did*
have such a word. *They* could imagine it.

Bemused, Perkar wondered if, as the Changeling ate streams,
the ocean could eat the Changeling. That might be worth knowing, a way of eventual escape even, except that whatever could
eat him might be worse, more powerful still.

Toward midday, he noticed another vessel approaching him
from the northeast bank. It grew quickly in his sight, a lean, long
craft with a lateen sail, a white triangle fragment of the overhead
sun.

He drew Harka, gazing off in the distance at nothing in particular. His regard was drawn inevitably back to the approaching
craft. Twice more he tried looking away, and twice more he
found himself staring at the ever-closer sail.

"They are a danger to me, then?" he asked the sword.

"*So it would seem,*" Harka replied.

He took the tiller and guided the boat toward the opposite

bank. The Changeling let him; he knew from experience that he could get close to shore if he wanted, though when the River deemed him *too* close he would stop him. Despite this maneuver, the approaching sail drew nearer and nearer. In a short time, the strange boat was just to the left of him. As he watched, the canvas came down, and two men began paddling furiously as a third watched him impassively from the bow.

"What do you want?" he called to them, when he judged them near enough to hear.

The man in the bow replied in a language Perkar had never heard before, but understood well. It was the language taught him by his dreams.

"I don't know that barbarous tongue, westlander," the man shouted back. "But if you can understand real speech and have any sense, you won't make trouble for us."

Perkar opened his mouth, and alien words licked off his tongue, first thickly, but swiftly learning more grace.

"I have no desire to cause you trouble," he declared.

"Well, then," the man retorted, as the two boats pulled almost within reaching distance. "In that case, you will abandon your ship now and save us the trouble of throwing you off. If you jump, too, you can leave your boat in a single piece rather than with your head and body separated."

"I have nothing of value to steal," Perkar said reasonably. "And I have no wish to fight you." Both statements were more than true. Though strange-looking, these men were Human Beings, not gods who would wing home to their mountain and be reclothed. They were men, and if they died the River would swallow their souls. Perhaps they would end like the watery fish he had speared, far back at the headwaters, memories of themselves in the current. Like the Kapaka.

Fury sparked at that. He realized they might well kill him, too, and *that* he no longer wished.

The man in the bow scowled, fiercely ridged eyebrows bunching above a hawklike nose, piercing black eyes. He held up a curved sword—heavy-looking, more like a giant cleaver than something to fight with. "Jump off or die," the stranger warned. One of the other men produced a sword, as well, while the third maneuvered the boat closer still.

Perkar drew Harka and stood, too. A month and a half in the boat had left him more than adept at standing in a rocking vessel.

"Please," he pleaded, though in him the anger was growing. "There is no need for this. I have nothing."

"You have your boat," the man countered easily, "and that will fetch a price worth fighting for. In fact, it might fetch a very high price as a curio. The Waterborn down in Nhol *like* curious things." His eyes narrowed. "And that sword; quite odd. Furthermore, you are clearly from far, far away. Why would you travel so far unless you have something to trade?"

It wasn't really a question, and Perkar realized that the man was not negotiating, but only trying to convince him to jump. Despite his belligerent attitude, he seemed reluctant to attack, even given the advantage he and his men had in numbers. He was perhaps thirty-five or forty, old enough to have experienced a few nasty surprises, to know that even the most promising situation could end in disaster. His men were young, younger than Perkar, though they had a hard look about them and numerous scars. The man's sons, perhaps?

"You can *see* I have nothing, or you are blind," he pointed out. "Let me go in peace. I can't jump in the River; he won't let me." Why wouldn't they *listen* to him?

"The River doesn't care about you—or anybody—except the Waterborn," the man asserted. He spat. "That for you. Get out of your boat or die."

He hesitated, wondering what would happen if he *did* jump overboard. Surely the Changeling would not let them take the boat. But if it *did* . . .

Perkar saw the man decide; it was a hardening of the eyes, a tightening of the gut, and then, as if by some signal, the two strangers leapt into his boat, swords drawn and already swinging.

Sudden, dark joy stabbed through Perkar as he shifted his

weight to account for the sudden motion of the boat, crouching as he did so. At last, someone to strike, someone to kill who *deserved* it. He brought Harka up to parry, slid the godsword on over his head to catch the strike of the second man. The first sword rang and slid away, but the younger man's weapon made a very peculiar sound as Harka cut straight through it. His eyes seeking danger, Perkar turned quickly enough to catch the first attacker's return stroke. The enemy sword shuddered and nicked deeply. Reversing again, he sliced back at the other pirate, who had not quite come to terms with his ruined sword and was swinging it anyway. Ignoring the wild attack, he cut into the man's exposed ribs just below the armpit. He sliced cleanly through, felt a slight jolt as the spine clove in two. Harka disengaged easily, caught a third attack by the first man—on whose face a sudden comprehension was just dawning. The parried sword slid into the side of the boat, *thunked* into the wood as Harka glittered through the sunshine, flinging droplets of blood behind, and opened the man's belly. Entrails spilled out like eels from a split sack, and the man stared at Perkar, wide-eyed. Perkar was turning yet again at Harka's insistence, but the weight of the younger man fell heavily against him, hands clawing at his head. Perkar brought his elbow in frantically—the fellow was too close for sword work—but it was more of a stumble than an attack; the young man slid against him, slicking him with blood. For the second time in his life, he was drenched in the stinking red fluid of another person's body.

He snarled and turned toward the boat, though Harka did not beckon him to. The third man was rowing desperately away, eyes wide with terror. Perkar shouted incoherently after him.

The older man was still alive. He lay in the bottom of the boat, trying to hold in his intestines. Perkar shuddered, ran his finger down the river of blood on his body. "This was your fault," he spat furiously. "You *made* me do this!"

The man just blinked at him.

Blood, Perkar suddenly thought. *The Changeling knew me because he tasted my blood.*

He tried not to let the thought form fully, tried not to puzzle it out. It was more instinct than anything else that drove him to grab his pack, sheath bloody Harka, and dive into the River. The bank was close, as close as it had been in a long time.

The River let him go at first, but it had done that before. It wasn't until he actually felt sand beneath his feet that he shrieked in jubilation. It had worked! The Changeling had mistaken him, cloaked in another's blood!

Two steps he took through the shallows, and the River took hold of him.

"No!" he hissed through his teeth. He kicked, strained with everything he had. Current clenched him, hauling him back out. In desperation he dove, clawed with his hands at the shallow bottom, and miraculously, his fingers brushed something hard. He tore at it, got a hold, pulled.

Unfortunately he could not hold onto the thing—it seemed to be a root—and raise his head above water, too. He knotted all his determination together, tied it about the root, and heaved, even as his lungs began to remind him frantically that breathing was a necessity. He pulled until his shoulder ached as if stung by ants, but finally he managed to drag himself far enough inland to get just his nose up, to sip a tiny amount of air. His arms were trembling now, but he was *so* close.

When he got his whole head above water, he knew he would succeed. It took a long time, until his body was weak and his mind reduced to a single thought—*pull!*—but at last he lay on the sand, the warm, dry sand. With the paltry energy left him, Perkar stumbled as far from the water as he could get, crashing into trees, torn by briars. When he finally stopped, it was because he could go no farther.

He could no longer see the River, but with the last of his strength he faced it. "You let the bit slip," he gasped. "I warned you." Then he sank down, resting against a tree trunk, trembling from exertion. Free.

VI

~~~~~~

A Visitor

"**W**ELL," Ghan asked, studying her face closely. "To what do we owe this renewed interest in matters intellectual?" His pen remained poised to continue its scratching upon the sheaf of paper open before him.

"I need to see those books, Ghan. Please."

"A little argument with your paramour, perhaps? A disagreement over 'lacies'?"

Hezhi suppressed a snarl. "Ghan," she snapped instead. "I don't have time to argue with you, do you understand? I know I upset you. I know you think I have better things to do than to play the court games. Don't you think I know that? But if you ever thought the least bit of me, if you ever cared about me at all, you have to help me. I have no time!"

Ghan's face changed oddly as she said this. She wasn't sure what emotions he displayed, so quickly did he master them—dismay? fear?

He regarded her for another moment, his face now carefully

blanked, and then tersely commanded, "Come." Grasping her hand—*her hand*—he practically dragged her off to the back room, where the index and valuable documents were kept. Shutting the door, he bolted it from the inside.

"You little fool," he hissed. "Don't you know better than to go shouting about like that? Who knows who might hear you?"

"What do you mean? What did I say?"

Ghan stepped back, his eyes dark with challenge. "Tell me," he said, his voice harsh. "Tell me why you have 'no time.' "

"I cannot," she breathed. Ghan *knew*? "I cannot. I know you have been Forbidden."

"Forbidding stops me from speaking, not from hearing. Tell me."

She studied her teacher, her heart sinking. Tears poised behind her eyes, cataracts waiting to fall. "I can't trust you," she sobbed suddenly. "I can't trust *anyone*. Not now."

"Hezhi," Ghan said more gently. "Hezhi, listen to me." He took her chin between thumb and forefinger and tugged it gently up. "I notice things, you know," he said at last. "I heard the talk about the ghost in the Hall of Moments. There are those who think it was after *you*. I saw, that time when you ordered that boy away from you, and he *went*, as if you had slapped him. You read books, many books, and all about the Royal Blood, about the old city. Can't you see I've been helping you all along? Child, you *must* trust me. I'm all that you have."

She stared at him, blinking away tears. It was true, of course, she knew that. Sometimes his help had been blatant, usually not. She had to trust him because he already knew—because she had to trust someone.

"We cannot get the books you want," Ghan went on. "The priesthood will not release them to me, and even if they were so inclined, they would certainly want to know who was reading them, and why. They would find you out, you see?"

"They will find me out anyway," Hezhi all but shrieked. "The next time they test me. The next time . . ."

"Is it that bad?" Ghan whispered almost wonderingly.

Lips pressed together defiantly, she pulled up her long sleeve, and there it was, blue and green in the pale illumination streaming weakly through the translucent skylight.

"By the River," Ghan breathed. Hand to his forehead, he sat back heavily onto a small stool, massaging his brow.

"What am I to do with you?" he muttered.

"You can't do anything," she rejoined, trying to seem brave. Despite her intentions, her voice sounded like a pathetic moan, even to her own ears.

"Why did you want the priest books? What did you think of?"

"Ghan," she said tremulously, "Ghan, I've *seen* them. I found a way down to where the Darkness Stair goes, to the old palace. I saw them, the Blessed. I can't be like that. I'll jump off the roof first."

She would, this time. She had promised herself.

"Hezhi, what did you *think* of?"

"That maybe . . . Maybe there is a way to stop it. To stop the Royal Blood from working. To keep the River asleep in me."

Ghan's head hung as if it weighed a hundredweight. She had never seen him look so old. "There *can't* be," he muttered.

"Why?"

"The priests would do it, don't you think?"

"They *do* do it, Ghan. They stop it in themselves!"

"By castration, before the change starts. That won't work for you. You aren't a man, and if you were, you would already be too old."

Her voice strengthened, as she gained a little courage. "If there is one way to stop it, there might be another." She watched him rub his head hopefully.

"I don't know. There might be. I don't believe so."

"It doesn't matter," she remarked bitterly. "Not if I can't see the books anyway."

Ghan looked up at her, meeting her eyes for the first time in several exchanges. "No," he said. "But *I* can look at them, if I go there. They have to let me, if I say it is required for the index."

"That would be dangerous for you," she replied.

"Yes. As this conversation, right now, is dangerous for me."
He gripped her shoulder, pointed his index finger squarely at her
nose, so that she almost went cross-eyed. "Stay calm, for a day
or two only. Stay off of the roof, and act normally. Work here in
the library, tell anyone who asks that I have demanded it. I will
find out what I can, do what I can. But you have to trust me. Me,
and no one else. Have they tested you once already?"

Hezhi nodded, dumbfounded by Ghan's sudden passion.

"Then they are watching you, you can be sure of that. Somewhere, in the shadows, following you. He will see you, Hezhi,
but you won't see him."

"Who?"

"The priests set watchers on children like you, children that
worry them. Members of the Jik sometimes."

"The Jik?" she repeated, her voice quavering.

"I know you've read about those Blessed who were discovered
too late. The noble children who went wild, caused destruction.
The priesthood won't let that happen again. When they fear it,
they turn loose the Jik—not to spy on foreign diplomats, not to
kill overly ambitious merchants—but to watch children, to stop
them while there is still time."

"It sounds like you agree with them," Hezhi murmured, suddenly unsure.

"I'm just explaining your danger and the reason for it," he explained quietly. "I have no wish to see my library and the rest of
the palace come down around my ears. But rather that than
know you were below the Darkness Stair. Bide, Hezhi, and let me
see what I may. And watch the shadows! Your half Giant will not
be able to protect you from one of the Jik."

WHEN they returned to the central room, she noticed Yen, a half-
dozen books open in front of him. He looked up and smiled at
her. She waved but did not approach him. Her life was compli-

cated enough without becoming better friends with the son of a
merchant. Instead, she went home, silently watched Qey go
about her tasks, and at last retreated to her own room, where she
could hear the comforting sounds of the house without danger of
having to *speak* to anyone.

As she lay there, turning thoughts and images over in her
mind, her ghost appeared, a man-shaped blur touched at the
edges by rainbow. She watched with some apprehension as he
meandered around the room, as if performing some stately spec-
tral dance. He did not approach her or threaten to touch her as
he had before. Eventually the shimmering that marked him
twisted, became thin, a line, vanished.

Left alone once more, she reflected on what small comfort
came from answers. After all, she now understood most of the
events of the past few months. Her power began to waken when
she began to bleed. The Riverghost had sensed her, lurked in the
fountain while her father summoned its lesser brethren, and then
come after her. Whether it meant somehow to feed on her or was
merely drawn to her like a moth to a flame was immaterial,
though she suspected the former, considering how the ghost in
her room was able to draw form and substance from the merest
contact with her blood. Who had the demon ghost once been?
Someone like her, of course. A child filled with forces she neither
wanted nor understood. She had lived below the Darkness
Stair—for how long? She had died there, and the River, torpid
and uncaring, had drunk her into himself.

She scratched at her own scale, her own sign of exile.

Evening found her still there, and in the entry room across the
courtyard, she heard a door open, and voices. She bolted up in
her bed. If it was the priests, she was doomed. She wondered,
wildly, if she could climb the wooden trellis to the roof, make her
way to the Great Hall, steal their victory from them. But it was
too late; footsteps slapped across the courtyard, hushed in soles
of soft leather.

Her visitor was no priest. The woman who uncertainly entered her room and leaned against the doorjamb was the last person she ever expected. Almost, in fact, she didn't recognize the woman. Slim, beautiful despite being a few years past her prime, coiled hair shot with a magnificent streak of gray. Eyes as wide and black as Hezhi's own, the same eyes, so many were wont to say.

"Mother?" Hezhi gasped, even then uncertain.

"So," the woman said, her voice cool, but edged with some almost concealed emotion. "You know me, at least. That is more than I expected."

Hezhi nodded her head, unable to speak. She tugged at her sleeve, making certain the scale was concealed.

The two women gazed at each other, neither speaking, for a long moment. The elder finally broke the silence. "You've grown into a pretty thing," she said. "Soon you will have many suitors."

"I have one already," Hezhi corrected quietly, sitting up and brushing at her disordered hair.

"The Yehd Nu boy? Yes, I've heard about that. You embarrassed him quite soundly."

Her mother's speech was glacial, each word carefully shaped as if just recalled from a distant memory. Hezhi noticed the discreet black stain beneath her nose, the dark cast to her lips.

"I didn't mean . . ." she stammered, but her mother held up a hand.

"No, you should keep him guessing. And soon . . ." She paused, wrinkled her angular face, brushed at it with a finely manicured hand. "Yes, soon you will have many suitors, and have your pick of them."

Hezhi nodded, still unwilling to offer anything to this ethereal creature, this woman she had seen only from afar for most of her life. When was the last time they had spoken? In her garden, two years ago? It seemed at least that long.

"Well, I . . ." Her mother seemed to search for words and frowned down at the floor as if she might find them there. When she looked back up, her glazed eyes held a frankness in them, an unspoken truth. "I just wanted to see you, Hezhi. It's been a long time since we talked." She smiled, a false and painful smile. "After all, I did bear you, didn't I? Nine months in my belly you were, though you struggled to escape much earlier." She shrugged. "I just wanted to see you, tell you I'm looking forward to you joining us soon. That will be nice, won't it?"

Hezhi could see Qey, across the courtyard, wringing her hands, pretending to slice onions. She was crying, but of course, she always cried when she sliced onions. Halfway across the courtyard was a handsome, smart-looking man in royal livery, trying not to seem uncomfortable. Her mother's bodyguard? Or a Jik? But no, the Jik she would never see; they were less visible than ghosts, and when their knives found your heart it was always from behind.

Her mother smiled at her for a score more uncomfortable breaths. "I just wanted to say hello," she explained. "You're really a very beautiful young woman."

"Thank you."

Her mother nodded. "I hope we see you soon," she concluded sluggishly, turned. Signaling her man with a slight crook of her wrist, she departed.

Her visit left Hezhi with a tight heart, a need for air. Dizziness crept up on her, and she realized her breathing was too hard, too fast. Why would her mother come see her now, of all times, after all these years? But Hezhi knew, she knew.

Even the most remote of mothers might want to see her child one last time.

Especially if she knew her child was soon to die. Or vanish.

GHAN had a harried look about him, as if he hadn't slept. His face was tightened into a frown more bitter than usual, and he ushered her into the back room without delay.

"It was more difficult than I imagined. I'm afraid I awoke some of my own sleeping enemies," he said tiredly.

Concern for the old man stole up through her other fears. "I never wanted to create trouble for you," she said.

"No, I created my own troubles long ago," he informed her. "Old debts can be put off for a time, but they must be paid eventually."

"They let you see the books?"

"Yes," he verified shortly.

She waited.

"There isn't much that can be done," he said at last. "Only one thing, really."

"But something?"

He shrugged. "It is a chance. Some of the older texts speak of a time before the Blessed were consigned . . ." A look of agony washed over his face, and his jaw worked soundlessly, like a mute gibbering. "You know," he gasped, after the spasm passed, "one can dance around a Forbidding, if one is clever. Sometimes I am not clever."

"Before they were sent *underneath*," Hezhi finished for him softly, wishing she could erase his pain.

"Yes." He seemed composed again. "Before that began, they were dealt with in other ways. Some were killed. Others fled Nhol entirely, or were exiled to some distant land."

"And now? Why not now?"

"There are uses for the Blessed," he muttered. "Under the right circumstances, their power can be controlled, manipulated. Used to enhance the Chakunge's power. More than that, though, was the nagging paranoia of the royal family. One does not let a rival power loose in the world."

"I don't . . ."

"Some evidence indicates that the . . . change"—Again he shuddered, lightly—"is so tied to the River that if one is not near him, if one is far away, it will not occur." He paused, watching her, letting that sink in.

"Leave Nhol?" It was a bewildering thought.

"Surely it has occurred to you," he said softly.

"I . . . *no*, I hadn't thought of that. How? Where would I go?" Even as she said this, her dreams came flashing back behind her eyes; deep forest, mountains, the gray-eyed man. Was that what they were about, her dreams?

"I made a wish . . ." she muttered.

"What?"

"The day I began bleeding, I drank Sacred Water. I wished for someone—a man, I guess—to come and get me, free me from my problems. It was a stupid wish, I know. It feels stupid talking about it. But after that, I began having dreams of a far-off place, of a strange man."

"You were bleeding," Ghan whispered. "Your first blood." He frowned, wrinkled his brow as if remembering something. "Blood is motion," he said softly, and it had the sound of something quoted. "Blood is motion, and thus spirit. Spirit is the roots of the world."

"What is that?" Hezhi asked.

"An old, old saying," Ghan said. "I never thought about it much. But the Royal Blood sets things moving, Hezhi. The River knows the feel and touch of Human blood, the scent of it. But the blood of his children he knows *very* well. You may have set something exceptionally deep in motion." He knitted his fingers tight, squeezed his palms together, nodded fretfully. "But what you get is not likely to be what you wished for."

"Why would the River help me at all? Why would it help me escape?"

Ghan quirked his mouth in a shallow grin. "The River is not a thoughtful or wakeful god. He is a very literal one, and it has been said that none can know his will. Not because he is mysterious, or even capricious, in the usual sense. But because he does not know his *own* will."

"Leave Nhol," Hezhi considered wonderingly. "I can't imagine it."

"But you can imagine the alternatives all too well," Ghan pointed out.

"I don't even know how to begin."

"Your Giant. He is loyal?"

"Tsem loves me," Hezhi said. "He has always been with me."

"In the palace, that means nothing. Do you trust him?"

"Yes," Hezhi said, "I do."

"Then leave and send him in to see me. He and I will make your plans."

"What of me? Am I to have no part in my own rescue?"

"Tsem and I can move outside of the city. You cannot."

Hezhi saw sense in that, reluctantly nodded acquiescence.

Ghan narrowed his eyes. "This man in your dreams. Describe him again."

Hezhi closed her eyes, concentrating. "He has very pale skin," she said. "Gray eyes, light brown hair. He wears armor sometimes. He has a sword. I think he is very far away; I have never dreamed about him here, in Nhol."

Ghan nodded. "These dreams of yours may mean something or they may not. Nhol is a large city, and even if this dream-man is here, he may be difficult to find. Though there must be precious few men in the city who match his description." He smiled and stretched out his hand to give her a squeeze. "Well, it's been long enough since I've been out of the palace anyway. This will be good for me."

He motioned for her to go on, his eyes thoughtful. Already seeing the city outside, perhaps, and the paths by which one might leave it.

"Ghan?" Hezhi murmured. "Ghan, why have you helped me?"

Ghan regarded her, his old face solemn. "I wish you wouldn't ask me questions I don't know the answers to," he sighed. "Not when I have a reputation for knowing everything."

VII

Paths of Stone, Mountains of Light

PERKAR spooned the soup greedily; he believed it to be the best thing he had ever eaten. Nearby, a scruffy brown dog watched him with more than passing interest.

"Otter Boy wants some," Win explained. Win was a little boy of perhaps seven years with a broad, happy face. Nearby, his mother, Ghaj, watched with evident amusement as she spun cotton onto a wooden spool. Hearing his name, Otter Boy stood, wagging and panting hopefully.

"Reminds me of my old dog, Kume," Perkar remarked. "When I was this hungry, I wouldn't give *him* any, either."

"They have dogs where you come from?" Win asked.

Ghaj snorted, glanced up from her work to show them her thick-featured face. "They have dogs everywhere," she opined.

"She's right, they do," Perkar agreed.

"Tell me more about where you're from," Win exclaimed.

"Don't be rude," Ghaj chided her son.

"It's all right," Perkar said.

Ghaj puckered her face in consternation. "He's *my* boy," she informed him. "I'll decide what is and is not acceptable."

"Oh," he said sheepishly, "sorry."

She nodded her forgiveness, but it was clear she had more on her mind. "I can't invite you to stay with us tonight," she told him. "Me a widow and you a foreigner—I don't need that sort of talk. There is an inn in town—sort of—L'uh, the stable master, rents a few rooms. You understand, I hope."

"I understand," he assured her. He also understood the suspicious way she kept eyeing his sword and the faded brown stains on his clothes.

"You do have some money?" she inquired.

He stopped with his spoon halfway to his mouth.

"What is money?" he asked.

Ghaj rolled her eyes. "A foreigner who doesn't even know what money *is*," she muttered. "Strange things the River sends me."

"Why can't he stay with us?" Win complained. "He can show me his sword."

"A sword isn't something to play with or to unsheath lightly," Perkar told the boy.

"How long will you stay in Nyel?" Ghaj asked.

Perkar considered. "Not long. I'll leave in the morning, I think."

Ghaj clucked her disapproval. "You must be in a big hurry to leave that soon. You're in no shape to travel."

"I have something to do," he told her. "Something I want to get finished as soon as I can, so I can go on with other things."

"I didn't ask for your life story," Ghaj chastened sourly. "I only wanted to know how long I have to put you up for."

Perkar finished off the soup and set the bowl down. Without hesitation, Otter Boy nosed down into it, tongue slurping. "I thought you just said . . ."

"Let them talk," Ghaj decided. "It'll only be out of jealousy anyway. Strangers don't stop here—they either stop in Wun or go on to Nhol, and the overland routes are nowhere near here."

"There is a path to Nhol, though?"

"A path, not much more. Most people go by boat."

"I lost my boat," he explained.

Ghaj grinned broadly, with genuine amusement. "So I guessed," she said, gesturing with the back of her hand at his still-damp and muddy clothing. "You know," she mused, "some of my husband's old clothes might fit you."

As it turned out, the shirt fit loosely and the kilt needed taking in. He accepted them gratefully, though he didn't much care for the kilt. How could one ride a horse in such a garment?

Ghaj was quick to suggest ways he could repay her kindness. She was low on firewood for cooking; two of her crawfish traps needed repair, and a new trash pit needed digging. He saw to all of these things, with the often dubious aid of Win. These chores he completed by evening, and when Ghaj served the late meal— River rice and steamed crawfish—he ate it with gusto. His muscles were beginning to ache, but to Perkar it was a delicious soreness, earned by doing something real and worthwhile. It reminded him of long days in his father's pasture, cutting hay and thatching it together for the winter, of hard work on a neighbor's damakuta and then a heavy meal and woti afterward. He had experienced pain enough, aching muscles to last a lifetime in the past few months—but *that* soreness had never brought him satisfaction.

"Tell me," Win begged. "Tell me more about your adventures."

"There isn't so much to tell about me," he told the boy. "But I can tell you some of the things I saw, coming down the River. I can tell you about the old Mang man I met."

"Tell me!" Win exclaimed delightedly. "Did you have to kill him with your sword?"

"No, he was very nice to me. He had a dog, too . . ."

He went on for a while, speaking of the vast open plains, gradually becoming desert, the occasional distant mountains, the
night that lightning had raged silently on every horizon without
ever a thunderclap or a raindrop. As he did so, a peculiar thing
happened. Remembering these things with his voice, he suddenly
marveled at them. When those sights had been laid out, actually
there for him to see, he had absorbed them with the eyes of a
corpse, indifferent. Wonder, long dormant, now quickened, and
he felt like both laughing and crying. Instead he talked on, until
Win's little eyes, fluttering closed and frantically opening again,
finally drooped still and stayed that way. Ghaj carried him up to
his loft bedroom.

"Let me show you where you will stay," Ghaj said when she
returned. She led him inside the house and motioned to a quilted
pallet on the floor. Perkar glanced around, puzzled.

"Where will you sleep?"

Ghaj grinned crookedly with her wide mouth. "The reason
people say those things about widows," she confided, "is because
they are true." He stood dumbly as she reached to her hem and
shucked her dress up over her head. "Besides," she added. "It's
not likely I'll meet another one like *you* anytime soon, and I can't
resist seeing how you're put together."

"I . . ." He felt a familiar shame, one almost forgotten in the
past months. How could he explain to her, about the goddess,
about his problems?

He was still searching for a way to tell her when she stepped
closer, reached out, and touched his cheek. "What's wrong?" she
asked. "I may not be as beautiful as you might like, I know . . ."

Her hand was warm, smelled of garlic and crawfish. Her eyes
were kind and just a little hungry, with disappointment already
threatening at the edges. Despite himself, despite what he knew,
he looked at her, took in her naked body with his eyes. Indeed,
she was like no woman he had ever dreamed of having. Her features were broad and thick, lips everted, cheekbones flat, angular.
Her body was thick, too, in every dimension, and she was not

young. The slightly swelling belly and the curve of her hips were stippled with pale stretch marks, as were her breasts, otherwise generous, enormous nipples charcoal in the moonlight. She was as much a Human woman as anyone could be, nothing like a goddess at all. He gasped aloud, closed his eyes at the sudden rush of blood in his body, at the fierce urge that overtook him then. Ghaj sighed with delight (and perhaps relief) as he sagged forward, embraced her, buried his head in the juncture of her neck and clavicle. She was salty, hot, her skin was a luxury like none he had imagined. He nearly sobbed with ecstasy as her lips closed around the lobe of his ear, as she pushed her hands up under his kilt.

"I . . ." he gasped as she took control of the situation, gently pushed him back onto the pallet.

"I know," she whispered. "It's been a long time since you were with a woman. It's been a long time for me, too. We have to try and be quiet, though. If we wake Win, we'll have less time for each other."

That made good sense to Perkar, but there were many times that night when he wondered how *anyone* in the entire world could still be asleep.

Later, when they were both exhausted, they held one another until limbs began to go numb and then settled for nestling. Perkar felt his quickening sense of wonder rise above him like a halo. Ghaj was now a beautiful woman, and he gazed at her through the night, noticed that her thick features had become sensual, her stubby hard fingers tender and evocative. The moon was set, sight replaced by touch and memory, when exhaustion drew up over his joy and hope like a warm comforter and settled him into dreams.

At Ghaj's earnest urging, he stayed another day and night, recovering his strength and enjoying Human company. He spent the day doing more chores and making Win a little bow and arrow so he could be like the great Ngangata of Perkar's stories.

That night, he and Ghaj made love again, and it was even nicer without the weirdness and uncertainty of the first time. He had never imagined that passion and comfort could be combined. After all, one could not be comfortable around a goddess.

He awoke to Ghaj's steady gaze, her dark skin buttered gold by the morning, her hair hanging mussed in her face. She was tracing her finger lightly over his chest, brushing the white mass of scar tissue where the lion had cut him open, the stiff ridge of it where the Huntress' spear had driven through him. When she noticed him awake, she smiled faintly. "So young, to have all these," she said, and lightly kissed the spear wound.

"Thank you," he said a bit later, as they were getting dressed.

"For what?"

"Everything. I know you don't understand, but this has been important for me. I've never . . ."

"You aren't going to tell me you were a virgin," she teased. "You were clumsy now and then, but not *that* clumsy."

"No," Perkar admitted, embarrassed. "No, not exactly. But it was important."

Ghaj walked over, gathered him in for a hug. "It was very nice," she said. "I enjoyed our time together. Come back through and if I'm not remarried, we'll enjoy each other again." She took his chin in her fingers, kissed him lightly. "You do know I could never ask you to stay? I like you, despite your foreign weirdness, but as a husband you wouldn't do me much good around here. Despite what I said, I *do* care what people say."

"I know. I'm flattered that it even crossed your mind, Ghaj."

"A sweet boy, despite your scars," she said, kissing him again.

Later, Win and Ghaj helped him get his things together. Ghaj replaced his dilapidated saddle pack with a woven shoulder-net, and after a bit of cobbling reduced some of her husband's too-large shoes to fit Perkar. Win was delighted with his bow. To Ghaj Perkar had nothing to give, save the little charm his mother had made him. He gave her that. "I wish I had better," he told her. "You've been very kind to me."

Ghaj's eyes twinkled. "Come back this way and I'll be 'kind' to you some more." She gave him another hug and a kiss that lingered *just* a little, and pointed him down the road.

"You'll be to the outskirts of Nhol by nightfall, if you walk briskly. You don't want to enter Nhol at night, so I suggest you go a little more than briskly. I also suggest you find one of the dockside taverns—they're used to strangers there and always have rooms. Take this." She handed him a little pouch. He shook it and it jingled.

"A Royal and a few soldiers," she informed him. "I can spare just that for you."

"It's more than I need. I can't . . ."

"Hush. In Nhol, without money, you'll be sleeping in an alley and have your throat slit before the first half a night. Take the coins, consider it pay for the work you've done around here, if you insist. And I suggest if you're going to stay long in the city that you find some way to pick up a few more soldiers. What I gave you won't go far at all."

He nodded. "Again, I'm grateful."

Ghaj called out to him once more as he was about to turn a bend in the trail. "Don't trust anyone in Nhol, Perkar."

He waved and called back that he wouldn't. Win followed him a little way, but not much beyond the edge of the bottomlands, where the trail climbed up out of the floodplain and onto the drier land around. He watched as the little boy's stubby legs took him quickly back away.

The sun was hot, but it did nothing to spoil Perkar's mood. Though the hard dirt trail was taking him to an unknown destiny, he felt ready to meet it now, hopeful even. The doom hanging over him like a thundercloud, if not departed, was at least letting a bit of light in.

In that light the day was beautiful, the strange scenery fascinating. It was a landscape of fields, and what fields they were! Grander than most pastures, they rolled out flat on both sides of the road, broken only by an occasional line of trees, the distant levee on his left, and strange streams as straight as arrow shafts.

It was only after he crossed a score of these streams, wondering at their perfect regularity, that he was struck with the idea that someone had *dug* them. The notion dumbfounded him, for though he could see the use of such unthinkably extensive ditches for watering crops, the labor involved was more than he could imagine. And yet the result was as staggering as the effort, for beyond the fields nothing grew but scrub, while the fields were green with strange plants.

And there were no cattle at all. What did these people do for milk, cheese—more important, Piraku? And yet the fields and their artificial rivers spoke eloquently of determination, ingenuity, and strength. Perhaps that, itself, was their Piraku.

Taking Ghaj's advice, he traveled as briskly as he could, but more than two score days with his butt in the bottom of a boat had not prepared him for a long walk. Near noon he stopped to rest, to eat the leaf-wrapped parcels of smoked catfish Ghaj had given him. In the shade of a cottonwood, he took Harka out to clean his blade.

"*You puzzle me,*" Harka told him.

"I puzzle myself, but go on."

"*All of that trouble to escape the Changeling, and yet you still follow the course he plotted for you.*"

"I said I would finish this, and I will," he replied. "But on *my* terms. That's important to me, to do things because I choose to."

"*Perhaps that is the chief difference between Humans and gods,*" Harka offered. "*We almost always do things because we must, because it is our nature.*"

"No difference," Perkar said. "Neither gods nor Humans like to be *told* what to do. Both follow their natures, and both want to be left alone to do it."

"*Human nature changes notoriously quickly, however. The nature of gods changes only slowly, through many passing seasons.*"

"Like the Changeling," Perkar noted.

"*He may not be the best example.*"

"Once I hoped to kill him," Perkar said. "Now it is enough for me merely to frustrate him. He wants something of me in Nhol. Very well, I will go to Nhol. But when I get there, I will be my own man. I will judge the situation for myself."

"Ngangata is right. You are most dangerous when you think."

"Perhaps. But in Nhol, I do not care whom I kill. I have no kin there, no friends."

"There is always me," Harka reminded him.

Perkar was forced to smile at the perversity of that. "If you die," he said, "I will most certainly be dead, too, and so I will not care. No, my only concern in Nhol is that I kill only those the Changeling does not *want* me to."

"Easier said than done."

"Not at all. I haven't felt even a flicker of guilt for killing those thieves a few days ago." That wasn't *quite* true, but to his own surprise, it was *almost* true.

"That isn't what I mean," Harka said. *"How can you pretend to know what the Changeling wants?"*

Perkar finished the fish and stood. "This girl who calls me. I think she must be one of these Waterborn. I think he wants me to save her from something. And so I will not."

"Perhaps he wants you to kill her. Perhaps it is she who wants to be saved."

"We'll see. We'll see when we get there. Right now I feel good, Harka, so keep your doubts to yourself. I *choose* to do this now—on the River I was compelled. I could walk back home if I wanted, I could go live with the Mang or become a fisherman. I pick my own doom from now on."

"Let us hope," Harka replied, *"that is merely a euphemism and not a prophecy."*

He grinned. "I care not!" he shouted, and brandished Harka above his head before returning him to his scabbard.

He reached the city walls not long before dusk, and found that while his dreams might have been competent to teach him a strange language, they were less adept at preparing him for the sight of the city. The walls alone were larger than any Human-made structure he had ever seen, dwarfing the largest damakuta a hundred times over. To that fact he added that they were clearly made of stone and not wood, and the effort put into building the stupendous stockade was, to him, even more difficult to envision than the artificial streams. As he approached it from a distance, he kept expecting that size to be an illusion that would resolve it-self when he got closer, reveal that the city was not really as large as it seemed, that the towers and great rising blocks of buildings that peered at him from *over* that great wall must be of more reasonable dimensions. And yet, the more closely he approached, the clearer it was that he was in a place where magnificent, impossible things were done. He began to understand, with a sinking feeling, why these people insisted on calling his own "barbarians." What he saw here made the difference between the dwellings of the Alwat and his father's damakuta seem insignifi-cant. Small wonder that the people of Nhol thought of his people in much the same way as his thought of the Alwat. And yet that thought gave him a bit of comfort, because he now understood—finally—that what people built didn't make them any more or less brave, worthy, or deserving. No man he had ever heard of had died any better than Digger and her kin or deserved more praise.

The gatehouse was a white-plastered cube the size of his fa-ther's stables; Perkar wondered how many warriors it might hold. He was greeted by only two; they looked at him as if he might be something the River had pulled in, something less than savory. Which, in its own way, was true enough.

"That kitchen knife of yours stays in its sheath here, do you understand?" The soldier spoke slowly, as if he thought Perkar might not comprehend him. "If you go near the great temple, any of the fanes, or within four streets of the palace, you may not wear it at all, unless you are employed by a member of the royal family to do so."

"I understand," he replied. "I am seeking employment for my

sword, actually. Can you direct me to someone whose business it is to hire?"

The second guard rolled his eyes. "You barbarians. Never been in a city before in your life, have you?"

"No," he confessed.

"Take my advice. Get a job on the docks, if you need money. That's good, honest work. The nobles don't usually hire foreign bodyguards, and when they do it's usually not very good for your continued well-being, if you understand me."

"I'm not sure I do," he said.

"Too bad," said the first guard, smiling in a way that didn't seem very genuine. "That's all the free advice we'll give today."

Perkar shrugged, a little put off by their rudeness, but still too overwhelmed by the city to take it personally.

"Go down to the docks, near Southtown," the second guard called after him anyway. "If someone wants your sword, they'll come looking for you there."

"Thank you," he shouted back, meaning it.

Passing through the thick, plastered walls, he entered a maze of confusion. His first instinct was to go back out, take several deep breaths, and reconsider his course of action. How could anyone find anything in such cluttered bedlam?

People were everywhere, as thick as ants on a piece of meat. They clustered in bunches or darted about, called to each other, all talking at once, it seemed. Beyond the gate was a small, cobbled square, buildings bunched at every side of it, enclosing it so that it more resembled a canyon than a yard. The only exits—save for the gate, of course—were a multitude of claustrophobically narrow paths between the buildings, cobbled like the square. Cobbled paths? Once again, he felt dismay at the sheer scale of Nhol.

He also felt horribly out of place. People were staring at him, rudely and openly. Some—particularly the children—even pointed and laughed. He grimaced uncomfortably. He *was* a stranger here, of exceedingly strange appearance, undoubtedly, though he had hoped the clothes Ghaj had given him would help. However, he noted that though the people swirling around him were dressed in a similar manner, most wore much more colorful clothing, and though the sun had darkened his skin considerably, it was many shades lighter than any other he saw.

He had not the faintest idea which of the little paths to take, and so he walked down the broadest one; as near as he could tell it led southeast, and the man had said something about Southtown.

The street was crowded, despite the late hour; night seemed to come quickly in the city, and Perkar was reminded of being at the bottom of the gorge at the River's headwaters. The buildings around him rose far above his head, perhaps four or five times his height. Balconies jutted off of these clifflike faces, here and there, and often people stood or sat out on them. Without fail, all of these upper observers followed Perkar's progress closely, and he wondered at first if they might be watchmen of some sort; but most were actually women, some of them rather old. It occurred to him that they might—strange as it seemed—*live* in those lofts, though he had originally supposed the upper rooms were for storing hay or grain.

As the sky darkened, the street reminded him more of the tunnels in the mountain than of a gorge. The heavens still held blue and gray, even a hint of crimson and argent, but smoke and shadows ruled the streets. Torches burned murkily in sconces near doorways, and the dragon-eyes of oil lamps stalked and hovered around him, revealing here a face, there a patch of clothing, the dark knots of the hands gripping the lantern handles. A fog of smoke from burning wood, oil, and tar lay heavily upon him, mingling with the stench of Human Beings, strange foods cooking, and a half-dozen other distinct but unrecognized odors.

The path he was on intersected a much larger one, and he finally tried to stop someone to ask directions. The person—a man who looked to be about his own age—disdainfully brushed off his inquiring hand and hurried on his way without even pausing. Perkar watched him go, dumbstruck. What manner of people *were* these? They looked like Ghaj, and Win, and Brother Horse, and yet they had not a smidgen of the same hospitality. He reminded himself that they also resembled the pirates who had tried to kill him, and began to proceed a bit more cautiously.

Two more men and a woman rebuffed him, and so at last he stopped a child.

For an instant, he thought the little girl was the one in his vision; she had the same black eyes and hair framing a heart-shaped face. But then he realized that her nose was a bit too broad, her eyes not as large, other details that he couldn't quite place but that added up to the wrong person. She stared up at him, half frightened, half curious.

"My mother says not to talk to foreigners," she said simply.

"Please," he pleaded, "I only want to know where the docks are, in Southtown."

She regarded him dubiously, but finally gave him an answer that involved a string of turns and unfamiliar street names.

"I don't know those streets," he told her. "Can you be more detailed?"

When she was done, Perkar didn't know whether he was thoroughly confused or knew where he was going. Thanking her, he followed her directions as best he could.

Not much later, he crossed a canal, a channel that had been lined with cut stones. He stared down from the bridge at it, agape. Boats were moving up and down the waterway—it was wider than the stream back home—poled by men and women. Some held cargo—fish, bundles of cloth—but most seemed to bear only a few passengers. He made out stairs descending at intervals from the street to the canal.

Beyond the canal, he turned where he thought the girl meant for him to, and the path climbed a hill. At the crest of it, he emerged from the early night of the streets onto an open plaza. There he was suddenly gifted with a broader view of the city, still visible in the pale and fading illumination of the sky. A thousand flat rooftops sprawled out below him, rectangular islands in an ink-dark sea. Many of the islands were inhabited; he could make out people tending fires, clothes and rugs hung on lines, flapping vaguely in the wind. A few of the roofs even had tents upon them, and he guessed that people might sleep in them, when the weather was warm. From many of the houses, pits of orange-yellow light gaped at his uphill vantage, interior courtyards cheerily lit from within.

Another hill rose to his right, and the structures clustered there loomed enormous. Massive vaults, sky-reaching towers, and long, unbroken walls of stone were somehow all joined into one, and formed a single building larger than the entire city of Wun. It scarcely looked like something Human Beings could live in, and the hair on his nape prickled at the sight of it. How must it be, in the center of such a thing? Like being in the mountain, in the Belly of the Raven, too far from sky and sunlight. He remembered the creatures who lived in the mountain all too well; spidery things, pale and sinister. Might not such creatures dwell there, in that hilltop edifice?

Was this the "palace" the guards spoke of? He remembered Brother Horse and his talk of the clan that ruled Nhol, men and women with a seeming of godhood upon them. Perhaps they were gods of shadow, of depth.

But there was a height, here, too. The hilltop monstrosity—the palace?—rolled down in blocky waves to the River, surrounded the whole of the way by a formidable stone wall. Where it touched the River, a monumental structure of cut stone reared up against the dying light. Perkar recognized it immediately as a mountain, or something made to resemble a mountain, but angular, like a building, as well. Water spewed from its summit, churning and gray, and poured like miniature rivers down its sloping faces. For an instant, Perkar felt dizzy, on the verge of some fantastic revelation. It was as if he were gazing at the very source of the Changeling, the mountain in the heart of Balat, where the gods lived. Yet it was the mountain not as it *was*, but as Human Beings might *make* it, of dressed stone, cornered, regular. He stared on, teased by inspiration but never quite comprehending the importance of what he saw. At last he shook his head, let his gaze stray.

The River was even wider here than at the point where the pirates had attacked him, the other shore obscured by distance and twilight. He saw several more canals—they all seemed to run toward the palace. He also made out, against the dim silver light of the water, a jumble of quays jutting out into the River like short, dark trails. They lay south of him, and so he continued on, sure that these were his destination, the false mountain still riddling at his brain.

He attempted to keep the location of the docks fixed in his senses as he descended the hill and lost sight of them. Despite his best efforts, he was soon confused again. He stopped several children to refine his course, and so at last, by the time night was truly pitch, he found himself near the water's edge and a strip of dirty, untidy buildings. There he sat down, his back to a wall, and gazed out at the dark River, freckled with the torchlight of a hundred boats. He sighed, his earlier elation gone with the sunlight. He felt very, very far from home.

"Well," he told the River. "Here I am. You killed my friends, bent my destiny, brought me across the whole world. Now what do you want? Where is this girl?"

His only answer was the sounds of the city, the faint lapping of waves on the quays.

PERKAR realized that he had dozed off; someone was nudging him awake with a foot. He gasped and reached for Harka.

"Hey, no, watch that!" a young voice called down. He squinted up but couldn't make out the face. Whoever it was, though, was dressed much like the soldiers who had met him at the gate; he could see that much in the feeble light of a nearby torch.

"I'm sorry," Perkar muttered vaguely, still confused.

"Sleeping on the street is a *bad* idea, barbarian," the voice informed him.

"I don't know my way around here," he explained. "I don't know where I should stay."

"Oh. Didn't your captain tell you?"

"Captain?"

"You came on a boat, didn't you?"

"Uh, no," Perkar said, rising to his feet. Someone passed close with a lantern, and he caught a glimpse of the soldier's face; very young, it seemed, smooth, kind. "No," he repeated, "I came overland."

"Overland? Well. The guards at the gate should have told you where to go then."

"They told me to go to the docks, near Southtown."

"You're a bit from there," the man told him. "Come along, I'm patrolling that way, if you want a guide."

"Yes!" Perkar agreed, nodding vigorously.

"Come on, then, stay close," the guard counseled.

After they had gone a few steps, Perkar spoke up again. "My name is Perkar, of the Barku Clan," he offered.

"Eh? Oh," the man responded. "Hang, son of Chwen, is mine. Where are you from, barbarian?"

"From the Cattle-Lands, at the edge of Balat," Perkar answered.

"Is that far away?"

"It took well over a month to get here on the River."

"I thought you said you came overland," the man said, a trifle suspiciously.

"From Nyel," Perkar amended. "I lost my boat at Nyel."

"Funny," Hang replied.

"How so?"

"Something I just heard—ah, watch them!" Hang stepped over a couple of men lying facedown in the street. They looked like natives; Perkar wondered why Hang didn't warn *them* not to sleep in the street, too, and said so.

Hang snorted. "They should know better, that's why, but

they're too drunk to have any sense, I imagine. I thought maybe you *didn't* know better."

"That was good of you," Perkar said.

The man shrugged, glanced slightly back at him as they walked along. "Most people don't like foreigners," he admitted. "I find them sort of interesting. My mother was a barbarian, you know."

"She was?"

"She was a Mang captive my father bought and eventually married."

"*Bought?*" Perkar asked incredulously, wondering if he had misunderstood.

"Paid a fair price, too, twelve Royals, he used to say. That's what he called her most of the time, 'Twelve Royals.' "

Perkar wasn't sure he was following, precisely, but he remembered his father's advice about keeping quiet rather than revealing his ignorance.

"I thought I might go trading up-River one day, so I don't mind meeting strangers, to learn a little about them."

"I see."

"What have you come to Nhol for?"

"To see it, I suppose," Perkar told him, not really knowing what else to say. Then he added, "I was hoping to get a little work for my sword."

The soldier nodded, and Perkar thought he caught a sidewise look of condescension from him. "You'll want to stay at the Crab Woman, then. That's not far, I'll show you to it and bid you good night."

They turned off of the street on the River and crossed several more streets inland. At last the soldier knocked on a heavy wooden door.

"This is the place, Perkar-from-faraway. Don't let them charge you more than a pair of soldiers a night. Remember that!"

"Thank you, I'll remember it," Perkar said. He was watching the fellow walk away when the door opened.

A large, rough man stood there, raking a practiced gaze over him.

"Barbarian sell-sword? Well, keep that thing leathered, you hear me? We get trouble from your kind all of the time, and we know how to deal with it. You've got no clan or brotherhood or tribe or whatever that'll find out what happened to you down *here* and avenge you, get that straight, right?"

Perkar frowned when he understood that he was being threatened, but let it pass. Piraku and its code of behavior were plainly not known to *any* of these people, though they insisted on calling *him* a barbarian. Best he should mostly watch and listen here, until he understood more about what codes of conduct *did* apply.

"I just want a bed to sleep in," he mumbled. "I've been walking all day."

"Four soldiers, here at the door," the man said gruffly.

At least he understood *this*. He had never dealt with metal coins before, but he had bargained for cattle often enough.

"A single soldier is all I can afford," he said.

"Well, then you can't afford to stay here," the man snapped. "Though we have a discount for albinos today. Three soldiers."

They settled on two, as the guardsman had indicated, and after paying he entered into the building's courtyard. Here, too, was a bit of familiarity. The courtyard was set up much like the hall of a damakuta, with heavy tables and benches. Men and some women sat at these, drinking from heavy clay bowls.

"You can have the room in the corner," the man indicated. "Beer and wine is a soldier a pint. Tell the serving boy if you want some."

"Where do I go to look for work?" Perkar asked, hesitantly.

"I *knew* it," the man grumbled. He sighed heavily. "Just stay around in here, keep your scabbard out where people can see it. If anyone is looking, they'll notice you."

"Thanks," Perkar said. Worn out and overloaded with sight, sound, and smell, he wound back through the mass of strangers to the door the man had indicated. It opened into a cell that was no larger than a storage shed, but held a pallet and a small lantern. He closed the door and, after a bit of fumbling about in the dark, found a bolt, slid it shut. He sank down to the mat, which stank of sweat and beer and possibly less appetizing things. He was musing on how a city could be so *huge* and rooms in it so *small* when, despite the smell and the constant noise of voices from outside, Perkar was soon deeply, mercifully asleep.

VIII

The Rooftop

GHAN was not in the library the next morning, and Hezhi knew what that meant; he was down in the city, planning her "escape." Her mind was still awhirl with the idea; she had stayed up late into the night, in the courtyard of her rooms, running her fingers upon the little Mang statuette. Somehow, the fierce little horse-woman made the almost unthinkable idea of leaving Nhol—of leaving the *palace*—seem possible, something she could survive. The little figure could not, however, allay her doubts; there were many of those. What would she do, wherever she went? Certainly she would not be a princess, waited on by servants. That and indexing in the library were all she knew how to do. Where else would her skills with books be useful? The Swamp Kingdoms, perhaps—they *might* have a few libraries. But the Swamp Kingdoms were too close to the River, still in his domain. Did the Mang have libraries? Probably not.

Hope and fear kept her company all night, and in the end it was knowing her only other choice was the underpalace that allowed hope to be the one that woke up with her. She would not be waited upon *there*, either, and no book could survive that flooded, terrible place.

Hope told her Ghan would think of something; hope was the statuette, the image of a creature, unfettered, unbindable.

The worst of it was that now that plans were in motion, she was helpless. After years of investigating her own life so that she could understand and control her fate, matters were again in the hands of others. She spent the morning thumbing vacantly through books whose pages she did not even see. Ghan's place was held by a plump young man from somewhere in the Butterfly Court, where the tax collectors carried out their business. He was pleasant and rather bland, and apparently of no help whatsoever to Yen, who came in about midmorning. Consequently, Yen brought his questions to Hezhi.

Yen was a fast learner, so his queries were no longer simple ones. She welcomed the challenge—it and Yen kept her mind and stomach off of wondering where Ghan and Tsem might be, what they might be doing. But once they had found the necessary texts—Second-Dynasty proscriptions for tertiary water fane drainage—her mind wandered off again into the land of what-will-be. She really couldn't help thinking that once she fled from Nhol, was exiled from it, she could marry whomever she wanted, even a merchant's son.

She also considered that, once she was no longer a princess, no one would *want* to marry her, not *even* a merchant's son. And of course, it could never be Yen, who was dedicated to his life here as a Royal Engineer. Still, it was a pleasant, even an entertaining, thought.

He looked up to ask her a question and caught her thoughtful gaze, and she blushed, fearing he could tell exactly what she was thinking.

"I'm sorry," he said sincerely. "I'm keeping you from something."

"No, no," she corrected, perhaps a bit too quickly. "I'm just distracted today. I have a lot to think about."

"Well, as I said," Yen began, making motions to leave.

"No, stay," she pleaded. "I wanted to ask you about something."

"Oh. Ask *me*?" Yen sounded very surprised. "An opinion, I hope, for of real knowledge I have no great supply."

"You know about this," she assured him.

He looked at her expectantly.

"It's just that I've never been out of the palace," she said at last. "The city is a mystery to me, even what I can see of it. Tsem—my servant—he tells me a bit, but of course *he's* never lived out there. I just wondered if you could tell me something about it. Anything."

"You've mentioned this before," Yen said, "and I didn't tell you before, but it puzzles me. I've seen nobles in the city many, many times. Why have you never been out?"

"I'm not old enough," she confessed, hoping the weight of what that meant to her was not apparent in her voice, on her features.

"Ah. But soon?"

"Yes. I suppose that's why I ask."

"Well, I don't know where to start. It all seems so plain to me, so common. Most people spend their whole lives wondering what the *inside* of the palace is like, you know. We don't think much about fishmongers and scorps, unless we have to."

"Scorps?"

"Scorpions. Thieves, cutthroats. Some parts of the city are rather dangerous, you know."

"The merchants' quarter, where you grew up?"

"No, not really. We have burglars, now and again, people who break into our houses to steal things, but they aren't really dangerous. They avoid the kind of trouble killing a rich man might bring down on them. They are very stealthy, crafty—but not dangerous. No, the scorps haunt the docks, the warehouse district, Southtown . . ."

"Would you come with me?" she asked him abruptly.

"What?"

"Just for a few moments, would you come with me?"

"Ah, I suppose. To where?"

"A place I know, where we can see the city, where you can point to things when you talk about them."

"Will that be all right? Without an escort?"

She had briefly forgotten about that. Tsem was with Ghan.

"Just for a short time. And no one will see us, I promise."

"If you promise," he said solemnly, "then I'm bound to believe you."

"THAT is my father's house," Yen said, pointing. "The one with the red awning, you see?"

Hezhi followed the line of Yen's finger, out and away from the rooftop garden. "Yes. Why, that's one of the largest houses there!"

"My father does well enough. Still, the least part of the palace makes it seem like a hovel."

She frowned. "But what of *those* houses?" she asked, indicating the thick, tiny huts of Southtown.

"Well, of course, those are *real* hovels," Yen told her. "One-room shacks with leaky roofs."

"What are the people there like?"

Yen shrugged. "I only know what I see—people from the rest of the city rarely venture into Southtown, you know. But the people there are scorps, beggars, cutpurses, prostitutes. The sort without the ambition to better themselves."

"Do they have a choice about that?" she asked. "*Can* they better themselves?"

Yen nodded easily. "I think so. We all have choices, you, me, the people in Southtown. I could have followed my father, been a trader, but see, I chose another path."

She wasn't so easily convinced. "Surely it must be very difficult to live there. I mean, someone from down there couldn't get appointed to the Royal Engineers, the way you did, could they? I

have trouble enough imagining life without slaves, servants, soldiers to protect me . . ."

Yen chuckled shortly. "Why bother to imagine that? That
would never be your lot."

The irony of that almost stung, but she could not, of course,
reveal her distress. "I try to imagine many things," she stated.

"As do I," Yen replied, and for a moment his eyes flashed in
a *most* peculiar way, a way that tickled her belly with warmth,
brought blood to her face.

"More," she demanded, tearing her eyes from the young man
and looking back out over the rooftops and streets.

"Well . . . the docks, there. I used to sit on them when I had
nothing else to do, watch the foreigners come in. Some of them
were so strange, they couldn't even speak, but only gabble in
their own barbaric languages."

"Tell me about them," she requested, resting her chin on the
walled edge of the court, watching sunlight flash on the River
like a thousand thousand golden eels. A great three-masted ship
was just heaving out of the channel, toward, dock, its sails
crumpling as it came, all but the lateen sail in back.

"There. What sort of ship is that?"

Yen nodded sagely. "Look at that craft, Lady. It is built for
sailing upon the ocean; see how most of the sails are rigged
square, but the one aft is triangular? That lets them sail *into*
the wind."

"That seems impossible," she remarked, watching the ship. It
wasn't headed straight for the dock, but was instead beginning a
peculiar little dance, switching back and forth, approaching the
shore as one might a lover one were very shy of meeting.

"See? They're doing it now. Notice the pennant at the top of
their mast? That will tell you how the wind is blowing."

It was true. The pennant streamed away from Nhol and the
docks, and yet the ship—the *large* ship—was somehow, if a bit
tediously, moving *into* the breeze, without oars or a hauling rope.

"Very clever," she breathed as she began to understand what

was involved. They were using the wind against itself, stealing strength from it rather than confronting it headlong. "Where is that ship from?"

"Well, I'm not quite certain. The south, for sure, but I can't make out the device on their pennant."

Hezhi squinted. "A serpent surrounding a quartered circle," she said.

Yen looked at her with new respect. "You have good eyesight, Lady. Well. That would be Dangun, one of the farthest of the Swamp Kingdoms, which actually borders on the coast. The ship, I think, is actually of Lhe manufacture."

"Lhe? South along the gulf? I've seen that on maps."

"Odd people, civilized in their own way, I suppose. They have skin as black as coal, as black as your hair and eyes. I like to watch them."

He did not look at her as he said this, but she was left wondering if Yen meant he liked to watch the Lhe sailors or her hair and eyes.

"And up-River?"

"The Mang, of course, and across the desert to the east the Dehshe, who resemble the Mang. They cut timber, though, and mine tin, so I suppose they are a bit more civilized than the plainsmen. Their boatmen are usually a quiet lot. Again, unlike the Mang."

"Have you ever met very pale men, with light hair and gray eyes?" she inquired.

"I've never laid eyes on such a man, though I have heard of them," Yen said. "They are said to live in the ice and snow at the very edge of the world, which colors them pale. The Mang speak of them as enemies, I think."

"They live north, then?"

"North and west, I think, from wherever the River rises."

"From the mountain?" Hezhi wondered. "They live at *She'leng*?"

Yen raised his open palms. "I know little of religious matters.

It is a constant source of irritation to the priests." He stepped nearer to her, hesitated, then reached out his fingers and took her chin in his palm. His eyes glowed, dark opals flecked with gold. Breath caught in her throat.

"We should go now," she managed.

"Yes," Yen told her. "In just a moment." He bent down, brushed his lips against hers. He did not *press* them wetly, as Wezh did, and they did not feel like wet liver. They felt sweet and warm, kind. And something else, something a little hungry . . .

She felt frozen as Yen drew away from her, unable to think.

"I'm sorry if that upset you," Yen told her, his voice husky. "I know we cannot court. But I wanted to kiss you once, at least."

"Once?"

He nodded. "Soon I will have no more excuses to come back to the library, at least not for many months; I will be supervising the construction. When I next see you, you will probably be married." He smiled thinly.

"Well," she gasped. "You should not have done it. If anyone saw . . ."

"But you promised no one would see."

She colored further. "I did not ask you up here for *that*," she insisted, turning her eyes back out to the cityscape, her heart doing hummingbird pirouettes in her breast. "But you may do it again, if you wish. Just once more."

From the corner of her eye, she saw him lean in again and, closing her eyes, turned to meet him.

She thought about that kiss for the rest of the day, the hours in the library seeming in turns frozen in time and rushing by. She was *still* considering it as she made her way back to her apartments. It was an odd feeling, the memory of that sweet, forbidden thing, another gift to go with the statue, another bit of madness in her life. The broad corridors of the palace seemed like the narrowest parapet of the Great Hall, a thin, tiny path that she could easily sway off of, out into the deep, the unknown. It seemed to her that Yen was right, though he had not been speaking of her, that her possibilities were virtually unlimited. She wanted to dream on and on of what might be, bathe in promise, yet at the same time, she knew she had to sober herself, become calmer for the adventure awaiting her.

No matter how often she told herself that, her feet still felt light.

Turning into the corridor where her rooms were, the stink of incense assailed her nostrils. The priests had just swept here, and the smoke still hung thick in the air. Certainly they had just been sweeping, as they did now and then. But Hezhi's eyes widened. The door to her rooms stood ajar a crack. Smoke drifted out, pungent gray coils of it. She could just see the fringe of Qey's skirt, silhouetted against the light from the doorway. She stood, staring, pulse hammering. All of her gauzy dreams were torn, just like that, and she realized exactly how fragile hope was. Trembling, she reached into her pocket, stroked the statuette, but it felt only like metal, unfeeling metal. The horse-woman was cold, her promise dissipated in that first sharp scent of incense.

She stood rooted until Qey turned, her face revealed in the doorway. Hezhi had that one glimpse of it as Qey recognized her, a sad, tortured look, pleading. A terrible flash of insight caught her, as if Qey's face were a light more blinding than the sun, and she understood she would never see the woman who had raised her again after this one last glimpse. The flash became an ache, a wish to be gathered up in Qey's arms once more, to eat breakfast just one more time, to tell her that she loved her.

This was the last she would see of Qey, and she would never see Tsem again at all.

Horse-woman clutched in her hand, she turned and fled, ran as she had never run before, just as a shout went up behind her, the high, boyish voice of a priest.

The halls echoed hollowly beneath her slapping feet, as if she were inside of a skull or the tombs beneath the temples one read about. It was as when she was a younger girl, with D'en, dashing through the empty places of the great palace, footsteps their only company. Now, however, the halls were crowded with footfalls.

D'en, she thought miserably. *I will certainly never see you again.*

Up a flight of stairs, and the next. She had no idea how close the priests were to catching her; the thundering of blood in her ears and the sound of her own flight obscured any clamor of pursuit. It didn't matter really, if she could just reach the rooftops before they did.

She burst into the afternoon light, gasping, tears just beginning to trickle. Frantically she clambered up the side of the upper court, where she and Yen had so recently kissed. Wind whispered through the cottonwood as if to welcome her back.

This may not be high enough, she thought, and so continued her ascent onto the red slate shingles that slanted down to the garden from higher regions of the palace.

She had nearly reached the ridge of the roof when a voice shouted behind her again. She turned, briefly, to see first one and then a second priest emerge from the stairs. Ignoring them, she finished climbing to the ridgebeam and began to run along it.

Here was her straight, narrow trail, illusion become real. It ran all along the top of the empty wing, a vertiginous path that led nowhere but to the roof of the Great Hall. There she would climb once more, put the distance of six ceilings and five floors between herself and the pavement. *That* would be high enough.

The shingles plunged steeply away from her left and right hands to join the flat roofs of lower floors. As she ran, she glimpsed little flashes of life in the courtyards below—a woman hanging laundry, a gardener watering potted plants, a man and a woman kissing. Such little things, and yet suddenly infinitely precious. As precious and precarious as her shattered hope. The only recognizable fragment of that hope was her chance to escape the priests—and D'en's fate. As she understood this her tears transformed from sorrowful to bitter.

Clambering up onto the roof of the Great Hall, she glanced back again. The priests were far behind her; *they* had not spent uncounted hours here, in the bright air above the palace. She would succeed, she had time.

She slipped a few times, ascending the steep, vaulted roof, but she knew where the handholds were, knew to go up the crease where a mighty strut supported the roof. A moment she had then, to think of Tsem, of how sad he would be, of how glad she was that he was in the city when the priests came. He would have killed them, and then he would have died, too. Now that wouldn't happen, nor would Ghan risk *his* life and freedom unnecessarily. She would solve her own problems, bear the weight of her birth on her own small soles.

Shuddering for breath, she completed the climb, and there took another moment to rest. The top of the dome was open, a great unwinking eye staring out from the Leng Court. Looking down, she could see its iris, the fountain, far below, the beckoning stones.

I mustn't fall in the fountain, she thought. *I mustn't give the River my blood while I yet live; I won't do that.*

She was still crying, but the tears now had the melancholy solace of happy tears, of the sort of crying that feels good. The priests were still pursuing, sluggishly. Gazing about her, she cherished the glorious view—the dusty desert reaches, the filmy green fields, the vast bustle of humanity that was Nhol. The sun resting in the River, half sunken, a floating tangerine.

Stepping up to the edge, she admired her little statue once more. The fierce grin seemed like laughter, like a secret joy they shared. Another wind whipped around her, and she felt her heart washed clean by it, filled with light and high, endless sky.

She spread wide her arms like wings, the long streak of her shadow fleeing eastward in the steeply slanting light.

IX

The Quickening of Dream

MORNING brought the city that Perkar remembered from his dreams, a forest of buildings flaming white in the sun. Yet already his pristine vision was faded, replaced by the reality of rude, incomprehensible people, dirty rooms, and the smell of the docks, a stench for which he had no name. Morning also brought with it a sense of immense inadequacy, for he had not the faintest idea what to *do*, how—or even what—to negotiate in this alien place. Until now, the River had provided him with direction and thus purpose. Now he lacked that. He wondered what would have happened had he stayed in the boat. Would it have sailed straight to where he was being called, to the task at hand? Or would he be in this same place, sitting at a thick, stained, knife-scarred table wondering what to do?

Midmorning actually provided him with part of an answer. He had been splitting his time between the table and its promise of employment and stepping outside, watching and wondering still at the immensity of Nhol. A few others in the Crab Woman seemed to be seeking work; a group of three rough-looking men, dark and scarred, conversed in low tones in a language he did not understand. Each wore his weapon in plain sight, as he did. Another, solitary man—he reminded Perkar of a ferret—sat scratching vaguely at his table with a knife. None of the four seemed much inclined to talk to him, and so he kept his distance, waiting and watching.

Around noon, four more men came in, three wearing plain kilts and one—a young, slim fellow—in tar-stained pants. Pants seemed a rarity in Nhol; these were the first he had seen. None of the four wore weapons, at least not visible ones, so he concluded that they were in the Crab Woman to drink rather than to look for "sellsword" jobs.

They chose a table near his, ordered beers. Casually he listened in on their conversation, which largely concerned an individual named "Lizard" who seemed to be their foreman. The four didn't like Lizard very much. As Perkar did not *know* Lizard, the conversation failed to capture his interest, and so his mind wandered with his gaze out beyond the door, to the people strolling past.

Until, that is, one of them mentioned his boat, and that took hold of his notice and kept hold of it.

"Strangest thing I ever saw," the pants-wearer was saying. "A whole crowd of us watched it, too; it's not like it was just me."

"Currents," an older fellow with a thin beard said. "Currents are strange."

"It was going against the current, no sail, no paddles, nobody even *in* it."

"And?" the bearded man responded.

"And that's it. It sailed right up Eel Canal, quiet as you please, six men in it yanking on the tiller."

"Priest stuff," one of the other men ascertained, and they all mumbled general agreement.

That was too much for Perkar. He rose and approached the table.

They nodded wary greetings, as if fearing he might want something.

"Excuse me," Perkar said. "I am Perkar of the Kar Barku Clan. I'm sorry to have been listening to you, but I *did* overhear you talking about a boat, sailing along without anyone in it."

"That's right," said the small man defensively, the one who had seen it. "It's true."

"What happened to it?"

The little man grinned. "Last I saw, two of the priests had come down from the temple with some of those brooms of theirs, the ones they burn."

Which meant nothing to him. "Where might that be?" he asked.

"*Might* be in the deep blue sea," the bearded man grunted. "But it's not. Back up that way, where the canal runs up to the palace."

"I'd like to see that," he told them.

"Well, that's nice," the bearded man said, and the others laughed.

Determined not to lose his temper, Perkar merely nodded at them. "Thanks," he said. Surely someone outside could tell him where Eel Canal was.

"Just go left, out the door, follow Shadowfish Street," the small man piped up. "That'll take you to Eel Canal. Just walk up that, you'll see it if the priests haven't managed to do something to it yet."

"Thanks again," Perkar said, and continued on out the door. Outside he glanced at the docks, several streets down, and turned left. He looked back—to memorize the landmarks near the Crab Woman, so that he could find his way back, and raised his eyebrows in astonishment. The largest man he had ever seen was just entering the tavern. He surely stood seven or more feet tall, massively muscled, thick, broad, with relatively short bowed legs. Despite his size, the glimpse of his face Perkar got reminded him of Ngangata. Heavy brows, sloping forehead.

Shaking his head in amazement, he went on in search of his boat.

Finding Eel Canal was no great feat, and neither was following it to the palace, though it was a long walk. There, perhaps a hundred paces from the base of a towering wall, was the Crow God's boat. Floating, empty and serene. Perkar wondered what had happened to the dead men he had left in it, but quickly put that thought away as something he didn't want to dwell much on. The boat was covered in streamers or ribbons of some sort, and no less than four blocks of some strange incense were burning on the canal wall nearest it. A young man was tending the incense and looking glumly at the boat. Perkar waved at him, and he stared back.

"Good day," Perkar said, not knowing how to wish "Piraku" in the language of Nhol. The man nodded back at him.

"You are watching this boat?"

"Yes" was the sullen reply.

Perkar was startled; the man was younger than he appeared, a boy really. "Why?"

"It was moving by itself," the boy explained. "It is either some gift from the River to the priesthood or a demon; we aren't sure yet."

"Perhaps it is inhabited by a god," Perkar offered, leaning against a nearby building, hoping that would not give any offense.

"Barbarian," the boy said, clearly disgusted. "The River is the *only* god."

"There are many gods where I come from," he replied reasonably.

"Demons, you mean. Ghosts, maybe. No gods."

He shrugged, remembering Balati, the Huntress, Karak. They certainly were not ghosts.

"Are you a shaman?" he asked, hoping that was the correct word.

"A witch, you mean? An old midwife? You *are* a barbarian. I am a *priest* of the River."

"Priest." Perkar knew the word—*ghun*—of course, but the concepts connected to it were vague. "What is a priest exactly?"

The man eyed him with a new, more intense disdain—which Perkar would not have thought possible. He spoke very slowly, spacing his words. "Priests ... serve ... the ... Ri-ver," he said.

"I know your language," Perkar said, restraining himself from snapping. "I don't know your *ways* as well."

"Why are you, an outlander, even concerned?"

"I'm curious."

The boy nodded. "I will tell you then. Listen to the sound of Running Water. Long ago, our people lived in the great desert. We had nothing, and monsters surrounded us. The daughter of one of our primitive chiefs had a child by the River, and he freed us from the demons, brought us here, to the River, and began the city of Nhol."

Perkar nodded. "My people have children by gods, as well."

The boy's face reddened again. "If you continue to blaspheme, I will cease speaking to you."

"I apologize," Perkar said. "You were saying?"

"The Chakunge—the Son from the Water—was the first of the Waterborn, the first of our kings. In them the blood of the River flows most deeply."

"And you priests? You are also Waterborn? Relatives of this Chakunge?"

"No," the boy said. "No, that is another story. The Waterborn, you see, are a part of the River and so they cannot *serve* him, worship him. They let us know his will, they wield his power. But to those of us who *serve* him, the River sent another man—a stranger. This man was known as Ghun Zhweng, the Ebon Priest. He taught us how to worship the River, built the Great Water Temple, established the flow of water into the palace. The River gave us his blood and thus our rulers, but it was Ghun Zhweng who brought us civilization. He gave us our rites, the spirit brooms, the knowledge of writing."

Perkar nodded. "I understand. The priests serve the River, the

Waterborn *are* the River. So, then, does your priesthood serve the Waterborn?"

"Yes, of course," the boy said—but Perkar sensed a hesitation in that answer. "Though we serve the River more directly, sometimes."

Perkar allowed himself to look puzzled, even exaggerated the expression.

"What I mean to say—" The priest frowned and looked down at his palms. "Do not mistake me," he said. "The Waterborn are the children of the River, and so we worship them, especially the Chakunge, the emperor—may he live a thousand years. But there are others who have far less of the blood, whom the River is not so much a part of. They are ruled by their coarser, Human half—which we as priests understand. We are also closer to the people—we mediate between the Waterborn and these people you see in the streets."

Perkar thought that somewhere in that rambling answer was the implication that the priesthood did not always bow to the will of the Waterborn—but he was confused enough not to be certain. What did seem certain was that this priesthood served the Changeling directly, though they were not related to him. Those who *were* of the Changeling's blood ruled the city.

This girl he was seeking, then. She was a part of the River. Who could her enemy be? Why did she call him?

"Do the Waterborn have any enemies?" Perkar asked.

That startled the young priest. "What do you mean? Barbarians like yourself, I suppose. Foreign tyrants who wish to conquer our city. Foes of the Waterborn are the foes of us all."

"None in the city? Criminals, treacherous men?"

The priest shook his head. "Absolutely not."

Perkar thought he had enough to absorb for the moment, and though the boy seemed to have warmed a bit to talking, he had not become much more pleasant.

"How long have you been a priest?" Perkar asked.

"I was initiated three years ago, and have attained the third stitch," he said, some pride glowing through the words.

Perkar nodded. "You seem very young to have such responsibility. Congratulations."

The boy—dark, of course, like everyone in Nhol—became a peculiar shade of purple. "I am twenty-two years of age," he snarled.

"But . . . your voice," Perkar stammered.

The priest appeared to be trying to decide whether to swallow his tongue. "I forgive you because you are a barbarian," he finally said in a tight voice. A tight, eleven-year-old voice. "Priests of the River are . . . *removed* from certain gross physical realms."

Perkar stared at the man in horror as that sank in. "You . . ." He didn't say it, didn't say *gelding*, for he had no desire to become engaged in a duel at the moment. He finally settled for a polite "Ah."

The man continued to glare at him for a moment, adjusted his robe and kilt, fiddling with the incense.

"Do you mind," Perkar said, uncomfortable now, "do you mind if I watch the boat for a while?"

"For what reason?"

"I want to see if it will move again. That would be interesting, I think."

The priest snorted. "Do what you will. It doesn't violate any laws, though I must caution you against approaching the boat. It belongs to the priesthood."

"I'll just watch then," he assured the priest, and sat down next to the wall. He was not certain why he did so, not sure why he shouldn't. It seemed reasonable that the boat would go where the River wanted *him* to, in which case he was where he belonged. Of course, he might be too late for whatever-it-was, or, without him in it, the boat might have wandered about aimlessly. Still, the immense palace was only a stone's throw away; the canal vanished into a black hole with a steel grate, and he suspected the water went into the royal dwellings themselves. Perhaps that was all the boat meant by being here, that he should enter the palace. Surveying it critically, Perkar could not imagine scaling its walls or avoiding the many guards and soldiers who would likely question him. In that case, he shouldn't be here, he should be back at the Crab Woman, pursuing the possibility that some noble might hire his sword. That was probably the only way he was likely to enter such a daunting fortress. And if he got in, if he found this girl, what then? She was the River's child, or at least of his blood. Here she was in his city. What would she need with him, a "barbarian" from a thousand leagues away? And most critically of all, when he found her, would he kill her or save her? He wondered, briefly, if he could kill a little girl, and was overcome by a sudden, almost dizzying burst of anger. *Yes,* he thought, remembering the ghost of his king, Eruka's empty eyes. *Yes, if it will thwart the River I can kill anyone.*

He was turning all of this over in his mind for at least the third time, when a great, deep voice rang out, just down the street.

"That *has* to be him," it said. Perkar was startled to see the Giant—or another man much like him—striding toward him. With the Giant was a small, wizened man in dark blue robes. It seemed that he had seen those robes back at the Crab Woman, too, and so it stood to reason they had followed him here intentionally. He scrambled to his feet, hand on Harka's hilt.

The old man was bald, Perkar could now see, though he had tied a sort of cloth around his head. It was he, not the Giant, who spoke when the two stopped before him.

"Gray eyes, light hair, pale skin," the old man muttered. "Well, well."

The Giant shook his massive head, parted his lips to reveal what resembled a mouthful of knucklebones. "There are many strangers at the docks. It is just a coincidence."

"Hezhi can tell us," the old man said. "If he isn't the one, what have we lost?"

"Everything, perhaps. Foreigners are thieves and cutthroats."

Perkar felt that he had been spoken of in the third person for long enough. "What are you two talking about?" he demanded.

The old man looked mildly surprised. "You speak our language passing well, for one from so far away, from the Cattle-Lands."

That stopped Perkar's ready retort. "You know my people?"

"By reputation only. I have read one or two of your . . ." He frowned. "Higaral?" he said at last, a question.

Perkar blinked. "*Ekaral,*" he corrected. "Songs."

"Yes. An officer of the Second Dynasty sailed up-River some time ago and lived with your folk for a while, wrote down a few of your *Ekaral* because he thought they might interest someone, I suppose."

The Giant growled and then looked abashed when the old man shot him a sharp look. The elder nodded, though, as if in agreement with whatever sentiment the Giant conveyed.

"We can talk about that later. Tsem reminds me that we have no time to discuss poetry. The other men in the Crab Woman told us we might find you here. I want to engage your services."

Perkar nodded. "So *you* are my destiny, caught up with me finally. Do you, by any chance, know a girl, perhaps twelve years old, with black eyes and a pointed chin?"

The Giant's jaw dropped, but the old man glanced furtively at the priest near the boat.

"Elsewhere," he hissed. "I wish to discuss this, but elsewhere." He gestured for Perkar to follow, and the Giant beckoned as well, with somewhat more insistence. Perkar pursed his lips, his only hesitation. This was what he was here for.

"THERE is much to explain," the old man said as they once again approached the docks. "Many questions I have for you, as well, but precious little time. So I must ask the most important ones first."

"My name is Perkar Kar Barku," Perkar informed him.

"Yes, yes." The old man nodded. "I am Ghan, and the half Giant is Tsem."

"Ghun, Tsem," he repeated.

"*Ghan,*" the old man said sharply, "*not* Ghun."

Teacher, not priest. And the Giant's name meant Iron.

"Ghan," Perkar repeated apologetically. But he marked that— this old man seemed no friend of the priests.

"You mention a young girl," Ghan went on sharply. "What do you know of her?"

Perkar considered his answer, but settled on telling at least part of the truth. "Not much. I dream about her, that's all. I have dreamed about her for months."

"You have been in Nhol for that long?"

Perkar shook his head ruefully. "I only just arrived."

"Why did you come to Nhol, Perkar?"

"I didn't have much choice," he answered. "The River brought me. It is a long story, an *Ekar,* but you say we don't have much time. So, shortly, the River took hold of my boat and brought me here."

Ghan raised his hand. "Did this make you bitter? Do you resent this?"

He grinned a little sourly and lied, though it was a lie twisted closely to truth. "It did. I think this girl called me, the way a shaman calls a familiar or a man a dog, and I came. I have had a long time to think about this, however. She was able to call *me*—as opposed to some other person—only because of certain acts I committed on my own. Acts that, for me, demand . . . *redressing.* I have determined that finishing out this part of my destiny—answering this girl's summons—is the first step in my atonement."

"Perhaps the last, as well," Ghan warned him. "What I will ask you to do is very dangerous."

"I assumed as much," Perkar said. "You said you are familiar with our songs. Do you also know the meaning of the word *Piraku?*"

"I read those long ago, and memory betrays," Ghan said, shaking his head.

"It means many things. Wealth, honor, glory. It means doing

what must be done, even if death is the only reward. It is what my people live and die by."

The Giant, Tsem, chewing his massive lip, suddenly erupted into speech. "This is ridiculous. We can't trust him, Master Ghan."

"If he is the man Hezhi dreamed of, we have no choice," Ghan muttered. "He may be of some help."

"I believe I am he," Perkar assured them. "Though I have no idea of what task I must perform."

"I will keep this story simple, too," Ghan promised. "I believe the girl you dream of is Hezhi Yehd Cha'dune, the daughter of the emperor of Nhol and its empire. As you say, I believe that she called you here to help her escape the city."

Perkar looked from one to the other of the two men. "Why must a princess escape her own city?" he asked.

Ghan shook his head. "It is complex, and not something Tsem or I may speak of. Hezhi can tell you, later, when all is well. But she must escape *today*. I'm afraid you must agree or disagree on what I've already told you."

Perkar nodded slowly. "I don't know anything about this city," he said. "I don't see what help I can be."

"Can you use *that*?" Ghan asked, pointing to Harka.

"Oh, yes," Perkar said. "I can use Harka."

"Harka?"

"The god who dwells in my sword."

Ghan lifted his eyebrows again, but did not dispute the existence of gods as the priest had.

"That may be your use. Frankly, I don't know, either. But Hezhi dreams of you, and I feel certain that there is a purpose to that." His face worked around some unspoken thought, and he let out a long, weary breath. "If only I could *know*," he groaned at last.

"I see her emerging from the River," Perkar whispered, closing his eyes. "The River is blood, and I am in it. The River is trying to swallow me, but it also offers me up, to her. She is weeping, and her tears are blood, too. She wants me to help her."

He opened his eyes again, so that sunlight could clean away the remembered vision. Ghan and Tsem were staring at him. The Giant's eyes were narrow. Ghan was nodding.

"I see no other choice," he said at last. "This is all moved by her blood, Tsem. If we do not trust *her*, we cannot save her."

Tsem almost snarled, but then his brutish face quieted. "You are wiser than I," he said at last.

"I doubt that," Ghan answered. "But I *am* more learned." His face hardened with decision.

"Perkar of the Clan Barku, we will trust you. We will help you earn your . . . perku?"

"Piraku," he corrected. "But I have a single question for you."

"Ask it then, quickly."

"The enemies of this girl. Is one of them the River himself?"

Ghan and the Giant both stared at him before the old man, almost imperceptibly, nodded yes.

Perkar smiled faintly. "I was told to trust no one in Nhol," he replied. "But I will do as destiny demands. Then perhaps my life will be my own again."

"Perhaps," Ghan allowed.

BY now they had retraced their steps to the docks. Ghan led them through the maze of quays, out to a small, single-masted vessel. He called out, and a sharp, weasely-looking man poked his head from the cabin.

"Ghan," he said, his voice pleasant-timbred, low, completely unweasellike.

"As we arranged," Ghan told him. He turned to Tsem. "Tsem, this is my cousin; you may call him Zeq'. He will take you and the princess down-River to my clan's holdings. I have prepared a letter for my family that contains both truths and lies—they would not help if they knew the complete truth. Have Hezhi familiarize you with its contents, so that what you say and know will be consistent with my story. My clan will then arrange overland transportation to Lhe. I have written another letter to the archivist there, whom I correspond with. I know that he will help us. In Lhe, Hezhi will be safe, and so will you."

"I can read it myself," Tsem rumbled. Ghan did not look as surprised as he might.

Ghan turned back to Zeq'. "This is Perkar, an outlander," he explained, though his cousin's suspicious stare made it plain that he had already ascertained that much. "I will pay his passage, too. His sword may prove useful if trouble comes."

Zeq' nodded at Perkar, doubt plain on his face.

"What of you, Master Ghan?" Tsem asked. "It will go badly for you if your part in this is discovered."

Ghan lifted his frail shoulders. "If all goes well, my part will never be known."

"Unless the priests question you. They can *make* you speak, you know."

"I do know."

"Then they will know where Hezhi has fled to."

"No," Ghan said. "Because the priests will never actually question me. Trust me about that."

Tsem regarded him thoughtfully. "Without you, my mistress has no chance at all. I will trust you." Tsem then turned his rugged features on Perkar. "Know this," he said softly. "Hezhi is the most precious thing that lives. If harm comes to her through you, nothing will stop me from snapping your neck. Not *that* sword or a hundred. Do you understand me?"

"I understand," Perkar said, holding his gaze steady on the Giant's own. Both of these men clearly loved this girl, were willing to give their lives for her. Could Perkar make the same commitment to a person in no way related to him, a person he had never met? The Giant didn't believe so, that was evident. And the Giant, of course, was right. Things were not as clear as he had hoped they would be; perhaps when he met the girl he would know for sure. In the meantime, how could he reassure the Giant without lying? For he did not want to lie to this strange, huge man, so like Ngangata.

"I have never met your princess," Perkar said softly. "But

many good people—friends of mine—died because of me. I can never be redeemed for that, my friend. I have no love for this River; it hurts someone I love, it took my life from me. You imply that your girl—this Hezhi—has somehow turned the River against herself. *I* believe that she intends to steal from him, rob him. I once swore to kill the Changeling Rivergod, Giant. That was stupid, and it led to all of the deaths I spoke of just now. But if she and I can steal from him—especially if it is her life we steal—then I will feel that I have taken at least that much revenge against him. I have been willing to die for less noble things than saving the life of a princess." *Or killing one, if need be,* he finished silently, though he felt a sudden, surprising guilt for the thought. But if what these men told him was true—if in saving this girl he was thwarting the River—then he would not betray his words. Only if he had been lied to would he have lied.

Tsem listened carefully, with narrowed eyes.

"I *love* her," he said at last. "Remember that, along with all of your other pretty words."

Ghan took Tsem's massive elbow. "Tsem, this is the time. You go back into the palace and get her. Dress her in those worker's clothes you told me about; cut her hair. Bring her down to the boat here, and Zeq' will do the rest."

"And me?" Perkar asked.

"I don't know why she brought you here," Ghan said, "if it was indeed she. It may be that the River *did* send you, at the behest of the priesthood or the emperor. I doubt that; it isn't their way to act in such a circuitous manner. Your presence here is so bizarre, so unlikely, that I trust it. As to what you are supposed to do, I rather think that will become obvious in the moments and days ahead. In the meantime, should anyone try to hinder your escape, kill them."

Ghan and Tsem turned and walked back into the city, Tsem with a smoldering backward glance.

"Well," Perkar told Harka. "Kill. That's something we can do, isn't it?"

"Just so long as you don't forget," Harka said. *"Some things even we cannot kill."*

JUST inside the gate, Tsem and Ghan parted ways. It was late enough in the day that Hezhi was probably back in her apartments, so Tsem steered himself toward that wing of the palace.

When he heard Qey weeping, he knew something was wrong. Suddenly frantic, he burst into the courtyard; Qey was there, and two of the priests.

"What?" Tsem demanded, despite the fact that they were priests, despite what they could have done to him for impertinence.

"Your charge ran away," one of the two informed him— darkly, though his voice was sweet. "Where *were* you?"

"Ran? Where?" But he knew, knew with a terrible sinking feeling in his gut.

"I don't know," the priest snapped impatiently. "Two priests followed her, but she has not returned."

Tsem nodded, blood pounding in his ears. The first priest never had the opportunity to cry out; Tsem's fist slammed into his temple with the force and effect of a sledgehammer. The second had time for a terrified squeal before Tsem lifted him up with both hands and snapped his neck like a chicken's. Then, ignoring Qey's sudden, rejuvenated hysteria, he ran as fast as his huge feet could carry him.

X

A Gift of Slaughter

SWAYING at the edge, Hezhi heard her name shouted. Not in the high, clear voice of a priest, but in Tsem's bass roar. She gasped, stepped back from her doom, and turned to see where the call came from.

Tsem was loping across the rooftop. As she watched, he caught the struggling priest by the hair. The priest yelped, and then Tsem broke his neck. The second priest, also looking back, screamed shrilly and continued screaming until Tsem caught him. Hezhi closed her eyes, unwilling to watch. When she opened them, the hapless priest had fetched up motionless against the parapet of an adjoining roof.

"Hezhi," Tsem bellowed again.

Trembling, she watched him approach, and without a backward glance at the long fall, she climbed back onto the slope and, sitting on her behind, began a controlled slide back to the roofbeam. Tsem caught her at the bottom, folded her into his huge arms.

"Did they hurt you, Princess?" he cooed.

"No, Tsem. No, they never touched me. I was ahead of them."

She tried not to look at the dead men and their bulging, surprised expressions when she and Tsem retraced their steps. Instead, she gave her attention to what Tsem was telling her, though it was difficult, with the relief and confusion that swam about in her skull.

"Ghan has arranged passage out of the city," he informed her. "It is all planned, you have no need to worry."

"There are probably more priests in the apartment . . ."

"Not anymore," Tsem growled. "Their ghosts, perhaps."

"Oh. Tsem, you shouldn't have done it. If they catch you now . . ."

"They won't, and if they do, they'll be very sorry. Now come."

They dropped back down into the courtyard with its familiar cottonwood, and there Hezhi's swirling head spilled weakness down into her knees and she nearly collapsed. Tsem scooped her up and started down the stairs.

The apartments were a nightmare. Qey was bawling and there were two more dead priests, one leaking blood from his mouth and the other with his face crushed unrecognizably. The thick scent of incense still hung in the air.

"Qey! Qey," Tsem roared, shaking her. "Cut her hair! Cut it off!"

The old woman, shaken almost out of her senses, looked vaguely at the two of them. "Her hair . . ." she repeated.

"Arr!" Tsem rushed into her room. "Where did you hide your work clothes? The ones I got for you?"

"Under the mattress," Hezhi called, still watching the quaking Qey.

"Qey," she whispered.

Qey's eyes sharpened a bit then, and she held out her arms. Hezhi rushed into them, ground her head against the woman's breast.

"Cut her hair," Qey suddenly muttered. She gently disengaged Hezhi and went to her sewing kit, returned with scissors.

"Turn around, little one," she whispered. Hezhi did so, felt the peculiar little grinding of her hair being all but sheared off, just at the nape of the neck.

Tsem burst back into the room with her clothes; she had rinsed them of the mud and slime of the underpalace, but they were still deeply stained.

"Put them on."

"Where are you taking her?" Qey wailed. "Where are you taking my little Hezhi?"

"Somewhere safe, Qey," Tsem told her hurriedly. "But you must know nothing, *nothing*, or they will hurt you to find out. Do you understand?"

"Come with us, Qey," Hezhi pleaded. "She can come with us, can't she, Tsem?"

"She may," Tsem said a little doubtfully.

Qey stared at them both, then gently shook her head. "No, little one, I can't do that."

"Why not?"

"I just can't. I would be in the way, I wouldn't know what to do."

"Take *care* of me, like you always have," she insisted.

"No." Qey stepped back, still shaking her head. "No, please, Hezhi, don't ask me to."

She meant to keep insisting until the old woman agreed, but the finality of Qey's tone convinced her. So, instead, she hurriedly doffed her skirt, pulled on the loose pants and smock.

"That's it," Tsem muttered nervously. "That's it, come on."

"Qey ..." Hezhi began, but the old woman shushed her, grasped her head, and planted a little kiss on her cheek.

"I love you, child," she said. "I love you very much. Go with Tsem and take care. Live, little one." Her tears had ceased, and now she seemed calm, in control.

"Come," Tsem insisted.

"Wait," Hezhi said. She searched back through her dress, found the little statue Yen had given her.

"All right, Tsem," she said, feeling stronger. "Let's go."

Tsem nodded and gestured. Together they set off down the hall, walking briskly, but not running for fear of attracting attention.

"WE'LL take the Ember Gate," Tsem explained. "You are Duwe, a boy from the docks. I paid you a soldier to help me carry four baskets of fish."

"Where is Ghan? Will he be at the boat?"

"Ghan has returned to his apartments. We will not see him. He has arranged everything."

"I have to say good-bye to Ghan."

"You can't, Princess, there is no time. Soon someone will notice the dead priests. Ghan left a letter for you."

"Ghan . . ." She sighed. She might never know what happened to him—or Qey.

They came to the Ember Gate, Hezhi walking with her head down, trying to seem humble, respectful. Two guards met them there.

"Who is this?" they asked, eyeing Hezhi suspiciously.

"Just a boy," Tsem replied. "I had too many fish to carry, so I gave him a soldier to help me."

"A boy, eh?"

Something was wrong; she already knew that. The guards seemed too alert, too suspicious, as if they had been warned to watch for her.

"You should know better than this, Tsem," one of them grunted.

Tsem grinned good-naturedly. "Well, you can't blame me for trying, can you? A man has to have a *little* something, doesn't he?" He ended his question with a wink and a bit of a leer.

The soldier shook his head. "We were warned about this," the guard said, drawing out his sword. The other followed suit.

"Princess," one of the guards commanded, "tell your servant to back away from us. Do it."

She hesitated, and she saw Tsem tense for a spring.

"Princess, he might kill one of us, but we have swords. Tell him."

You fool, Hezhi thought. *I can no longer tell Tsem anything.*

Tsem confirmed that by taking that moment to lunge. The guard saw it coming, backpedaled away from the Giant, his sword slashing down. Tsem caught the blow on his left arm, and blood started instantly. The other guard stepped around and behind Tsem, sword raising up.

Hezhi shrieked and lashed out, though her fists were clenched at her side. In her mind, her shriek was a spear, hurtling through one guard and then the other.

The effect was instantaneous. The guard stepping behind Tsem dropped his sword and curled around his belly, gagging. The other, dancing away from Tsem, doubled over and disgorged, first his breakfast and then a stream of blood.

Whatever it was she had done struck Tsem, as well, though a lesser blow; he staggered and crumpled to his knees, eyes glazing. Blood was pouring from his arm.

"Tsem!" she gasped.

"I'm all right," he muttered, rising back onto his feet. "Come on, we have to hurry."

"I didn't mean to hurt you, too."

"Doesn't matter," he said, looking dully at his slashed arm. "Come on."

"Wrap your arm," Hezhi said.

"Later."

"No! Someone will see!"

Comprehension flickered in the half Giant's eyes, and he tore one of the guard's surcoats off. Both of the men still seemed to be alive, though in terrible pain. She felt a stab of remorse, and then remembered that they had meant to kill Tsem, had been *doing* it, and the guilt died, stillborn.

The scale on her arm ached as if burning. Tsem wrapped his arm, took her by the shoulder with his free hand. Together they passed through the now-unguarded gate, and for the first time in her life, Hezhi entered the city of Nhol.

GHE stared down at the dead priests in disgust and dismay. They never even understood they were dying; he could see that on their frozen, stupid faces. It was his own fault, as well. He had spent too much time with Hezhi instead of following the old man and the Giant; by the time he had found them, understood what they were up to and had taken measures to have the boat seized and the gates guarded, he had lost touch with Tsem. Yes, he had allowed himself to be distracted by a silly boyhood whim, and now priests were dead. And yet, he had done the impossible, kissed a princess, the daughter of the Chakunge himself. What gutter rat in Southtown wouldn't give his knife arm for that? Not that he could *tell* anyone, but *he* would know.

Ghe caught the motion easily; it was the old woman, of course, the one he had found just staring down at the dead bodies. Why hadn't he noticed the scissors? He *was* distracted.

He disarmed the old woman as she stabbed—overhand, of course—and watched her crumple as the blade of his hand struck the base of her skull. She would live, to pay for her idiocy on a torture rack. *He* had things to do.

He hoped the guards at the gate would stop them, but if not, the boat should have been seized by now. There were only two men guarding it, its owner and a barbarian sellsword.

Ghe checked his weapons to make sure they were all accounted for, and without sparing the *-nata* priests a second glance, he loped hurriedly down the corridor. He still had much to prove, to the other Jik and to the priesthood. He should have taken Hezhi just after their lips met, while she was happy, before the palace was littered with bodies, but sentimentality and uncertainty had stopped him. No, *hope*. Hope that the stupid girl wouldn't go through with it, but stay in the palace and accept whatever destiny the River granted her. Now he had much to explain.

PERKAR was sitting on the edge of the dock, watching the water ebb and flow against the pilings when Zeq' gave a sort of strangled yelp. He looked back to see what the matter was. Whatever it was wasn't back there; Zeq's distended eyes were staring out at the street. He followed the boatman's terrified gaze.

Eight men were marching down the street. They were dressed in identical kilts striped black and dark blue, blue tunics stiff over steel breastplates. Their dark hair was shoved up under plain steel caps.

"Who are they?" he called back to Zeq'.

"Nunewag," Zeq' replied stiffly. "The emperor's elite guard."

The men showed no sign of halting or explaining themselves. The situation seemed clear enough to Perkar; these troops had been sent by the emperor to find his daughter. Serving the emperor, they served the River. They, at least, were unambiguously his enemies. Still, they were Human Beings, and so it was with some small reluctance that he walked over to the gangplank connecting the ship with the dock. He drew Harka.

The apparent leader of the men—the one in front, at least—looked up at him and said dryly, "Barbarian, I give you one chance to escape being a ghost. We are the Nunewag, the emperor's personal guard, on his business."

"What business *is* that?"

The leader made a disgusted face. "Barbarian, if that is any concern of yours, then I will have to arrest you. Do you understand me?"

"I understand that this man has not given you permission to

board his boat," Perkar said as easily as he could. He knew that if he appeared calm, that would most likely rattle them. In point of fact, he *was* calm, and Perkar wondered—not for the first time—if Harka had some hand in that, too.

The leader of the soldiers waved his hand and the others began to spread out quickly so they could flank Perkar, though they would have to leap to the boat to do so.

"Take them the fight," Harka advised. *"Don't let them pin us on the boat. Despite the advantage we have at the moment, we will lose it if any of them manage to get behind us on the boat. Better to have them behind us out on the street, where we have room to move."*

He saw no reason to argue with Harka. He waited until the men were actually in position to jump before he made his own move. Skirling the fierce war whoop of his father, he charged down the plank.

The leader faced him first and was consequently the first to die. Harka met the oncoming blade, slid down to its guard, sheared through that, arm, and breastplate. The man's dying face was more incredulous than shocked, as if the great opening in his chest were less an issue than the wholly unfair way it had been achieved. Perkar's charge did not slow; he whirled away from the crumpling man and continued it, crushing physically into two warriors who did not have their swordpoints up yet. One actually fell and the other stumbled away as Perkar beheaded a third. Then something cold and hard slid into his kidney. Snarling, he spun, felt the blade in his back tear a gash, swung backhanded and decapitated that assailant, too.

If they had all rushed him then, it might well have been the end. But he bellowed and whirled, yanked the offending sword from his body, and though he staggered and his knees nearly buckled, the men seemed to take note not of that but of the fact that he was still on his feet, while three of them lay dead. In a few heartbeats, their eight had become five, and those five looked nervous.

Perkar felt the pain ebb then, and strength returning. By the time they chose to renew their attack—circling him now—he had cleared his head of the pain and felt ready to deal with them again.

As soon as the circle closed on him, he let Harka pick the most dangerous point, hurled himself at it, sword cutting brightly. He broke another sword and cut off its wielder's arm, sliced deeply into the thigh of another, though he took a hard slash into his own ribs, felt a flood of warmth wash down his side. He wished he had his hauberk; that would have deflected the last cut.

Now, effectively, they were three. They were stubborn men, and one of them managed to wound him again—this time rather high in the chest—before he finished them and sagged back against the dock, coughing up blood. He turned to ask Zeq' if he might get a drink of water, when he realized that the boat was already leaving the quay, Zeq' madly working the sail.

"Wait!" Perkar called after him.

"I'm sorry, my friend," Zeq' yelled back. "There is nothing I can do for you. You're already dead, you just don't know it yet!"

"I won't die," Perkar insisted. "Come back!"

"I didn't bargain for this," Zeq' yelled. "They probably already caught the Giant and the girl. It's over, barbarian! I'll tell people of your battle."

"I don't care about that!" he howled. "Just come back!"

Zeq' didn't answer. His sail caught a breeze blowing out from the shore, and his little boat began to pick up speed.

He made to shriek one last time but blew out a clot of blood instead.

"*Careful,*" Harka cautioned. "*That last one got your lung.*"

"How quickly will I heal?"

"*Quickly enough. We have five heartstrings left between us. If you can wait a little while before getting run through again, you'll have six.*"

"How long?"

"*Half a day.*"

"I'm waiting here," he said stubbornly. "For as long as I can. If I have to fight more soldiers, I'll fight them."

Back to a piling, Harka on his knees and eyes alert, Perkar waited. A crowd of thirty or more people stood, staring at him and the corpses of the king's guard. Two of the latter lay moaning, and two passersby were helping them staunch the blood flowing from their arm and thighs, respectively. He doubted if either would live. Belatedly, he felt a stab of remorse, then wondered why the possibility of regret never occurred to him *before* a fight anymore. He had heard that killing grew easier as one became accustomed to it. It was certainly easier when your enemies attacked you in such a dishonorable fashion, eight against one. Of course, he had Harka, but *they* hadn't known that. They had believed him a lone barbarian with a normal weapon. Such was their misfortune, to be both without Piraku and wrong at the same moment.

A member of the city guard appeared in the crowd and gaped at the dead men and at Perkar. He made as if to draw his sword and come forward, but Perkar shook his head, a silent *no*. That was apparently enough for the guard. He took his hand from his hilt and vanished up the street, surely seeking reinforcements.

"Hurry up with your girl, Giant," he muttered.

THE blood was soaking through Tsem's makeshift bandage before they had crossed five streets, but Tsem seemed untroubled by his wound. He rushed ahead of Hezhi, and people scrambled from his path.

For her, the city was a series of broken patterns, faces, colors rushing by her. She had no time to comprehend it, to chart it out in some way she could understand. The newness was too steeped in blood, pain, fury, and fear. What should have been a moment of discovery was instead just another tunnel she was rushing down, seeking her life.

They ran, it seemed, forever, and the air changed as they went

on, became thicker, scented with fish and truly unpleasant smells
that chewed at the back of her brain.

"Almost," Tsem said, triumph and worry both audible to her
ear, so familiar with his voice. A crowd burst apart before them,
as much from the force of Tsem's presence as from his mass.

The scene revealed then was a strange one, and oddly enough,
the first thing that Hezhi noticed, the thing that she would always remember, was the River, right there, lapping at a wooden
walkway no more than ten steps away. Looking at him, from
level ground and not from above, the River was somehow more
awesome, a sheet of power that lay over every bit of the world
but for that upon which she stood. Rivergulls complained above,
fighting the wind forcing them from shore and whatever meals
they might find there.

Next she saw the bodies, the blood, and, last of all, *him*. He
was the man from her dream, there was never any question,
though at the moment he looked absolutely unlike any image
that had ever come to her. Spattered in blood, his face an odd,
angry red, wearing some sort of peasant garb, he sat watching
them and the crowd, looking across the bodies as if they were a
field of grain he had just reaped, as if he were resting a bit before
gathering it up, his sword a red sickle on his knee. It was he,
though; she smelled a hard, sweet metallic smell that was not just
blood but *his* blood, and she knew it, as if she had smelled it or
even tasted it before. That was the River in her, she knew, recog-
nizing him, not *her* eyes, not *her* nose.

What's more, he knew her, too. His strange gray eyes flashed,
a weird little smile played across his lips.

The River, the bodies, the man—there was a stroke or two
missing from the painting, she understood, and Tsem's stunned
grunt of consternation suggested what it might be. The gray-eyed
man confirmed her guess, in a wintery voice.

"Our friend Zeq' should be out in the channel about now," he
said. "Seems he didn't care much for the elite guard's attention."

"How did they know?" Tsem bellowed. "Who told them?"

Hezhi was becoming aware of the crowd, a sea of faces staring at them, angry, curious, frightened.

"I don't know," Perkar said. "I only know we have to leave some other way, and quickly." He frowned. "You're hurt."

"They caught us at the gate to the palace, too."

The man stood and strode over to the two, so that they need not shout. "A city guardsman just came by," he said. "He probably went for reinforcements."

"Probably," Tsem answered, glancing around at the carnage, at the man's clearly hideous wounds.

Closer, he looked more like his dream image, though the dream image had been more boyish somehow, younger. Perhaps it was the blood that made him look older. His eyes focused on hers again, and then he dropped to one knee.

"Perkar Kar Barku," he said. "I believe you summoned me, Princess."

Hezhi opened her mouth—she did not know what her reply would have been—when there was a hoarse shout up the street.

"Guards coming!" someone in the crowd cried, and she couldn't tell if she and her companions were being warned or whether the person was eager to see another slaughter.

"This way," Tsem bellowed, and once more they were running, pounding over the cobblestone streets. Above them, the dark sheet of night was drawing over the sky, hastened by clouds flying in on some high, furious wind. She glanced now and then at Perkar, wanting to ask him so much, wondering how he could still be alive with such terrible wounds.

"The South Gate is our only chance," Tsem gasped. "It will be least guarded. Perhaps the barbarian and I can fight our way through."

South Gate? Something about the South Gate rattled memories, didn't it? She tried desperately to *think*. They rounded a corner—Perkar was hanging back, trying to discourage the crowd—fully half of them were following the trio, clearly hoping to see more fighting. Tsem, ahead of her, nearly slipped in a puddle of some nameless gunk . . .

That jarred her memory. "Tsem!" she yelled. "Tsem, the sewers!"

"What?" He stopped and turned toward her, shuddering. She remembered that running was difficult for him.

"The new part of the city drainage—the one Yen is working on—it runs out past South Gate."

"I don't understand, Princess."

"We can cross *under* the wall. Just help me find Caul Street."

XI

~~~~~~

The Changeling

AFTER all that had happened that day it was the dank tunnels Perkar and his companions descended into that brought shivers to his spine. The closeness and the dark evoked memories he had no wish to recall.

"That grate up there is beneath Moon Street," Hezhi called, gesturing at a cataract of light falling through from above.

Passing beneath it, Perkar glanced up, saw perhaps ten faces crowded against the fading light. They still had followers from the Riverside, it seemed. Which was unfortunate, since that would certainly attract the attention of soldiers, sooner or later.

"How much farther?" Tsem called.

"Not too far. They just began construction of the new section, so the outer grill should have been removed. It comes out a few hundred yards from the wall."

"What if it's guarded, too?" Perkar asked.

"I don't know."

"We might have done better at the gate," he observed. "Fighting *up* a ladder will be real trouble."

"They will have bows at the gate," Tsem informed him.

"Ah."

"Anyway," the girl, Hezhi, put in, "we won't have to climb up. The duct should open from a hillside."

Perkar was curious as to why a princess should know the ins and outs of the sewers. For that matter, a part of him was fascinated by the very concept of these underground ditches built to drain the city of rain, floods, and Human waste. It was not something he would have ever thought of or searched for, that much was certain.

The three of them slogged on.

"The girl looks like a god," Harka volunteered.

"What?" he whispered, low, so that the others would not think him insane.

"She is not a god, but she certainly resembles one. This is very odd."

"Is she my enemy, Harka?" Perkar barely sighed. "Did the River send me to serve her or stop her?"

"Perhaps the River did not summon you at all. Perhaps it was always she."

"You say she resembles a goddess. Is she more powerful than the River? Could she force her will upon him?"

Harka hesitated before answering. *"No,"* he said finally.

"Everyone who pursues her serves the River. The emperor's guard, the priesthood. Yet she is of *his* blood."

"A rebellious child?"

"Why should a barbarian be summoned from half a world away to kill a rebellious child?"

"Perhaps no one who serves the River can do it. Perhaps only an outlander."

"Still, that feels wrong. In my dreams, she wanted me to help her. That means I should kill her."

"Only if she is your enemy, and not the River. Remember what Brother Horse said, about a god so large his head doesn't know what his feet are doing?"

"I wanted this to be simpler," he muttered, somewhat more loudly than the rest of his conversation with his sword. Tsem sent him a sharp glance over his shoulder.

"You always do," Harka said. *"It is your chief character flaw."*

That should not have come as a shock to Perkar, but it did. "We'll think about that later," he muttered. He crinkled his nose, and then, in a louder voice, asked, "What's that smell?"

"Sewage," Tsem answered.

"No, no," Hezhi gasped. "I smell it, too. Incense, or a priest's broom."

"Above us?" Tsem said hopefully. "At the gate?"

"We don't pass beneath the gate," she said. Her voice sounded choked, as if she were about to cry. Small wonder; a girl her age shouldn't see this much killing, be caught up in so much terror. She was right, too. The smoke was coming from up the tunnel, not wafting down through one of the infrequent grills.

"What does this mean?" Perkar asked.

"Priests," Tsem said grimly, "and probably soldiers, too."

They hurried on regardless, Tsem in the lead, Perkar to the rear, Hezhi between them, protected by their bodies, hands, and sword.

Tsem slowed up after a moment, breathing heavily. Perkar didn't think the Giant looked very well.

"There," Tsem said. They could see the end of the tunnel, though it was faint due to the darkness outside of the city. It was just light enough to make out the figures silhouetted there. The smell of smoke was stronger.

GHE slowed as his opponents did, rubbing his chin thoughtfully. He had caught up with them at last, though they had led him a merry chase. Of course Hezhi would remember these sewers—after all, he had brought them to her attention. He fingered the tip of his sword, to make certain the toxin smeared on it was still there. Satisfied that it was, he slipped on toward where the three stood. Clearly they were aware of the priests, were deciding what to do about them. Perhaps the girl would try to use her sorcerous powers, the ones she had used against the guards at the gate. If so, she would fail, for the priests were now thoroughly protected from such attacks. The same smoke that swept away ghosts and demons would contain her power, or so the priests assured him. No, Ghe was much more worried about the barbarian, the one who reportedly had killed eight of the king's elite. He felt the elite were overrated, especially by themselves, but that was still an incredible feat, one that Ghe *might* be able to duplicate if he managed to strike first, before they were aware. As he would do now. He slipped closer still, until he could see the weave in the outlander's shirt.

"SOMETHING," Harka warned.

"What?"

"I don't know. The smoke confuses me."

HEZHI turned at Perkar's muttered word. Was he talking to her? His gray eyes were staring, shocked. A bloody spike projected from his chest, right where his heart should be. He crumpled, and from behind him stepped a shadow in the shape of a man. She shrieked and leapt away as something swung out—a fist, she guessed later—and struck her in the mouth. Then the shadow leapt on toward Tsem. She reeled back crazily, trying to regain her balance; her mouth tasted coppery, and she realized with horror that it was filling with blood. She spat and fell into the water almost simultaneously.

Pushing up on the palms of her hands, she tried desperately to seize the images around her, force sense into them. The shadow was dancing around Tsem, and she saw the flicker of a blade. Anger surged up from her feet, through the *thing* in her, and she sent it to stab the black-clad man. He did stumble; but she felt the power drain out of her attack, as if the very air were sucking it up. *The smoke,* she thought. *They sweep me as if I were a ghost.*

Tsem was leaning heavily against the wall, how badly hurt she could not tell.

The shadow recovered, stood, walked toward her.

"Well, Princess," he said. "The priests assured me that you would not be able to do even that much. I'm impressed. Best I kill you now, I think, before you can prove them wrong again."

At that, Tsem groaned in anguish, lurched toward them, and fell. The shadow-man laughed. "Strength and size don't count for much," he observed.

Chills prickled all over Hezhi. She knew his voice.

"Yen?" she gasped.

The shadow bowed. "My name is actually Ghe," he confided. "But I was Yen to you. When I was assigned to watch you, in case you ascended early or disastrously. Becoming your acquaintance seemed the best way."

"But . . ." Hezhi groped for words. How could this be Yen, so kind, who had given her the statuette? "Yen, no. I'm just leaving. I'm not ever coming back. Please, let us go."

The man's voice softened a bit. "Princess, I'm sorry, I truly am. I grew to like you, playing at Yen. But I am *not* Yen, not at all like that. I kill people; that is what I do. And the priests tell me to kill you."

The priests were creeping closer, the smell of their smoke more overpowering. Desperately she launched another attack at Yen, but this time she felt it drowned in the smoke instantly. He didn't even react.

"I *am* sorry. I'll try to make it quick, and I'll leave an offering for your ghost."

"Leave an offering for your own," another voice growled. Hezhi gaped. Perkar, the dead man, stood behind them, sword in hand. He did not look happy.

*　　*　　*

FOR a whole heartbeat, Ghe stared at the walking corpse. He recalled feeling the heart split, and even if he had missed, the toxin
on his blade was known to paralyze and kill in less than fifty
heartbeats. *The blade had come out the front!* An unaccustomed
fear stabbed through Ghe, and he lashed out quickly, hoping to
hamstring this demon. His blade met the other, his priest-blessed
blade, and it shivered. Ghe knew that it had almost shattered,
would have shattered if the impact had been oblique. Desperately
he attacked with the *wintsem*, the net of steel, a combination of
strokes that would end inevitably with his point in the man. The
last stroke went too low, because Ghe was afraid to meet the
strange weapon head on, and so his final lunge took his blade
into the barbarian's belly rather than some more immediately vi-
tal spot. Ghe yanked to withdraw his steel, had one look at the
foreigner's face, realized what he had done. The pale man's blade
was already descending toward his unprotected neck.

Li, think kindly of my ghost, he had time to think, before his
head fell into the dirty water. Even then, for just a moment, he
thought he saw something strange: a column of flame, leaping
out of the muck, towering over Hezhi. Then something inexorable swallowed him up.

HEZHI saw the pillar of light draw up from the floor, from a
glowing, iridescent stain floating on it. With dull surprise she understood that it was her blood, the blood from her mouth. She
heard the gasps from the priests; saw Yen's head parted from his
body, still shrouded in its black hood. The flame took form, congealed, became a creature from a nightmare, tentacles, horn,
many-colored plates. It shuddered, stretched wide its ten crablike
legs, and, before she could draw another breath, turned to her.

A flaming broom struck the thing, slowed only slightly as it
passed through, but the creature lost its form momentarily,
flowed and then came back together. Soundlessly it glided toward
the priests.

Hezhi sank down to her knees, held herself with both arms, moaning.

"A GOD," Perkar breathed as the thing appeared. He lurched toward it, swayed back. The assassin had hurt him badly.

"*Careful,*" Harka warned. "*It isn't a god precisely, but it has many of the same qualities. And we only have three heartstrings left.*"

"Is it like the girl?"

"*Yes, somewhat. More like the ghost-fish in the River, but stronger.*"

"Heartstrings?" He saw that he had a brief reprieve; the thing had turned on the priests, obviously annoyed by the silly burning broom one of them cast at it.

"*No mortal heartstrings at all, no Ti to sever. It is a ghost!*"

"Can we fight it?"

"*It has seven immortal strands. We will probably lose.*"

Terrible things were happening down the corridor. He stumbled over to the girl. "Are you all right? Can you run?"

"Tsem," she muttered. "See to Tsem."

He nodded and quickly crossed to the Giant. To his credit, Tsem was already struggling to his feet. A sword wound gaped in his abdomen.

"We have to get past that thing," Perkar told him. "While it is killing the priests."

Tsem nodded, leaned against the wall. "Come on, Princess," he said. "Come let me carry you."

She didn't respond, other than to look at them, confused. Tsem bent down and lifted her up.

"I'm sorry to spoil your beautiful clothes, Princess," Perkar heard him whisper.

They stepped over two dead priests, who appeared to have been boiled alive, and Perkar wondered how Harka could possibly protect him from *that*. The thing was a shimmering presence, up in front of them.

"When it finishes the priests, I'll take it, try to drive it from the tunnel," Perkar told Tsem. "Then you *run*, do you understand? You have no hope against a creature like that." Perkar realized that he had made his decision. Whatever murky purpose the River had proposed for him, he could not bring himself to slay Hezhi and her guardian. Tsem was too much like Ngangata. Harka was right—he always wanted things to be simple, and he did the simple things even when they did not *feel* right. Helping Hezhi and Tsem *felt* right. Helping the priests and their assassin did not. In its own way, that was simple enough for him.

Tsem nodded weary assent.

The last of the priests fell at the mouth of the tunnel, and Perkar relinquished his wildest hope—that the thing would pursue its tormentors out into the sand he could barely see beyond. He gritted his teeth and prepared to charge. Then he whooped, because the monster *did* glide out of the end of the tunnel. There was a furious clatter around it, which puzzled him momentarily until he placed the strange sound. Arrows, smacking into the stone surface of the duct. Soldiers, firing from outside.

Standing at the lip of the tunnel, the world yawning wide before them, Perkar quickly assessed the tableau. Ten or so soldiers were hurriedly trading bows for swords; three more were running like frightened dogs. A wisp of rose curled against the western horizon was all that remained of the day, stars and moon smothered by churning clouds. The landscape was sand, scrub, and beyond that, green fields.

Shrieks went up as the demon fell among the men, and Perkar, remembering his battle with the Huntress, felt a brief, diluted pity.

They ran. Despite Tsem's huge frame and powerful legs, his wounds and weight were taking their toll; the giant was soon staggering. The shouts behind them were still too near.

"Come on," Perkar said. "I'll carry her."

"No," Tsem gasped. "No, I have her."

"Where? Where do we go?"

"West," he said. "West into the desert."

Where the Giant came by his energy, Perkar did not know, but he kept going. He resisted the urge to look back, knowing that Harka would warn him if the god-creature came close enough to be a danger. The sounds of combat died away behind them, just as they entered one of the fields. Knee-high plants, gray in the darkness, shivered in the wind.

"*Best turn, Perkar,*" Harka said.

Perkar slowed and drew a long breath. "Keep going," he told Tsem. "Just keep going."

Waiting, legs braced wide, he watched for the thing. "At least I'll fight some part of the Changeling," he muttered.

"*Too bad the soldiers didn't occupy it longer,*" Harka said. "*If we could have managed to get farther from the River . . .*"

"How much farther?"

"*Farther than we can get, I'm afraid. See, there it is.*"

Perkar could make it out, running up one of the irrigation canals, a dancing, deadly, many-colored flame. Of *course* up one of the canals—the canals were part of the stinking River. He should move, fight it out in the field, where it might have less power. He glanced back at Tsem and Hezhi: They were still paralleling the watercourse, unaware. It might pass him by and follow them instead. He tightened his grip on Harka.

"*Look,*" Harka seemed to whisper, though the "voice" in his ear was no softer than it ever was. "*See its heart-strings?*"

"I do," Perkar said. Seven strands of living light knotted together behind the ephemeral, monstrous form, bearing down on where he waited.

The ghost hesitated, perhaps puzzled by him. Staring at it towering over him, venomous, deadly, he saw no point in waiting for *it* to attack *him*. He shouted and slashed, Harka flaring with light, cascades of flame enveloping him. His blow went deep into nothing, until Harka's edge struck a heartstrand, and *that* split with a force that nearly tore the sword from his hands. Something struck into him, too, a deep flare of heat, liquid metal filling his bones, a pain unreal in its intensity.

"*Fight, fight,*" Harka urged frantically. "*We have two heart-strings left!*"

Grimly Perkar struck back into the withering light.

Hᴇᴢʜɪ felt Tsem's blood soaking her, seeping through her clothes, sticky against her skin. Like honey. She wanted it all to stop, for Yen to be Yen and still alive, for Tsem to be un-wounded, to have never even met the inhuman Perkar. She shut her eyes tight, wishing, wishing.

Tsem gasped and stumbled, nearly cried out. Two more steps, and the great legs folded them to the earth.

"Princess," he whispered. "I'm sorry. I have to rest, just for a moment. Keep this way, and I'll follow."

"Tsem!" she urged. "No, Tsem."

He set her gently on her feet and then sank back to a sitting position. "Go on," he said.

Back behind them a shout rang out. Turning, she saw the ghost, a scintillating cloud, and the black shadow of a man silhouetted against it.

"This is what comes of my wishes," she muttered. "This."

A hot surge of anger cut through, knifing up from below her fear and helplessness. Men were dying all around her, and she was curled up, wishing it all away—when she was the one who had wished it all into existence. Her mouth set in a little line, fists clenched, she stalked back toward Perkar and the ghost. She was *not* helpless. She was Hezhi Yehd Cha'dune, and ancestors of hers had tumbled cities.

She suddenly felt the River, pulsing along beside her in the irrigation canal, felt as if it were part of her own bloodstream. She drank from it, her arms and legs flaring with energy, stretching out and out until she could embrace the canal, the field, Perkar, the demon. The demon she *did* embrace, tightly, angrily.

It knew its danger; she felt its slow mind understand, and it flickered past Perkar, a spider made of lightning. She heard Perkar groan, but her attention was not on him anymore. She was actually smiling when her hand that was more than a hand reached out and into the ghost, seized the knotted strands of light within it and *squeezed*. Fire rushed up her arms, a brass drum crashing in her head with each heartbeat. The demon writhed in her grip, lashed at her, died. When it died, she ate it up. It was a fine meal, demon.

Hezhi cackled gleefully as her embrace grew to include everything around her, even things she could not see. The soldiers pursuing them, the walls of the city—and it was flowing out yet, a pool spreading.

She slapped at the soldiers first, though what she really wanted were the priests. The priests, who created Yen, the betrayer, the priests who put D'en down in the dark, who held her down, naked on the bed. She could make rubble of Nhol, and she would, she would. Feeling the walls, she marveled at how easily they might crumble. The soldiers were dead now, their feeble little lights gone. With sudden delight, Hezhi sensed what must be a priest, a sort of blank place, the shadow of a person. He was standing on the wall, watching her, chanting. She danced and shouted as she pulled him apart, sent the shreds of his spirit scattering around the city.

Nearer her, Perkar was still alive. He felt strange, stronger somehow than the others. Of course he did; Yen stabbed him in the heart and he was still alive. He was probably the only one here who could stop her, she mused. And so, laughing, she turned her attention to him, as he came unsteadily toward her. Yes, there was a little knot tying him to his sword. A simple enough thing to sever . . .

She lived in that instant for a long while, stretched out, her head in the mountains, her body as long as the world. A hideous and beautiful cruelty saturated her, a delicious thing.

I will live awake, she reveled. *I am awake!* Flesh and bone could know hunger better and deeper than any spirit, any ghost. That was why gods wore flesh, was it not? And she had been sleeping, sleeping in this flesh for so long! But even the pain of denial felt wonderful—as a memory to make the feast more pleasurable.

Perkar was quite close. Best kill him quickly.

Tsem grasped her from behind gently. She hadn't noticed him, so familiar was he, so close to her.

"Do not touch me, Tsem," she snarled.

"Princess," he wheezed, "Princess, please."

How feebly Tsem's heart beat! How slowly his flame flickered. The tiniest thought from her would end it. But even with her new vision, her anger and her pristine malice, she did not desire that. Tsem should live, should be her right hand in the new city she would build. She would need one loyal servant, at least. And so instead of snuffing him out, she reached in, intent upon fixing him, strengthening his weak strands. Healing him.

And she could not. She could twist, tear, break. But she could not heal Tsem.

In that instant—that long frozen moment, Perkar still stepping toward her with glacial slowness—she stood again on the roof of the Great Hall, gazing down. How simple to jump this time, to consume herself, not with death, but with *power*, with complete certainty. Life without doubt or fear, if she jumped. The little girl would die, but a terrible and exquisite creature would be born in her place, a goddess.

But she was Hezhi, and she had faced this before. Suddenly the difference between death and power seemed illusory. She would have certainty, but not hope or love or longing. Only certainty and hunger. A rat had certainty and hunger, a ghost did, too. She had always, always wanted more. Love, purpose, comfort.

And so, like all of the other times, she stepped back from the precipice, and as she did so a hard, clear wind blew out of her. When it was gone, when she shrank back to what she was, the earth rushing to slap her, Tsem caught her up, hugged her to his bloody chest.

PERKAR watched in astonishment as the monster suddenly writhed, clenched in upon itself, and then flew apart.

"Harka?"

"Behind us!" the sword said, snapping his head around with the force of the danger behind him. Hezhi stood there, a tiny figure in the dark. But around her, something rushed and swirled, heaved like black water. Perkar's face tingled as from a rush of cold wind. *"She will kill us,"* Harka stated flatly. *"Unless you are very swift indeed."*

For an instant, Perkar's mouth worked. As in the cavern beneath Balat, everything was coming too quickly, far too quickly for him to comprehend. But Harka was showing him now—the living mass of strands within Hezhi, the rope of shuddering lightning feeding into her from the canal. Strangling a cry, he began to run.

He had been right all along. If he was meant to save Hezhi, then he should kill her. Brother Horse's words seemed to jab at him from the maelstrom of his thoughts. About the River walking free, one day, destroying everything. And it was Hezhi's feet the River was to walk upon.

His own legs betrayed him after only a few steps. Grimly he struggled back up, steeling himself for the girl's assault. She had many more strands than the monster he had just faced. He had no chance, but he had to try, for Apad, for Eruka. For the king.

He staggered on, and no attack came. With each step he summoned more of his anger, her face in his dreams that allowed him no sleep. If he could only land a single stroke before he died, his ghost might know at least some peace.

When he was less than a score of steps from her, the strands suddenly unknotted, whipped about like a whirlwind untangling, and swirled back into the water. Hezhi trembled, her eyes wide, sightless, and fell. Her face bore a little smile that seemed almost triumphant. Perkar raised Harka and advanced.

"Can I kill her now?" he gasped.

"With a single stroke. But she is no longer . . ."

"That is all I need to know." He stepped forward.

Tsem saw him approach, seemed puzzled an instant before his

dull eyes gleamed with understanding. The Giant snarled, raised his bandaged arm to ward off the blow, curled his huge body to protect her. Perkar took the final step, felt Harka, hard and effective in his hands.

"I'm sorry," he said to the Giant. "But this ends now."

The Giant did not answer, but followed the gleam of Harka in the moonlight as Perkar raised him.

For the king, he thought again, summoning the image of that hollow ghost, caparisoned and parading at the Changeling's whim. Focusing his anger to make the stroke clean, merciful. Tsem certainly deserved that. But the memory that lit behind his eyes was not of the king, it was of the woman in the cave, the touch of her gaze upon his as her life swiftly ebbed.

An instant before it would have been combat. Now it was murder. Tsem's loyalty did not deserve murder. He closed his eyes and gritted his teeth. *This is weakness,* he told himself. *Avoiding what must be done.* But the steadfast light in Tsem's eyes was more adamant than any shield, and the anger in Perkar splintered against it like the flawed weapon it was. Trembling, he lowered Harka, plunging the blade into the black soil, following it down to his knees. A sob of frustration tore loose from his throat. He did not understand—*anything.* But he couldn't kill Tsem and Hezhi, whatever sort of monster she might have been a moment ago.

"Come on," he said to Tsem. "Can you still walk?"

Tsem nodded his head in dull affirmation and, still wary, stood, his charge tiny in his huge grip. With Perkar trailing, they walked away from Nhol, away from the River. None of them looked back.

NEAR midnight, Tsem finally collapsed, moaning once and then toppling almost gracefully. Perkar disengaged Hezhi from the massive arms. She seemed to be nearly unconscious herself.

He did what he could for Tsem's wounds. The cut into his arm was deep, to the bone, and still bleeding. Perkar bound it up tightly. The gut wound was more of a problem; the giant was certainly bleeding inside. The blade had slid into intestines, mostly. Perkar did the only thing he knew. He was too tired and thirsty himself to go much farther, especially carrying Hezhi. He found water in an irrigation ditch and drank as if he had never touched water to his lips before. Then he gathered scrub and brush for a fire.

The Giant shrieked in his sleep when Perkar plunged the burning tip of a branch through his wound, careful to follow the line of the sword puncture. The smell of searing flesh caught at Perkar's nose and nearly made him gag.

When Tsem's shriek died down, Perkar heard a whicker out in the darkness, a sound he would know anywhere. Horses.

Shakily he rose to his feet. The pursuit had come quickly, more quickly than he had imagined. Above him, the clouds were parting as if the stars and moon wanted to watch his last battle. He smiled, mocking that grandiose thought; of course the sky had no care for him. But the Pale Queen was there, resplendent in a double halo, and he found some contentment in the thought that he would die beneath her.

"I'm sorry, Hezhi," he muttered down to the girl. "I'm really not very good at this sort of thing, when it comes right down to it."

She surprised him by speaking. "I didn't mean to call you," she said. "It was . . . I didn't know what I was doing."

"It's all right," he assured her. "It's done now. I'm not angry, just sorry I couldn't have been more help. Seems that the River's plan for you was lacking in detail."

"The River had no plan for me," she shot back bitterly, "save that I should become a monster."

He shrugged. "There are horsemen out there—one at least, and he just rode off, I think, to find the rest. They'll be back soon, in force. When they come, hide somewhere; they may think you went on while I stayed here to hold them off."

"I will stay," she replied.

"No. Do as I say."

Hezhi gazed at the sprawling Giant. "Is he dead?" she asked.

"He wasn't a moment ago; I might have killed him trying to close his wound." He paused. "Among my people he would be counted a very brave man."

Hezhi nodded, tiredly. "I killed him," she said.

"If he is dead, he died for you," Perkar said. "That isn't the same as you killing him. Believe me, I've had ample time to consider the difference, and the difference is great. We all have to die, Hezhi. It's worth dying a little earlier if the reasons are good enough. His were; he told me he loved you."

"Yes," she agreed. "He did."

"Hide now," Perkar whispered. "Hear? The horses are returning."

It sounded like a score of them, at least. He took a deep, painful breath. His heart beat weirdly, and he couldn't shake the memory of feeling it *stop*, of seeing the bloody point of a knife slide out the front of his breast.

"Maybe I'll die this time," he told Harka.

"And me working so hard to keep you alive? Very ungrateful."

"I get sick when I think about the things that have happened to my body," Perkar said. "No one should have to carry the memory of being stabbed through the heart. Death should soothe that away."

"I won't apologize," Harka said. *"Someday you will thank me."*

"I would thank you now, if I could be rid of you."

"Careful. You'll hurt my feelings."

He threw back his head and howled. "Come and get me, walking dead men! I'll pile your bodies around my feet, I'll trample on your sightless eyes!" He wondered if Eruka would be proud of him, quoting verse even as the end came. He howled again.

A horseman broke from the trees, another, and another. The lead horseman grinned at him, a smile that nearly split his head in half.

"If you insist, I suppose," the rider said. "Though that isn't really what we had in mind for the night's entertainment."

Perkar was actually struck dumb. More riders filed into the clearing, wild-looking men on lean, beautiful mounts, hair braided and ornamented with copper, silver, gold. They were all showing him their teeth, fierce, wolflike smiles.

"Ngangata?" Perkar choked out at last.

"Nice to be recognized by such a great hero," Ngangata replied, leaning with braced hands, palms on his saddle. "And I would spend some time singing your praises, except for the fact that a contingent of Nholish cavalry will be on us in about two hundred heartbeats. Brother Horse and a few others will slow them down, but we had best ride."

"Do you have mounts for us?"

Ngangata nodded, and a stallion and a mare were brought up.

"The Giant has to go, too," Perkar insisted.

"Is he alive?"

One of the Mang warriors knelt at Tsem's side. He spat something at Ngangata, who replied in the same tongue. Another steed was brought up, and three men wrestled Tsem up onto its back.

"They say he won't live out the night," Ngangata explained. "But they will bring him anyway, so that he can die on horseback."

XII

~~~~~~~~~~~~~~~~~~~~~~~~~~~~~~~~

The Song of Perkar

Tsem surprised everyone. He *did* live through the night, and a second, as they put leagues between themselves and Nhol. And, Hezhi reminded herself, the River. She felt a dull ache with each footstep of the horse, with each breath of the old Mang warrior she clung to. She was not certain what the cause of her pain was, whether it was the loss of Qey and Ghan and everything she knew or whether it was the *thing* in her crying out for its father, for her to awaken it again. During the third day, when they had to tie her to the saddle to keep her from leaping off and running back toward Nhol, it seemed certain to be the latter.

Midmorning that day, the company stopped and dismounted near a tree—an unremarkable cottonwood, gnarled and ancient, roots feeding in a meager wash. The desert stretched out and away from them, a pitted and striated landscape of rust and yellow sand.

"What are they doing?" she asked the old man—Brother Horse, he was named.

"Offering to the god of the tree," he explained.

"The what?"

The men began burning bundles of grass; one placed a little bowl of something amongst the questing white roots of the tree.

"This is the first one—or the last, depending on which direction you're going," Brother Horse explained. "The god on the borderland, the edge of the empire of Nhol."

"The edge of the River's hunger, then," Perkar said from nearby on his own horse.

Brother Horse chuckled. "Not the edge of his hunger, but the edge of his reach. From here on the desert lives again."

"Then I shall offer, too," Perkar said. He smiled at Hezhi, seemed happy. Dismounting, he joined the other men. She felt only a terrible anxiety, as if some unthinkable thing were about to occur.

When they remounted, rode *past* the tree, an appalling, wrenching pain pushed her violently into oblivion.

When she awoke—not sure how much later—the pain was still fading, like the sting from a hard slap. She felt for her scale. It was still there, still itching faintly.

"Ah," Brother Horse said when he felt her stir. "Let me have a look at you." He called a halt, dismounted, reached leathery brown hands to help her down. Her feet felt light and sensitive on the hot sand.

"Yes, yes," Brother Horse said, smiling at her and mussing her hair.

"What? Yes, what?"

"Well, you see, child, I can see gods—always been able to. When I first saw you I said 'Now, that girl has something in her.' I could *see* it in there, you understand?"

She nodded. As she could see her father, when he called the Riverghosts, perhaps.

"Well, it's still there, but it's gone quiet. Can you feel that?"

She felt a faint tickle of joy, despite herself. "Yes," she said, "I think I can."

"Good. Come on now, cheer up. The River has lost his grip on you, too, and your friend may live yet!"

Hezhi actually felt herself grin.

"Back up!" Brother Horse ordered, boosting her up onto the beast's back. When he was mounted, too, he gave a great shout, one that frightened her and delighted her at the same time. The animal beneath her surged, and she was reminded of Tsem carrying her. Yet this was different, a rushing thing that she had not understood or appreciated during their midnight ride out of Nhol. The landscape raced by, the horse a half-tamed thunderbolt beneath her. She did not shriek herself, but she almost did, and felt a brief, almost terrible shining joy, somehow more solid and real than the joy of a goddess. She thought of the little statue, the horse-woman, and *was* her, proud, fierce. *Free.*

"Now tell me," Perkar insisted, days later. A pair of boys and a girl laughed nearby, chased a wooden hoop across the red sand of the village square. Sparks swept up from the fire, twining up an invisible tree of wind to join the darkening sky. A cool dry breeze padded down from the mesa, breathed across them promises of autumn, coursed on east.

Perkar, Brother Horse, Ngangata, and a Mang warrior named Yuu'han gathered about the fire in what Brother Horse named a Wheel of Words. Hezhi sat outside of the circle as Brother Horse's eldest daughter, Duk, plaited up what little hair Qey had left her.

"Tell," Perkar repeated. "I don't believe that you just *happened* upon me."

"Why not?" Ngangata asked. "Isn't that the lot of a hero's friend?"

"Riding to the rescue? That sounds more like the *hero* to me," Perkar rejoined. " 'The Song of Ngangata.' I like the sound of that."

"No songs about me, please," Ngangata said.

"Well," Brother Horse told them, "you can sing a song about *me*, then."

Perkar looked at both men in exasperation. Brother Horse grinned, took a drink of cactus beer, and finally relented.

"Your friend here was frantic when he discovered you gone, don't ask me why. He insisted that we follow you. I refused, of course—I am an old man, much too old to ride out against Nholish cavalry."

"To be sure," Perkar muttered sarcastically. "*Much* too old to ride circles around them, widdershins and back."

Brother Horse glowered at Perkar. "How long did you beg me to tell you this story?"

"My apologies, ancient one," Perkar said. "Please continue."

Brother Horse nodded with apparent satisfaction. "I did agree to take Ngangata—at great risk to my own life—as far as a village I knew of, there to bargain with my great-nieces and nephews and other assorted kin for a horse to ride to Nhol. A half day's ride, a day walking. I guessed that the Woodpecker Goddess would not notice me in such a short time."

He grinned, showing his yellowed, broken teeth to best advantage, quaffed another mouthful of beer. "Well, of course, halfway there—just past Lies-in-a-Square Rock—there came a whirlwind and a sound of feathers, and my old heart stopped dead in my chest. I was beginning a dignified defense of my actions . . ."

"He was on his knees, begging," Ngangata clarified.

"*Dignified* defense of my actions," Brother Horse repeated with a wicked glance aside to the Alwa-Man, "when I realized that the god standing before me was not Nuchiinuh but a black god, feathered, yes, but not a woodpecker. It was Raven, I knew that right away.

" 'Lord Raven,' said I, 'to what do I owe my great fortune?' And he said, 'No doubt you define "fortune" differently than *I* do,' and he stared at me with those yellow eyes of his."

"Karak? Karak came to you?"

Ngangata nodded, while Brother Horse patiently drank some more beer.

"I'll shorten this up," Brother Horse said, "because I can smell supper nearly ready. Raven-god told me he had been watching us all, from afar, because it pleased him to do so. He said that I should assist Ngangata in reaching Nhol, since he had foreseen that we would be needed. In turn, I explained my infirmities . . ."

"He asked Karak what was in it for him," Ngangata elucidated.

"I explained my infirmities," Brother Horse continued stubbornly. "When I was done, Raven asked me how infirm I might become if someone were to alert Nuchiinuh that I was wandering about unprotected. I didn't like the tack of that conversation, I'll tell you. But *then* Raven made a kindly offer to speak to the Woodpecker Goddess on my behalf. He told me that she owed him many favors, and that he would spend a few so that I could live out my years among my people again. Well, you know, I hadn't really thought about it all that much, but I *did* miss my relatives, alone out on that island. I could also see that great things were happening, a grand adventure calling me to one last heroic task . . ."

"Karak convinced him to help," Ngangata summed up.

"*You* tell the rest of it then," Brother Horse grunted, lifting his beer cup.

Ngangata complied. "Brother Horse convinced some of his relatives to come along, promised them war honors if they came— and some old treasure of his, buried somewhere, I think. The rest isn't much to tell. We rode straight across the desert to Nhol, while you meandered down the Changeling."

"Yes, but how did you *find* me?"

"Karak told us to watch for you on land. That was cryptic and *I* thought not much help. We sat up on a hill where we could see the whole west side of Nhol."

"From that far away? How could you recognize us, or even see us?"

"I can *see* gods, remember?" Brother Horse reminded him, his voice becoming ever so slightly slurred. "I know that sword of yours, and there are no other gods in that miserable land except the Waterborn"—he looked suddenly embarrassed and winked apologetically at Hezhi—"I'm sorry, child, I don't mean to offend you."

Hezhi shrugged her little shoulders and shook her head to say that there had been no affront.

"So," Brother Horse went on, "I thought that anything I saw that looked like a god would be you, probably."

Perkar shook his head in amazement. "And so you watched that entire time? Without sleeping?"

"Ah . . . not exactly."

"He actually *was* asleep," Ngangata put in. "But then Yuu'han, here, saw a burst of light, strange godlike light."

"The ghost," Hezhi murmured, the first words she had spoken that evening. "The ghost from my blood."

Ngangata nodded agreement. "We found that out later; it was too dark for us to see anything else, really. We woke Brother Horse up, though, and after a good bit of squinting he swore he could see Perkar and a goddess, a goddess growing larger and larger."

They all glanced at Hezhi, who shifted uncomfortably and stared down at the dirt.

"You all leave the girl be," Brother Horse snapped. "She's been through enough, lost plenty. No need to keep reminding her of unpleasant things."

"It's just that I'm the cause of it all," Hezhi blurted. "All of you, traveling across the world, risking your lives, killing people, all because I made a stupid wish. It wasn't even a *real* wish, just an impulse. And Tsem, hurt so badly . . ."

Perkar watched her eyes wander off, wondered how she was not crying and wished she would. Whatever kept her from crying seemed to hurt her more than a good bawl.

"Now," Brother Horse puffed out. "Come here. Come here and sit with us."

She stared over at the fire for a long moment, her black eyes drinking away the flames. Then slowly she disengaged herself from Duk—who understood not a word of their conversation, which was in Nholish—and hesitantly approached the fire. Brother Horse patted the spot next to him.

"Don't waste your energy on that kind of thinking," he told her. "You didn't pull all of the threads that tightened up this net. You only pulled one of them. Take me. What did you have to do with my altercation with the Woodpecker Goddess? Nothing, that's what. It happened six years ago, long before all of this began. Perkar, he was tied up in something gone wrong long before your blood set the River in motion. And Raven, who knows why he does what *he* does? But the certain thing is he does nothing at *your* whim or mine. Ngangata never even knew you, and he had precious little reason to help Perkar—no offense, Perkar—but he came along anyway."

"But, Tsem," she whispered, and then sobbed. "Qey, Ghan . . . all of those soldiers . . ." She buried her face in Brother Horse's shirt and began to shudder with much-needed crying. Embarrassed, Perkar excused himself, wandering off from the fire. He went on out of the square, threading between scrubby junipers and wiry bushes, let the faint wind settle on his shoulders.

All those soldiers, she said. But *he* killed them. He should feel something, he knew, remorse, guilt the like of which had raged in him after the Kapaka's expedition had all but died. Instead he felt only a vague regret, sorrow that the men had stood in his way, but no awful grief.

"Everyone dies," Harka offered.

"And everyone lives," Perkar retorted. "That's no answer."

"What about this, then? You've finally learned to shoulder what you do and move on, without wailing about the burden."

"I like that better," Perkar admitted, "though it seems a bit self-serving."

"Better to serve yourself than someone else," Harka pointed out. *"I should know."*

"Can I free you, Harka? Is there any way to do that?"

"If there is, I don't know of it. But thanks for the thought."

"It wasn't just for you, but you are welcome."

Later, returning to the village, he noticed a low, familiar chanting issuing from a clump of scrubby pines. He nearly passed on, but after reflecting for a moment, he sat down on a convenient rock and waited, watched the crimson slice of the sun flatten against the black rocks in the west.

After a while, the chanting stopped, and Ngangata emerged from the trees, bowstave in hand. He nodded at Perkar when he saw him. The two men regarded each other, Ngangata standing, Perkar seated on the stone.

"It should be time to eat," Ngangata said after some time had elapsed.

He nodded. Wondering what it was, precisely, he wanted to say. He frowned in concentration.

"Come on," Ngangata said, his voice soft, like the evening air.

Perkar shook his head. "No, I . . . Brother Horse was right, you know. You had no sane reason for coming to help me."

Ngangata's mouth quirked up. He glanced off at the horizon, at the faded sun, and it seemed a long time before his black gaze, once so frightening, came back to meet Perkar's eyes.

"Perkar," he sighed at last. "You think too much. Too much. Now let's go eat; my bow and I are starving."

Perkar stood a bit unsteadily. His vision was a trifle blurred, as if some dust had blown into his eyes. He brushed off his kilt, took a few, slow steps to join Ngangata. "Thank you," he said.

Ngangata looked down at his own feet, nodded. "Come on. Food." And when he smiled, Perkar felt his own face respond, smiling back.

"PRINCESS?"

Hezhi woke to the familiar voice, wondered if she had overslept again, if Ghan would be angry, what Qey was preparing for breakfast. Reality intruded quickly, the red desert, unfamiliar voices buzzing in the background. But Tsem, Tsem was familiar. And awake.

"Tsem!" Hezhi fell forward across his chest, buried her face in his monstrous shoulder. "Please live, Tsem."

The half Giant chuckled wanly. "That is what I hope to do, Princess, believe me." He glanced blearily around at the cedar posts, the soot-darkened walls of the little house they were in.

"I don't know where we are," Tsem admitted.

"Let me get you some water," she offered, "and I'll tell you." She patted him on the shoulder and went outside, down the hill to the spring Duk had shown her. So much she had to tell Tsem, and so much of it was unexplainable. So much unknown. Where were Ghan and Qey now? Being tortured for their part in her escape? Dead already? She might never know. Fetching the water back, she took a moment to regret her refusal of power. Whatever else she would have done, she would have saved Ghan and Qey. But if the fire in her had burned that far, she would have been lost, and many, many people would have died.

Tsem accepted the water thirstily and listened with wide eyes as she explained where they were, what had occurred while he slept.

"What will we do?" he asked, when she had finished.

"I don't know," she replied. "But I hope you will stay with me. I can't bear to lose you, too."

"Of course, Princess. I am your servant."

"No," she refuted. "I am no princess and you are no servant, not out here. If you stay with me here, it must be because you choose to."

Tsem nodded and sat up, gazing silently out the bright rectangle of the door.

"I should like to step outside," he said at last.

"I don't know . . ."

"Please."

She was scant help in aiding Tsem to his feet, but in reality he seemed to need only her moral support. Out in the sun, he leaned against the clay-plastered wall of the hut, gazed around at the distant horizon.

"I would like to find my mother's people," he said at last. "Someday. She used to tell me about them . . ."

"We can do that," Hezhi said.

"Not necessarily right away," Tsem put in. "But someday."

"Someday," she agreed, and grinned. She laid her hand on his shoulder, and together they contemplated the distance.

EPILOGUE

~~~~~~

Autumn

A MONTH passed, and the sky grew clearer, the winds colder. Some days brought clouds of geese and ducks, winging from the north in search of a warmer sun. Others brought the cold fingers of winter the birds were fleeing. The Mang worked hard in that month, chinking up houses, trekking to the wetlands nearer the River to gather nuts and berries, ranging in the uplands for meat and pine nuts.

Tsem recovered slowly, but after the first week the Mang healer attending him announced that he would certainly live—though he hinted that the debts he had incurred with certain gods would have to be repaid. Perkar, eager to do his part, organized a hunting expedition with Ngangata and a few younger Mang men. It was decided that a few women would accompany them, as well, and Hezhi, unskilled as she was, begged to be included.

Two days brought them to a lightly forested canyon, and there they made a strong camp, set up tents, dug firepits, built skinning frames for the hides they hoped the men would bring in. Hezhi set about learning the things Mang women did: gathering nuts, digging roots, tanning hides. The work was hard, and many times, early on, kindled nostalgia for the palace, where she was waited on by servants. The women she worked with were cordial but a little impatient with her. They seemed to expect her to already know how to do things. Hezhi was a quick learner, however, and before many days had passed the women began including her in their storytelling sessions, laughing now and then at her highly imperfect Mang, but never with any malice. The men returned every few days, always with game, and the women murmured much about the skill of Ngangata and his bow. Perkar was less esteemed, but he also killed much game, often entering the camp, flushed with his success, "like a little boy, just learning to hunt," the women would exclaim.

Half a month passed at the camp, and Hezhi began to feel a certain contentment, the days settling on her shoulders like a warm coat, her fingers learning their tasks as her tongue became comfortable with the language of the Horse People. One of the young warriors began flirting with her, and she became the object of good-natured gossip, though she kept a good distance from the young man. The lesson she had learned with Yen—Ghe?—was not one she would unlearn quickly. It was one of three pains still throbbing in her. The palace and her family were already fading. They were, as the saying went, more of her skin than her heart. But she missed Qey and Ghan, feared for them. She wondered often what the letter Ghan had left her contained—it had gone with Zeq' and his boat when he had fled.

Toward evening of the twentieth day in camp, Hezhi was scraping clean an antelope skin when the packhorses began to pace nervously in their corral. Many of the women stopped in their tasks, gazing down the canyon to see who or what might be approaching. They soon made out two riders, and one of the older women, astute in such matters, recognized Brother Horse and Yuu'han, his grandnephew.

That evening they held a celebration. Fortuitously, the hunters returned that same day, and so a deer was dressed and roasted. Brother Horse brought with him beer, candy, copper bells for the men and their horses, cloth and knives for the women. To Hezhi he gave one of the knives, a small, sharp blade.

"They tell me you learn quickly," he said. "Every Mang woman needs a good skinning knife."

"Thank you," she said, meaning it. The knife borrowed from Duk had always been that, and she was astonished at how happy she was to have her own.

"Well," Brother Horse went on, when she had accepted her present. "I have something else for you, as well." He drew forth a small bundle from his pack. "A friend of yours sent this along."

"A friend of mine?"

"Yes. Yuu'han and I rode down to Nhol, to buy sugar and knives."

"Nhol?" She took the package, fumbled it open with eager fingers. Saltwater started in her eyes when she saw what was enclosed. There was a book—*The Mang Wastes*—and a ten-score roll of blank paper. The latter was accompanied by pen and powdered ink. There was a note, as well.

"Hezhi," the note began.

I have lived a long life, but there has never been much joy in it. What pleasure I did find was usually in the paper and ink surrounding me. And so I thank you for an unaccustomed sort of happiness. I never intended to love you, you know, for I have learned that love is rarely pleasurable. It was not when I thought you dead. I cursed myself daily. Yet now I hear you live and are safe, and I no longer regret my affection. I would, of course, never say these things to you, but pen and paper may speak when I am silent.

I know you must worry about your nurse, Qey, but she is well. The soldiers found her half dead amongst dead priests and believed her to be the victim of your crazed bodyguard as much as they. Neither has anyone pointed a finger at me. The massacre at the South Gate is little talked about, and your name is spoken only as Hezhinata.

I have sent along a paper and pen with the Mang; I only hope they do not use it to wipe themselves with along the way back to you. It is my hope that you will compose a letter or two to an old man, telling him of the things you see. There must yet be wonders he has not read of.

You must not return to Nhol, Hezhi. Nothing pleasant awaits you here. I have confidence in you, know that you will make a life for yourself wherever you go. You have that in you, and it is all you, nothing of the River you leave behind. Be blessed by whatever gods there are in your travels, and try to think kindly of me, though I was never as good to you as I should have been.

—Ghan

She read the letter and read it again, never sure whether to laugh or cry. It did not really matter; either would have contained the same mixture of joy and melancholy. She gave Brother Horse a hug and thanked him again. Grinning, he patted her shoulder and then started to rejoin his family in drinking. He turned, though, gazed at her seriously.

"You may become Mang, if you wish," he said. "I will adopt you as my daughter, and we will find a good, capable husband for you. Who knows? Now and then I see the sparkle of power in you—not like it *was*, of course, not enough to change you, but perhaps enough to make you a shamaness, to earn an honest living that doesn't involve scraping hides."

"I'm learning to like scraping hides, thank you," she replied. "But I thank you for your offer. It is very kind, since I know I would be a burden, at least for a time."

"Families have broad shoulders," Brother Horse replied, "made to bear burdens."

"I don't know what I will do yet," she mused. "I think Perkar and I must speak."

"You are not bound to him," Brother Horse said.

"No, not bound exactly," she half agreed. "But there are debts we share, responsibilities we hold together."

Brother Horse shook his head. "Such young people to be so serious. Enjoy yourselves, before your bones turn into dry sticks and your skin into leather."

Hezhi smiled. "I will try," she promised.

PERKAR edged around the skinning frame, admiring the hide from all sides. "You've done a nice job with this," he said. "One would never know you were once a princess."

She attempted a smile, but it fell into a flat line.

"Sorry," he hastened to add.

"No," Hezhi said. "It isn't that. Being a princess never meant much to me. It might have, I suppose, if . . ." But the *if* hung in the air.

He pretended to examine the skin more closely, embarrassed.

"What are your plans, Perkar?" she asked abruptly. "Do you plan to hunt with the Mang from now on?"

"No." He had been thinking about that, of course. "No. I'm repaying debts right now, and I thought to begin with the closest, the ones I owe here. I'm also told that winter is hard on the western steppes. When spring comes, I'll go back to my father's land, to my own people. I have much to atone for there, many things to set right."

"Many things that I share blame for as well," Hezhi said.

"This has been discussed," he told her. "I believe you to be blameless."

"If I am, you are as well. But if you bear responsibility, so do I, Perkar. You can't have it both ways. We did this *together*, you and I. No matter what Brother Horse says, this skein was wound by the two of us, out of our fears and desires. I barely know you, but we belong together, at least for a time."

He tried out a chuckle and found it wanting. "How old are you?" he said. "Why not rest for a few years, be a child awhile longer?"

The girl looked back at him wearily. "That is already lost to me," she said quietly.

"Lost things can be found," he replied. But he knew what she meant. He would never again be that boy with his first sword, whooping in his father's pasture.

"I don't know," he went on, when she didn't reply. "We have many months to think about it. It might be that you will change your mind."

"I might," she conceded. "I did promise Tsem a few things. But I want you to think on this."

Perkar grunted. "You know," he said, "you frighten me a bit."

"I? I thought *you* were a demon, when I first met you."

"Perhaps I am, when I wield Harka. I don't know. But you . . ."

"How do I frighten you?"

"Who knows? All that time, on the River, your face the only clear thing in my mind. I can't see you without remembering that, without remembering that I hated you for a while."

"You still hate me?"

"No. It is just a memory. A clear memory." He settled down, cross-legged.

Hezhi hesitated for an instant, eyes turned from him. "You were going to kill me," she blurted suddenly.

Perkar grinned sardonically. "We were going to kill each other, weren't we?"

Hezhi nodded, but choked suddenly, gasped with an obvious effort to fight back tears. Perkar stared at her with open dismay. She bit her lip and began to scrabble to her feet. Perkar, to his own vast surprise, reached his hand out gently, laid it upon her shoulder. After a tiny hesitation, he knelt and drew her to him, felt her heart beating in her slight form like a thrush's wings. She sobbed, once, into his shoulder, and he felt a sudden tightness in his own throat.

"I'm sorry," he sighed, as he hugged her awkwardly. "I'm sorry. I know it hurts, all of it."

"I never *meant* to . . ." she mumbled, sniffling.

"Shh. Never mind," he soothed back. For a moment they stayed that way, and Perkar realized that though he had come half a world to find her, he had never really *touched* Hezhi.

"Listen," he said seriously, disengaging but leaving his hand on her shoulder, "all of this talk about duty and responsibility is fine, but I would be happier if we could at least *like* each other."

Hezhi nodded, reached up to brush at the dampness beneath her black eyes. "I can do that," she said, her tone a shade less certain than her words.

Perkar smiled, but boyishly this time, with none of his world-weary hardness. "I can do that, too. Maybe . . ." He crinkled his brow. "Maybe we need each other to heal from this; I don't know. But when I go home, I hope you will come with me."

"I would like that," she replied.

Suddenly embarrassed, Perkar turned his attention back to the skinning frame. "I thought I might go for a ride," he confided. "I like this horse the Mang gave me. He reminds me of one I used to have." He glanced over at the girl. "Would you like to come with me?"

Hezhi surveyed her work. Overhead, a late flight of geese arrowed through the turquoise sky.

"Yes," she said, her eyes distant. "Yes, I think I would."

He rose and offered her his hand, but she stood on her own before taking it, grinning.

"Where shall we ride to?" she asked.

It was his turn to smile. "Anywhere," he said. "Wherever we choose."

They turned together toward where the horses waited.

About the Author

Born in Meridian, Mississippi, on April 11, 1963, J. Gregory Keyes spent his early years roaming the forests of his native state as well as the red-rock cliffs of the Navajo Indian reservation in Arizona. Storytelling in his family and on the reservation sparked an interest both in writing and in the ancient. Pursuing the ancient, he obtained a B.A. in anthropology from Mississippi State University. Moving to Athens, Georgia, he worked ironing newspapers and as a night guard to support his wife, Nell, in her metalworking/jewelry degree, and also began seriously pursuing writing in his spare time.

Returning to anthropology, he earned a master's from the University of Georgia, concentrating on mythology and belief systems, long-standing interests that also inspire his fiction. He currently teaches introductory anthropology and a course on reconstructing Southeastern Indian agriculture while pursuing his Ph.D.

In leisure time, Keyes enjoys ethnic cooking—particularly Central American, Szechuan, and Turkish cuisine—heirloom gardening, and *kapucha toli*, a Choctaw Indian sport involving heavy wooden sticks and few rules.